CW00498288

# Dark Desire

Alice Renaud
Alan Souter
Nancy Golinski
Dee S. Knight
S.K. White
Virginia Wallace
F. Burn
Gibby Campbell
Deborah Kelsey
Zia Westfield
Estelle Pettersen

www.blackvelvetseductions.com

ISBN 978-1-914301-31-5


Published 2022

Published by Black Velvet Seductions Publishing

Dark Desire Copyright 2022 Alice Renaud, Alan Souter, Nancy Golinski, Dee S. Knight, S.K. White, Virginia Wallace, F. Burn, Gibby Campbell, Deborah Kelsey, Zia Westfield, Estelle Pettersen
Cover design Copyright 2022 Jessica Greeley

All rights reserved. No part of this book may be used or reproduced in any manner whatsoever without written permission, except in the case of brief quotations embodied in critical articles or reviews.

This book is licensed for your personal enjoyment only. This book may not be re-sold or given away to other people. If you would like to share this book with another person, please purchase an additional copy for each recipient. If you're reading this book and did not purchase it, or it was not purchased for your use only, then please return to your favorite book retailer and purchase your own copy. Thank you for respecting the hard work of this author.

All characters in this book are completely fictional. They exist only in the imagination of the author. Any similarity to any actual person or persons, living or dead, is completely coincidental.

www.blackvelvetseductions.com

Contents Warning
Some of the stories in this book contain scenes and subjects some
readers may find uncomfortable or disturbing

# Contents

www.blackvelvetseductions.com

# Introduction

Our latest anthology, *Dark Desire,* is possibly our most daring publication to date. In the twelve stories, our authors delve into the dark crevasses of their imaginations, probing into dark themes, creating strange new worlds and inventing larger than life characters.

These stories explore relationships, unafraid of taking the genre of romance to a darker, deeper level. We meet:

Jillian, a wife and mother, who serves as an assassin for her clan of werewolves.

A shifter mermaid who is forced to team up with a vampire to steal a magical weapon, but can she resist his lethal charm?

A cocky rodeo cowboy, who falls into the clutches of a hard-core Dominatrix.

Gina, who following an accident, can see the dead. Can she find a positive? Maybe find true love?

Lily, who wakes from a coma with dark dream memories of a stranger. Is he the love of her life?

A shifter who finds a woman who can change the world's destiny. Can he protect her, or will a supernatural battle destroy them all?

Kat who talks to herself and mentally responds as her mother. Murder and arson lead her to a cop, but could he be much more?

Two Nazi officers who meet for dinner on Christmas eve and reveal their darkest desires.

Lovers, on a crazed road trip, murder and havoc at every turn as an expression of their true love.

Tasha whose world is rocked by a mysterious teacher. His dark secret only makes her want him more.

Harper who is visiting an Island known for a wolf's mysterious healing powers. Will this lead to a dangerous game?

Two young people fleeing for a better life; a six-gun, an outlaw and a Tarot card binding their fates together.

Buckle up as we journey into the unknown and discover the shadowy forces that hauntingly dwell within the provocative pages of Dark Desire.

Richard Savage
CEO, Black Velvet Seductions

# Blood of the Ocean
## Alice Renaud

Arian slid through the dark waters of the canal with barely a ripple. She was very quiet, even for a mermaid. So quiet that even the fishes didn't hear her.

The two drunken humans on the boat never stood a chance.

She swam right up to the prow without them noticing. They were too busy swigging from bottles of champagne and slapping each other on the back.

"Priceless," the younger man hiccupped. He lifted the object he held in his hand. It shone in the gloom like a miniature golden sun.

"Biggest diamond I've ever seen," said his companion, a stocky, older fellow. "We're made for life!"

Arian grinned at the thieves' foolishness. They'd been clever enough to steal the jewel from the London wizards, but they had no idea what they'd taken. This was no diamond. It was a Heart-Revealer, a magical crystal that could turn emotions into colored light.

And now it was hers.

She gripped the side of the boat and hauled herself up. The two men gasped and staggered back. The older man dropped his bottle, which exploded into a thousand shards of glass, splattering the deck with champagne.

"What the fuck is this monster?" the younger one shouted.

Arian opened her mouth wide to reveal her razor-sharp teeth. "I'm your worst nightmare."

She jumped on him and bit him on the wrist, hard. He screamed and dropped the jewel. She snatched it in her webbed hand and plunged into the canal. The whole episode hadn't lasted more than a minute.

She could hear the shouting and swearing as she swam away underwater, but she knew they had no chance of catching her. Elation ran through her veins, bright and swift. It was so easy to steal from fools.

She sped down the canal like a dark, silent arrow, enjoying the rush of cool water against her skin. Bert would be happy. Although… he had probably already planned a tougher assignment for her. He often said she'd lose her edge if she only did easy jobs.

Unease crawled over her skin, setting her teeth on edge. She had to keep him happy. Her very survival depended on it. He was her only protector in the vast, dark city of London. The only thing that stood between her and a nasty, short and brutish life on the streets.

The canal ended in a marina screened off from the River Thames by stone quays and Victorian-era brick warehouses, now repurposed into high-end apartments. Boats of all shapes and sizes bobbed on the dark water – luxurious yachts, barges, wooden flat-bottomed canal boats painted in bright colors, and even a couple of skiffs. Arian swam up to the largest yacht and tapped the white hull three times.

Bert's mean face appeared overhead. His eyes shone with greed when he saw the crystal in Arian's hand. "Good girl! Up you come."

A rope ladder dropped over the side. Arian put the Heart-Revealer into her mouth and climbed, slowly, because webbed hands and feet are not designed for that exercise. She felt very exposed, shimmying up the side of the boat. It was a relief to drop onto the hardwood deck.

She took the jewel out of her mouth. Bert extended his hand. She shook her head.

"Money first."

He glowered at her. "You're one hard-nosed bitch, Arian. Still, I guess you've earned it."

He walked over to a bench, lifted the cover and pulled out a black suitcase. He brought it over to Arian, placed it at her feet and opened it. It was full of banknotes.

She crouched and flicked through the wads. Satisfied that he hadn't cheated her, she closed the suitcase with a click. Another successful job. Another pile of cash in her bank account. Another layer of protection. Little by little, she was building her refuge, each banknote a brick in the wall that would keep her safe in the human world.

Perhaps one day she'd have enough to stop waking up at night in a sweat, wondering if Bert had withdrawn his protection… if one of his heavies was coming to kill her… or kidnap her and exhibit her in a freak show. Bert had threatened to do that many times when she'd displeased him.

But today he had no reason to complain. She straightened and handed him the jewel. "It's a pleasure doing business with you," she said, with as much fake warmth as she could muster.

Golden light spilled from the crystal, revealing the gangster's pleasure. "Magnificent," he said. "The wizards will pay a high price for this."

Arian's mind lit up with curiosity. Bert rarely talked about his clients. "Presumably they're different wizards from the ones who owned this jewel?"

"Oh, yeah." Bert pocketed the crystal and chuckled. "These sorcerers are from Ireland. They want to take over London, I think." He said it casually, as if magical wars were nothing to worry about.

Anxiety slithered in Arian's belly. She'd no wish to get caught in the crossfire. "They'll have a job beating Ariel Wolfsbane and the other London warlocks. This toy won't help them much against fireballs."

"I know." Bert had a gleam in his eye that told her he was planning another operation. A big one.

He pulled his phone from his jacket and tapped on it. "These Irish wizards, who pay very well, are after something else. A weapon that could give them the edge in their battle with Ariel and his crew. Look at this."

He showed her the phone. Arian came closer. The object on the screen was another large crystal, lit up from the inside. It shimmered and changed colour every few seconds, from blue to green to purple, then back to blue. It looked like a pretty paperweight, or a New Age bedside lamp.

But she knew it was nothing of the kind. Her worries hardened into a ball of fear, deep in the pit of her stomach. "It's the Blood of the Ocean!"

"I knew you'd recognise it." Bert pocketed his phone with a satisfied smile. "A weapon designed by your people, long ago. The Irish wizards want me – that is, you – to steal it from its current owner. They say it contains the power of the sea itself. Enough to blast Ariel and his warlocks to kingdom come."

His voice dripped with venom. Ariel Wolfsbane, the leader of the London warlocks, took a dim view of Bert's traffic in stolen magical artefacts. He'd thwarted many of his operations, and it was said that he'd sworn to capture Bert and throw him into his deepest dungeon. No wonder the gangster wanted to help the Irish wizards destroy the London warlocks.

But if this weapon were unleashed in London, civilians could get hurt. She opened her mouth to say that she wouldn't have anything to do with the Blood of the Ocean, but Bert raised a hand to silence her. "The wizards will pay fifteen million pounds for it. Five million will be for you."

The sum stunned her and snuffed out the words she'd been about to say. Five million. She wouldn't need to work again. She'd be safe. She could even send some money to her people, and perhaps in time they'd forgive her and allow her to come back to her native islands.

She was careful to keep the elation off her face. Perhaps she could obtain even more. "Why do I get only five million, if I do all the work?"

Bert laughed. "Don't argue with me, fishface. I deserve a bigger share, because I'm the one who sets up the deal with the wizards. And if Ariel and his brothers catch us, I'm the one who will go down to the dungeons, or worse. They'll let you off, because they don't want to upset the merfolk. You guys are outside human laws, which is handy."

Icy water dripped down Arian's spine at the thought of getting caught. She wasn't afraid of what the warlocks could do to her, but if her people heard of her crime, they'd banish her forever. She'd never see her home or her family again. She was taking a big risk too. "Why is your share two-thirds of the prize? Why not half as usual?"

Bert gave her a look that chilled her blood. "You're getting bolshie, Arian. Keep arguing with me and I might sell you to a travelling circus. Did I say we were splitting fifty-fifty? We're splitting three ways. Because there's no way you can do this on your own, you stinking shrimp. For this job, I've found you a partner."

Arian's immediate instinct was to say no. She worked alone. But the cold fear in her veins made her pause. She couldn't risk antagonising Bert. And this job was big, bigger than any she'd ever done before. Perhaps on this one occasion she could use some help. The reward would still be large, but the risk would be lower. "I need to meet him, or her, before I say yes or no."

"Sure." Bert walked to the cabin that stood a few feet away and opened the door with a flourish.

The most handsome man that Arian had ever seen stepped onto the deck.

He was so good looking that for a moment she forgot all about the job, Bert, and even the suitcase of cash at her feet. She was lost in the perfect planes of his face… the glossy waves of his black hair… the diamond-hard light in his dark eyes. Her gaze travelled lower, taking in his broad shoulders in the tailored black suit, his narrow waist and long, lean legs.

"Arian, this is Victor. Your partner in crime. Victor, this is Arian, a mermaid from the Morvann Islands, as you can tell."

Bert's voice broke the spell, and she dragged her eyes back to the man's face. He smiled, revealing teeth even longer and sharper than hers.

Shock and fear hit her in the stomach like a tidal wave. She opened her mouth to scream, then found that her emotions had swallowed up her voice. She gulped air to steady herself, then hissed at Bert like a furious cat. "You are kidding me! You want me to team up with a *vampire?*"

The gangster shrugged. "What's the big deal? Victor doesn't drink human blood. Or merfolk blood."

A horrible image popped into Arian's mind. Victor's sharp canines, piercing the skin of a young mermaid…

Anger surged, pushing the fear aside. "I'd like to see him try!"

Victor's smile didn't waver. "I would never attack another sentient being." A beat, then he added with a smirk, "Anyway, I avoid marine creatures. Red meat is more my thing."

He actually dared to joke about his evil, blood-sucking ways. His insolence heated up her anger. "And what does vampire blood taste like?"

The fiend lowered his voice, almost into a purr. "We taste wonderful, Arian. A heavenly drink that will make you believe you've gone straight to paradise without bothering to die first."

He gazed at her with those dark, half-lidded eyes, and suddenly another image formed in her mind. She was biting into his neck, licking the delicious blood that poured from the open wound… She was a carnivore, like him.

And he sure looked good enough to eat.

Victor's hyper-refined senses were in turmoil. Arian smelled amazing. Hot sands and cool seas, salt and spice and all things nice. He'd lied through his pointed teeth when he'd said he wouldn't drink her blood. If her scent could turn his head, what would a taste of her do? He'd sink his fangs into her smooth, black flesh anytime. But only if she gave permission. He only preyed on the willing.

He allowed his gaze to linger on the polished column of her throat, and on the pulse that beat there, just beneath her skin. She had an unusual colouring for a mermaid. He'd read lots about them, and even seen a few, when Ariel had sent him on a diplomatic mission to the Morvann Islands. In their aquatic shape, they were usually one colour all over. But Arian's onyx-dark skin was embellished with pale grey strands that gleamed like silver under the electric lights. He allowed his gaze to glide lower, over the buds of her breasts, down to her belly and the apex of her legs. She was as smooth as marble there. He wondered what she would feel like if he slid a finger inside her… if he dipped his tongue in her opening…

He'd been fascinated by the merfolk for many years, and meeting them in the flesh had been a dream come true. But none of them had managed to heat up his cool blood. Only this Arian was awakening the cravings that lay deep inside his resurrected body.

Bert, clearing his throat, brought him back to reality. "Well. I'll just leave you two to get better acquainted. You can debrief her, Victor. You know everything about the mission."

He scuttled away, and Victor's sharp ears soon caught the thump of his feet on the jetty. The scumbag couldn't wait to get away from him. Which was wise, as Victor would have liked nothing better than to rip out his throat and throw him to the fishes.

But Ariel Wolfsbane and his brother Auric wanted Bert alive. So Victor had to repress his murderous instincts and play the game until he could help the warlocks catch the gangster red-handed.

Unfortunately the lovely, lithe mermaid in front of him had to be a pawn in that game. An emotion he hadn't felt for a very long time welled up in him. It took him a few seconds to identify it as regret. He wished that he didn't have to get Arian involved, but he had no choice. Bert had insisted that she was to be his partner for this job.

He shoved the uncomfortable feeling down. She was no innocent. She worked for Bert, so she must have plenty of crimes on her conscience.

And she looked pretty fierce as she stood there glaring at him with her beautiful dark eyes.

"Is it true that you don't drink human blood?" she asked.

"Only if it is offered willingly, and even then I never take enough to hurt the donor," he answered. It was the truth. He had never bitten a human against their will. He was the cleanest-living vamp in England, which was why Ariel Wolfsbane had selected him to be his undercover agent.

She took a few steps towards him. If he'd had a pulse, it would have sped up at having her so close. Close enough for him to notice that flecks of silver dotted her irises, and that she had a small scar at the side of the mouth. He had to fight the temptation to lift his hand and trace it with his finger. He wondered where she'd acquired it. An accident? A fight? Mermaids were very tough and healed fast. Injuries didn't usually leave a trace unless they were serious. Bert wasn't known for his kindness. Had he beaten her up? His fists clenched at his sides of their own accord. Bert would pay for it if he had hurt her.

Her single nostril flared, and he realised that she was sniffing him. Amusement bubbled up in him. He was usually the one doing the smelling. But, of course, mermaids were predators too.

The thought sent a small wave of heat into his belly.

Her nostril closed, and he saw her shoulders relax. "You're not lying. If you'd killed and drunk human blood recently, I would know. But people probably don't offer you their blood very often, so how do you survive?"

There was genuine curiosity in her voice. It warmed him up. He wanted her to be interested in him... to like him. He told himself it was because it would make the job easier, as well as safer, if she didn't hate his guts.

"In the countryside, I hunt. Mostly rabbits and deer. In the city, I buy blood from butchers and slaughterhouses."

She nodded, apparently satisfied. "I can work with a clean-living vamp."

His heart lifted a little at her words. "And I can certainly work with a strong and beautiful mermaid."

She snorted like a well-bred horse. "You can keep your smooth talk, Victor. We're partners on this job, that's all." She jerked a thumb in the direction of the jetty. "Bert told you to debrief me. Tell me everything you know about the target."

"Sure." He sat down, extracted a map from his jacket and laid it on the polished deck. Then he produced a small electric torch, turned it on and placed it next to the map. Arian crouched to get on the same level as him. Her foot-long, flexible tail curled around her webbed feet. Victor couldn't help staring at the silver-coloured tip. A merman on the Morvann Islands had told him that the tips of mermaids' tails were hyper-sensitive. He wondered how Arian would react if he took it in his hand and stroked it... or licked it"This is Paynes Lake, a few miles west of London. I know it." Her voice yanked him out of the little fantasy bubble he'd created. She was studying the map, her eyes as bright as jewels in the torch's light. "There are two islands in the middle; they're owned by a reclusive billionaire, Sir James Romberg."

He was impressed. "You're very well informed."

She shrugged. "Everyone in our line of work knows about Romberg. He's a collector of rare magical objects. Does he own the Blood of the Ocean, then?"

"He does." Victor tapped the map with his finger. "His house is on the main island, but the treasure is held in his private collection, which is housed in a building on the smaller island. The room has security cameras and alarms, and guards patrol the island twenty-four hours a day."

Arian frowned. "It's going to be difficult to get in."

Victor couldn't tell her that stealing the treasure would be the easiest thing in the world, because Romberg would let them take it. Romberg was a friend of Ariel Wolfsbane. They'd arranged for Victor to take the Blood of the Ocean and bring it to Bert. As soon as the gangster had the treasure in his hands, the warlocks would pounce and he'd go down… very deep, and for a very long time.

Unfortunately Bert wouldn't believe that Victor could steal the Blood by himself. So he had given him Arian as a partner.

He gazed into her dark mermaid face. She looked worried, and a stab of guilt pierced him, sharper than anything he'd felt in the past two hundred years. He hated that he had to lie to her. But he'd no choice. The best he could do for her would be to convince Ariel to let her go and not tell her people of her crime. And hope that the chief warlock would agree.

"You've gone very quiet, even for someone who's been dead for centuries." Arian leaned towards him. "You must have a plan up your sleeve. Vamps are known for their resourcefulness."

"Indeed." He shoved the guilt into the darkest room of his mind and shut the door. "I have watched the islands for weeks and studied Romberg's movements. Our chance will come in two days' time. That evening, Romberg is giving a big party at his home. Many VIP guests are coming, and most of the guards will be diverted to the main island to ensure their security. There will be a window of opportunity when the guests leave. The guards will be busy escorting them to their boats.

The remaining guards may be distracted by the sight of the famous actresses and models who are coming."

Arian let out a low whistle. "You're very well informed."

Of course, he was. Romberg had told him his plans for the party in great detail. In particular, he had informed him of the time when the private collection would be left unguarded.

He made a deprecating gesture with his hands. "I've been chatting to the guards. They spend a lot of their downtime in a pub called the Swan and Bottle, on the west shore of the lake. A few free drinks always loosen the tongues... and I can be very charming, you know. People like to talk to me."

She smiled. Something stirred in him at the sight of her needle-sharp teeth. He'd never been attracted to female vampires. They were too cold, in all the meanings of the word. Human women were pleasant company, but so weak compared to him. Too easy to seduce, and he always had to be careful, in case a careless bite sent them from his bed to their grave. But here, at last, was a live, warm female who could be his equal.

"It's great you've got all that intel, but I'd like to see the place for myself. Watch the guards do their rounds and time them." She sounded very calm, as if stealing priceless treasures was routine for her.

And, of course, it was. Regret snuffed out his growing excitement. She was a hardened criminal, and he was about to betray her. They could never be together.

He forced the words out of his mouth. He needed to focus on his mission, not on these inconvenient feelings that kept bubbling up to the surface. "Of course. We can go there tomorrow night. Meet me at the Swan and Bottle after nightfall."

She nodded. "OK. We can find a hideout, stake out the place, and finalise our plans."

She got up as if to leave. The pang of regret took him by surprise. He wanted her to stay. He wanted to spend time with her... get to know her better. "We can talk some more now, if you like."

She gazed down at him with dark, inscrutable eyes. "It will be dawn soon."

He glanced at the sky. She was right. Grey light was seeping into the world. Shit. Those midsummer nights were so short. "You're right. It's time I went home." Chilly disappointment seeped into him. She was the most unusual, fascinating female he'd met in centuries, and now he had to leave.

"Do vampires really burst into flames in the sunlight?" she asked.

She sounded curious, which only intensified his yearning to stay… to tell her about himself. But he'd die if he remained in the open much longer. "Unfortunately, yes. I'd better go."

"It's a shame." Her white teeth flashed in the growing light. "I would like to learn more about you. You're the first vamp I've met. You're not what I expected."

Her words, and her soft tone, dropped into his belly like embers, dispelling the chill and intensifying his longing for her. "I look forward to tomorrow night. I hope I can continue to surprise you."

"I'm sure you will."

Her smile kept him warm through the long walk along the docks and back to his underground flat in Tower Hill. He reached it just before sunrise and collapsed into bed, his mind full of Arian. He would have dreamed about her if vampires had been able to dream.

***

Arian stretched her neck to peer through the reeds. "There are more guards than I'd hoped for."

Victor didn't answer straight away. His brain didn't want to focus on the guards. His brain wanted to study the woman lying on her stomach in the grass, a few tantalising inches away from him.

Because now Arian was in her human shape. She was a slim, dark, very attractive young woman, with a mane of black hair, long, toned legs, and a pert bottom encased in cut-off jean shorts.

He hadn't expected to find her so alluring. After all, he'd bedded – and tasted – hundreds of women over the centuries. None had ever had the impact that Arian had on him.

She shifted her gaze to him. Her eyes were the same as they were in her aquatic shape, enticing pools of darkness lit up by flickering silver stars. She may have looked human, but her eyes were all mermaid. So was her scent, which whispered to him of cool waters and warm, glistening flesh spread out on hot sand…

"Earth to Victor. I'm worried about the guards."

He wrenched his mind away from her enchanting body and dragged up the reply he'd prepared. He knew she'd ask the question. "Don't fret. Two-thirds of them will be diverted to the main island on the night of the party. And I know the ones who will be left won't be the strongest, or the brightest." Their employer Romberg had made sure of that. The guards weren't in on the plot, but they wouldn't be much trouble.

Arian chewed her bottom lip. Her teeth were a little sharper than a human woman's. He imagined these white canines piercing his skin... her pink tongue licking his blood...

"OK. So what's the plan?"

Her impatient tone pulled him back to their task. He had to get a grip. He couldn't let his fantasies get in the way of the mission. "I've timed the guards' rounds. At ten to midnight there will only be one guard near the door. You will sneak up on him and take him out of action." He paused. "Best not to kill him, though. We don't want to trigger a murder investigation."

She nodded. "Don't worry. I'm no murderer. I can disable humans without doing too much damage."

Relief trickled through him. He didn't want her to be bad. Not truly bad. He had enough cold-blooded killers in his life. Most of them his own kind. "When you've taken care of the guard, I will get into the building. I know how to switch off the alarms. And the security cameras won't detect me. I'll be in and out before you know it."

Arian couldn't detach her eyes from Victor's beautiful face. His eyes glittered like black diamonds in the twilight. The long, summer grass, dotted with oxeye daisies and Queen Anne's lace, framed his perfect body as if he were a painting. But he was real. Very real...

She'd arrived early at the meeting point and had waited with growing impatience for the sun to set. He'd appeared just as the last rays were sinking beneath the horizon, and her heart had jumped. Actually jumped, as if she were a young mermaid on a date with a handsome merman.

It was crazy. She'd only known him for a few hours, and he was a bloody vampire. But something in him called to her. Perhaps because he too was a freak and a criminal. A loner, on the fringes of society, just like her. He didn't look down on her. He accepted her just as she was.

And he was so calm, so confident. She'd no doubt that he could steal the Blood of the Ocean. Bert had chosen a good partner for her.

Pity she was having second thoughts about the job. She sat up and gazed across the water at the island. It was now shrouded in shadows, but the building was brightly lit and shone in the gloom like a beacon. All the guards had vanished, except one. She brought her binoculars to her eyes. He was young and looked bored. After a while he took his phone out and fiddled with it instead of keeping watch. It seemed Victor was right. The magical jewel was not as well defended as she'd thought.

"What will you do with your share of the prize?" she asked.

Victor rolled onto his back and folded his arms behind his head. She tried, and failed, to notice how his biceps strained against the sleeves of his jacket. "I'll retire. Find an honest job. Build a nice little crypt somewhere and live out the next centuries in peace. You?"

She hesitated. She never shared her dreams and fears with anyone. Since she'd left the Morvann Islands, she'd guarded her mouth and her heart. But now all the unspoken words and feelings of the past six years rose inside her, yearning to be let out. "I thought maybe I could buy my people's forgiveness. So they'd let me come back."

He turned his head towards her. His face softened. Before meeting him, she wouldn't have believed that a vamp could feel compassion, but it seemed that he did. "They banished you?"

She found that she couldn't speak through the lump in her throat, so she nodded.

"But why?" he asked. "Why do such a terrible thing to one of their own?"

His sympathy reached inside her and dissolved the barriers that she'd built around her soul. No one outside the islands knew anything about her past. But now she was ready to open the gate and let her darkest secret out. He wasn't a merman, or even a human. After this job was done, she'd probably never see him again. She could afford to unburden herself. "You won't tell anyone?"

"Of course not." He turned onto his side and propped his head up on his hand. "You can trust me."

His eyes shone with sincerity. She took a deep breath and began her story. "Six years ago, a man came to my home, Regor Island in the Morvann archipelago. We were surprised because humans don't normally visit it. It is uninhabited – at least that's what they think. My Clan lives underwater; unlike other mermen Clans we rarely switch to our human shape to go on land. But this man turned out to be a wizard. He knew about us and presented himself to the leader of the Clan. He was very handsome, and very charming."

The memory triggered a hot wave of embarrassment, and she paused. She'd been so young, so naïve, and so ready to believe his honeyed lies.

Victor was listening, his face open and friendly. She sensed that no judgement or condemnation would come from him, no matter what she said. This gave her the courage to continue.

"I fell in love with him. I thought that he loved me. I would have done anything for him. But it wasn't me he wanted. It was a magical object my Clan owned, a statuette that could talk and even foretell the future…"

Embarrassment turned into burning shame, and she let her sentence trail off.

"Let me guess." Victor's voice was soft and contained nothing but gentleness. "He convinced you to steal the statuette for him?"

Arian heaved a sigh. "Yes. I took that treasure, that belonged to my people, and gave it to him. He left for London and told me to meet him there. I fled before the theft was discovered and hid for three days in a cave on the mainland, so my Clan wouldn't be able to find me. Then I went to London and waited for my lover."

Bitter anger surged through her shame, and she almost choked on the words. "But he never came. He'd only used me to get what he wanted."

"Bastard." Victor spit the word out. His fangs gleamed in the light of the rising moon. "Tell me his name. If I find him, I'll kill him."

The ferocity in his tone warmed her, as if he'd enveloped her in a blood-soaked hug. No one had ever fought for her. "He gave me a false name, I realised that when I tried to track him down."

For a moment they remained silent. Arian felt lighter, as if she'd taken a weight off her heart and buried it in the shadows that lay thick between them. But she hadn't quite finished her story. "I was alone and lost in London, and I had no money. I lived on the streets and stole food and clothes. Eventually Bert caught me. When he realised that I was a shifter mermaid, he ordered me to work for him. I didn't feel I had any choice but to obey. By then my people had found where I was staying and sent me a message. They said I was banished from the Morvann Islands."

Grief flooded her, drowning all other emotions. Her eyes were prickling, and she swiped them with the back of her hand.

Suddenly he was kneeling in front of her, and his arms were around her. She froze in shock and put her hands on his shoulders to push him off… but he only held her tighter. A powerful thrill ran through her entire body, from the top of her head to the tips of her toes. Something in her that had been frozen melted… and longing rushed into her veins. All her senses were full of him. His hard muscles against her chest. His scent, a designer fragrance shot through with an earthier, more exotic perfume, that evoked ancient palaces and cool forests under the moon. His eyes, so close to hers she could see right into their velvety depths. And his lips, half open, as red and tempting as a forbidden fruit…

She could have fought it. She could have pulled away or slapped him. But the deep well of loneliness within her demanded to be filled… and he felt, smelled, looked so damn good…

She allowed her head to move forward, just a couple of inches.

He angled his head to cover her mouth with his. His sharp canines grazed her bottom lip, and a shiver of excitement made her gasp.

He stroked her back, in a slow, deliberate motion that sent flames coursing over her skin. His tongue entered her mouth and explored it, slowly, deliciously. She laced her hands behind his neck and closed her eyes. The lake, the heist, her Clan, her sorrow and the bad memories… all had vanished. There was only room for him, and the sensations he aroused in her.

Breaking up their kiss was like coming out of a dream. She didn't know whether their clinch had lasted a few minutes or several hours. Her bottom lip smarted. She touched it and saw a drop of blood on her finger. She looked at him. His eyes burned bright, with an intensity that sent an arrow of fire into her loins.

"You taste delicious." His voice had grown huskier. "Like the essence of the sea."

He'd drunk her blood… and found it to his liking. Far from repelling her, the thought only increased her excitement.

She traced the outline of his jaw and was gratified to see him quiver at her touch. "I want to taste your blood too."

A slow, sensual smile spread over his lips. "You're a bad girl, Arian. A very bad girl."

The heat between her thighs grew. To mate with a vampire… what a delicious transgression that would be.

Then his beautiful face grew serious. "Our blood is a priceless gift. It gives health and long life. I have never given it to a female… of any species."

A cold blast of disappointment cooled her libido. She'd presumed too much. She didn't mean that much to him. He probably just saw her as a curiosity, another exotic notch on his bedpost.

Victor's silent heart contracted in his chest as he watched Arian's features crumple. He'd said it all wrong, and now he'd upset her. He took her hands. "But for you, I might make an exception."

Light returned to her enchanting eyes, and he felt his undead soul lift. He hadn't planned to kiss her. But when he'd seen her so distraught, an old instinct had taken over… an instinct from his human days, that he'd thought buried and long forgotten. He'd reached out to comfort her, with no intention of doing anything else… but his body, and hers, had other ideas. The kiss still burned on his lips, and in his blood. That small, fleeting taste of her made him hunger for more. But she'd been hurt before, and she deserved more than a one-night stand, or even a short affair.

"Arian." He relished the sound of her name in his mouth. "You're very special. I would love to spend time with you and get to know you better. In all my long time on and under the earth, I've never met anyone who makes me feel like you do."

Her smile was as radiant as the moon above their heads. Then a shadow descended on her face. "I sense a "but" coming."

This was it. He'd reached the crossroads. He could continue lying to her, or he could tell her the truth about who he was. But he'd sworn an oath to Ariel not to reveal their plan to anyone. The conflicting impulses fought inside his chest like two angry cats.

Her silver-starred eyes searched his. "Victor?"

He reached a decision. He wouldn't tell her everything, but he would offer her a choice. A chance to turn away from this life of crime she'd fallen into. A chance to become the person she was meant to be.

"I've been having second thoughts about this job." He paused, waiting for her reaction.

"Me too!" She let go of his hands and sat back. Her pulse beat fast and frantic at the base of her neck. "The Blood of the Ocean is a powerful weapon. In the wrong hands, it could do a lot of damage." Her hands twisted in her lap. "Those wizards want to use it in a magical war. Lots of civilians could get hurt."

Victor felt his shoulders relax. He hadn't realised how tense he'd become as he waited for her answer. Relief blossomed in him. She shared his values. She could be redeemed.

There could be a future for them.

"You're right. I don't think we can take the risk of giving the Blood to Bert." He leaned towards her and whispered, even though no one could hear them. "So why don't we keep it for ourselves?"

Her nostrils flared with excitement. She bit her lip. "I've thought about it. But it will be risky."

A bead of bright blood appeared at the corner of her mouth. His throat tightened, suddenly parched. How he longed to taste her again.

With effort, he reined in his vampiric instincts. When the mission was over, he'd have all the time in this world to woo her and make her his. "Fortune favors the brave. When we tell your Clan that you've stopped a bunch of evil wizards from getting their hands on a dangerous weapon, they'll realise you're not a bad person."

She clasped her hands over her heart. "They'd forgive me for sure if I brought them the Blood of the Ocean. It once belonged to my people. Let's do it, Victor. Let's steal the jewel and take it to the Morvann Islands."

That wasn't the plan. The plan was to give the magical treasure to Ariel. But he couldn't tell her that, not yet. The important thing was that she'd agreed to help him secure the jewel and keep it safe from Bert's clutches.

Surely, once the merfolk learned how she'd rescued the Blood of the Ocean, they would see that she deserved a second chance.

He extracted the map and torch from his pockets. "OK. Let's go over the plan one more time."

Once they'd ironed out every detail, Arian folded the map and gave it back to him. "I don't need it; I've memorised it. I know where to go and what to do."

He turned the torch off, plunging them back into the velvety gloom. Clouds hid the moon, and he prayed that tomorrow would be a dark night too. "Do you want to get some sleep? You can stay here if you like, I'll watch over you." He'd never watched a woman sleep, never wanted that kind of intimacy. But with her, it was different. He wanted to be at her side, every night, from now to eternity.

"No." She crept towards him, enveloping him with her salty, sultry scent. "We've still got a few hours of night left. I'd like you to tell me about yourself."

Happiness unfurled in his chest. She was interested in him as a person, not just as a partner in crime or an exciting erotic option. "You want to know more about me?"

"Sure." She settled next to him, so close that he could feel the heat from her body. "I want to learn about your life, your death, and the time since then, when you've been, er…"

"Differently alive?" he suggested, and was gratified to hear her giggle. He cast his mind back two hundred years into the past. "OK. I was born in 1792 and died in 1824."

"Wow." She whistled softly. "You were a Regency rake! Tell me all about it."

So he did. They talked, and then they kissed again. Then they talked some more until the first glimmers of dawn appeared in the sky and it was time for them to part.

***

Arian scanned the lake before her. It lay dark and still as a mirror, barely broken here and there by the faintest of ripples. She glanced up. The thick clouds hid the moon and stars. Perfect. The Lady of the Sea, the ancestral guardian spirit of mermen, was with her tonight. She slid into the water, dragging her waterproof bag with her. It took her less than five minutes to reach the smaller island. She hid among the reeds and peeped through the tangled vegetation.

A young guard was standing a few feet away, looking at his phone. She lifted her bag onto the shore, hauled herself out of the water, and pounced.

He dropped his phone and gasped in horror when her webbed arms closed around him. She grinned to show him her sharp teeth. "One move, one scream, and you're dead."

He didn't attempt to fight her. She took his gun and made him sit down in the bushes, then she tied him up and gagged him with the rope and cloth she'd brought in her bag. "Good. Now you stay here, nice and quiet, and don't get yourself noticed until I'm gone."

She retreated to the edge of the water and hid among the reeds. Slow minutes passed. A knot of anxiety formed in her throat. Where was Victor? Had something happened to him? Her stomach lurched. The thought of him being captured or hurt was like a dagger between her ribs… a real, physical pain. This, more than the kisses and the long conversations, forced her to face the truth. She had fallen for him.

A vampire. It was crazy. Yet she couldn't help it. She had to be with him… she had to follow him, as the tide follows the moon. They'd found each other in the shadows, two creatures of the night, and they belonged together. Now they had to find a place where their dark romance could bloom. The Blood of the Ocean would make it possible. But if they failed… The pain in her abdomen intensified. She couldn't wait any longer. She had to find Victor.

But just as she was about to get up, the moon emerged from a cloud, revealing a dark shape against the building. His tall silhouette and the stealthy grace of his movements told her it was Victor. She breathed out, giddy with relief, but she knew it wasn't over yet. He still had to steal the jewel.

Victor stopped at the door and fiddled with the digital security lock. He'd told her he'd broken the code a while back, and clearly it was true, because very soon he was in.

She waited. All her muscles were tense and all her nerves on edge as she listened and watched, ready to attack any guards that turned up. But all she heard was the wind whistling in the reeds and the thump of her own heart.

At last Victor reappeared and shot across the grass towards her. "I've got the Blood of the Ocean," he whispered as he crouched next to her.

A powerful wave of relief and joy washed the tension away. Thank the Lady of the Sea, he was safe. But they had to get away fast, before the guards raised the alarm. "Where's your boat?"

His canines gleamed in the shadows. "A boat would have attracted attention. I came the same way as you."

She'd been so anxious, and focused on watching out for guards, that she hadn't looked at him properly. Only now did she notice that he was wearing a wetsuit and was dripping wet. "You can swim underwater?"

He chuckled. "I didn't have to swim. I don't need to breathe, remember? I walked. C'mon!"

He got up and went into the water. She followed him.

He did indeed walk on the bottom of the lake, and she swam next to him, torn between amusement and admiration. An image flashed into her head. She and Victor lying on the sand under the sea, near her native island, making love among the green fronds of kelp and the white seashells…

But she knew it was a pipe dream. Even if her people took her back, they'd never accept a vampire as her mate. A cold pit opened in her stomach. But she'd lived without her folk for years. She could survive without them. Victor would be enough for her.

When they came out of the lake, they waited for a while on the shore, silent and dripping, to make sure no one was coming after them.

"All good," Victor said finally. "Before we go, I need to confess something."

His face was grave in the moonlight, and a twinge of foreboding registered in Arian's chest. She tried to keep her voice light. "I didn't know that vampires did confessions."

He didn't smile. "I know you don't want to hand over the jewel to Bert. But I need to meet him and pretend to give him the Blood of the Ocean."

Arian stared at him, confusion swirling in her head. "Why? It's a huge risk. What if he's not on his own? We can take him on, but not a whole bunch of heavies."

Victor dragged a hand through his damp hair. "I asked him to meet us alone. In order not to attract attention, I said. You're right, he might ignore my request." He heaved a sigh. "I had never intended to give him the jewel, Arian. I have a plan. The jewel will be safe, I promise, and you will be free, and your people will know the good deed that you've done. But for my plan to be successful, we have to take the jewel to Bert."

He paused. His eyes searched her face. "You will have to trust me on this, Arian."

The way he said her name, intense and low, lit up a flame at the base of her spine. She tried to figure out what the plan might be. Perhaps Victor was going to give the jewel to someone else? Or perhaps he intended to keep it. But if that was the case, meeting Bert made no sense.

"Please, Arian." He put both hands on her shoulders and gazed into her eyes. "I can't tell you the plan, because I swore not to reveal it to anyone. And the man I made this promise to… well, let's say he wouldn't take it well if I betrayed his trust, and even I would not take the risk of pissing him off. But the Blood of the Ocean will be safe from Bert and the Irish wizards, and we will be safe too. I swear it on my past human life."

This was the most solemn oath a vampire could take. Arian felt she stood at a crossroads. She could refuse to believe him. She could turn her back on him, leave, and return to her life of crime and loneliness. Or she could choose to trust him.

Her head told her to take the first path. It was the safest option. She wouldn't take a risk, and she wouldn't get hurt. But she would remain a thief and an exile.

And she would never see Victor again.

The thought was like an abyss gaping under her feet. She had to see him again. She had to touch, smell, and taste him again. She wouldn't know peace until he was hers – body, mind, and whatever remained of his soul.

She took a deep breath. She felt she was launching herself off a cliff. "I trust you."

The light of his smile radiated into her very bones. "Thank you, Arian. You won't regret it."

He kissed her brow, and her entire being soared, as if he'd removed all the dead weight from her soul and set her free. "Let's go."

But first, they had to go home and change. In Arian's case, that meant changing her shape as well as her clothes.

A few hours later, they met up at the Underground train station near the address that Bert had given Victor. The clock on the platform stated that it was two o'clock in the morning. They had three hours before sunrise.

The crime lord had chosen to meet them in one of his properties, an ordinary brick end-of-terrace house in an anonymous suburb of London. It was close to the Thames, and the river's salty, muddy smell followed them as they made their way along the dark and empty street. Arian glanced over her shoulder, calculating how long it would take her to reach the water, should things go pear-shaped. She hoped Victor knew what he was doing. They were gambling with their lives by double-crossing Bert.

Victor took her hand, as if he'd read her mind and wanted to reassure her. The contact of his smooth, cool skin reignited her flagging courage. She was the meanest mermaid the Morvann Islands had produced, and she was in league with a vampire. It was Bert who should be worried. He was a monster, but only a human monster. She and Victor were the real deal.

But she couldn't stop her throat from tightening when they entered the narrow hallway that smelled of damp and of overcooked vegetables.

"In here." Bert's voice came from an open door to the right.

Victor let go of her hand and stepped through. She followed him, her hands balled into fists at her side. Ready to fight or run.

The room was large, sparsely furnished, and looked like it hadn't seen a hoover or a duster in a long time. Bert sat in a corner, in a faded armchair below a naked lightbulb. His face lit up when he saw them. "Have you got the Blood of the Ocean?"

Victor stopped in the middle of the room and pulled the jewel out of his coat. It glowed like a star fallen to earth. Shimmering, changing light bathed the dingy room, transforming it into a palace fit for kings. Arian let out a sigh of wonder. No photograph could have done justice to this living, shining beauty.

Bert's entire being radiated greed. He extended his hand. "Give it to me. The Irish wizards will be so pleased. We're going to be rich!"

Victor took one step towards him and froze. He seemed to be waiting for something.

A man in police uniform came out of the wall and laid a hand on Bert's shoulder. Arian, stunned, tried to make sense of what her eyes were telling her. The tall cop, built like a heavyweight boxer, couldn't simply have walked through the bricks. Yet here he was, and his booming voice reverberated around the room.

"Bert Simmons, I arrest you for theft, conspiracy to steal, and handling stolen magical goods."

Then another man materialized on Bert's right. He was as tall as the cop, but of slimmer build, and wore a sharp black suit. Bert's gaze went from one man to the other, and his face contorted in horror.

"Auric and Ariel Wolfsbane? What the hell?" Then his features twisted with rage and he let out a scream. "Kevin! Tom!"

The man in black laughed. It was a beautiful sound, silvery and ethereal, yet it sent a shiver down Arian's spine, as if she'd walked into a frost-covered forest. "Your thugs won't come, Bert. They're fast asleep in the cellar." He gestured at the policeman, who brandished a pair of handcuffs. "You have a choice. You can go with my brother Auric peacefully and be dealt with according to British human law. Or you can come with me."

Bert recoiled from him as if he were a snake. "I won't go to your dungeon, Ariel. I'll take a human prison anytime."

The gaze he turned on Victor and Arian was so filled with venom that Arian half expected poison to drip onto his cheeks. "You betrayed me, you blood-sucking, slimy vermin. You'll pay for this."

Ariel's musical, chilling laugh echoed around them. "No, they won't. Auric and I will make sure of it. You'll never hurt anyone ever again, Bert."

Bert glanced at the warlock, and whatever he saw in his eyes made him fall silent. His shoulders slumped. Without a word, he presented his hands to Auric, who clapped the handcuffs on his wrists.

The policeman gave Victor and Arian a nod. "Thanks for your help, folks."

And with that, he marched his prisoner out of the house.

Arian found she was breathing more easily, as though the air in the room had become fresher. She turned to Victor. "So that was your plan."

He nodded. "I'm sorry. I couldn't tell you, because I had promised Ariel not to reveal it to anyone."

She laid a hand on his arm. "I get it. It was better that way – the less I knew, the safer it was for me."

He took her hand and kissed it. "I was hoping you'd understand. I will never keep secrets from you again."

His smile filled her with joy. She had been right to trust him. They were a team, and always would be.

Victor didn't need a living, beating heart to feel that Arian was the best thing that had ever happened to him. He would do anything to make her happy. He turned to Ariel.

"We won't get the money now. But there is another reward I'd like to ask for Arian. She was kicked out of her Clan for stealing. Now she has helped us recover the Blood of the Ocean, will you speak to the mermen and convince them to forgive her?"

Ariel's hard, perfect face softened. "Of course." He bowed to Arian. "I am grateful for your help. I have influence with the mermen – one of my best friends is married to their leader, Caltha." A smile tugged at the corner of his mouth. "I can convince the mermen to let you come back to the islands… if that's what you want?"

Victor's entire immortal body ached as he gazed at Arian's pensive face. If she went back to her people for good, they'd never be together. The mermen would never accept a vampire. But her happiness was more important than his. He'd let her go, if it was her wish, even if it destroyed him.

Arian dropped her eyes to the floor. "I want to go back to the islands… but with Victor." Her voice faded to a murmur. "You're a powerful warlock. If there was any way he could become more like me…"

"You want me to change him into an aquatic vampire?" Ariel looked amused. "I couldn't do that on my own. But there is one magical jewel that can give him the power to live under the sea. Swim like a merman. Fish like a merman." He grinned. "Love like a merman."

Victor realized that he was shaking from head to foot. Despair had given way to a bright, trembling hope. "Where is that jewel? Tell me where it is; I'll move heaven and earth to find it."

"There's no need." Humour danced in Ariel's dark eyes. "You're holding it."

Victor gazed at the shimmering treasure in his hand. Wonder bloomed in his mind. "This can make me into a creature of the sea?"

"Yes." Ariel came closer. "It's what it does. Well, it's one of the things it can do. It's not called the Blood of the Ocean for nothing. But, of course, you need a spell to unlock its power and trigger the transformation." He winked at Victor. "Luckily for you, my friend, I know that spell."

"Say it." Arian's voice was low, pleading. "Make Victor into someone... something... I could bring to the Morvann Islands and introduce to my Clan."

She took Victor's free hand. Her love was like an April shower. It had awakened his ancient, dormant heart, and now it was making it blossom. He lifted his gaze to Ariel. "Please do it."

The warlock rested his hand on the jewel and sang an incantation in a language that Victor didn't recognize. As the beautiful melody rose and fell, the Blood of the Ocean glowed brighter and brighter. Its light radiated into every corner of the room, and in every corner of Victor's being. Then suddenly the light pooled around his body, and its magic penetrated his flesh. He felt he was slipping into a dream, though he was wide awake. In the dream, his veins ran with saltwater... his teeth changed into pearls... and his bones were made into corals. Ariel's music still resonated in his ears, but now other sounds mingled with it. The cries of seabirds, the crash of the waves, and the distant songs of the humpback whales flooded him. He was at one with the sea, and with all sea creatures. Including the one at his side.

"Victor! Your eyes have turned green!" Arian exclaimed with awe. "As green as emeralds."

He opened his mouth to speak, but what came out was a stream of musical clicks and whistles. The language of the mermen.

And now an aquamarine light surged from him and bathed the room in an otherworldly glow. Silvery shapes of fishes and dolphins darted above their heads, as if they were all standing at the bottom of the ocean.

Then Ariel fell silent. In a second the light vanished, leaving them stranded in the dingy room. Victor blinked. The dream had ended. The magic had left his body. But he knew it had changed him forever.

"I can speak your language," he said to Arian, in her native tongue.

She squeezed his hand and let out a little "Oh" of surprise. "Look!"

Victor gazed at his webbed fingers. He wiggled his toes inside his shoes, and realized they were webbed too. "I'm an aquatic vampire," he said. Joy danced inside him and erupted into laughter. "I am reborn – again!"

Arian threw her arms around his neck and kissed him. "Now we can be together for good."

He kissed his mermaid back, and for a while the whole world disappeared, until they heard Ariel's polite cough.

"If you don't mind... Could I have the Blood of the Ocean now, so I can return it to its rightful owner?"

Victor and Arian broke off their embrace. Victor handed Ariel the jewel. "Please take it, with my heartfelt thanks."

The warlock pocketed the treasure and smiled. "One good turn deserves another. Bert is behind bars, the Blood of the Ocean is safe, and you two have a new life ahead of you."

Victor stroked Arian's dark hair. "As man and wife."

Her sharp teeth flashed. "As mermaid and mervampire. Now that will give my folk something to talk about!"

Then she kissed him again... and nipped his lip to taste his blood.

## The End

# Wonder Town Station
## Alan Souter

Bob Cramer and Chelsey Pickles sat on wooden benches at either end of the train station's outdoor platform. The station was an antique, all gables and windows that looked like they were last washed when McKinley was president. Under icy moonlight, it stood like a final bastion against defeat. The two bundled young people, huddled on those benches, did nothing to dispel that mood.

No lights shone in the windows of any of the clapboard and brick commercial ventures that lined both sides of the paved street a quarter mile away. It seemed as if all the town's imagination and building skills had been invested in the train station. Then the townsfolk had scurried back to their places of livelihood to await a cascade of good fortune to dismount from the Pullman rail cars and spread prosperity like a new coat of paint. Even the town's name, Wonder, held promise.

It didn't happen. Oh, the drummers and sales opportunities-men piled off, pasting on fresh smiles and warming up fresh patter. The land speculators stepped down from the coach seats to sniff the dirt, and ask, casual-like, about the weather. Even a Chautauqua tent preacher looked up the Methodist Ladies Baking Club at a meeting to see how many had been saved. Noting a number of horses in town hauling buggies, spring wagons, hay mows and buckboards, an automobile dealer wondered about the possibility of a Ford dealership stirring the progressives' blood.

Nope, it didn't happen. People with old ideas had built a new town, dead certain the ideas that had worked before would work again. The freshly laid Acheson, Topeka and Santa Fe train tracks proved the town fathers' plan was sound. They disregarded the non-profit producing spring-fed water stored up in a tall tank near the station that gave the Santa Fe an important stop for their thirsty steam engines called "Wonder Tank."

***

Bob and Chelsey did not know each other, not to speak to, at least. Bob had grown up in Clermont, just over the western forest and a patch of rolling hills. He had moved to Wonder when his father sold the farm for a good profit to build and stock the Wonder Emporium and Merchandise Store. Bob knew his numbers and had four years of high school at the Cranbrook School for Boys. He had filled out, tall and muscular, with a smooth face, gray eyes and large, capable hands. He made money every time the rodeo came to the county fair in Clermont.

The end of Wonder's boom came to Bob after his mother visited Clermont, brought cholera home and gave it to his father. They both passed within two days of each other. The store was deeded to Bob, lock, stock and debt.

Bob looked up as the stationmaster – an elderly, upright gentlemen behind a well-trimmed silver-white mustache, wearing his long blue coat and stationmaster cap – paused at Bob's shoulder.

"I'm heading home, Bob. I'd leave ya the key, but the railroad doesn't want no bums using the station as their bedroom an' toilet. You sure you'll be okay?"

"I'm fine, Mister Hardy."

"I saw your ticket was one way. Y'got kin in Kansas City?"

"It's a business trip. I don't know when I'll be comin' back."

"If you're placin' any orders, I sure wish you'd fetch back some of those molasses cookies. I surely love them."

"I'll remember that, Mister Hardy."

Bob watched the elderly gent lock the station door and then head for the steps at the end of the platform. The red lantern hung high on a pole next to the tracks caught his eye. Wonder was still a flag stop on the Santa Fe line. That lantern signaled the engineer that a passenger or some freight was ready to be picked up.

He glanced toward the other end of the platform. The girl looked ready to leave Wonder, with two suitcases next to her on the bench. She looked kind of familiar, but bundled up like that it was hard to tell. He was hardly a ladies' man. Since his parents died, he had the full responsibility for the store. His father had had a handle on all the items on the shelves. He knew who ordered what. Did the brine get stirred in the pickle barrel? Was their stove gasoline in the drum outside for automobile drivers? What about those dozens of new canned foods, and ice for the meat chest?

He'd scraped all his cash and squirreled enough away to pay his way to Kansas City and to look for a new start if he lived cheap. It was all there, wrapped in brown paper in his satchel, success or failure. He looked at the girl again. What was she running from? Or was she just visiting some maiden aunt?

***

Chelsey Pickles, all milk-fed sweetness, chestnut hair cut short, and her mother's splendid figure, hidden by shy choice, sat wrapped in a huge army coat buttoned to the neck. When she and her mother had arrived in Wonder, they'd been the victims of bad timing. Expecting a boom town on the railroad line, they arrived to establish their Frock and Chapeau Shoppe, supplied with fashion knockoffs from a French cousin in Paris, to be a grand success.

Their new French name was *Piqulé* (pronounced *Peeclay*), ready to lure the new sophisticates arriving in lush Pullman cars and smarten up the local farm and shop women. Sadly, Wonder's husbands locked their purses tight when it came to women's frillies. Any extra pennies went in the mason jar toward one of them gasoline tractors, a new milking stool, or seed to get crops out of the land. This was the sad story of Wonder's commerce. They needed something to prime the pump. The Farmers Bank held paper on virtually everyone of value. More folks were leaving on that train every day.

Soon, Chelsey was working as a domestic for some of the more affluent homes, and the frock shop had yet to receive the promised French fashions from Paris. She took to drink, and Chelsey became "pickled" to Wonder's church-sober population.

Sewn into her undergarments was all the cash they had to buy fancy dresses and hats, gloves and stockings in Kansas City. Every penny was there, with just enough to get along on for maybe three days. She tightened her wrapped arms around her midsection against the cold and felt the cash crackle.

***

The two young people sat well apart on the train station's covered platform under the fly-specked Edison bulb in its tin shade. Bob stamped his cold feet to get some circulation going. Chelsey glanced over in his direction. He looked behind them at the station waiting room door and at the Edison bulb burning behind its frosted glass panel.

He shouted at her. "It's too cold to wait out here."

She remained silent and watchful.

With his satchel in hand, Bob tried the wooden door—it was locked. He took a breath, backed a step and kicked the lock. The effort threw him back, almost off the platform. The door had quivered. From two paces back, he came at the lock again and swung his boot. With a twang, the lock sprung loose and the door flew open.

"Bravo!" shouted Chelsey—and covered her mouth instantly, smelling the whiskey on her breath. Her cheeks colored.

Regaining his balance and grinning her way, Bob grabbed up his satchel and strode inside. Noting her absence, he poked his head out.

"C'mon, I ain't gonna bite ya. There's a stove and everything in here."

Chelsey Pickles followed with her two suitcases. The inside smelled musty, like folks coming and going never bothered to step into this shelter. A potbelly stove sat on a sheet of iron next to a half-full wood box. Bob found blue-tip matches on a shelf behind the barred ticket window.

"We're in business. If you would tear up some of those old magazines to act as kindling, we'll get a blaze going."

His enthusiasm blanketed over her nervousness at being alone with a man in this lonely station. She set to work tearing up the magazines and soon, between the two of them, they had a formidable fire heating the iron stove. They stripped off their coats and pulled a heavy wooden bench closer to the heat. As the flames danced across their faces, they smiled at each other. All fear was displaced by the comfort that coursed through their frigid limbs.

"I'm Bob Cramer, I own the merchandise store."

Chelsey licked her dry lips and said, louder than she meant to, "I am Chelsey *Piqulé*—that's French for 'Pickles.' We own the frock shop."

Bob had forgotten his wide brim Stetson and whipped it off. "I've seen some of your fancy dresses in the window—you being across the street from my store—handsome… uh… frocks, I must say."

"Everybody stops and looks," she replied, "but no husbands are prying loose any cash to buy one. And our prices are too expensive for butter and egg money the wives might save. Too fancy for this town until it grows some more. We're just getting by selling bolts of gingham, cotton and such like for their sewing machines."

Turning his hat brim in his hands, Bob spoke to the floor. "When my folks passed, they left the store to me, along with the debt piled up to stock it. I don't really own the store, but I do own the debt to the Farmer's Bank and Trust. They've run out of trust."

Chelsey shrugged. "I'm washin' floors and makin' beds for extra pennies. I'm headin' to Kansas City"—she paused to make up a quick lie—"to get a real job to send back money." Chelsey bent forward to take off a soaked shoe—and a half pint bottle of Old Overholt Irish Whiskey fell out of her jacket's inside pocket. It lay between them, half full. She quickly looked up at him.

Bob saw the shame. He said, "That's a great idea for a night like this. Mind if I take a pull?"

"P-please do." She hurried on. "It's for medicinal purposes. Mom's worried I'll catch the grippe."

Bob took a sip and handed back the bottle. "Just the ticket, thanks." He looked sheepish and then looked at the floor between his boots. "I'm just headin' for Kansas City. Period."

"Shakin' off Wonder's dust for good, are ya?"

Bob chanced a look her way. She could see his eyes were tired and shone bright with held-back tears. "I hate it. My father taught me better. I got a kid watching the store while I'm gone. Maybe I'll come back. Maybe not." He met Chelsey's questioning look. She put her hand on his shoulder.

The door slammed open and in shambled three trail dust covered cowboys, lugging their gear, saddles, and worn boots with jingling spurs. They came up short when they spied Bob and Chelsey.

"Waaaal, lookee what we got here! Fellow travelers! Didn't see no horseflesh out front or back, so you must belong to that slice of civ-il-ization up the road. That right?"

Bob offered, "That's right."

The cowboy who had spoken was tall, lank and bearded, wearing bat-wing chaps scarred by every cactus and ocotillo plant between Wonder and the Mexican border. His shirt and jeans were sweated to his body. A shorter version of sweat and dust next to him unscrewed his Stetson, that had once been black, from his beer-keg head, and with a bright smile that fastened on Chelsey, barked out, "They speak English! They speak English! No need for the Spanish book in my saddle bag."

The third trail rider dropped his saddle from his narrow shoulders, wiped his hairy forearm across his lips and swept his gray sombrero from his blond locks as he thoroughly appraised Chelsey's body, lingering at the places that interested him most, as if she were a carcass of hanging beef. Chelsey turned half away from him and his turquoise eyes, wide and bright.

"We been rude boys," the tall speaker said, gesturing with his hat as he spoke. "I'm Long Tom, this short—sorry, *compact*—gent is Hank. When he ain't tight, he's a tolerable cook. The blond lover here without hardly any meat on his bones is the Yellow Kid."

Hank eased his gun belt on his prodigious hips and laughed hard,

"Any women he's ever kissed, he had t'chase 'em down. That's why he's so skinny."

Chelsey's eyes were wide, and she had snatched up her army coat to hold in front of her.

The Yellow Kid looked around. "These benches look damned uncomfortable. I'll have t'drape my hoogans over 'em to get a good night's sleep." He leered at Chelsey, "Care t'share a blanket, sweet cheeks?"

Long Tom opened the stove's front grate and fanned the fire with his sombrero. "Hell, Kid, stop makin' a fool out of yourself and help set up camp."

The Yellow Kid laughed hard. "Hell, Tom, we stumbled into one fine campsite!" He reached out and grasped Chelsey's coat by its front buttons. "C'mon, buttercup, show us what you got!"

Bob grabbed the Kid by the arm, spun him around and caught him with a hard left cross. The Kid dropped like a stone. Long Tom drew his Colt revolver and bounced the barrel off Bob's head. Bob joined the Kid on the floor. Chelsey cried out and dropped down next to the young storekeeper and shouted, "You scum!"

Bleeding from the mouth and nose, the Yellow Kid reached for a scabbard at his belt and drew out a ten-inch Bowie knife. "I'm gonna mark that son of a bitch!"

Long Tom stepped between the two fighters. "You ain't markin' nobody, Kid. He ain't got no gun, nor knife. Leave him be."

"I don't care! I'm gonna take an ear. He won't be so purty then!"

As this was going on, Hank had been squatting, digging through Chelsey's suitcase. "Forget the kid, Tom. We ain't got a peso between us. These travelers must have some cash." Hank suddenly sat back on the floor.

"Whoa, lookee here, she's a card shark! He held up a package of playing cards.

Chelsey cried out. "Those aren't playing cards! Those are tarot cards! I can tell fortunes!"

The Yellow Kid froze with a handful of the semiconscious Bob's hair, the Bowie knife in his other hand. Long Tom reached for his revolver to club the Kid senseless if necessary. Hank just ginned like a child at the pictures on the unfamiliar playing cards that told the future.

Chelsey nodded. "Really, I can," she said, looking from face to face.

Long Tom held up three. "They're all face cards. How can you tell who won?"

Chelsey shook her head. "Nobody 'wins,' and yet everybody can win if their question is answered accurately."

The Yellow Kid stroked his blond goatee beard. "How do they work? Deal a hand and maybe we can come up with pot that's real interesting. After all, we got a lot of time t'kill before those three thousand head of cows catch up to us."

Chelsey blinked. "That's a lot of cows."

Long Tom nodded. "Don't you worry about them cows. We been ridin' point for the last three days, and a little entertainment's gonna go a long way."

Against her feelings of fear, Chelsey spread out the cards. The four of them sat in a circle while Bob leaned back against a bench, holding his damaged head.

She began her recitation. "There are seventy-eight tarot cards in a deck. Twenty-two are called Major Arcana cards. The fifty-six Minor Arcana cards are divided into four suits called wands, cups, swords, and pentacles. Each suit contains fourteen cards, comprising of ten numbered cards plus a Page, a Knight, a Queen, and a King."

Long Tom slid his revolver back into its holster. He repeated, "Page, Knight, Queen, and King. No aces up the sleeve?"

"You can't cheat at tarot," Chelsey replied.

Bob was still woozy and watched her as the Yellow Kid, sitting next to her on the floor, stared at the cards with their fanciful illustrations.

As she went on with her explanation of tarot, Hank watched the Kid's hands. They were nervous hands the short, fat cook had seen before. In spite of Chelsey's hypnotic lecture, the brightly colored tarot cards and their exotic promises, the Kid's breath quickened. He was planning. She was a pretty girl, and four months on the trail strained a man, especially a sick one like the Yellow Kid.

Long Tom glanced up at the station's regulator wall clock and said, "The red lantern. The train won't stop if the lantern is down. Hank, get up and cut that lantern down. We don't want no visitors."

The Kid wiped his forearm across his lips. "We don't want no train to stop! Get rid of the lantern!" His eyes were getting wild.

Hank stood up and went out the door. Five minutes later, he returned, but left the door ajar to hear it go on by. "No more lantern."

The Yellow Kid snickered and leaned close to Chelsey. "Hell, you smell fresh as a new peach."

Her hands trembled as she dealt out a spread of tarot cards on the floor. In the center, the knight night on his white charger carrying his black flag caught all their attention. Long Tom peered at it hard. He looked down at the girl.

"What's that iron man on the white horse mean?"

Chelsey picked up the card. "You've heard of the knight in shining armor, haven't you?" He offered a blank stare. She nodded. "Okay, long ago, hundreds of years ago, there was this round table around which the knights—he's a knight—gathered to tell stories of their quests, their good deeds and bold battles. This knight is Sir Lancelot, the bravest of them all. And a savvy lover."

"Hot damn!" Yellow Kid clapped his hands together. Hear that! The jasper on the white horse has a hot pecker too! What about that black flag?"

She made a stern face. "That is the flag of death he brings to his every adversary."

Kid looked puzzled. "Ad-ver-sary. What kind of critter is that?"

She shook her fist. "Dangerous knights, fierce dragons, anyone who crossed his path and challenged him to a duel!"

"This gets better and better!" the Kid shouted. "Sweet cheeks, you got a reward comin'!"

Hank looked nervous. Long Tom hesitated, but made no move toward his gun. He just stared as Chelsey pushed herself away from the Kid, sliding backward on the floor.

Bob shouted, "Stop, Kid! All eyes went to him, standing with his back to the platform door. In his extended hand was a small, nickel-plated revolver.

"Whoa," shouted Long Tom. "Where'd that pop gun come from?"

Bob shouted, "Chelsey, come here. Be quick!"

Chelsey gathered her legs under her and dodged the Yellow Kid's reaching hands. She stumbled over next to Bob. While she ran to Bob, Long Tom edged over to the right. The Kid scrabbled up his gun belt and grasped his Colt. Hank just froze with his gun belt at his feet.

Long Tom, his hand hovering over his holstered revolver, shouted, "Ya can't get us all with that pop gun.'

Bob gripped the small caliber revolver. "I got five tries!"

From alongside him, Chelsey cried out, "Bravo, Bob! We're no dogfall, Mister Kid!" She dropped to her knees and grasped Hank's revolver from its holster on the floor. "Now we got ten tries!"

The front door slammed open, followed by the stationmaster. "What the hell's going on here?" Behind him, another man pushed into the waiting room.

Hank sat on the bench, his head in his hands and gun belt on the floor. Long Tom slowly raised his hands, staring at the pair of long-barreled Colts, cocked and leveled by Sheriff Chauncy F. DePew.

The Yellow Kid winced behind his hands held in front of his face. He pleaded, "Make her put that hogleg down. It might go off!"

***

On Wonder's Main Street, dentists, grocers and lawyers opened their shop front doors. The milk wagon turned out of the dairy, and a pair of schoolteachers rode toward the school in a one-horse buggy. Doc Overton parked his locomobile in front of his dispensary. They all looked up toward a gunshot that came from the train station.

Some idlers having their morning beer came through the swinging doors of McCann's Tavern and followed the other rubbernecks toward the station, standing out against the morning sky and a sliver of sun. One observer noted the red lantern was at the top of its pole in time to signal a stop for the daily passenger and peddler freight the town counted on. The squeal of its brakes made some of the approaching citizens smile as they checked their pocket watches. Right on time.

Inside the station, the results of the gunshot were plain and simple. Sheriff DePew covered Long Tom, Hank the cook, and the Yellow Kid on a bench. The Kid had a stunned expression, holding his sombrero with a bullet hole just above the hat band. His tousled blond hair had a new part sizzled right down the center.

"I'm sorry, I'm sorry," Chelsey was muttering, her eyes squeezed closed. "I didn't mean to shoot him. Is he dead? "

Bob moved her out onto the station platform as the freight cars were unloading. She had her arms wrapped around him, and he reciprocated. "No, Chelsey, you shot the hat off his head. He'll live." Bob paused and looked past Chelsey.

"I may be wrong, but if I read the stencils on the unloaded boxes they say *Paris, France. Manipuler avec soin.*"

Chelsey gushed. "Oh my gosh! Those are our dresses and hats from Paris." She turned to Bob. "You saved my life to see this!"

"Did you see that in the tarot cards?"

Chelsey reddened across her cheeks. "I didn't see nothing in those cards. They aren't mine. I was taking them to my aunt in Kansas. I only know what a few of the pictures mean."

"How about that knight in shining armor that was in the Yellow Kid's hand?"

Her eyes narrowed, "That's the Death card. Sort of a hopeful wish, I guess."

"You're lucky you had time to memorize some of those cards."

"Girls named Pickles have a lot of time on their hands."

The stationmaster hurried out to the platform. He spied the couple on the bench. "Bob, you be sure to stop at the sheriff's office. He says there's wanted paper on the Yellow Kid in Texas and Montana. He also said Wonder don't have a medal for bravery, but you sure can get a few thousand dollars in reward on that murderin' rattlesnake. Oh, sorry, Miss Pickles. I gotta get to the newspaper. Just come in overnight on the wire. We got three thousand head of cattle gonna be here in three weeks to ship out on the Santa Fe. Looks like we're goin' to be a cattle town for a spell. Hallelujah!"

Bob took her in his arms. "Looks like we're stuck in Wonder for a while. What would you think of Cramer for a new last name?" He felt her shiver.

"Shouldn't we do some courtin', just a little, for appearance's sake?"

Chelsey reached into her coat pocket and pulled out a tarot card. "This is the Lovers card. It means love, harmony, trust, honor, the beginning of romance, and optimism. Are you ready for all that in one turn of the card?"

He held her closer, their lips only an inch apart. "Miss Pickles, can you cook?"

"I make a mean stack of flapjacks. That's about it,"

"It's a deal, Mrs. Cramer" Their lips crushed together.

The locomotive tooted its whistle and jangled its bell as it hauled the peddler freight and departing passengers away from Wonder train station. Alongside the bright rails lay a broken half-pint bottle of Old Overholt Irish Whiskey.

## The End

# Grow Where You're Planted
## Nancy Golinski

Gina only looked down for a second. That's all it took. She was reaching for her phone, which had slipped out of her purse, when she heard the sickening crash. Her car had just slammed into a guard rail. The force triggered the airbag, which pushed her head back against the headrest.

It took a moment for reality to sink in. Then she unbuckled her seatbelt and stepped out to observe the damage. The front end was twisted under. One tire rim was completely bent, and she could see a green liquid trickling out from underneath.

Gina kicked the tire in frustration. She had stretched her finances just to buy the hunk of junk, and there was no way she could afford any repairs now. As she rubbed the back of her head, she watched a state trooper pulling up.

The cop got out and approached. He was wearing one of those goofy hats, and she swayed on her feet as she looked up at him.

"You okay, miss?"

"Yah. I'm fine, but my car isn't. I got distracted and hit the rail."

"Have you been drinking?"

"No. I was just reaching for my phone when the accident happened."

He nodded and opened a notebook. "You weren't texting, were you?"

"No. But I was getting ready to." Gina never lied. It was an idiosyncrasy that got her into a lot of trouble. She quickly covered her mouth with one hand and rubbed the back of her neck with the other.

The cop tilted his head down and eyed her over the top of his sunglasses. Then he smiled. "I'm going to have to write you a ticket. The good news is you'll have a report to file with your insurance company. I'll also call a tow truck for your car and an ambulance to take you to the hospital."

She sighed. "I understand. No ambulance, though. I can't afford it. I don't have health insurance."

He frowned. "You really should get checked out by a doctor. You seem a bit unsteady, and even a fender bender can do serious damage that's not always obvious."

"Well, I guess I can go to an urgent care. They're cheaper." Then she mumbled, "Grow where you're planted."

The trooper gave her a funny look.

It was one of Gina's favorite sayings, and she often repeated it to herself. Her life wasn't quite where she wanted it to be, but she still made the best of things. Someday she would have a nice house, but for now she settled on a cute efficiency apartment in the city. Someday she would be a singer in a successful band, but for now she sang in one that did gigs at nursing homes and birthday parties. Gina always made the best of any situation.

The cop finished writing her ticket as the tow truck pulled up. He handed it to her and then offered to drive her to an urgent care center. The man was only a few years older than her, but he acted all fatherly as he dropped her off at the entrance.

"I hope everything checks out okay with the doctor," he said. "Don't worry. Your day will get better. These things happen all the time."

She smiled and thanked him as she stepped out of the car. Then she waved, before walking into the building. Gina had every intention of ditching as soon as the police car was gone. She already had her phone out to order an Uber, but a blinding headache stopped her at the door. Maybe she should get checked out. She turned and walked up to the reception desk.

"Can I help you?" A disinterested employee was sitting there reading a magazine.

"Hi. I was just in a car accident. I want to be seen by someone just to be safe. I don't have insurance."

The man eyed her from behind the plastic partition. Gina didn't have any obvious cuts or bruises. He pushed some forms across the desk. "Fill these out and bring them back when you're done. It's fifty dollars for the visit, and we take credit cards. There's a line ahead of you, so it's going to be a while."

Gina took the forms and grabbed a seat. She looked around the waiting room. There was a mom sitting with two small children, a construction worker with an arm packed in ice, and an old man sitting in the corner. She ignored them all and started on the forms. A television was hanging on the wall, and she could hear the faint murmur of a game show playing.

As she penned her answers, she could hear another odd noise. It sounded like water gurgling. Gina paid no attention to it until the noise grew louder. Now there were sharp gasps interspersed with gurgles. She looked up, but nothing seemed amiss. Then her eyes landed on the old dude in the corner. He was clutching his chest and struggling to breathe. His body looked oddly gray, but there was a dark shade of purple clouding his cheeks. The man dropped to the floor and started shaking. The noise grew even louder, and it sounded like rattling pipes.

Gina flew out of her chair and went to grab the receptionist. He had stepped away from the desk, so she pounded on the plastic. Finally, he arrived, and Gina gasped, "Help! There's a man dying out here."

The receptionist hit a button on the desk and ran through the door. He was followed by two other employees in white lab coats. "Where?" they yelled.

Gina pointed to the man in the corner. He was now lying completely still, and she could see an odd dark substance swirling around him.

The three medical people looked to where she pointed. "There's no one there, honey." They were now giving each other knowing looks.

The receptionist asked, "Did you by chance hit your head in that accident?"

Gina nodded.

"Well, why didn't you say so? We always take head injuries first. They can be serious." He took her arm and gently led her back to an exam room.

A half hour later they were done. The doctor confirmed she had a concussion.

"No kidding. I barely hit my head. But I do have a headache. That's a sign, isn't it? And is it normal to hallucinate when you have a concussion?" She was babbling and couldn't stop herself.

The doctor smiled. "It doesn't take much to cause a concussion. As for hallucinations, they're not typical, but they have been known to happen. You're going to need to rest for a few days. You can take an over-the-counter medication for the headache, and try to stay cool and away from bright lights. Keep moving, though, as that will help stimulate the brain. If the hallucinations continue, call your primary doctor."

Gina ordered the Uber while she waited for them to process her credit card. Then she headed out the door. In her peripheral vision, she could still see the old man lying on the floor. The dark substance was almost completely covering him now. She shook her head at the hallucination and headed outside.

As soon as she got home, she took some aspirin. She was feeling antsy and upset, but it wasn't because of the car accident. She had faith her concussion would heal, but tomorrow she had to go to her great-uncle's funeral. She hadn't been particularly close to the man, but it was an obligatory event, and her family would be there.

Therein lay the problem. They were your typical, overbearing Italian family, and they did not like Gina singing in a band. Instead, they wanted her to get a boring but sensible job. She shuddered at the thought. She was a free spirit, and there was no way she could do such a thing. But her mom nagged her continuously, and her dad talked about secure income and paying bills. They would have a fit when they learned she'd wrecked her car.

Gina sighed. There was no way she could show up in an Uber. She would call her cousin, Jimmy, instead. He could take her to the funeral, and he would keep quiet about the accident. Jimmy was a free spirit just like her.

When she went to bed, she briefly thought about the hallucination. She chalked it up to her creative mind and was able to finally fall asleep.

***

The next morning she woke to the phone ringing. It was her insurance agent letting her know the car would be fixed. She would have to pay the hefty deductible, and if she wanted a rental car, she would have to pay a daily fee. Gina gave her credit card number for the deductible and politely declined the rental. She would figure something else out.

After an invigorating shower, she dried her hair and slapped on a black knit dress. It was the most versatile piece in her wardrobe. She could wear it to job interviews, cocktail parties, a night on the town, and even today's funeral. Gina applied a bit of makeup and threw her hair up into a sixties-style bun. That, paired with the funky jewelry she put on, would surely drive her mother crazy. She smiled at her reflection in the mirror.

Jimmy was only five minutes late picking her up. He chuckled when he saw her hairdo. They chatted the entire way to the church and only quieted down at the entrance. Like good Catholics, they dipped their fingers in the holy water, made the sign of the cross, and genuflected. Then they dropped into a pew right behind Gina's parents.

The service started shortly after. It was long, and by the time Communion rolled around, Gina was bored. She looked around the church and noted a hot guy at four o'clock. He had on a military uniform, and she wondered if he was one of her great-uncle's "children." Her uncle had served in Vietnam. After the war he became involved in the VA and volunteered as a counselor for soldiers with PTSD. He often told stories about these men and women and what they were going through.

The hottie suddenly looked her way, and their eyes locked. Gina felt a shiver and quickly turned away. She pretended to be interested in the Virgin Mary statue on the left side of the church. Then her eyes glanced down at the group of people sitting there. They did not appear to be part of the funeral. They had their heads bent and were clutching rosaries. Their lips were moving as if in prayer, and they were all the same shade of gray. It reminded her of the old man from yesterday. Then she noticed the black mist. It was creeping out from the confessional and was moving in a spiral formation. It was just about to reach the oldsters, when the bells began to toll.

The funeral had ended. Gina tore her gaze away and dutifully followed her family out of the church. The casket led the way, and she watched as her dad and brothers lifted it into the hearse. The American flag on top fluttered softly in the wind.

A line of cars followed the hearse to the cemetery. Somehow Gina got stuck in a car with her mom. She listened as the woman droned on and on about the ceremony, the flowers, and what people were wearing. She loved her mom, she really did, but they had nothing in common other than genetics. When Mrs. Rini started lecturing her on current fashions, Gina rubbed her head and made a silent prayer for patience.

As soon as the cars were parked, she made her escape. She told her mom she would stand and let the older relatives sit. Then she made a beeline for the back of the crowd. She stood off to one side and listened as people began to speak about her uncle. It was hot out, and her head was hurting. She regretted not taking a seat when she had the chance.

Gina noticed a marble bench close by. It was tempting to go sit on it, but the bench was part of a tombstone. She idly read the name, Harvey Smith, and the dates, 1966 to 1982. She ran the numbers through her head and realized he had died young. That was sad, but at least his family had a sense of humor. They had inscribed "May your feet find rest where Harvey's soul finds rest" on the bench. That made her smile. She yawned and tried to concentrate on the priest's words. She noted the military guy was standing fairly close to her.

Then out of nowhere, she heard it. There was a low grunting noise coming from the bench. She turned and watched in horror as a gray hand slithered out of the ground and grasped the edge of the seat. A body slowly followed and began to pull up out of the ground. As it did, her nose was assaulted by the rankest of smells. She had to bend over and clutch her stomach to keep from heaving.

It felt like her feet were frozen to the ground. This had to be another hallucination but damned if it wasn't a doozy. She squeezed her eyes shut, but the noise grew louder. She finally opened them and watched as the body freed itself. The head turned her way, and she gasped in horror. Half the face was gone, as if completely blown off, and the other half had a dangling eye that stared right at her. There was no mouth, but the thing was still grunting and wailing. Then the head tipped back, and it let out a primordial howl.

Gina screamed in response, but just then a twenty-one-gun salute was going off for her uncle, so nobody heard. She turned without thinking and started running. As she ran, she noticed other hands coming out of graves all over the cemetery. There were wailing noises everywhere, and she could see the dark swirl in the distance. It appeared to be reaching out to grab her. Gina's breath hitched in terror, and she kept running until she cleared the cemetery entrance. Outside, things seemed quiet, and she stopped to catch her breath. Then she heard footsteps running toward her.

"Are you okay?" It was the military guy.

She could only nod as she continued to catch her breath. Over his shoulder, she could see gray beings slowly walking toward them. "Oh my God, they're coming," she said.

He looked behind him and then back at her. "It's okay."

She didn't wait to hear more. She took off down the road, and he didn't follow. She made it four blocks before she had to stop again. She was on a downtown street with shops all around. There were no gray beings in sight. There was a coffee shop across the street, though, and she decided to go in there to rest.

Gina ordered an iced latte and grabbed a seat by the window. As she calmed down, she thought about what had occurred. It had to be more hallucinations, but they were so vivid. She worried this was more than just a concussion. What if she was developing schizophrenia? She seemed to remember a psychology class that talked about the disease. It tended to show up at a young age, and she was only twenty-two. Then there was the whole military guy issue. He had clearly seen her meltdown and probably thought she was crazy. What if he told her family what happened?

Sure enough, her phone started chirping as she sipped her coffee. One text was from Jimmy wanting to know where she was and if she needed a ride. Another was from her dad, who told her to get to the Knights of Columbus for the reception, or there would be hell to pay. The last was from her mom, who refused to text and instead called and left a message. It went on for two minutes and ended with, "That nice marine, Mike, told me you got upset but would be okay. Really, your great-uncle was old, and there's no reason to be upset, Gins. But what about this Mike guy? Are you two dating?"

Gina groaned. Leave it to her mom to see a match where none existed. She downed her drink, used the restroom, and then got her bearings. The K of C hall was only a few blocks away. She would walk it and save the money on an Uber. The exercise would help clear her mind. She sent a quick text to Jimmy and headed out.

By the time she reached the reception, it was in full swing, but she was still feeling jittery. Maybe the latte had been a bad idea. She took a deep breath, walked in, and was immediately bombarded by her family.

"Where were you?"

"Why didn't you let your cousin drive you?"

"Why didn't you drive your own car?"

Gina listened to the questions and finally fessed up about the car accident from yesterday. They stared at her in shock.

"It wasn't serious, but the car needs some work, so that's why I had Jimmy drive me. I hit my head in the accident, and I was feeling sick at the cemetery, so that's why I left."

She was hoping her responses would appease everyone, but of course they didn't. Her parents started lecturing her on safe driving, buying a better car, and ultimately getting a real job to pay for it. She let them drone on and on. It was nothing she hadn't heard before. Out of the corner of her eye she noticed the cute guy, aka Mike, hovering close by and listening. She arched one eyebrow at him until he turned and walked away.

An hour later Gina was doing something she almost never did. She was getting drunk. The doctor had told her to stay away from alcohol, but this was more than any girl could bear. As she sipped her gin fizzie, she watched Mike approach.

"You okay?" he asked.

"No, and I don't want to socialize, so go away."

"Oh. Okay. Sorry." He turned to leave, but then he stopped and turned back. "You really shouldn't have gone into the cemetery without your shield on. I know you were grieving your uncle and all, but that was risky. They spotted you a mile away."

She sighed. Why were the handsome ones always so messed up? He was definitely one of her uncle's "children," but she was half in the bag, so she politely asked, "Who spotted me?"

Mike stared at her. "Oh my God. Is this your first time?"

She noticed his hands were clenched in fists, never a good sign, and she quickly stood up. "Okay. Good chat. I've gotta go now."

He followed as she walked away. "It *is* your first time. No wonder you didn't have your shield on. You've never seen the dead before, have you?"

She stopped and turned. "Please tell me you're talking about my uncle's casket."

He stared at her.

She hesitated but then whispered, "That's what they were? Dead?" How did you know I saw anything?"

He gave a sad smile. "Because I see them too."

She stared at him for a beat. Nope. No can do. She wasn't going there. "Okay then." She turned to walk away, but Mike grabbed her arm.

"Please wait."

Just then Jimmy walked up. "This guy bothering you, Gins?"

She laughed. "God, you're such a Guido sometimes, Jimmy. But no. He was just leaving."

They both looked pointedly at Mike, who had the decency to blush. "Okay. I'll leave you alone. You can reach me at the VA if you ever need to talk. Just call the Sutton office and ask for Mike Santos. Tell them you need to talk about the dead, and they'll give you my number." Then he was gone.

Jimmy looked at her. "Talk about the dead?"

"Don't ask," she laughed. Then she made a crazy motion with her finger in front of her head.

The reception lasted another hour. Everyone was getting drunk, and at one point Gina's mom linked arms with her and asked about Mike.

"Oh, Mom. He's crazy. He keeps talking about seeing dead people."

Her mom didn't bat an eye. "You could do worse, dear."

Gina sighed. Yep. It had been an all-around stellar twenty-four hours. She needed to get home and go to bed. Tomorrow would be a better day.

***

It certainly started off that way. A friend from the band dropped off an old car he wasn't using, which solved her transportation problem. They had a gig that night, and she was looking forward to it. She also had to work at the local hospital that morning, and she dearly loved the job. Her brother was a nurse there and pulled some strings to get her in. Gina's job was to deliver the meals to the patient rooms. It was easy work and only part-time, but they were able to schedule around her singing gigs, which was nice. She also liked chatting with the patients. She was caring and compassionate by nature.

Her first stop was the oncology floor. Sadly, not a lot of meals were delivered there, as most patients could only tolerate liquids while they were receiving treatment.

Gina got off the elevator and pushed the cart toward the unit. One wheel was wonky and making a squeaking noise. It was loud, and she made a mental note to have maintenance fix it. But over the sound she started to hear something else. It was a shuffling noise like someone was following her, only they couldn't pick up their feet.

This, in and of itself, was not surprising in a hospital setting, but Gina started to feel apprehensive. When the foul smell hit her nose, her heart sank. Not again. She slowly turned and looked behind her.

Sure enough, there was a woman standing there with a festering, black tumor on her neck. She was reaching out her arms toward Gina, and she was tinted in the now-familiar shade of gray.

Gina turned back around and wheeled her cart toward the unit at a fast pace. There was no way she could lose this job. She would ignore the lady and deliver those meals if it was the last thing she did. As she worked, she realized more gray beings had joined the woman and were slowly parading behind her. She tried not to look, but the smell was awful, and when she turned a corner, she saw more ahead. They all looked to be suffering terribly.

Gina finally gave up, abandoned her cart, and ran toward the elevator. She furiously pushed the button to shut the door, and just as it was closing, a dark swirl swept in. Everything went dark in front of her, and she screamed. She vaguely heard the words, "Help me," before she passed out.

Gina woke ten minutes later in a bed in the emergency department. Her brother was hovering over her.

"Jesus, Gins. What happened? An orderly found you unconscious in the elevator."

She rubbed her head and anxiously looked around the cubicle. There were no gray beings. "I told you. I was in a car accident yesterday and hit my head. The doctor said I had a concussion. I must have passed out while making deliveries."

Her brother touched her forehead. "You should have stayed home and rested. Your supervisor would have understood."

She sat up and waved the comment away. "I need the money, Joe. You know that."

He sighed. "You really need to get it together. You know Mom and Dad are not going to like this."

"Then don't tell them."

"I won't, on one condition."

"What?"

"That you go home and rest today."

"Okay. Easy enough."

"Promise me, Gins. No singing. No projects. Just go home, put on a movie, and sleep."

"Fine. I promise." She stood up and reached over and hugged her brother.

"I'll call you later to see how you're doing," he said.

She left the hospital and got in the car. She drove home as promised and put a movie on. She called the band leader and told him she wouldn't be there that night. Fortunately, they had a back-up singer. Then she hesitated. The hallucinations were getting out of hand, and she needed answers. After a mini war in her mind, Gina finally gave in and called the Sutton VA office. Mike called her back an hour later.

They agreed to meet for coffee in the same café she had stopped at yesterday. Mike was already there when she arrived and asked what she was having. He ordered and paid, which was a nice gesture. Then they found a seat in the back and sipped their drinks in silence. She was running through her mind what to say and what to ask, but a small part of her couldn't help but notice his sexy brown eyes. They were dripping pure empathy, which made her want to cry.

Finally, Gina composed herself enough to speak. "So, am I going crazy or something?"

"No. You're not," he reassured her. "But I know how you feel. I felt the same when I first started seeing them."

She motioned for him to continue.

"I served in Iraq and was thrown during an explosion. The back of my head hit the side of a building. I started seeing them right after that. They're tough to ignore, and I didn't know how to make a shield back then, so the dead were following me all over the place. I tried to keep it to myself, but sometimes you have to run and scream, you know?"

She wryly nodded.

"The Marines finally clued in and discharged me. I ended up here and in your uncle's care. He was the only one who believed me and didn't think I was hallucinating. He got me in touch with the other sensitives."

"Sensitives?"

"People who can see the dead."

"Huh. So that's actually a thing. I mean, I've heard of psychics and all, but I always thought they were scammers."

He grinned. "There's some of those too, but sensitives are for real. So how did you lift your veil?"

"Excuse me?"

"There's a veil that separates our world from the spirit world. When it's lifted, you can see them. Yours obviously just lifted. How?"

She thought about it. "I was just in a car accident. I hit the back of my head on the headrest. It wasn't much of an impact, though. It hardly seemed enough to cause this craziness."

"Sometimes it doesn't take much. You might have been sensitive to begin with, and this might have taken you over the edge."

"So what are these gray beings? Just random dead people? Shouldn't there be more of them?"

"No. Most of the dead cross over. For whatever reason, these ones don't. They are suffering and desperately want their pain to end."

She frowned. "Cross over to where? Heaven?"

"Who knows? We do know most dead go into a light. I've seen it happen myself. When I was still in Iraq, I saw a tank get blown up. Then I saw this bright light and all these spirits floating up and into that beam. It was so beautiful and peaceful to watch."

Gina felt tears in her eyes. "That's lovely. So these gray beings, why don't they get the light? Are they evil?"

"Some are. But some aren't. There doesn't seem to be any rhyme or reason to it. All we know is, once they realize you can see them, they come after you and try to get your help."

"Oh. That's sad. Can we help them?"

"I guess. I know some sensitives have tried, but it's risky."

"Why?"

"Think of it as trying to save a drowning victim. If you go in after them, they are in a panic and flailing about. They can pull you under with them. It's kind of like what you described on the phone with the elevator."

Gina shuddered. "Yah. That wasn't good. Okay. So tell me about this shield."

His face lit up. "You are definitely going to need to practice building one. It's a mind exercise where you picture a circle of mirrors all around you. The mirrors face out and reflect the negative energy back on the dead. When it's up, they have no idea you can see them. Inside your circle is safe and full of light." He proceeded to walk her through the exercise in her mind. When he was satisfied she had the hang of it, he added. "You will need to pull it up anytime you go into a hot spot."

"Hot spot?"

"Yes. Places where the dead are likely to be. Cemeteries. Hospitals. Battle sites. Any place where a terrible homicide occurred. Even freeways are out, as lots of car crashes occur there. I haven't driven on a freeway in years. It's tough for me to keep my shield up and drive at the same time, and they're everywhere on a freeway."

Gina shook her head. She couldn't decide if he was crazy, or if this was for real. Come to think of it, the same could be said of her. Was she crazy, or was this for real? Finally, she stood up and thanked him. "Can I call you again?"

"Sure. Anytime." He stood and gave her a hug, and a delicious shiver ran up and down her spine.

\*\*\*

They started hanging out after that. Gina had to quit her hospital job, which infuriated her parents, but they liked she was spending time with Mike. He was the one who helped her land a new job at a florist shop. It was perfect. Her creative side was great at arranging bouquets, and her social side enjoyed interacting with the customers. The ones that touched her the most were those who came in to order arrangements for a funeral. She spent extra time with these customers and tried to ease their pain. In the back of her mind, she wondered if their loved ones had crossed over or were still hanging around.

Meanwhile, Mike helped her fine-tune her shield skills. He also introduced her to other sensitives, and it was like being welcomed into a whole new group of friends. They hung out together, swapped stories, and gave advice on safe places to shop and eat to avoid the gray beings. They were able to warn her about which singing gigs she should avoid, and they even came to some of her shows.

Mike, in particular, was supportive of her singing. "You have such a beautiful voice. It's mesmerizing."

Gina blushed. He was paying her more and more compliments, and he often swung his arm across her shoulders when they were out. Her family was convinced the two were dating, but she wasn't so sure. For one thing, they had never even kissed. For another, they had only been thrown together due to the circumstances. Sure, there was an interest there on both sides, and they were definitely vibing, but did she really want to get serious with this guy? Part of her still thought the whole "sensitive" thing was crazy. If it was real, and each day brought more and more proof that it was, then there had to be a reason. Why would they be given this gift and not use it?

She broached the topic at a friend's house when they were all sitting around a table having dinner. "Has anyone ever tried to help these spirits?"

"I tried once," said Tom. He was a quiet, older man who rarely spoke, and Gina was surprised he did now.

"How did it go?"

"I was able to get them to a light, but they were too terrified to cross over."

Gina frowned. "That is so sad. I wonder why?"

Mike shrugged. "Who knows. I read a bunch of books on the topic, and the consensus seems to be unfinished business, but they're hard to talk to, as they panic, so it's tough to figure out what that business might be."

The group continued to discuss it and finally agreed it was best to not even try.

Gina was less convinced. "I don't know. I think I might want to attempt to help one at least once."

They tried to dissuade her, but she could be stubborn when she wanted.

Mike finally spoke up. "Well, if you're determined, then I don't want you to do it alone. I will help you." They smiled at each other, and the group moved on to other topics.

***

Gina decided to start with Harvey Smith. In her mind, the spirit had brought Mike into her life, and she felt she owed the dead guy.

Mike was sitting next to her on the couch in her apartment. "Let me see what I can find out about him." He proceeded to type away on his computer at an alarming speed.

Gina sat back and watched with amusement. She was slowly learning more about Mike, and now she could add ninja typing skills to the list. She also knew he had an older brother who was a lawyer, had wonderful parents, and ran his own tech company.

It only took him ten minutes to get what they needed. Harvey had committed suicide.

"Well, that explains why half his head was gone. I bet he shot himself," said Gina

"I wonder what his unfinished business could be?" added Mike. "I mean, he clearly wanted to die."

"Yah, but maybe he regretted it after," she said. Then her brow furrowed with sadness, "Oh no. I hope it's not like what the Catholics preach. If you commit suicide, you don't go to heaven. That would be so sad. I mean, suicidal people are depressed. It's not like they can help it."

Mike looked worried. "If that's the case, then maybe we shouldn't focus on him. Why risk it if we can't get him to the light?"

But Gina was determined. "No. For some reason, I think we should start with him."

Mike smiled. "Okay. I know there's no use arguing with you when you've made up your mind, stubborn Italian girl."

"Oh, is that right?"

"Yes, it is." Then he leaned over and kissed her. It was their first really intimate moment, and she felt her heart leap in her chest.

"I like kissing you," she said. Then she abruptly changed the topic. "Now, how do you propose we get into that cemetery teeming with spirits? We can't talk to Harvey with our shields up, can we?"

"No. But I've been giving it some thought. We can both go into the cemetery with our shields. Then when we get to Harvey's grave, you'll keep yours up and expand it to surround me and the grave. Once you've done that, I'll drop mine and try to talk to Harvey."

Gina thought about it. "I don't know. It's a great idea, but I don't think my skills are that good yet. Maybe you should be the one to protect us, and I'll talk to Harvey."

Mike didn't like it, but he finally agreed it was the wiser option. They practiced for a week, although more time was spent making out than actually working on the shield. By Saturday they were definitely a couple. They were also ready to talk to Harvey.

They opted to go late in the afternoon. As they walked, Gina realized she was putting a tremendous amount of trust in Mike. It felt right. She liked everything about him and was slowly falling in love. They held hands as they entered the gate.

Once they reached Harvey's bench, they set up. Gina stood next to it, and Mike stood further away. He expanded his shield like they practiced, and she dropped her own. Then they watched as Harvey slowly made his entrance.

The stench was overwhelming. Gina tried not to gag and was breathing in short, shallow breaths. She started talking a mile a minute and had no idea what she was saying. It was an intense moment that seemed to go on forever. What's worse, it didn't look like Harvey was hearing her. Instead, he started wailing and clawing at the air with one hand.

Gina kept jabbering until Harvey's other hand came into view. It was mostly skeletal bone and rotting flesh clinging to the edges, but the long, pointy fingers were wrapped around a hard and solid-looking object. It took a second for Gina to realize what it was. Harvey had a gun, and it was pointing right at her.

Mike must have seen it too, as his shield suddenly came down. He lunged for Gina and started pulling her away, but not before Harvey reached out and clawed his shirt. Then the two were running through the cemetery with spirits in hot pursuit. At one point Mike fell flat on his face. Gina stood over him and threw her shield up in anger. It worked, and they were able to stagger out of the cemetery together. Nothing followed when they reached the gate, but they could see masses of spirits behind them, and the dark swirl was all around the trees and tombstones.

"Oh my God, are you okay?" asked Gina. She pulled up his shirt, and both looked down at the deep scratches on Mike's stomach.

"Harvey Wallbanger, you prick," yelled Mike. "You're lucky I don't go back in there and kick your ass."

Gina's worry immediately washed away, and she started howling with laughter. "You just gave him a nickname."

Mike glanced over at her, and then he starting laughing as well. "Yah, I guess I did. I could go for a few drinks right now. You wanna hit a bar?"

She shook her head. "One thing you need to know about me, seeing as how we're dating, is that I try not to drink. I'm a lightweight."

"Good to know. So all I have to do is get you drunk, and then I can take advantage of you?"

"Nah. You can do that to me sober."

That's all Mike needed to hear. He rushed her back to his place, and they were in such a hurry, they ended up banging on the hallway floor. Afterward, they crawled into bed and cuddled under a blanket. They forgot all about Harvey and instead talked about their lives, hopes, and dreams. It was a lovely moment, but Gina finally had to get up to pee.

When she came out of the bathroom, Mike handed her a pair of pajamas. "I'm assuming you're spending the night."

She grinned. "Sure. Got a toothbrush?"

While they got ready for bed, she waved her arm around the room. "How can you afford such a nice place? I thought you were on the VA dime." He lived in a two-bedroom condo right on the lake. It was beautiful.

"I told you, I have a tech business. It does pretty well."

She frowned. "What kind of tech stuff do you do?"

He pulled the sheets down on the bed. "We build firewalls and security systems to keep out the hackers."

She started laughing. "So you basically develop shields in your real life too."

"Yah, I guess I do. It's like you with your singing. When I'm on a computer and figuring things out, I feel so alive."

"Wish I could use what I'm good at to make a real living," she sighed.

"Maybe you can, Gins. I don't think you realized this, but when Harvey started going all batshit crazy, you began singing him a lullaby. I think he was calming down, but I didn't want to risk it, so I stepped in."

She was stunned. "I did? No kidding. I have no recollection of that."

"I think when we go back, you should just sing to him."

"Wait, you want to go back? What about the gun?"

Mike got in bed and motioned for her to join him. "Well, think about it. His family wouldn't bury him with a gun. It's gotta be some kind of spiritual visual aid or something. We'll check with the group and get their opinion. I think if you try singing to him, he'll calm down enough so you can talk to him."

They brainstormed their options well into the night. They also ran it by the other sensitives, and by the following Saturday, they had their plan in place.

***

This time they went at the crack of dawn. They followed the same plan, only Gina started singing as soon as her shield was down. She sang every lullaby she knew and then segued into pop rock songs.

It worked. Harvey came out gnashing and howling, but then it slowed to an occasional whimper. The gun also shimmered, and Gina was calm enough to see it was transparent. She kept right on singing, and finally Harvey sat down on the bench and croaked out a question.

"Who are you?"

"My name's Gina Rini. I'm here to help you. That guy over there is Mike Santos." She could see tears flowing down what was left of Harvey's face.

"I haven't talked to anyone in so long. It's nice."

He appeared to be catching his breath or shoring up energy, so she softly sang as she waited.

"I like your singing, Gina. Do you know any AC/DC?"

She laughed. "Sure." Then she started belting out "Back in Black." She could hear Mike chuckling off to one side.

"So how can you help me?" asked Harvey.

"Well. We're hoping we can get you into the light. We think you will be at peace there."

Harvey shook his head, while pieces of flesh fell from his chin. "No. I can't go into the light. It's a trap. It will take me straight to hell."

"Why would you say that, Harvey? The light is good."

"I know, but I committed suicide. I was taught that would send me to hell."

She sighed. "I was taught the same thing, but I just don't believe it. You were depressed when you were alive, right?"

He nodded.

"Then your sadness led to the suicide. You were just trying to ease your pain. I think God would take that into consideration and forgive you for it."

Harvey seemed to be thinking things through. "But you don't know for sure, right? And I'm dead, and I don't know either."

"True, but are you happy here? Seems to me it must be super lonely. Do you talk to the other spirits?"

"No. We mostly keep to ourselves. And I am lonely. So unbelievably lonely."

She nodded. "Your parents have passed on, you know. If you went to the light, you would probably get to see them again."

He moaned, and the sound shook the leaves in the trees. "If I knew for sure, I would go. Maybe you could come visit me all the time, and then I wouldn't be so lonely."

"I can't do that, Harvey."

"Why not?" Then he sighed, "You're dating that guy over there, aren't you?"

She smiled. "Yah. He used to be a Marine."

"Oh boy. Tell him I'm sorry I scratched him."

"I'll tell him. We have to go now, but promise me you'll think about the light. It's a risk you would take, but I think it would be worth it. You don't want to stay here forever, do you?"

He sighed and croaked, "I'll think about it."

Gina walked over to Mike, and then they left the cemetery. Outside the gate, they stared at each other.

"Oh my God, you actually talked to him. Your singing worked."

"I know, right? Now we just need to figure out how to get him to find peace."

"No easy task," muttered Mike.

Gina couldn't agree more.

\*\*\*

A week later they were back and armed with anything they could find on the topic of an afterlife. Gina was ready to share it all with Harvey, but he surprised her.

"I've thought about it, and I want to leave," he sighed. "It sucks here. Maybe I need to face the consequences of my actions, anyway. If hell is what I get, so be it."

"I really hope that's not the case, Harvey. I just don't think God would have sent me here if I was helping you move on to hell."

The spirit smiled at her. "So you believe in God, then?"

"Yah. I guess I do."

"Cool. I hope you're right."

She nodded. "Now we just need to find some light."

He laughed. "Oh, it's always been here." He pointed to the west. "I've just always ignored it."

"No kidding. I wonder why I can't see it?"

Harvey smiled. "Maybe because you're still alive. Do you mind singing to me as I cross? It really soothes my nerves."

"Sure. What song do you want to hear?"

" 'Crazy Train' by Ozzy Osbourne. You heard of it?"

She laughed. "Of course I have. An appropriate choice. Okay then, here goes."

She softly sang the song as Harvey walked toward the west side of his grave. Then she saw it. The light was faint at first, but the closer Harvey got, the brighter it became, until it seemed to pierce through the entire cemetery. The dark spirals all around them pulled away, and then Harvey was gone.

Mike walked over and touched Gina's face. She was surprised to feel the tears on her cheeks. "We did it," was all she could think to say.

He nodded. "Come on. Let's get out of here. He kept his shield on until they were safely out of the cemetery. Then he hugged her. "That was unbelievable."

"I know, right?"

"He had it bad for you. I was worried he wouldn't go, because he was crushing on you so hard."

Gina laughed. "Sounds like someone is jealous."

"Nah. Tough to be jealous of a sad spirit. If anything I'm still angry he scratched me, though."

"Poor baby. Let's go back to your place, and I'll kiss your wounds."

Mike grinned. "Now you're talking." He took her hand and led her to the car. "You know, Gins, I really don't think we could have done this if it wasn't for your singing."

She shrugged. "Maybe."

"No, seriously. It's like that verse you're so fond of saying. Grow where you're planted. You love to sing, and this is a way you can do it and help others."

She laughed. "Sure. Now if only there was a way to make money at it."

They stared at each other, and the wheels began to turn in their minds.

***

Six months later, and the Spiritual Travel Agency was born. It was a company dedicated to sending lost spirits on to the afterworld. Gina and Mike were the co-directors, but they had several sensitives working for them and a waiting list of customers a mile long.

Mike had worked out the details. They all knew of desperate spirits, plus there were many people complaining of hauntings. He put up a website and got the word out. Their company investigated hauntings, tried to communicate with the gray beings, and helped them move on, if at all possible. Some were willing to go, while others flat out refused. Gina still talked to them and was often able to convince spirits to tone down their behavior.

Of course, her family all thought she was crazy.

"You're doing what?" asked her father.

"That's a scam, Gins. How can you do that to people?" asked her brother.

Her mom was the most supportive. "Well, it sounds odd to me, but if people are willing to pay you for that kind of thing, I say why not? Now tell me about Mike. When do you think you two will get married? Seems to be the next logical step now that you're in business together. You *are* dating, right? I mean, you're living together for goodness' sake. Please don't tell me this is another one of your platonic friends. Honestly, Gins, I just don't understand what you young girls are all about these days."

Gina groaned and made a face at the phone. Her mom droned on as Gina looked over at the man in question. He was typing away on the computer and had a happy expression on his face. They had just come back from a "save" two hours ago. As soon as they'd got home, she'd jumped him. Nothing made her hornier than a save, and Mike was not complaining.

As her mother continued to yap on the phone, Gina thought over things. It was way too early to be thinking about marriage. Besides, she was content right where she was, and doing what she was doing. Life was great. One could even go so far as to say it was blooming with the possibilities.

## The End

# Seen and Unseen
## Anne Krist

### Chapter One

Merle Haggard's smooth voice came from the radio as Katherine Hahn swung her Jeep Cherokee into the parking lot of LiveWell Industries. This late at night, she didn't bother finding a regular space in back to park but instead stopped right in front of the door. While the manufacturing plant was about to finish for the night, she would be by herself in the company offices.

Kat flipped the key to off and opened her door and was struck in the face like a hammer by the heat. No one thought of northern Idaho as having heatwaves with temperatures in the hundreds, but this year they'd had several weeks of it, starting early in the spring. At least, unlike her native Virginia, the humidity was low and—usually, at least—it was accompanied by a breeze. And fortunately the heat didn't normally last long.

Today, it hung in the air with nary a wisp of wind. She blew a puff past her bottom lip that riffed her bangs and grabbed her purse from the passenger seat.

Using her key to the office door, she entered and locked up after herself. The building wasn't very large, but it always gave her the creeps to be alone here at night.

*One little thing to do and I'm outta here.* She hurried down the hall and to her office.

*You could have waited until tomorrow.* Her mom's voice sounded in her head.

*I know, I know, I know. But I want to get out the monthly report before then and back up the files.*

*Okay. You know, you work too hard.*

After unlocking her office door, she stepped in, then pushed it closed but not latched. Flipping on her desk lamp instead of the overhead light, she sat down and booted her computer.

Ten minutes and a few seconds later she shut down the computer and slid the thumb drive into her purse. Turning out her lamp, she froze as voices came to her from down the hall.

"I won't be told what to do," said an unfamiliar male voice, a few octaves above normal conversational range. He sounded angry.

*Or scared?* her mom whispered.

Another voice sounded, though it was softer and muffled. Kat couldn't make out anything for a few seconds, and then Harlan's voice could be heard. "You'll be sorry!"

A door slammed, startling Kat. The argument, or whatever it was, scared her a bit. Harlan Waters, the CEO and her boss of two years, had always been a friendly, mild-mannered kind of guy. He was her mentor and helper when she first moved to Milford, and she didn't think she had ever heard him angry.

Without wasting another minute, Kat exited her office, locked the door and then left the building.

Taillights headed down the sharply sloped driveway to the main road. Securing the front door, a frisson of fear ran up her spine as more headlights swung past her and then around, lighting her and the reception desk in the lobby behind her. Shading her eyes, she turned and stepped toward her Jeep. A car pulled up alongside and the window rolled down.

"Kat? What are you doing here?"

*Careful,* her mother warned.

*Yes, Mom.* Though she had no fear of Harlan.

"Hey, Harlan. I thought I'd pick up the paperwork so I could finish the monthly report before I came in tomorrow."

He stared at her a moment and then his shoulders relaxed. "No need. You work too hard, Kat. Go on home and worry about the report in the morning."

She smiled. She wanted to know why he was there so late, and who the man was he had been arguing with, but something *told* her to keep quiet. "Okay. You're the boss. See you in the morning."

"Careful going home now." Harlan rolled up the window and drove off.

"Curiouser and curiouser," Kat murmured.

***

The phone rang the next morning just as Kat sliced a banana atop the Cheerios in her bowl. "Hello?"

"Kat, it's Amanda." Amanda Gilchrist and her husband Brendan lived a few houses down the street. Amanda produced beautiful fiber art that she sold for big sums all around the world. Brendan was a detective in their small town of Milford, Idaho.

*Too bad Brendan doesn't have a brother. A man like him would be perfect for you.*

Kat sighed. Her mother had always been on the lookout for Kat's "perfect man." Unfortunately, the trait continued, even now.

*Good morning, Mom. How are you this morning?*

*Still dead, Daughter. I sure wish I could have just one little cup of coffee.*

"Kat? Are you there?"

Kat laughed. "Sorry, I was woolgathering, thinking about all I have to do at work this morning."

"That's what I'm calling about. Kat, a terrible thing has happened. There's been a fire at LiveWell. The offices have been destroyed."

Kat grasped the counter edge. "What? How? When?"

"Brendan called a few minutes ago and asked if I could get in touch with you. They're going to need to talk with you as soon as you can get there. He would have called himself, but he wanted me to soften the blow." Amanda took a deep breath. "Kat, there's a body."

"Oh my God! Whose?"

"I don't know. That's all Brendan told me. Can you leave soon, though?"

"Yes, of course. I'll put on my shoes and go right now."

"Thanks. Brendan will be there, so just ask for him. If you need me for anything at all, please let me know."

Kat ended the call and regretfully set aside her breakfast. After a quick trip to the bedroom to slip on her shoes, she also grabbed her purse and headed to the garage in back of the house.

"No comments, Mama?"

Nothing but silence. "Well, that makes sense. Since I'm really talking to myself, you can't comment on anything I don't already know. Bet you we'll both have something to talk about in a few minutes."

## Chapter Two

"I'm sorry, miss, but you can't go any farther." The police officer stopped Kat at the crime scene tape that had the whole office parking area closed off.

"But I work here."

He shook his head. "Sorry."

Kat searched the gathered officers and suited men near the door. "Can you tell Detective Gilchrist that Kat Hahn is here if he wants to talk to me?"

At his nod, Kat walked back to her car. Faces dotted the windows of the manufacturing plant halfway up the hill at the back of the property, and a crowd stood outside, watching the activity at the offices. Police cruisers and two firetrucks filled the parking area not marked off. Water ran freely out the door and down the asphalt.

"What's going on, Kat? Do you know?" Ellen Harris, Harlan's admin, came up beside her. Her appearance was tidy, as always, with her Pendleton plaid skirts and crisp white blouses. Her light brown hair, sprinkled with bits of gray now, settled in a bun resting on her nape. She must have decided years ago to settle on that for her "work fashion," because in the years Kat had worked at LiveWell, Ellen's outfits had been just that, varying only in the color plaid in the skirts and her scarves and lapel pins. Her watch, stud diamond earrings, and low-heel black pumps completed Ellen's external persona. Kat often wondered if the woman let loose when she was home and wore wild colors and torn jeans or if she maintained her staid exterior all the time.

"All I know is that there was a fire in the offices, and I heard that a body was found." She spoke without thinking. Maybe Brendan wouldn't want that piece of information out?

*Take better care, Daughter. This is serious business.*

*Yes, Mom.* Sheesh. She needed to stop talking to herself. It was bound to get her in trouble someday.

"A body?" Ellen asked, sounding as flustered as Kat had ever heard her. "Oh, my. Do you know who it is?"

Kat looked up to see Brendan exit the building, followed by a tall man with a slight limp. Brendan said something to the policeman Kat had spoken to when she arrived and then looked at her. Nodding, he led the tall man toward her.

"I hope to know something shortly," Kat said to Ellen. She straightened from where she'd been leaning against her car. One of the firetrucks backed up, sounding its warning beeps, and then left. A couple of police cars followed. They must know something if people were leaving.

Brendan stepped up before her. "Kat, thanks very much for coming in early. You're the only person I know personally who works here."

"It's not a problem at all. Brendan, this is Ellen Harris. She's Harlan Waters' admin. She probably knows everything that goes on around here and everyone working here."

Brendan's brow wrinkled. "I thought you were Waters' admin."

She shook her head. "No, I do the bookkeeping and finance stuff."

"Okay," he said. He turned to Ellen. "Ms. Harris, I'm Detective Gilchrist. Would you mind stepping over here and answering a few questions, please? And Kat, this is one of our new people, Detective Lancaster. He'll interview you, if you don't mind."

Kat looked up into soft brown eyes. A scar marked his face above his left brow, making it look perpetually raised. He smiled, turning an interesting face into a truly handsome one. His left hand held a small spiral notepad. Scars crisscrossed the back of his hand, and his pinky finger missed its top knuckle. What in the world…?

"Would you be more comfortable sitting in the car?" he asked her.

Kat wondered if standing was difficult for him, so she agreed. She sat behind the steering wheel, and the detective slid into the passenger seat, using his right leg to keep the door propped open. He made her car feel tiny, and he hadn't even closed the door.

\*\*\*

"May I have your full name and what you do here?" he asked Kat. She had the most gorgeous blue eyes, and her hair had shone in the sun. This close, he noticed streaks of gold and darker, richer reds. He'd always been a sucker for redheads.

"Katherine Jane Hahn. I do the books for LiveWell. My title is bookkeeper, but I do a variety of things, from handling payroll, accounts payable and deliverable, and any financial reports Mr. Waters needs. LiveWell is a small company, though they're trying to expand right now with a new product. I imagine they will be hiring more help soon and divide the labor."

"How long have you worked here?"

"Two years. I moved to Milford for this job."

She kept fiddling with her earring. Was that a sign of nervousness? "Where did you move from?"

"Virginia."

Kyle fixed her with his gaze. "That's a very long way to come to work for a company that's not only small but also not that well-known."

"My father had heart trouble, and his doctor used one of LiveWell's monitors on him. He spoke well of the product, and out of curiosity, I looked them up. They had a position open, and I was ready for a change. I applied for the open position they had, and Harlan offered me the job. My dad died shortly after he started using their monitor, but I was still impressed enough that when my mother also passed, a couple of years ago, I came out."

She called her boss by his first name? "What is your relationship with Waters?" He stopped taking notes and focused on her as she answered. Her cheeks tinged pink and she narrowed her lips.

"He is my boss. That's it. We have business meetings. Once in a while he'll call and ask for a special report. Most of the time I work through Ellen, his admin. Outside of work, Harlan and I don't have a relationship."

Kyle nodded. "Okay. Where were you between midnight and five a.m.?"

"I stopped by here on my way home from the gym last night and left—"

"You were here last night?"

She huffed out a breath. "As I was about to tell you, I stopped by here around eleven-thirty."

"You work out pretty late, don't you?"

"It was the time I had available. I've been helping at the lentil festival, over in Washington, and it's demanding on my free time."

*Does she not have a boyfriend, if she's doing all this stuff alone? Idaho men must be blind to let this woman get by.*

"Not a Montana man," he murmured.

"What did you say?" She swiveled in her seat so that she faced him full on. His breath nearly stopped.

"Nothing. Go on, please."

"I loaded all of the month's files on my thumb drive and took them home."

"Did you notice anything unusual?"

"I didn't think anyone was here," she said. "There were no cars out front." Her brows creased, and she tapped her lips with her index finger as she stared out the open door. Brendan was leading the admin into the building. Hopefully, she'd be able to identify the dead guy. They hadn't taken him off yet, because the coroner hadn't arrived. *Small towns.*

"Yes, I know," she whispered. "I am telling him everything." If he hadn't been paying close attention, he might have missed her nearly silent comment.

"I was only here ten minutes or so. But I heard what sounded like an argument between Harlan and someone else. It was a man, but not a voice I recognized."

Kyle unconsciously straightened up. "What did you hear?"

"The man said, 'I won't be told what to do.' There was muffled talking, and then Harlan said, 'You'll be sorry.'"

"He said 'You'll be sorry' to the man he was talking with? Did you hear anything else?"

"A slamming door. It couldn't have been Harlan's door, because whoever left would have had to go past my office to get out, and no one did. Plus, I'd locked the front door when I went into the building, and it was still locked when I came out."

"Could the slamming door have been Waters' private exit? The one that accesses the back parking area?"

She looked at him. There was no hint of fear in her eyes, just curiosity.

"Is it Harlan's body in there?"

If this had been anyone else, he would have informed the person that he was asking the questions. But he couldn't look into those blue eyes and say anything harsh to her. Hell, it was all he could do to resist touching her, her hand, her knee, her soft-looking lips.

"Honestly? We don't know."

## Chapter Three

When Kat looked up, the detective was watching the front of the office building. She turned there, also, seeing Brendan and Ellen come out. Ellen's demeanor was serious, but she didn't seem to be emotional, as such. Kat assumed the woman had been asked to try to identify the dead body. Kat would be beside herself if she'd been asked to do anything like that.

"Do me a favor?" Detective Lancaster asked.

"What's that, Detective?" Kat answered in a low voice.

"Don't tell anyone you took the files home. And also, call me Kyle? Please?"

Kat snapped her attention back to him. She was sitting on his left side and once more noticed the scar above his eye. The wicked deformity must have measured three inches and disappeared into the hair at his temple. This close, smaller pockmarks and more scars along the left side extended from his ear to his neck. What had happened to this man?

"That's two favors," she replied. "But I believe I can handle it. Do you think I'm in trouble for having the company files?"

"I think you might be in danger for having them." At last, he turned those amazingly soft brown eyes on her again. Simultaneously, her heart sped up and she calmed down. *How is that possible?*

"You live near Brendan, don't you?"

Kat nodded. "A few houses away and on the opposite side of the street."

"Here's my card." Digging into his inside jacket pocket, he produced a business card. While handing it to her, he asked, "Would you review the files you have? Go back a couple of months and just see if there's anything hinky. If you see something right off, call me. If nothing obvious pops out this afternoon, tell me all about it at Brendan and Amanda's this evening."

Her hand froze, fingers on one end of the card while the detective's fingers held the other end.

"What are you talking about?"

"They're old friends of mine and they're having me for a barbecue tonight to welcome me to Milford. I hope you'll be my plus one." He smiled and Kat melted into her seat. "I don't know anyone else, but even if I did, I'd still like you to join us."

Kat didn't know what to say so she said nothing. His smile waned a bit. "Is that too weird, for this situation?"

"Um… No, I don't think so. I suppose it would be all right, if it's okay with Amanda." He released the card and she tucked it into her bag.

"I'm sure she will enjoy having another woman there. Dinner is planned for six-thirty. I look forward to seeing you under more pleasant circumstances. And Kat? Thanks for your help."

By then, Brendan and Ellen had reached them. Both Kat and Kyle climbed out of the Jeep.

"Kat, you might as well go home," Ellen said. "All of the main offices are in ashes. What's left is dripping in water." Closer, the woman did seem lost and a little shaken up.

"Did you know…?"

"It's Mike Forester."

"Oh, dear." Kat didn't know Forester except by name and seeing him from afar at company picnics. She'd heard he was very nice and also a brilliant engineer.

"Did you know him, Kat?" Brendan asked. Detective Lancaster had moved away from her, slightly behind Brendan. She wished he stood closer. She needed that calmness he exuded. Or was that only her imagination? He was handsome as sin and he had just asked her to dinner, though maybe that was because she was part of this horrible situation?

*Don't read too much into it, one way or another. Just enjoy dinner tonight.*

*Yes, Mom.* She sighed. Hearing the admonishment just as her mother would have given it was almost the same as having her close again. *Close and alive, let's not forget that part.*

"Not really," Kat said to Brendan. "But then, here are a lot of people here I didn't have much contact with."

"Unless you need me for something else, detectives?" Ellen turned an inquisitive raised brow toward Brendan.

"No, Ms. Harris. If you think of anything, please call. You have my card."

Without another word, Ellen walked to her car and, after buckling in, she started the engine and pulled away. At the end of the long drive, another car screeched around the corner and stopped just as Ellen came to the stop sign where the driveway met the main road. The two drivers sat adjacent and appeared to be talking.

"If I'm not mistaken, that's Harlan Waters." Brendan muttered.

"We haven't been able to reach him all morning," Kyle Lancaster explained. "Brendan, Kat was here last night."

Brendan turned surprised eyes her way. "You were?"

At her nod, Kyle picked up her story. "She came in late to pick up some paperwork. She has the company files at home on a thumb drive."

"In fact," Kat added, "I forgot to tell you that Harlan can verify the time I left. I was closing up when he pulled around the building. We spoke briefly. A second car had just left the campus. I assumed it was the man Harlan argued with."

Kyle gave a low whistle. "It's even more important that you keep to yourself the fact that you have company files."

"You're making me nervous."

He reached out and touched her arm. Sparks flew up to her shoulder and then to points south. She blinked, shocked. Even Kyle looked stunned.

"I, uh, invited Kat to dinner tonight," he said to Brendan. "I hope that's all right?"

"No, that's great," Brendan replied. "We're happy to have you join us, Kat. Amanda will have relief from all the Montana ranch talk." He smiled at her but then watched Harlan's progress up the drive and to the parking area. "Time to make the doughnuts, Kyle."

He strode off toward Harlan as he climbed out of his sedan. Wiping his hands down his face, he shook his head and stared at the ruined building.

"Thanks for your help," Kyle said again as he followed Brendan. Then he turned and walked backward a few steps. "See you tonight." With a flash of that earth-shattering smile, he was back in detective mode, and Kat was left with a stuttering heartbeat and a sudden shortness of breath.

## Chapter Four

Kat arrived at Amanda's house at six o'clock, with a six-pack of the beer Brendan favored and a quart Mason jar of sweet tea, which Amanda enjoyed. Kyle had already arrived and rushed to help her carry the drinks.

"How are you feeling after everything that happened this morning?"

"At a loss, I'm afraid. Am I just supposed to stay home now? Harlan didn't call with any instructions or to ask questions about the report I was supposed to have done today. Of course, I guess the offices being shut down will change everything."

Kyle placed the beer and tea in the refrigerator. "Did you get a chance to look over any files?"

"I started, but I don't know what I'm looking for. I can—"

"That's enough, you two. No work talk. We need a break. Thanks so much for the tea, Kat. You know how much I love it."

"No work talk. Yes, ma'am," Brendan said with a grin. Amanda slapped his shoulder playfully and took the tea and paper plates and napkins out with her.

"Come on, Kat. Brendan already has the grill fired up. He and I will probably have to go back to work after we eat."

"Oh! I'm sorry to hear that," Kat said, and found she meant it. All day she had looked forward to seeing Kyle again and getting better acquainted.

Kyle stepped closer and linked his fingers with hers. "Me too."

"Kyle, will you bring a Coke out with you, please?" called Brendan.

Brendan grinned. "A sure sign we are going back to work. He wants a Coke instead of a beer."

He chose a can from the refrigerator and led Kat outside, guiding her with his hand on her lower back. In some cases, Kat would have felt crowded by the gesture. With Kyle, all she knew was warmth. After the events of the day, she wished she could curl up next to him and have him warm her from the inside out.

The rest of the evening was filled with laughter and great burgers. Kat had never made friends easily, so the laid-back fellowship she found with Amanda and Brendan had been a surprising treat.

As hot as the day had been, the evening air cooled to the point of needing a sweater, something she had forgotten to bring. The scent of zinnias and sweet William came to her on a breeze that drifted across the patio, and she shivered but didn't want to go inside. The loam from freshly turned earth piqued her nostrils. Dusk hovered. Full, content, and relaxed, Kat felt her eyelids start to droop.

"We'd better go," Brendan said to Kyle half an hour later.

Kat sat straight and gazed at Kyle. Lucky for her, he gazed right back. "I'll walk you home," he said in a low voice.

"There's no need," Kat said. "I just live a few houses down."

*Let him.*

Her inner mother again. She'd been silent all night.

"I'm going to walk Kat home," Kyle told Brendan. "Can you just drive down to pick me up?"

"I should stay and help to clean up," Kat insisted, raising her brows at Amanda for confirmation.

Amanda waved a paper plate at her. "Nothing much to clean up. We served the potato salad out of the container it's going to be stored in, and the same for all the condiments. Go on with Kyle."

With a smile, Kat took Kyle's hand and stood.

"Thanks so much for dinner."

"Yes," Kyle said. "It was much appreciated." He looked at Brendan. "I'll be out front of her house in a few minutes."

***

Holding Kat's hand felt so good, so right. Kyle was sixteen again and Mindy Anderson had agreed to go to the prom. Butterflies filled his stomach. He felt elated and nauseated at the same time. God help him, his hands had been sweaty, and he'd stuttered a hello to her parents. But the moment she'd taken his hand, all was right and good in his world. That's what holding Kat's hand did for him. Because of that, he kept his steps particularly short and slow. Yes, he had to leave in a few minutes, but he wanted to drag out their time as much as possible.

"I'm glad you came tonight," he said.

"I am, too. You know how it is when you're working—you get caught up in all kinds of things that keep you from visiting with friends. I really like Amanda and Brendan, but I can't remember the last time we visited. Between Brendan's on-call schedule, their kids, my job… But we should make time. I'm going to try harder."

"I hope you'll carve out some time for relaxation and fun stuff. And I hope you'll include me when you do."

*This is so important. Tell him yes!*

"I will. Give me time!"

Brendan pulled her to stop in front of her next-door neighbor. "This is the second time you've talked to yourself," he said. "Give me a hint of what's going on?"

Kat took a deep breath. "You'll think I'm crazy."

He smiled and gave her hand a shake. "No, I won't."

She dipped her head. "Okay, then. We might as well get crazy out right up front. My mother and I were the closest of friends. We lived up the street from one another in Virginia and she was my best friend as well as my mom. She died just before I moved to Idaho. But I have conversations with her in my head."

Kyle simply raised his brows. "So, you don't talk to yourself, you talk to your mother?"

"Well, no. Of course, I talk to myself. I mean, I can picture Mama's face and her voice, and I just give myself advice that she would give me. We knew each other very well, you know?"

"What kind of advice does she give you?" He took a step closer and fixed his gaze on her lips."

"Right now, she'd say to take you at least to the porch. Not to kiss you in the middle of the street."

"Good advice," Kyle murmured. Silently, he picked up the pace and practically ran.

"Right here," Kat called out, laughing.

When he got her on the porch, he took her in his arms. "What does your mother say now?"

"Kiss—Oh! I don't feel so well all of a sudden."

*Go inside.*

"I hear her say to go inside."

Kyle leaned back so he could see her face. All mirth left his expression. "I think she's right. You're pale as a ghost."

Kat pulled her keys from her pocket and handed them to Kyle, who fit one of them into the lock and opened her door.

"Do you smell that?" Kat scrunched her face and walked from the living room into the kitchen.

"Smell what?"

"That smell. It's cloying, heavy. Like… like I don't know what. Gardenias?" Her shoulders dropped. "It's gone now." She turned to him with a bright smile. "Everything's fine."

"Just the same, I'm going to check out the place."

Kat didn't object, so he walked through all the rooms. In what looked like an office, Kat held up the thumb drive and put it in the back of the middle drawer of her desk. He went into the guest bathroom.

"Do you always keep the window open in here?"

Kat peered around him. "The latch is broken. I keep meaning to get it fixed. It slides up a tiny bit in the course of the day."

"Hold on a minute." Kyle squeezed through the doorway past her. After a loud crack sounded in the kitchen, he returned with a portion of a broom handle. As he forced it between the bottom window and the top sill, he said, "I'll buy you a new broom, but this will keep the window from opening."

Kat nodded her head in appreciation. "I wouldn't have thought of that—thanks! And that broom had seen better days anyway. I'll get one this weekend."

He inspected the closet in her bedroom and pulled back both the shower curtains before facing her, hands on her shoulders. "All clear."

She gazed at him so trustingly, he nearly leaned down to kiss her again. A taste of her would be his reward after the security check.

"No monsters under the bed?"

"All safe, m'lady. All of your windows are secured, and your back door, too. Be sure to lock up after me, okay?"

Her smile was as soft as the kiss she placed on his lips. "Thanks for looking out for me."

"I'll call tomorrow?"

"I hope you do."

Kyle walked to the front door. The lights from Brendan's car lighted the yard. He grinned. "Tell your mom goodnight from me."

Her laughter was the last thing her heard after he closed the door. Her laughter and the sound of the deadbolt being thrown.

## Chapter Five

Kat sat straight up in bed. Her breathing sounded fast in the silent room and her heart raced. Her eyes were wide as she searched every corner of her bedroom, and she strained to hear anything. The results were nil. Still… *Something woke me.*

Unsatisfied, she threw her feet over the edge of the bed and slid them into her slippers. Reaching for the robe at the end of the bed, she stood and pulled it on, then tightened the sash. The moonless night kept the room dark as sin. A flashlight would be on the counter in the kitchen, and she knew the way through her house blindfolded. Or at least, that's what she'd always told herself. This would be the test.

She eased away from the safety of the bed. When she was little, she believed with all her heart that if she pulled the covers over her head and couldn't see the monsters, they couldn't see her. Growing up put that idea in the fantasy stage. She faced reality now.

Tinkling glass hitting the floor stiffened her spine. Something had broken a window? The sound came from the guest bathroom, and more followed now. *Where did I leave my mobile?*

*On the charger.*

Great. The charger was in the outlet beside the flashlight.

She stepped as quickly and as quietly as she could, going down the hallway, past the bathroom in question. Someone was trying to get in the house. Get into her house, where she'd always felt safe. No more.

Practically running now, she grabbed the flashlight with one hand and the phone with the other. She pushed 9-1—

*Not now,* her mother instructed. *Get outside. Use the back door.*

*I almost have this call—*

*Now, Katherine Jane! Out the back door!*

Her mother always meant business when she used Kat's middle name. Without another word, Kat hurried to the back door and slid the deadbolt. She opened the door enough to slip through and then pushed it closed.

*Not along the back of the house. Go through the bushes and to the Mitchells' backyard. They'll call the police.*

Kat stopped a moment to wonder how she knew to do that. Her initial reaction had been to run down the back of the house and to the street. But the voice she heard was her mom's, and so she obeyed.

A narrow path led through lilac bushes serving as a property divider. Hiding the light from the flashlight as well as she could and yet not attract attention, she maneuvered the trip to the Mitchells' front door. Her knock sounded like explosions in the quiet night. It must have to their dogs, too, because they set up an uproar from the backyard. A light came on overhead and a wary Don Mitchell peeked past the front curtains.

"Kat, what's wrong?" he asked when he opened the door.

"I think someone is breaking into my house. May I use your phone?"

Mitchell sent sharp looks over her shoulders and into the darkness beyond his porch. "Of course! Come in." He swung wide the door and stepped aside. Then he closed and locked it.

"What's going on?" his wife, Harriet, asked.

Don was already punching 9-1-1 into the face of his landline telephone as he responded, "There's a burglary at Kat's."

Harriet made all the common comfort sounds, patting Kat down onto the couch and going into the kitchen. "I'll start a pot of coffee."

Her mother's voice sounded relieved when she whispered, *Good. Brendan and Kyle are here.*

She'd no sooner spoken in Kat's head when Harriett rushed to the front door in response to a firm, loud knock. Without asking permission, Kyle practically ran past Harriett and Brendan to get to her.

"Are you all right?"

Her voice was shaky, and she couldn't loosen the grip on either her phone or the flashlight—which she still had on—but she wasn't hurt. "Fine. I'm fine."

As though he didn't believe her, Kyle ran his hands down her arms and then back up, caressing her neck and head. Then he gently pried her fingers off the two items in her lap and pressed the switch on the flashlight off.

Brendan had been talking quietly with Don by the door, but now he moved to stand in front of her beside Kyle.

"What happened, Kat?" Brendan took the lead, of course. Kyle crossed his arms, tucking his hands under his armpits.

*Is he angry? Or trying not to touch me again? I wish he'd touch me! And I wish there were a splash of whiskey in the coffee Harriett just set on the table beside me.*

"Thanks, Harriett." She took up the cup and sipped the blistering hot liquid. She was cold through and through. She took a deep breath and looked up into four sets of eyes, all regarding her. "I woke up sharply. You know, like something had startled me awake but I didn't know what. Then my mother… uh… I mean, I had a feeling that I needed to get out. So, I ran into the kitchen to grab both the cell and the flashlight and then came through the lilacs to here."

Kat took a chance to glance at Kyle. He was the only person in the world with whom she'd shared that she talked to herself, or rather, to an imaginary friend she thought of as her mother. The whole fiasco was bound to come out. The whole world would think she was crazy now.

"Why didn't you just run through the front door? It was closer than going to the kitchen for anything." Brendan and Amanda had been to her home many times and knew the layout well.

She rubbed her temple and frowned. "I don't know. Something told me to go out the back."

"The intuition might have saved your life. We found footprints in the bushes adjacent to your door."

"Officers are at your house right now," Kyle told her. "We think there were two intruders. They broke the window in the bathroom to enter."

"The one you fixed last night?"

He nodded. "Looks like I didn't stop them."

## Chapter Six

"Is there anything else you can tell us, Kat?" A frown marred Brendan's expression.

"I don't think so," she said. "I didn't wait around to discover much, I'm afraid."

"I'm glad you didn't." Kyle reached out and squeezed her shoulder. His simple touch spread the warmth she needed throughout her body.

Brendan cleared his throat and Kyle took his hand back. Just then, an officer came to the Mitchells' door. Brendan and Kyle moved to talk to him, but a minute brought them back.

"We couldn't find fingerprints or any useable evidence at all," Brendan said. "I'm going to walk through again, though, just to give everything another look. Amanda wants you to stay at our house for the rest of the night."

"Oh, no, I couldn't—"

"You can't stay at your place, and we would feel better if you were safe. Would you rather go somewhere else?"

Kat considered. She could go to the Best Western or Fairfield Inn, but if she were honest, she'd feel better being with friends. "That's very kind, thank you. If I went with you, could I go home for a change of clothes?"

"Sure, let's go now."

She hugged Harriett. "I'm so sorry for interrupting your night. Thank you very much for helping me."

"Of course, dear. I do hope the police can get this whole thing solved."

Kat pulled the belt around her robe tighter as Don shook hands with both Kyle and Brendan. She thanked him as she left and then followed Brendan to the sidewalk and around the corner to her house.

Blue and red lights flashed across the front of her bungalow, lighting up the night in a frightening mishmash of dark Halloween-like colors. Or maybe she was reflecting the way she felt onto the pattern of lights. The lightbar atop one cruiser turned off as the car started and pulled away from the curb. That left one police unit and Brendan's car.

"Don was just calling the station when you arrived," she said, perplexed. "How did you get here so fast?"

"Amanda called me at the station about twenty minutes ago." Brendan flipped Kat a glance. "She said there was some trouble at your house and to get back here quick. She told me you were at the Mitchells."

Kat's forehead wrinkled. "How did she know? I was just escaping my house twenty minutes ago."

"I think you should ask her." He pulled open her front door and checked in with the officer standing there. "We're going to get a change of clothes for Ms. Hahn. She'll be at my residence for the remainder of the night." At the officer's acknowledgment, Brendan led Kat back to her bedroom.

She tugged a small duffel from under the bed and threw in a change of underwear, her shoes, a blouse and a pair of jeans. In a makeup bag, she tucked her toothbrush and toothpaste, deodorant, and her brush, and then tossed that into the duffel. "Ready."

"Kyle, why don't you walk Kat down to the house? I'll be there in a few minutes."

"One more thing," she said. She walked into her office, pulled open the drawer, and grabbed the thumb drive. Slinging her purse over her shoulder, she stepped outside. "Thank you, Brendan."

He smiled, looking tired. "Get some rest. I'll see you later this morning."

With a start she realized the time—well after midnight. Brendan and Kyle had already had a long day, and it wasn't over yet.

Kyle took her bag. They started walking down the street they'd walked up just a few hours ago. "Have you made any progress on the murder?"

"No." His mouth was set in a firm, narrow line. "You took the thumb drive. You think it's related to the break-in?"

"I've lived in Milford for two years, and there hasn't been any trouble in this part of town. Suddenly I come home with that thing and my house is broken into? That window latch hasn't worked for a couple of months and no one has bothered it. Now, all of a sudden, it's the point of entry? I have to think they're related. I'm keeping it with me from now on."

"Smart woman. I'm just glad you're okay. Do you think the breaking glass is what woke you up?"

"Not sure."

One thing she was sure of, though. She wasn't ready to confide something she had discovered earlier. Her mother had "whispered" things that she, Kat, had no knowledge of. Her escape from the house and the warning to go through the bushes to the Mitchells' house had not been Kat pretending to talk to her mother. It was Kat's mother actually talking to her.

\*\*\*

Kat was keeping something back, Kyle was sure of it. "You're sure you're all right?"

They arrived at Brendan and Amanda's front door and Amanda opened the door before they had a chance to knock.

"Come in," she said.

"Thanks so much for offering your guest room." Kat said. Now that the events were nearing an end, Kyle watched as energy drained from her, from loosened shoulders to her eyelids barely staying up.

"I'll just take her bag back," Kyle murmured. He knew where the guest room was, thanks to having stayed a few nights with the Gilchrists when he first arrived in town. Once there, he flipped down the bedspread and sheet, having dropped her duffel at the foot of the bed. The mattress was comfortable. Despite the coffee she'd had at the Mitchells', he thought she'd be dead to the world as soon as she covered up.

"She's done for," Amanda murmured as she led Kat into the room. "I'll be right out."

Kyle moved down the hall and stood waiting in the living room for Amanda to return. "Is there anything I can do for you before I head back to Kat's?" he asked her.

"No, I think we have everything under control," Amanda replied. She smiled. "Take care of my husband, huh?"

Kyle grinned. "Always. Just like we used to as kids."

"I'm glad you moved here, Kyle."

He cast a glance to the wall that separated them from the guest room. "I am, too."

On the walk up the street to Kat's house, no longer bathed in blue and red lights, he considered her suspicion that the break-in was connected to the murder and fire at LiveWell Industries. He and Brendan had come to the same conclusion earlier that evening. Someone believed Kat knew something or had proof of something that she didn't herself realize. Later today—hopefully after a few hours' sleep at some point—he meant to go over those business files with her. The answer to all this mess was there. He'd lay money on it.

## Chapter Seven

Kat's head hurt, and her back ached from having been at the computer so long. Kyle sat beside her, examining the work files right along with her. Why didn't his eyes feel crossed as hers did?

"I can't take much more without a break," she said. She tried not to sound whiny, but maybe she did, just a little.

Kyle stretched and then rubbed circles with his palm at the top of her back. Given her druthers, she would curl into his touch and purr like a kitten who'd just had warm milk, but they sat in her office. Brendan could show up at any time, and Kat was quite sure he would not appreciate seeing his burglary victim with her head on his detective's shoulder.

"Tell you what," Kyle said, "why don't you make us some coffee? I'll take another quick look in the reports files and then join you for a break. I could use one, too."

"Deal," Kat replied. "Though now I feel like a slouch. You already put plywood up at the bathroom window, and you had much less sleep last night than I did."

"True, but I'm used to long hours with little sleep, and I wasn't the one who had a trauma last night."

"Okay," she said. "I appreciate all the help." She stood and had to grab the desk edge to catch herself.

"Whoa!" Kyle stood too and caressed her cheek. "You've been sitting too long."

Kat stood upright and found her balance. "I'm fine."

"Okay, I'll be right out."

The landline rang as she entered the kitchen. "Hello?" Freeing the long cord, she squeezed the receiver between her jaw and shoulder and filled the Mr. Coffee with water.

"Kat? It's Ellen Harris. I heard through the grapevine that you had some unfortunate excitement last night. Are you all right?"

"Yes, Ellen. I'm fine. Thanks for calling." She measured in the grounds and started the brewing cycle.

"Nothing was taken? You weren't hurt in any way?"

"No, the burglars were disappointed, I'm sure. The police were here so fast, I think they only had time to get in and hurry out."

"They? So, the police think there was more than one intruder?"

"Yes. They found tracks in both the front and back with different sized shoes."

"I see." Ellen was silent for a few seconds.

"Did you need me for anything, Ellen? How are things going at LiveWell? Is Harlan making arrangements for temporary offices?"

"Nothing has been decided yet. With the new monitor project and all the extra work that's entailed, we've hit a perfect storm. There's too much to do at the moment and nowhere good to do it."

"I understand. I should have had the monthly report in yesterday, but the police have asked me to go over the files and I don't have it done yet. Please tell Harlan that I will get it to him this afternoon or early tomorrow morning."

"How are you able to generate a report, Kat? You can't access the system from home."

Being able to use VPN to access company files was pretty important, and Kat wondered how Ellen didn't remember giving her that secure access last year, when new regulations overwhelmed them in paperwork and harsh deadlines. But with the thumb drive, she had everything she needed for the monthly report. Because she was delayed in producing it, she'd uploaded the files from the drive to the cloud server that morning.

"You gave me access last year, remember?"

"Oh, oh, yes, now you mention it. Well, Kat. Take care. I'll let you know when we're set up to work again. And bring that report to my home when it's completed, okay?"

"I sure will. Take care, Ellen."

"You as well."

*Download those files now.*

*What?*

*Now, Daughter. Don't waste any time.*

Kat walked across the kitchen to hang up the receiver and then continued to the office. "Kyle, I just spoke with Ellen Harris. I have a feeling we need to download the server data right now."

He took one look at her expression and moved out of the way. "Go to it. I think I've found a problem."

***

Kyle heard the phone ring. That Kat had a landline was one of the things he liked about her—a little old-fashioned and just as sweet, but still smart and independent. Not many single women would pick up and move nearly all the way across the country just because they were ready for something new. For most of the women he knew, wanting something new meant changing their diet or taking a class at the local college.

There was the talking to herself and making believe she carried on a conversation with her mother, but hey, everyone had their little quirks. He sang country and western music at the top of his lungs in the shower, or on horseback, or alone in the car. Come to think of it, he'd been singing an old George Strait song when his Humvee was blown to smithereens in Iraq. He could remember most everything about that day except the song. Maybe his subconscious knew it would be ruined for him now.

Without realizing what he was doing, Kyle saw a possible problem. He'd need Kat to tell him if what he saw was something or nothing.

***

Once started, the download took its time. Nearly ten minutes had gone by, and her hard drive storage indicator gradually was climbing to the red line/full mark. The entire time, she bounced her knees and kept her hands in her lap, squeezing and unsqueezing. Finally, he covered her hands with one of his.

"It'll be okay."

"I hope so." Worry creased her brows and she turned in her chair to face him full on. "I have to tell you something."

"About the case?"

She nodded. "Sort of."

He took her hands in both of his. Hers were like ice. "Go on."

"Last night… Last night, my mother told me to get out of the house."

"You mean, you knew to get out and you pretended your mom told you?"

She shook her head. "No. That's what I've always thought was going on. But, Kyle, last night my mother told me things I couldn't possibly have known. I made it to the kitchen and started to call the police on my cell. She told me to get out the back door, not the front, and she used my full name. I would never do that, talking to myself. Then, when I would have run to the street along the back of the house, she told me to go through the lilacs to the Mitchells'. There's no way I would have known all that. Nor was I in the presence of mind to think through it all."

Kyle tried to keep his voice even and calm. This sounded like more than a quirk.

"So…?"

"It's been my mother talking to me all this time. I don't know how, but I haven't been talking to myself. And it was she who insisted that I hurry and download the company data."

## Chapter Eight

All in all, Kyle took the news about her mother's presence in Kat's life better than she had expected. He asked a few questions, mostly about whether she would have known to do everything she had the previous night on instinct, and didn't she feel the need to download all the files because she intuited something from her conversation with Ellen.

Kat explained as well as she could, but the long and short of it was that she was perhaps the least intuitive person she knew. Also, though she could appear calm, she wasn't always the best person in a crisis. In the end, he didn't agree that her dead mother spoke to her in my mind, but he didn't come out and disagree with the notion, either.

They did take a short break and have coffee, but quickly sat back in front of the computer, needing to notice if the hard drive filled up or anything else went wrong.

"I found a discrepancy in the number of files in your report folder," Kyle told her as they watched the hard drive capacity indicator stop just below the dangerous red section. "The cloud server files for May showed one file less than the same folder for June."

"It shouldn't show a file short. I add the new month's report but drop the report for the previous year into an archive folder."

"I saw that. But there is a file missing. It was something about a progress report for the HM45."

"That's the new monitor we're developing. It's supposed to open all kinds of new avenues for business. Remember I told you that when the new product comes out, I'll be getting different responsibilities?"

"So why would that report be removed?"

"I don't know." Something was just out of reach in her mind. Something important.

*Who worked on it?*

Would she ever get used to having her actual mother in her head?

"Oh my God, Kyle. Mike Forester was the lead developer on the HM45 project."

He pulled out his cell. "Brendan is going over the autopsy report and everything collected at the scene. I'd better let him know what's going on."

He stepped into the living room. Kat leaned back and closed her eyes for a few moments to give them a rest. Then, just for the heck of it, she tried logging in, using her VPN login. She was denied.

*Thanks, Mom.*

Kyle returned and sat beside her. "Brendan wants us to find the last incident of the report and bring him a copy. I think we should email one, too."

"Multiple layers of protection. I like it." Quickly, she found the file Kyle mentioned in the May reports. While he attached the same file to an email message and added a note to Brendan, Kat skimmed the data.

Most made no sense to her, but one phrase stood out like a blinking neon sign: catastrophic failure. From what she could glean, a microchip in the monitoring unit kept failing. In the comments section of the report, Mike noted that presently they had no solution or suggested replacement that could meet the timeline Harlan set forth. Mike's suggestion was to revamp the design and plan for next year's release. Obviously, Harlan hadn't taken Mike up on his suggestion. As far as she knew, the big unveiling was still to be at the end of the year.

"Was Mike Forester the man arguing with Harlan Waters the other night?"

"I don't know." Kat shook her head. "I don't think I've ever talked with the man, so I wouldn't be able to recognize his voice."

Kyle stood and folded the report to store in his inside jacket pocket. "Do you want to come to the station with me to see Brendan?"

"No, unless you need me to answer questions. You really know everything I know right now. I'd rather get through the monthly report. Did you see? I'm locked out of the system. At least remotely. I have a feeling I might need to look for work soon." She grinned. "And that's my own feeling, not my mom's."

"I think your organization just presented us with a motive for murder. Brendan told me that Mr. Forester had severe head trauma before the building burned. No smoke in his lungs."

"Oh my gosh!"

He took her hand and tugged her up out of the chair and into his arms. "You were damned lucky your mom was watching out for you. I'm so glad you're safe. Please keep your cell with you. When you finish the report, take it with you to Amanda's. I'll meet you there when I finish at the station. Maybe you can introduce me to your favorite restaurant tonight."

"Hmm, I'd like that."

He lowered his head, stopping a breath away from her lips. "May I?"

Instead of answering, Kat rose to her toes and kissed him. At least, she took the first kiss, which was kind of sweet but also glorious. The second kiss was commanded by Kyle, and it sent her into orbit.

"Don't go anywhere but Amanda's without me," he whispered. "We're not out of the woods yet."

"Promise," she said in return.

***

"Kat, where are you?"

Why was Ellen calling again? Did she have any idea that Harlan appeared to be the killer?

"I'm finishing up in my office. I can get that report to you this afternoon."

"No problem. In fact, I'm out running around right now. Why don't I stop by and pick it up?"

"Oh. Okay. You remember where I live?"

"Yes. I'll be there in about fifteen minutes."

The final page of the report came off the printer just as the doorbell rang. "That was a lot less than fifteen minutes," Kat muttered. But when she opened her door, Amanda stood there with her toddler in a stroller and her five-month-old in a carrier that fit on top.

"Hi. Come on in."

"I can't stay. I just wanted to tell you that I sense trouble in the air. Brendan told me last night that he told you about me. I hope you don't think I'm too weird, you know, that I can see things."

Kat laughed. "Amanda, you don't know weird. When this whole mess is cleared up, I want to talk to you. My mom might even want to talk to you."

Amanda's forehead wrinkled but she smiled through her confusion. "I 'see' many interesting coffee sessions in our future."

Just then, a car pulled up to the curb. "Can you hold on a second, Amanda? I have orders to stay at your house until Kyle can meet me. That is, if you don't mind?"

"Of course not. We were just finishing our walk when I had the urge to stop by."

"Let me give this report to Ellen Harris and grab my purse and phone and I'll be ready to go."

## Chapter Nine

Ellen walked up to the house. "What lovely children," she said to Amanda.

"Amanda, this is Ellen Harris, the CEO's admin at LiveWell. Ellen, this is Amanda Gilchrist. Her husband is Detective Gilchrist. I'll be right with you, Amanda."

Kat went into the house, pushing the door to. From her office, she could hear only muffled voices, nothing distinct. Yet the hair stood up on her nape. That was the same sound she'd heard that night in her office. Ellen had been with Harlan that night. Good God! The cloying smell of gardenias filled the room, nearly making her gag.

She grabbed her phone and found Kyle in her contact list. His phone rang and rang. "Kyle, Kyle, answer!" she whispered.

"I thought I'd come to see what was holding you up," Ellen said from behind her.

Kat's heart sank into her stomach. Dots danced before her eyes. Her knees turned to pudding. Shielding the phone with her body, she laid it on the desk. Picking up the monthly report, she turned in place.

"Just checking to be sure everything is here," she said. "I think you'll find that it is."

"I'm sure," Ellen said as she slid a small revolver from her purse. "You've always been so efficient. It's unfortunate that we have to lose you."

"Now, Ellen." Try as she may, Kat couldn't keep the waver from her voice. "Detective Gilchrist's wife is just out front. There isn't anything you can do to me."

"Wrong. I poked the baby and must have woken it up. It started causing a fuss and she said to tell you that she would see you at her house. No, all I have to do is knock you out. He'll do the rest." At Ellen's gesture toward the office window, Kat saw Harlan use a cigarette lighter to set a stick wrapped with newspapers afire. His gloved hand crashed through the glass.

"Hurry up," he said in a low voice.

"If only you hadn't been at the office the other night. That's why we had to come and make sure you couldn't put two and two together. Harlan tried to climb through the window, and I waited out front in case you came that way, but no joy for us. Then I figured what had worked for Mike would work for you."

She pursed her lips in a pouty way. "Too bad those burglars had to come back to finish the job. If only I had been here to identify them."

Ellen raised her arm with the butt of the gun aimed at Kat's head. Kat squeezed her eyes closed, not wanting to know when the weapon would crash into her head. Instead, without warning, Ellen flew backward, across the hallway and into the wall. Her arm flailed up and the gun flew into the guest bedroom.

"For Christ's sake, Ellen, stop screwing around. Hit her."

"I can't move," Ellen struggled to say.

*Do I really have to tell you to get out?*

*Um... No.*

Her front door crashed into the wall as Kat stepped over Ellen's legs, which had all the appearance of being pinned to the floor.

"Kat!? Katherine Jane Hahn!" Kyle raced around the corner.

"I'm here. And look who else is here," she said proudly. "Mom and I captured your murderers."

***

After dinner at Kat's favorite Italian restaurant, she and Kyle walked up Main Street, hand in hand. "Dinner was very good," Kyle said.

"It was." She smiled up at him. "So was the company. Thanks so much for taking me out tonight. After the past several days, dinner out was even more special than it would have been otherwise."

"Two broken windows in one week," he teased. "The building supply company is going to love you."

"Well, I do aim to please."

"And you do." He leaned over and kissed her temple.

"After saving the day, I hope I'm up for a better reward than a PG kiss."

"Right here on Main Street? Maybe when we get home would be better." He dropped her hand but wrapped his arm around her shoulders to make up for it.

He didn't know how it had happened, but the first time he'd seen her, he knew Kat was the woman he wanted. The woman he'd fought through his injuries and come home for. It had been his lucky day when Brendan called him at his dad's and lured him into coming to Milford for a job on their force. He'd saved him from a lonely homecoming to a future filled with hope and joy. That is, if Kat felt the same about him.

"And also, I'm not sure you *totally* saved the day on your own." He quickly held up his hand to ward off her comments, which he could see she was about to make. "Not that you don't deserve credit for calling me and finding a way to leave your phone open. But I have to tell you, Amanda called Brendan just as you were calling me, so we were already on our way."

"I wondered why she left me alone with that lunatic."

"She knew something bad was going on, but she didn't want the children there when it happened."

"Don't blame her," Kat said. "But other than her phone call, I saved the day."

Kyle chuckled. "I believe your mom was the force behind tossing Ellen across the hall, knocking her gun away, and keeping her pinned to the floor."

"Yeah, you're right. I wonder how she did that? If she can move things, maybe she'll fix dinner some night." She slapped her hand over her mouth and laughed.

"What?"

"I won't tell you what Mom just said about my idea."

Kyle pulled her into a storefront doorway. "What would she say about what I have in mind for her daughter tonight?"

"I'm not sure." She sighed. "I love her dearly, but I hope she keeps her opinions and advice to herself."

"And closes her eyes." With that, he kissed her, silently promising good things for later that night and for a life together.

The End

# Linked
## S. K. White

### Part One: Swirl

Heavy droplets flooded the windshield. Lily flipped on the highest speed to squelch the raindrops' assault. The wipers moaned and screeched in their frantic effort to clear the path. She swiped the clouded glass with her palm to free the foggy obstruction and reveal oncoming traffic.

"Shit!" Lily jerked the steering wheel back into her lane and drew in a deep breath to relief her clenched jaw. She switched her playlist to *Lily's Meditations* to calm her racing heartbeat. "Inhale… one, two, three. Exhale… one, two, three."

Lily squinted as the bright beams hit her pupils from an oncoming car. She quickly glanced right to avoid the blast. "Asshole!" Lily leaned forward and clamped her fingers tightly around the steering wheel. She glimpsed down at her speedometer and eased off the gas. She leaned back in the car seat and nervously tapped her finger to the soothing melody. The taillights ahead grew farther and farther away, and the headlights behind her turned off the road. Sweet darkness surrounded her; finally, she was alone on the perilous stretch of blacktop.

Lily switched programs on her playlist, unclenched, and belted out her favorite tune. Droplets sprinkled the glass. She twisted the knob and turned down the speed to a slow, steady cadence. A yellow triangle warned to take the impending corner at forty-five mph. She glimpsed down at her speed and tapped the brake.

Suddenly, a bright light blinded her; then within seconds, a loud bang echoed as heavy metal slammed into the side of her car. Her seatbelt tugged and tightened as her body thrashed to and fro. Time stopped. Lily's eyes locked onto items flying past her. Lip gloss, broken glass, sunglasses, and an empty coffee mug sailed in slow motion through the air. The car tumbled over the guardrail, rolled down the embankment, and landed with a thud. Her body jerked and tingled. Her eyes fixed on a strange image, and then slowly turned dark.

Minute's passed by until Lily flinched and drew in a deep breath. She paused and wailed at the sharp pain in her right arm and ribcage. She scrutinized her surroundings.

"What happened? Where am I?"

She raised her left arm and swiped the fluid from her eyes. Lily glanced down at the dark goo and tapped the source of the trickle erupting from the gash in her throbbing head. She wiped the blood from her eyes and blinked to clear its remains. Afterward, Lily clutched her wounded arm and stepped in slow, measured movements to minimize the impact. She scanned the terrain and searched for lights, houses, or any sign of civilization. Finding neither, she followed the centerline on the asphalt, put one painful step in front of the other and chanted *"Inhale-step, exhale-stop, inhale-step, exhale-stop."*

Lily kept a slow and steady pace until dizziness took hold. She stumbled, staggered off the yellow line and stopped. Lily lifted her head, glared into the empty darkness, and slid her foot back on the yellow line. She trudged ahead, one foot at a time, and slowly found her rhythm once again. Suddenly, Lily's ears perked; she froze and strained to hear an echo in the distance.

The sound drew closer and closer and shouted, "Hey!"

Lily raised her head, blinked to clear her vision and shrieked, "Hello?"

The rich tone of bass grew louder. "Are you okay?" He reached for her. "Here. Let me help you." Lily glimpsed up at his face and collapsed in his arms. He glanced down at her. "It will be all right. I'm here."

The good Samaritan carefully lifted her into his arms and carried her down the highway. He spotted a building out in the field and stopped next to a barbwire fence. The tall, dark-haired man traveled down the fence line with his wounded discovery until he spied a break in the fence. He lifted the makeshift latch and opened the entrance, then packed the injured woman down the long gravel driveway and laid her down on the grass beside the porch of the log cabin.

Determined, the man-pounded on the door, but silence answered back.

He peeked in the windows and spotted cobwebs and dust. "Abandoned." He turned the locked doorknob and snatched a rock off the ground, then he struck the glass window on the door and cleared the broken shards from the windowpane.

The interloper unlocked the door, slowly cracked it open, and crept inside the dingy room. He glimpsed at a lantern on the table, searched the cabin in all the appropriate places for a match and growled. "Great. No matches."

Unexpectedly, the lantern instantly lit up. Puzzled, he turned around. "What the fuck?" Seconds later, a fire in the fireplace erupted. He turned his head from side to side and grumbled, "What the hell is going on?"

The perplexed man checked the bathroom. "Weird. No one's here?" His mind raced. "Oh shit. The woman."

He rushed outside, leaned over his wounded discovery and whispered, "I'm still here." He picked her up and packed her into the cabin.

He ripped the blanket off the bed and laid her on the sheet, then slipped outside, shook out the dusty blanket, and gently covered her chilled, broken body. He glanced around the grubby cabin and mumbled, "This can't be sanitary. She doesn't need an infection on top of all her other injuries." He opened a closet door, pulled out an old, dilapidated broom and rusty dustpan, and swept the floor. Then he emptied the dustpan filled with dried mud and broken glass in the trash, lifted the broom and cleared the cobwebs. He snatched a rag from the kitchen drawer and dusted the layers of neglected dust bunnies off the furniture.

The ambitious man ambled to the sink with his grimy rag and pumped the handle. Dirty water sprayed out. He pumped harder until the water cleared. "Looks like it's been a while since anyone was here." He rinsed out his rag, grabbed a dried-out old bar of soap out of the tarnished soap-dish, and washed out the filthy rag.

Once cleaned, he lathered it up again and scrubbed the kitchen counter and tabletop. Afterward, he scrutinized his housekeeping skills and dipped his chin twice. "Not perfect, but much better." The mildly contented housekeeper sat down in the wooden chair, rested his head on the freshly cleaned kitchen table, and closed his weary eyes. "Just a few minutes of shut-eye."

*** 

The sun peeked through the broken window. The green-eyed Samaritan lifted an eyelid and shot straight up. He turned to the pretty light-brown-haired woman sleeping on the bed and wrinkled his forehead.

"Who are you?" He stood and crept beside the bed. The handsome man bent down and swiped the hair out of her eyes. "What happened to you?"

He stepped into the kitchen, snatched a pan off the shelf, rinsed it out and filled it. He grabbed a washcloth out of the bathroom and dipped it in the cool water, cleaned the dried blood off his patient's head and left arm. He lifted her right arm. Still unconscious, she whimpered. He gently ripped the sleeve off and checked her arm.

"I'm sorry, but it's broken."

The man leaped outside and scrounged for pieces of wood but found nothing. He strode back in and spied two perfectly sized wooden slats and a roll of gauze on the kitchen table. "This is really fucked-up." Once again, he searched the perimeter, but discovered no one.

He bandaged her head, then splinted and elevated her arm using old, raggedy kitchen towels. Afterward, he trod into the bathroom and gazed at his reflection in the bathroom mirror. He touched the huge bump on the back of his head and swiped dried blood.

"Head wound. That explains this strange delusion." The man lifted his shirt and gasped. He spun around and checked his back. "Holy shit. I'm black and blue all over." He wiped off the dirty glass mirror with his sleeve, bent in closer, and stared at his bloodshot eyes. "What happened to me?" He placed his hands on the door frame and frowned at the young woman on the bed. "What happened to us?"

The disoriented good Samaritan flopped down in the chair. "All these bruises, and no pain?" Instantly, a pain seized his body, and he doubled over. "Okay, okay. Please... no pain." In seconds, the man sat up, pain-free. "Thank you. Whoever or whatever you are." Silence answered back. He planted his head in his hands and contemplated. *I must be dead.* He glanced over at the woman. *Are we dead or am I stuck in a nightmare and can't wake up? Sleep. I just need more sleep.* He stumbled to the bed, climbed in next to the beautiful stranger and shut his eyes.

***

Moonlight crept through the open curtain. Lily turned her head to take in the view. A sharp pain hit. She glanced at her splinted arm and slowly reached her left hand up to her bandaged head. "Where am I?" The strange man roused and turned over. She kicked him with her left foot and winced. "Ouch. Dammit."

He jumped. "What?"

"Who are you?" Lily kicked again and grimaced. "What am I doing here?"

He sat up. "Huh?" He tossed his head from side to side. "I... I found you on the highway and brought you here."

"What happened to me?"

"Okay... uh... first things first." He bit his lip and sighed. "I don't know what happened to you. I found you staggering down the road and you... you collapsed in my arms."

"Oh. So, you don't know what happened?"

"No. I don't."

"Well. I suppose I need to thank you then." She twisted her face. "Thank you.... what's your name?"

"Colin. My name is Colin Hayes."

"Thank you, Colin." She sniffed. "Do you think I was in an accident?"

"Yeah. Some kind of accident? But I didn't see any cars in the area."

She shrugged. "Maybe I fell hiking?"

"Maybe. But the mountain is at least five miles from here. You couldn't have traveled on foot that far in your condition."

"Maybe someone dumped me off on the road?"

"It's possible... I guess." He crumpled his forehead. "Do you ride horses?"

"No. Never ridden."

"Okay, let's count that one out." He held his stare. "By the way, what's your name?"

"My name is Lily. Lily Wallace."

"Well, Lily. We've got ourselves a mystery."

"Yeah." She glanced over at the fireplace. "Thanks for lighting the fire."

"Feels pretty good, huh?" He lowered his chin, stared into the crackling flames and pondered. *Shit. I don't remember ever lighting or stoking that fire.*

Lily cleared her throat. "How long have you lived here?"

He raised his head. "Haven't been here long."

She smiled and adjusted her blanket. The firelight caught the side of her face, and Colin gazed at the glint in her hazel eyes. A lock of her tussled hair clung to the side of her cheek. She grunted as she tried to swipe it away. Colin reached his hand out. "Here. Let me."

The corners of her mouth lifted in gratitude. He gently freed the strays and tucked them behind her ear. The shimmer of moonlight cast a shadow of a nearby tree branch upon her face and danced with the wind. He blinked as the butterflies in his stomach churned and thought, *How can I tell her what's really going on when I don't understand it myself?* He stared mesmerized at her beauty. *It's strange. There's something so familiar about her.* The wind heaved and howled outside. The limbs on the oak tree crackled and bent in protest as their warped and knotted image cast a haunting shadow across her face and extended across the wooden headboard. He eyed the headboard, and ruminated, *I need to stay quiet until I figure it out. She's worried enough already.*

She scrunched her nose. "Everything all right?"

He snapped out of his trance. "Oh… just tired."

"It's late. We should get some sleep." She yawned. "Looks like we bunk here together." Lily cocked her head and eyeballed his side of the bed. "Only one bed."

"Yeah." He slowly lifted his index finger, raised his brows and risibly drew a line right down the middle. "Don't worry, m'lady. I shan't cross over this line."

Lily giggled and moaned. "Stop that. It hurts to laugh."

He bowed and conjured a very bad interpretation of an Old English accent. "As you wish."

"Ouch!" She tittered and scrunched her nose. "Asshole."

Colin smirked. "Goodnight, Lily."

"Goodnight, Sir Colin."

He shook his head and grew a sly grin. Moments later, his eyelids grew heavy, and he fell into a deep, deep sleep. Within seconds, his cryptic dream began….

Colin hopped into his Ford 250 four-wheel drive and started the engine. He turned on his radio and hit playlist twenty-three—the perfect party-mood appetizer. Colin pulled out and headed for his favorite hang-out—a local bar filled with bros, brews, and babes. Raindrops sprinkled the windshield. He flipped on the wipers and traveled mindlessly down the familiar stretch of road.

Without warning, the raindrops blasted his glass. Colin eased up on the gas pedal. His phone buzzed. He reached down to tap the phone icon but smacked the side of the phone and his phone fell out of the holder. "Shit!" He glanced at the empty road, then back down at the floor. He stretched his hand out to grab the phone off the floorboard and stopped.

A flash of light caught his eye…

Suddenly, a sleeping Colin woke up, shot straight up in bed, and gasped. "No!" He turned his head right and left. The fire crackled and snapped. He glanced down at Lily and mumbled, "It was just a dream." Colin laid back down and stared at the wooden beams on the ceiling. "Just a dream."

He propped his head on his arm, gazed over at the endless fire, and watched the flames dance. He glimpsed down at Lily as she softly snored. "She's way above my paygrade." He dropped down on the pillow and eyed the wooden beam above. "Don't even think about it, dumbass. You'll only get hurt."

He stared at a crack in the center beam. Something dark emerged from the deep crevice. He focused on the impending intruder. A dark, shadowy fog poured out of the crack and spread out over the wooden boards between two beams. The centrifugal black fog sparkled and swirled. He raised his head off the pillow and focused on the swirling mass, but two seconds later, he blinked, and the swirling dark fog had vanished. Colin lay back down on the pillow and stared at the abandoned spot. His eyelids grew heavy and once again drifted back to sleep.

***

The early morning sun aroused the sleeping savior. Colin quickly spied his arm around Lily's waist and jerked it off. He lifted his hand, wiped the moisture from his nighttime drool off onto his jeans, then nonchalantly lay flat on his back.

Lily lifted an eyelid and groaned, "No…" She scrunched her nose and slowly opened both her eyes. "What time is it?"

"Dawn."

"I know that." She scowled. "But what time?"

He glanced around the room. "Your guess is as good as mine."

"No clocks?"

Colin shook his head. "No phone. And… no clocks anywhere?"

"You have no phone?"

He smacked his lips. "Nada."

"I have no cell phone?"

Colin lifted his shoulders. "Nope."

"I always have my phone."

"Me too." He patted his jean pockets and huffed, "All gone."

"Shit. No way to call for help. Colin, we're on our own."

"Yep." He jumped off the bed. "Guess I'll have to walk to town."

"No! Don't leave me here."

He sat back down. "Okay. We're doing all right here. I'll wait until you're stronger."

"Thank you." She paused. "Not like I have to get home to someone."

He gawked. "No husband or boyfriend?"

"Had one." She creased her forehead. "But didn't work out."

"Family?"

"Not close," she said. "They live in another town up north."

"Me too." He stuttered. "I... I mean, my family lives in another town several miles away. Colin smirked. "No wife or girlfriend, either."

"No way. No girlfriend?"

"Well..." he stammered. "Nothing serious."

"So, there is a girl?"

"No." He furrowed his brow. "Just a friend. We hook up once in a while."

Lily giggled. "She a fuck buddy?"

He grew wide-eyed. "Maybe?"

"I'm just kidding, Colin." She tilted her head. "You know you're entitled to have someone."

"Okay." He paused. "What about you? You hook up?"

"Nope. Done with that shit." She flared her nostrils. "That's all my ex did was hookup with one here, one there, and one everywhere."

"Oh... damn. He was one of those." Colin lifted a brow. "Well, if I'm in a relationship, I don't cheat. Never have. Never will."

She held her stare. "Never?"

"Never. If I had someone like you..." he stopped and lowered his voice. "Wouldn't do it."

Lily grew a grin. "That's good."

"His loss." He turned around and muttered, "My gain."

"Help me up." She lifted her head off the pillow. "I need to stretch my legs."

Colin spun around. "Are you sure?"

"Yeah. It's not good to lie here. I need to move around." Colin rushed over and lifted her to her feet. She cringed. "I think my ribs are bruised." She drew in a deep breath and stopped. "I hope not broken."

He lifted her shirt. "Looks like they could be bruised." He touched her ribs. "Maybe cracked?"

"If they were broken or cracked, I wouldn't be able to move this well."

"Probably right," he said. "Hopefully, just mildly bruised." Colin lifted his hand. "Hold on. We need to sling your arm." He dashed into the kitchen, opened the bottom drawer, and pulled out a dish towel. "Spotted this when I was cleaning." He tied the white cotton dish towel around her neck.

She eased her splinted arm inside. "Perfect. My mom had these dish towels. She called them flour-sack towels."

Colin smiled. "My grandmother had them too."

Lily walked into the kitchen holding Colin's arm with her good arm. She pointed to the cupboard. "I'd like a glass of water."

Colin opened the cupboard. A row of sparkling clean glasses lined the shelf. He mumbled, "What the…?" Then, he slowly pulled out a glass and thought, *Those weren't there before.* He pumped the handle, filled the glass with cold, clear water, and held it up.

"Anything wrong?"

He handed it to her. "No. Fresh and cold."

She sipped the cold water. "Yep. Fresh and cold." Lily handed him the half-empty glass, and he assisted her back to the bed. She grumbled, "Good enough for today." She eased herself underneath the blanket and propped her broken arm on the stack of towels. Lily lifted her left hand, tugged at the bandage on her head, and pulled it off. "How does it look?"

He wiped the blood-caked hair away and checked her gash. "Healing nicely."

"Good." She turned towards him and gazed into his emerald eyes. "Do we need to bandage it again?"

He sat down on the edge of the bed. "No. It looks like it's stopped bleeding. I think we can let the air get to it."

She cupped her hand on his scratchy stubble. "Good bedside manner, doc."

Colin tucked the loose hair behind her ear. "Guess I need a shave."

"No need. Don't need to on my account."

"Couldn't even if I wanted." He pointed to the bathroom. "No razor or shaving cream. Hell, we don't have much here."

"We have each other."

He grew a wide smile and prepared his mangled Old English accent. "You flirting with me, m'lady?"

"Yes, I am, Sir Colin."

He leaned in, brushed her cheek with his lips and whispered, "Don't start something you're not going to finish, m'lady."

She pressed her lips against his ear. "Never do. Never did, Sir Colin."

"I'll hold you to that… m'lady." He dropped back, gazed into her eyes, and kissed her left hand. "But for now, my good lady, you need to rest and give yourself time to heal. I want you healthy and happy." He cupped her face in his hands, bent over, and kissed her forehead. "I'm not going anywhere. If you want me to stay. I stay."

"Okay, Colin." She snuggled down in the bed. "I will rest and be good."

Colin slipped over to the other side of the bed, snuggled in, and glimpsed over. "Before my parents moved, I grew up a few miles from here."

"Really? What did you do for fun?"

"Mostly rode horses. I had an old buckskin mare named Bucket. That old girl knocked over her feed every time. She did it on purpose."

"Kept you hoppin'?"

He squinched his face. "Don't they all?"

"Just who are they?"

"All the females in my life." He scoffed. "Dad was deployed overseas most of the time, so I had to fend for myself against three older sisters. In other words, I grew up in a house full of women. And they definitely kept me hoppin'."

She giggled. "You mean they put you in your place?"

"What place?" He sighed. "I was lucky if they let me have a seat at the table."

"Poor Colin. Did you have to eat all alone in the kitchen?"

"Me and my dog ate with Bucket." He glanced over, tipped an air-cowboy hat and conjured up his best Texan accent. "Yep. Poor Colin ate with Bucket and my old cow-dog Bailey in the barn."

"You're quite the bullshitter, aren't you?"

"Been known to spin a few tales." He arched his brow. "But only in fun."

"Thought you never lied."

"Don't lie." He held a firm stare. "Sooner or later, I'll always tell you if it's bullshit." He raised his finger in the air. "Here goes." The bossy older sisters are true. Bucket and Bailey are too. But I didn't eat in the barn. Well, when I did, it was by choice; usually, when I needed to get away from too much estrogen. At least, the humankind."

"I take it Bailey was a male?"

Colin bobbed wide-eyed. "Definitely." He leaned in closer. "Hey, care to hear a few more bullshit stories?"

Lily waved her hand. "Let 'er rip."

Colin spent the rest of the afternoon and evening entertaining her with stories in various accents. Then after sunset, he tucked her in. "Goodnight, m'lady."

"Goodnight, my sweet knight."

"Sweet?" He cocked his head and lifted his shoulders. "Don't know how sweet." He winked, placed his hands on the bed and bent closer. "But definitely faithful… and impishly truthful."

"Okay." She giggled. "Goodnight, my impishly truthful, faithful knight in shining armor."

He stretched out on the bed and folded his arms. "Night."

She rubbed the side of his blue jeans with her hand and tapped his leg. Colin turned his head towards her, cracked a smile, grabbed her hand, and kissed it. "Sweet dreams, Lily."

He stared at the spot on the ceiling and matched Lily—breath for breath—as she drifted deeper and deeper. Within minutes, his eyelids fell victim to her rhythm, and the two lightly snored in unison.

\*\*\*

Two hours later, Colin thrashed and moaned. He jerked and opened his eyes. The dark spot on the ceiling swirled and grew brighter and brighter. A light erupted from its center and raced towards Colin's head. He threw up his hands to block its impact, but in a flash, it disappeared, leaving only darkness behind.

Colin jumped up and headed for the bathroom. He placed his hands on the edge of the sink and gazed into the mirror. "I'm going crazy." He pumped the handle and splashed cool water over his face. He snatched a towel off the hook, dried off, and quietly returned to bed. Colin turned on his side and shut his eyes tight.

\*\*\*

The next morning, Lily climbed out of bed. Colin jolted awake. "Lily, what are you doing?"

"Getting up. What does it look like?"

"You feel okay?" He scowled. "Don't hurt yourself."

"I feel much better today." She spun around. "See."

"Wow. You do heal fast."

"I'm going to take a shower now." She unbuttoned her jeans, pulled and tugged at the denim one-handed, and kicked them off. "Are you coming?"

Colin jumped up. "Hold on." Her sling tangled around her shirt. He rushed over to help. She ripped off the white kitchen towel and threw it on the floor. He stepped back. "Okay. Guess you don't need my help."

She cocked her head, slid her shirt off, and lowered the straps of her bra. Colin's eyes widened. She grew a sly smile and turned around. "Aren't you going to undo it?"

He raised his hands in surrender and eyeballed her. She bobbed. He tentatively unfastened her bra and maintained his stare. She pulled the strap over her splint and handed it to him. He stuck it on a bathroom hook. Lily kicked off her panties and ogled Colin. He bent down, picked them up, and placed them on top of the bra. She pulled back the shower curtain and bellowed, "Bathtub. No shower! No faucet?"

He spied a bucket next to the tub and shrugged. "I'll heat the water."

Colin gathered wood off the porch, built a fire in the cast iron cook stove with the help of a burning stick from the fireplace and heated several buckets of water in an old soup pot he retrieved from the kitchen.

Lily strode over to the bed, flopped down on her stomach, and tantalizingly scissor-kicked her legs in the air. Colin snuck in a few peeks at her naked body while he cunningly filled the rest of the tub with cold water. Upon completion, he dipped his hand in the bath water and announced, "Your bath awaits, M'lady."

Lily bowed, promenaded over to the tub and stretched her hand out. Colin lightly received her hand and assisted. She climbed in, propped her injured arm on the side of the claw tub, and soaked in her soothing bath.

Several minutes later, Colin packed in another bucket. "Let me warm your tub?" He gazed down at the outline of her curves and lingered on her nipples peeking through the water's surface. The blood rushed to his groin. He slowly poured in the freshly heated water and growled in a low deep voice. "Feel better?"

She lifted her eyelids and purred. "Mmm… it certainly does." She swirled the water with her hand and flicked it with her fingers. "Climb in."

He glimpsed down at the wet spot on his shirt and shot her a devious grin. Colin peeled off his shirt and tossed it on the floor. She eyed his bruises. "How did you get those?"

"Don't know. Rough living, I guess." He removed his jeans. Lily gazed at his offering and smiled. He slowly slid into the water behind her and snarked. "A bit crowded." She lifted her toned, round bottom, and he scooted underneath her. She sat on his lap, leaned back, and rested her head on his shoulder. He lay back against the porcelain and wrapped his arms around her waist. "You okay?"

"Fine."

He gazed at her breasts floating in the water and craved the feel of her hardening nipples. Colin inched his way up her side and rounded her soft breasts. He glanced at her closed eyes and gently circled her aroused nipple with his fingertip. She softly groaned, grabbed his other hand, and placed it between her legs. He kissed her neck and massaged her sweet spot. Lily arched her back, clutched the side of the tub with her left hand, and moaned.

She arrived, turned her body around, and climbed on top of him. He kissed her slowly, cupped his hands around her bottom and assisted her up and down motion. Colin inhaled her scent and closed his eyes. His desire built and built with each thrust; then, overcome with passion, he erupted and emptied body and soul into the woman he hoped to love someday.

Afterward, Colin relaxed, caressed Lily, and opened his eyes. Lily's hazel eyes met his. He smiled and proclaimed, "God, Lily, you're beautiful."

She nuzzled the nap of his neck and whispered, "And you, Colin, are everything a woman could ever want."

After basking in the afterglow, Colin eased Lily out of the tub and held her firmly around the waist. "Careful. Looks like our fun spilled over onto the floor."

She giggled. "They say it's not the size of the vessel, but the motion of the ocean."

Colin twisted his face. "My good lady, no one's ever complained about the size of my vessel."

"And none here." She lifted her chin. "For, my good captain, you have a mighty fine vessel and steer her well."

Colin snickered. "Damn straight. Precise navigation."

He dried her off, whisked her into his arms and carried her over to the bed. He placed her underneath the covers and slipped in beside her. "Care for another voyage aboard my mighty vessel, M'lady? She grew a wily smile and bobbed. The two embraced and Lily set sail for the rest of the afternoon aboard his mighty vessel.

Later, the couple emerged from their sanctuary just in time to watch the stars blanket the evening sky covered in diamonds. Colin held her close, and the two counted shooting stars and orbiting satellites. A chill filled the night air. Lily shivered, so the two held hands and opened the cabin door. A bottle of merlot, two wine glasses, and a platter of cheese and apple slices greeted them on the table.

Lily glanced over at Colin. "How did you do this?"

He shrugged. "Not me. But someone wants us to have a romantic evening."

"Who knows we're here?"

"Neighbors, I imagine." He checked the bathroom and hedged once again. "They certainly come in and out easily without a trace."

"Well." Lily waltzed over and lifted the bottle. "Let's not waste it." She examined the label. "It looks like a fine wine."

Colin collected the platter and two glasses off the table and headed for the bed. He propped up the pillows, undressed, and raised both glasses in the air. "Care to join me?"

Lily disrobed, sashayed over with the bottle, and handed it to Colin. The two sipped wine and feasted on sliced apples and cheese.

Colin slid the last two pieces of apple towards him and placed a sliver of cheddar cheese on each slice. He lifted the first wedge to her lips and raised an eyebrow. She opened her mouth, and he tenderly popped it in. Lily chewed her apple slice and cooed; then, she grabbed the last piece and raised it to his lips.

He wrapped his lips around the cheesy slice and deviously licked and sucked the remains off her finger. Lily embraced the sensuous sensation. Colin kissed her hand and slowly made his way to her left shoulder. He gathered her hair in his hands and gently placed it on the other side.

Colin brushed the nape of her neck with his lips, captured her earlobe and teased it with his tongue. He released her lobe and kissed the back of her neck. His hot breath sent shivers up and down her body. Colin slowly made his way to the front and kissed her lips. The tip of his tongue lightly touched hers.

Lily clutched the hair on the back of his neck, drew him closer, and passionately returned his kiss. Her hunger grew. She opened her legs, ready to receive him. He slid down to her eager breasts, wrapped his lips around her nipple, and aroused it with his tongue. On the brink, she grasped his buttocks with her left hand and enticed his entry.

Colin lifted his head, accepted her invitation, and initiated a slow burn. He tantalized her sweet spot with feathery strokes. Lily moaned as her arrival grew near. Colin slightly entered her and slowly inched deeper, but kept his tempo. Lily's intensity grew stronger and stronger.

Finally, she could no longer hold back. She pressed her hand firmly against his tight butt, and he dove in deeper. She let out a primal cry and detonated. A burning Colin thrust in deep, picked up his pace, and soon released with a passionate groan. He collapsed beside her, wrapped his arm around her waist, and leaned up to her ear. "I love you, Lily."

She squeezed his hand. "I love you more." The two caressed and surrendered to the lure of a sweet slumber.

A few hours later, Colin jerked awake and gazed at Lily sleeping soundly on his chest. He kissed her forehead and slipped out from under her. The wind howled outside as raindrops rushed through the broken window. Colin spied a sheet of plastic and duct tape on the table and roared, "Of course! As usual, whatever we need just magically appears." He snatched the materials off the table, tossed his head from side to side, and huffed, "And always materializes just in the nick of time."

He taped up the windowpane and threw the roll of tape on the table. "There! Happy?" Colin raised his hands in the air and quietly groused, "Am I just a pawn in your sick game?"

Silence answered back. He shook his head and crawled back into bed. He crossed his arms and stared at the crack in the beam. Once again, a shadowy fog emerged from the crack and transformed into particles of sparkling lights that swirled in between the beams. Their hypnotic swirl lulled him into a relaxing trance. His eyes grew heavy, slowly shut tight, and the nightmare began…

The music blasted in his Ford truck. The wipers struggled to remove the raindrops from his windshield. He turned up the fan on defrost to clear the fog buildup on the glass. His phone buzzed. He stretched his hand out to answer the phone but knocked it out of the holder. Colin glanced up at the empty road, unbuckled his seatbelt and reached for his phone on the floor. He turned his head towards a flash of bright light and shot back up in his seat. He jerked his wheel to round the corner. The truck skidded and slammed into the side of a car. Colin's airbag deployed as he hurled towards the steering wheel and bounced back against the headrest. The truck and car catapulted over the embankment…

Colin woke up, gasped, and opened his eyes.

"Please…no!" The swirl on the ceiling faded. He glared at the abandoned spot. "I'm dead. Are we both dead? Did I kill her!" Silence answered back. Tears rushed down his face. He cuddled close to Lily. "God, Lily, I'm so, so, sorry." She stirred and groaned. He kissed her cheek. "How could you ever forgive me? Baby, I'm so sorry." He held her tight and silently chanted "I'm so sorry" over and over until he slowly drifted back to sleep.

***

The next morning, Colin glanced over at an empty bed. He shot up and checked the bathroom. "Lily!" Only the cold remains of used water from the night before filled the tub. He rushed outside. "Lily?"

The frosty ground laced the dried grass and stung his bare feet. Undeterred, he ran to the back of the cabin. "Lily."

Colin dashed back inside and noticed there were no wine glasses or cheese platter littering the kitchen. He glared at the bed and discovered one pillow propped against the headboard. There were no towels or women's clothing strewn about. He flopped down in the chair and placed his head in his hands.

"Lily! Where are you?" He glimpsed up and spied a glass of half-filled water on the counter. "There! There's your cold fresh water." Colin raced over and lifted it up. "See! I'm not dreaming. You were here."

His nostrils flared and his chest grew tight. The blood rushed to his head as he squeezed the shaky glass. Water spilled over onto his hand. He glared at the droplets and snarled, "Fuck!"

Colin reared back and threw the offending reminder across the room. The glass hit the wall. Shattered pieces slowly floated through the air. He blinked and bent forward for a closer look. The shards sparkled as they cut through the globules of water. Then, once freed from their bondage, the slivers glided unimpeded through the open air. They twisted and turned in slow motion and aligned in single file. Afterward, the perfectly aligned pieces glistened, circled the globule of water and spun faster and faster, creating a shimmering surface.

Images of Colin's accident projected off the surface like a movie screen. Colin watched as his battered body flew through the shattered windshield and landed among the broken glass. He spied solid pieces of shattered glass lift off the hood and freeze in mid-flight. In seconds, the shards shot out of the shimmering surface and raced towards him. He shut his eyes ready for impact. The solid projectiles stopped inches from his head. Colin gingerly opened his eyes and reared his head back for a better look. The frozen pieces of glass remained suspended in midair for several seconds; then, in the blink of an eye, they suddenly dropped to the floor.

He glanced over at the shimmering surface left behind. The surface slowly liquified and spattered to the floor in a defused puddle. He grabbed a chair and pulled it closer to the menacing glass fragments.

Colin warily sat down and stared at the shattered pieces on the scuffed hardwood floor. One by one, each piece slid back together like a completed jigsaw puzzle. The sealed pieces sparked and lit up until the photo of a person slowly came into view.

Colin leaned down and cried, "Lily!" Suddenly, the glass dimmed, and the image burned out. Colin shook his head. "This is fucking crazy." He clenched his fists, thrust his head back, and yelled, "What do you want from me!" He dropped his head and closed his eyes. "Give her back to me. I just want Lily."

Colin held his head in his hands, opened his eyes, and stared blankly at the wooden floor. "Lily, if you can hear me, please come back. I need you. Forgive me." Tears flowed down his cheek, and his stomach heaved. He rushed into the bathroom and retched. Afterward, feeling inconsolable guilt, despair, and exhaustion, he plopped down on the edge of the bed and glanced upward. "Without her, this is hell." He dropped his head. "I'm in hell! If I killed her… I deserve it." He slowly lifted his head and flared his nostrils. "Do you hear me! I deserve it!"

## Part Two: Rise…

The whoosh and beeps of the machine next to the bed echoed in the room. Lily twitched her fingers. The nurse bent down. "Lily, if you can hear me, lift your hand." Lily lifted her index finger and slowly raised her hand. The nurse checked the monitor and removed the eye guards and tape. Lily blinked and squinted from the bright lights. The nurse stroked her hand. "Okay, Lily. I'll get the doctor, and we'll remove the breathing tube." Lily blinked and dipped her chin. The nurse opened the door and motioned for the doctor.

After the on-call physician arrived, he checked Lily's status and explained the procedure. He suctioned, deflated the cuff, and leaned down. "Lily, I'm going to remove your breathing tube now. On the count of three, I want you to take a deep breath, then exhale or cough. Ready?" Lily dipped twice. He counted. "One, two, three."

Lily drew in a deep breath and exhaled. The doctor gently pulled out the breathing tube. Lily coughed several times, opened her eyes wider, and dropped her chin. He grew a smile. "Well done, Lily. I'll be in later to check on you." He turned and walked out.

The nurse moved the cart out of the way. "Hon, your throat is going to be a little sore. I'll bring you something to ease the irritation." Lily blinked and slightly lifted the corners of her mouth. The nurse patted her arm. "You've been here for a while, but you're doing much better. Please stay still and let your body rest. I'm giving you a little something for the pain. This should help the irritation in your throat too. The doctor will come in later this afternoon and check you. He'll answer any questions you might have. For now, let's get a bit of rest."

The nurse injected meds into her IV and turned around. "This medication will also help you sleep." She dropped the empty syringe into the receptacle and rolled the cart next to the door. "I'll be back with something for your throat."

The nurse rolled the cart out into the hallway and shut the door. Lily shifted her eyes from side to side. Cords and wires attached to the monitor stretched out and ended taped to her body. The continuous clicks and beeps from the monitor, a casted arm, bandaged head, and sore ribs foretold the extent of her injuries. Teardrops rolled down her cheek. She grunted, lifted her index finger, and wiped away the moisture.

The nurse popped back in, holding a light-green popsicle. "Like a cool treat for your throat? Hope you like lemon-lime. That's all that was left." Lily smiled and nodded. The nurse handed Lily the stick, pointed to a plastic tray, and said, "You can just put the stick on the stand. I'll be back later."

Lily sucked on the cold treat. The cold liquid trickled down and eased her dry, irritated throat. Her eyelids grew heavy from the meds as they kicked in. She set the half-eaten popsicle down on a mustard-colored tray next to a plastic glass and pitcher. Then Lily sunk down on her pillow and drifted to sleep.

Later that afternoon, a doctor quietly entered, checked her vitals, and glimpsed down at his tablet. Lily opened her drowsy lids and glanced over. He turned around and walked to the bed.

"Lily, I'm Doctor Troy." Lily's chin dipped and her forehead wrinkled. He cocked his head and lowered his voice. "I'm going to decrease the dosage on your sedatives and pain meds. We kept you in a coma for a while to let your brain injury heal. It's time to wing you off. You've healed nicely."

Lily blinked and bobbed. The doctor stuck his stylus in his pocket. "It will be a day or two before you'll feel like talking. That's okay. It's normal. There's a notepad and pen next to the bed if you need anything. Just buzz the nurse. She'll get it for you. For now, let's get some rest. Plenty of time for questions and answers later." The doctor slipped the buzzer next to Lily's hand. "I'll check on you in the morning during my rounds." He flashed a half grin and strolled over to the door. "See you in the morning."

Lily waved, lightly rubbed the side of the buzzer with her index finger and let the drone of the monitor lull her back to sleep. Within seconds, her lucid dream began…

Lily stroked Colin's chest hairs with her fingertips. He glanced down at her. "I love you, Lily."

She kissed his muscular pec, glanced up at him and said, "Love you too." He tucked a lock of her long hair behind her ear, bent closer and kissed her lips. She climbed on top of him and gazed into his green eyes. "Make love to me, Colin. He cupped her bottom and rolled her underneath him.

All of the sudden, Lily jerked awake. Memories of Colin flooded back. Her body stiffened and her heart raced. "Colin." She glimpsed over at the monitor, then gazed down at the cast on her arm. She inhaled and bemoaned, "Was I in an accident?"

A light crept through a crack in the bathroom door and revealed a beautiful bouquet on the counter. Lily turned her head towards the clock on the wall and squeaked, "Three-thirty?" She glanced at the window and spied streetlights beaming through the glass pane. "Nighttime." Lily closed her eyes, drew in a cleansing breath, and replayed images of Colin in her mind until the medication kicked in once again.

The next morning, after Dr. Troy's morning rounds, Lily screeched out a thank you as he shut the door, then afterward, swallowed hard and coughed. She quickly turned her head, spotted a mustard-colored plastic pitcher and a matching glass with a straw. She pushed the buzzer.

The nurse entered, and Lily pointed to the glass on the cart and croaked, "Water please." The nurse poured water into the plastic glass and raised the straw next to her lips. Lily lifted her hand and grasped the straw. She sipped the water slowly and swallowed. The cool water stung, but refreshed. Lily coughed and, in a hoarse voice, uttered, "So good."

The nurse smiled and consoled. "You're getting your voice back." She dipped her chin at the glass. "Are you done, dear?" Lily bobbed. The nurse set down the glass, lifted the notepad and pen, and lay it down beside her arm. "Just write down what you need if your voice gets tired." Lily nodded. The nurse made a quick check on the monitor and left.

Lily gazed circumspectly at the glass of cool water for several minutes. *Colin.* A righthanded Lily picked up the pen with her left hand, eyed the pad, and clumsily scribbled, "Where's Colin?" She dropped the pen and pushed the buzzer.

A new nurse peeked in the doorway, and Lily pointed to the notepad. The nurse grinned, picked it up, and read aloud. "Where's Colin?" Lily nodded. The nurse placed the notepad down beside Lily. "I'll see if I can find out. I just got on duty so I'm not up to speed yet." Lily bobbed, and the nurse left.

Lily stared at her cast. Thoughts of Colin's makeshift splint drew a smile. The door opened, and Lily's dad popped his head in. "They called and said you were awake." He pointed to the flowers. "I see you got the flowers. Sweetheart, I'm so glad you're awake." He strolled over to her bedside and pulled up a chair. "You gave me quite a scare."

Lily hissed, "How long?"

"Three weeks." He patted her left hand. "You were in a coma for three weeks."

She lifted her notepad and handed it to her father. "Where's Colin?"

Lily's father glanced down at the note. "Colin?" He furrowed his brow. "The man who hit you?"

Lily scrunched her nose and nodded. He swung his head from side to side. "We can talk about that later. You just concentrate on you."

Lily shook her head vigorously. Her father twisted his mouth. "Sweetheart, I think he's still in a coma." Lily scowled. He squeezed her hand. "You have always worried about everybody but yourself." Lily's father pressed his lips together and relented. "Very well… I'll go find out how he's doing."

She raised her brows and grinned. He tapped his thighs, stood up, and sighed. "Okay sweet girl. Wish me luck."

"Good luck." She blew him a kiss. "Thanks, Dad." Lily's father flashed her a quick wave and shut the door. Lily wiped a tear from her cheek and glimpsed down at her cast. Her mind raced—Colin hit me? Accident? Has to be a car accident. Why can't I remember the accident?

Fifteen minutes later, Lily's father opened the door and sat in the chair next to the bed. "They couldn't tell me. Patient confidentiality." He shrugged and bent in close to her ear. "But… I snuck around and found his name on a tag on the door. Honey, it looks like he's still in his coma."

Lily's raspy voice growled, "What happened?"

"His truck went into a skid from the rain and plowed into you. You both went over the embankment. The police said he wasn't wearing his seatbelt. He was beat up pretty bad. I saw his folks a few days after the accident in the waiting room. They said Colin had some internal damage, but mostly a head injury." Lily exhaled and frowned. Her father stood. "I think you've had enough for today. I'll be back tomorrow to visit. You have the nurse call me if you need anything." He kissed her on the cheek. "Get some rest." She waved goodbye with her one good hand as he shut the door.


## Part Three: Forever…


Lily grasped the covers and jerked them off. She pulled out her IV, yanked off the sensors, pressed against the bar with her left hand and sat up. Then she slid her left leg off the bed, pushed off with her good hand, and stood. She tucked her casted arm next to her stomach and stumbled to the door. Lily opened it and ambled down the hall.

A nurse rushed to her side. "No, no. You mustn't walk by yourself." She motioned to the desk nurse to get a wheelchair. "We must do this together." A desk nurse dropped off a wheelchair and slipped into Lily's room to turn off the alarm on Lily's blaring monitor.

Lily pointed down the hallway and throatily squealed, "Take me to Colin's room."

The nurse tilted her head. "Colin Hayes?"

"Yes," Lily screeched. "I need to see him."

"Are you family?"

"Girlfriend." Lily swallowed hard and lied. "I'm his fiancée."

"Okay." She turned the wheelchair. "But not today. Neither one of you is ready for a visit."

Lily planted her feet firm. "Now!"

"Alright, we'll just swing by there. But only for a minute." She turned the chair and wheeled down the hall to room 214. The nurse opened the door and rolled her next to his bed.

Lily grabbed his swollen hand, squeezed it, bent close and whispered, "I'm right here, babe." She glanced at the breathing tube, the bandages, and all the tubes and wires hooked up to him. "You fight, Colin. Fight for us." Tears streamed down her face. She sniffed. "I love you."

The nurse stroked Lily on the back. "Lily, we need to let him rest now so he can come back." Lily lifted her head and nodded. The nurse handed Lily a tissue and wheeled her back to her room. She helped Lily into her bed and wagged her finger. "You need to rest too, so you can be there for Colin when he wakes up."

Lily cleared her throat. "When will he wake up?"

"That's up to him." The consoling nurse lifted her shoulders. "He'll be back when his body's ready. We just need to give his body time."

Lily snuggled down in her bed. The nurse handed her the TV remote, and Lily hit the power button.

Three hours later, the on-duty nurse did her nightly check. Afterward, Lily turned off her monitor, waited a few minutes, and threw back the covers. She hobbled to the door, checked both ways, and crept to room 214. She pulled up a chair and rested her head on Colin's chest. Lily stroked his chest and whispered, "Come back to me."

After an hour, voices and rolling wheels echoed down the hallway. Squeaky wheels and muffled laughter grew closer and closer. Lily squeezed his hand, kissed Colin on the cheek, and muttered, "I love you." She stood, regained her balance, and snuck back to her room.

Night after night, a stealthy Lily checked on her beloved; but each night, Colin still remained in his coma. Then, on her final morning at the hospital, Lily popped into Colin's room and bent next to his ear. "See you tonight."

Colin raised his finger. Lily shrieked, "Colin, can you hear me?" His finger wiggled. She cleared her recovering raspy throat and said, "I'm here. It's Lily." He raised his fingers.

Lily raced out into the hall. "He's waking." She rushed back in and squeezed his hand. "Colin. I'm right here."

The nurse rushed in and checked his vitals. The on-call doctor shooed Lily out into the hall and checked him. Lily stood at the door. The doctor removed Colin's eye guard and checked his pupils. Colin lifted his fingers on command. The doctor glanced over at Lily and nodded. She wiped the tears off her face. "Colin, I'm here."

Colin flashed her a hint of a smile as he fought to stay awake. He exhaled and cogitated, *She's alive! My Lily's alive.*

Lily's father walked down the hallway and stood behind her. "Are you ready?"

"No, Dad. I have to stay." She pointed at Colin. "He's awake. If he wants me to stay. I stay."

"Lily, he needs to rest." He grasped his daughter's shoulders. "Honey, you can come back tomorrow."

"No! I need to stay with him. He needs me."

"Let's get you to your apartment so you can rest." He squeezed her shoulders. "I'll bring you back tonight."

Lily spun around. "All right. But let me go tell him first." The doctor finished his examination, removed his breathing tube, and informed her to keep it short.

Lily sat in the chair beside his bed and grabbed his hand. "Colin, Dad wants me to go rest and come back later." Colin blinked and dipped his chin. She leaned over and kissed him. "If you want me to stay. I stay."

The corners of his mouth lifted. After a brief pause, he drew in a breath, swallowed hard, and mouthed, "Go rest. See you tonight."

She bobbed. "Tonight."

Lily and her father walked down the hall. He turned towards her. "How long have you known Colin?"

"Not long." She shrugged. "But it feels like I've known him all my life."

"So, you knew each other before the accident?"

"Dad! What is this?" She scowled. "An interrogation? What does it matter? Leave the badge at home."

He threw up his hands. "Okay! Okay… I just thought it odd. You never told me about him before."

"Well!" She sighed. "Dad, I'm a full-grown adult. I'm not going to talk about my sex life with my father."

"Please don't." He wrinkled his forehead. "But hopefully you'd let me know if you loved the guy, and it was serious."

Lily put her hand on his chest. "Dad. Thank you for coming to stay with me. I really appreciate it, but I do have a life you know. And, yes, I do love Colin. And I intend to have you meet him." She crooked her mouth. "Let's let him heal first."

"How long have you two dated?"

She rolled her eyes and groused, "Long enough."

Later that night, Lily's father reluctantly dropped her off at the hospital with strict instructions from his daughter to wait until she called. Lily crept into Colin's room, sat beside him, and held his hand. He cracked open his eyelids and gave her a half-grin. She grasped a glass off the cart and stuck the straw close to his lips. His green eyes twinkled as he wrestled with the straw and took a sip.

Colin squeezed her hand and mouthed, "Thank you."

She leaned up to his ear. "Do you remember me?"

He raised his brows and rasped, "I love you, M'lady."

She grew a wide smile. "Me too, Sir Colin."

A tear ran down his cheek. "I'm sorry, baby."

"I'm not." She wiped his cheek. "I wouldn't have found you. It was meant to be."

His lip quivered as thoughts of guilt raced through his soul. Right at that moment, Colin realized his guilt had become a powerful, dark, swirling force that had manifested itself during the hours he was vulnerable and lost in the grip of a coma. That guilt had become a relentless demon that led his soul down a dark path—a deep, dark path. It was Lily's sweet voice and love that brought him back from his endless pit of despair. He stopped, gazed at the love in Lily's eyes, and cried out. "How could you ever forgive me? I hurt you."

"Forgive you! Nonsense. It was an accident." She stroked the side of his face. "The best accident of my life."

He grasped her hand and kissed it. "I love you."

Lily flashed him an artful grin. "You sure know how to get a girl's attention." She winked and leaned in closer. "Besides, you'll just have to spend the rest of our lives making it up to me."

He mouthed. "Gladly."

"Rest, baby. I want you strong and able-bodied." She lightly patted his chest, slid her hand slowly down to his nether regions, and stopped. "We have some catching up to do and plenty of voyages to take with that magnificent vessel of yours." She winked. "Captain."

He bit his lip and mustered up a wily grin. She raised her left hand and closed his eyelids with her fingertips. "Sleep, my captain, my mighty captain, and let that amazing body heal." She laid her head on Colin's chest and let the rhythm of his heartbeat soothe her. The two drifted off to sleep and their nexus began once again…

*** 

Colin leaned down to grab his phone. Bright lights flashed. He jerked his head up to turn the wheel and round the sharp corner. His truck hydroplaned from the pouring rain and slammed into the driver's side of the car. The impact shoved them both down the embankment. Lily's car rolled and landed with a thud. The truck smacked up against it. Colin splayed over the hood. His eyes opened. He stared over the glass-covered, bent and battered hood, and spied Lily's head pressed against the car window. She gazed into his shell-shocked green eyes. Their pupils dilated, locked in on each other, and focused. An unexplained energy passed between them and surged from head to toe. Their bodies tingled, heaved, and quivered for several seconds. Then, a flickering light erupted, and images of their life together flashed before their eyes. Afterward, the flashing bright light stopped, slowly eclipsed, and all went dark.

Colin and Lily woke up. Their eyes met and immediately dilated. Suddenly, a flash of light erupted from their pupils and projected images of their past, present, and future lives together.

After the flicker slowly faded away, Lily raised her head off Colin's chest. He furrowed his brow and muttered, "Did you see it?"

"Yes. While we were sleeping, I saw the accident again; then, I saw our entire life together. It was just like that night." She shook her head and wrinkled her forehead. "But a moment ago… I saw several lifetimes together."

He nodded. "Me too. First this life. Then, all of our other lives together.

"Exactly." She shook her head. "How?"

"I don't know?" He cleared his gravelly throat. "But somehow we're linked."

"So many lives together." She scrunched her nose. "No one will believe us."

"I know."

"This is our secret," she whispered. "Our business."

"It will remain our secret." He cocked his head and flashed a Cheshire cat grin. "One of the secrets of the great unknown."

"Yeah." She smiled. "No one will ever understand it."

"We're still trying to understand it ourselves." He patted her arm. "You know… I think, right after the collision, something mystical happened to us. In the twinkling of an eye, two souls bonded once again and fell in love."

"Yes!" Lily placed her hand on top of his. "And… I think the coma gave us time to process what happened to us during the accident, find each other once again, reconnect through shared dreams while unconscious, and fulfill our destiny."

He licked his dry lips and pointed to the plastic glass. Lily lifted the straw to his mouth, and he sipped the refreshing water. Afterward, he stroked her leg and cleared his throat. "Lily, I don't know how… but I know it was meant to be, and that's good enough for me."

"Me too." She sat the plastic glass down. "I don't care how or why. I'm just glad we found each other again and we're together."

"Yes, we definitely are." He kissed her hand and flashed his twinkling emerald eyes. "Happily, linked forever."

"Forever." Lily's pupils instantly dilated, and her bewitching twinkle answered back. Afterward, she cracked a resolute smile and whispered, "Yes. Together forever. Our destiny."

The end… or is it?

The Wheel of Life
S. K. White

Love can't be forgotten,
we rise, we fall,
and turn the wheel,
only to discover,
that in the end,
all life is…
or ever really was…
is just a circle,
lessons repeated over and over,
until we finally get it right.

Trigger Warning:
The Ritual contains scenes of graphic violence

# The Ritual
# Virginia Wallace

## Chapter One

The North Carolina sun shone brightly, scorching everything beneath its gaze with searing tendrils of blistering light.

There was no breeze today, and the air was dead silent. Even the midday symphony of cicada clacking was absent, here in this tiny clearing. This was a forgotten place, a place pulled out of time and even memory.

This place was the epicenter of Nowhere Land, its sadly glorious, un-remembered capital.

The clearing was completely surrounded by cypress swamps, their stagnant muck penetrated here and there by towering trees bearded with dry Spanish moss. The air reeked of sulfur, with a suffocating, rotten-egg stench.

In the center of the overgrown clearing sat a tiny brick building covered in peeling paint, with a rotting tar-paper roof and a few small, barred windows. Its door had a chain slung across it, for its own lock had long ago succumbed to rust. The sign on the door had once read "U.S. Post Office", but alas it had long ago been rendered illegible by time and decay.

Only a narrow gravel road led to the clearing, overgrown with weeds and barely visible beneath the shadows of the towering trees. The swamp seemed languidly determined to devour the road, for the muck and stagnant water were steadily eroding its edges for miles beyond the forgotten clearing.

This place looked as though it would remain forever forgotten, inhabited only by ghosts. It appeared unlikely that mankind would ever trespass here again. Indeed, such would have seemed an insult.

But men are nothing if not prone to giving insult, and ever heedless of the respect due forgotten, secret places.

There was only silence …

And then there arose a roar in the distance, the unmistakable sound of a truck tearing down the gravel road.

Suddenly awakened from their torpor, the cicadas began clacking furiously. They increased their volume until the truck reached the clearing, skidding to a stop in front of the abandoned post office.

The truck was a shiny new king cab, painted black, with tinted windows. A hot breeze arose, as though the offended, hidden place meant to gently blow the interlopers away.

The truck's engine rumbled to a stop as the doors opened, and two men climbed out. They were both dressed in black, with dapper pants, and shirts with the sleeves rolled up. They wore matching sunglasses, and they both had short-cropped dark hair. At a glance, they looked like photocopies of the same man, a man who was used to going incognito and could easily fade into the shadows.

The two men stood with arms crossed, waiting.

After a few minutes, another truck came tearing down the road. This one was also a king cab, but it was white. There was a shield painted on the door, shining in resplendent shades of gold. *Alcott County Sheriff's Department*, read the lettering on the shield.

The truck came to a stop, just as roughly as the black truck had. The men in black made no motion as the front doors opened, and two people climbed out.

One was a portly, aging man. The other was a pretty, young woman, decidedly Latin in appearance, with her black hair pulled up into a tight bun. The old man wore a wide-brimmed hat, but the young woman did not; it seemed that her dark sunglasses and stern expression were sufficient to stave off the hot sunrays.

Both the man and woman wore matching brown uniforms, with a gold star stitched onto the breast pocket. *Sheriff*, read the lettering on the old man's shield. The woman's read *Sheriff's Deputy*. The old man was armed with a holstered, semi-automatic pistol, but the woman was not.

*She* was carrying a shotgun, which she shouldered with a calm sense of self-assurance.

The sheriff threw open the back door of the truck and irritably reached inside.

"*Get* your ass out here!" he ordered, dragging someone out.

That "someone" was a lanky, young-ish man. He was tall, with a boyish face and uncombed blond hair. His expression was mild, even as he was being dragged across the overgrown lawn by the chains shackling his hands behind his back. He tried to gain his footing as he was dragged along, but he couldn't manage it with the leg shackles on.

The men in black watched calmly as the old man dragged his prisoner slowly toward the decrepit building. The young woman stepped smartly forward and unlocked the padlock holding the chain over the door. She kicked in the warped-shut door and stepped inside.

As the sheriff dragged the prisoner over the threshold, the deputy walked around the single room inside, smashing the windows out with the butt of her shotgun to let some air in. When she was finished, she slung the shotgun by its strap across her shoulder and stood at attention in the corner, still and silent.

"Sit your ass down!" ordered the sheriff, throwing his captive into a rickety chair. "And don't speak 'less you're spoken *to*, y'hear?"

"Of course," said the young man pleasantly.

The prisoner wasn't un-handsome, despite being so lanky and his hair being such a mess. In fact, most women would have said that he was rather attractive in his own peculiar way. He just sat there, smiling pleasantly at the scowling sheriff.

That's when the men in black stepped inside. They calmly sat down on similarly dilapidated chairs, across the table from the young man.

"Hello," said one of them. "I'm Bill, and this is Bob."

"Not your real names, I'm betting," replied the young man, speaking with a pleasant southern accent. "But that's okay. Federal Bureau of Investigation, I assume?"

"That's neither here nor there," said Bob coolly. "You're Herbert Ray Bartlett, right?"

"Call me Bert," said the young man, in a friendly tone. "Please, what can I do for you?"

"You've been charged," said Bill, "with more counts of first-degree murder than I've seen any one man rack up in my entire career. But we're missing details, Bert, and we're also missing your accomplice. We know who she is now. We could never find a match for her fingerprints before, not until her neighbor—Deputy Rodriguez, here—tipped us off about some suspicious activity. We printed her home, and positively matched her to most of the murders you committed. Sheriff Fleury was kind enough to play host for the day, so we could bring you here to shed some light on the situation."

"You could have done this at the jail, I think," said Bert, his eyes narrowing and his tone growing colder. "It *is* air-conditioned, you know. And as far as accomplices go, I don't know what you're talking about."

"We wanted this … *interview* off the books," said Bob. He pulled out his phone and opened a file on it.

"This *is* your accomplice, Bert," he said firmly, "is it not?"

Bert took a long, long look at the photo on the phone.

"I have no idea what you're talking about," he said at last, looking away.

"You left her out of the story," said Bill grimly. "Now, let's put her *in* it, shall we?"

"Put who in the story?" asked Bert.

"YOU *KNOW* WHO!!!" roared Sheriff Fleury.

Bert looked down at the table, sweating. His jaw was tense, and his face red; clearly something –or someone—was at stake here, and he wasn't happy about it. His expression was an odd mix of rage and terror.

"Look," said Bill patiently, "if you cooperate, you can both reduce your own sentence and offer your courtroom testimony in exchange for reducing hers. But that's only IF your assistance leads to her capture. If it doesn't you're *both* fucked, and her capture is only a matter of time. Got it?"

"That's not what I want," hissed Bert from between clenched teeth, "and it won't be what *she* wants. I love her too much to sell her short, so no. Take your offer, sit on it, and twirl."

"Then what *do* you want?" asked Bob, assuming a falsely intimate tone.

"We always hated it," said Bert, his eyes radiating resentment, "when people begged for their lives …"

Gone now was the mask of geniality, of easy-going courtesy. Something near and dear to Bert Bartlett was at stake, and his intense, focused demeanor betrayed his fear.

"Why did you hate it when people begged for their lives?" prodded Bill.

"Because it's PATHETIC!" snapped Bert. "Living life means accepting that it could end any minute. If you're scared to die, then you never really lived. I'm alive, and *so* is she. And that's why I won't take your offer, and *neither* will she."

"Then what do you want?" repeated Bob.

"Death penalty," said Bert, his mask of courtesy slowly emerging once more.

"Execution?!" asked Bob. "You *want* that?"

"I'll do whatever it takes to hang her, and me with her," said Bert, now fully back in possession of his affable smile. "We're not afraid of dying. I've never loved anyone so much in my life, and prison is the last thing I want for her. I can tell you about murders in both Virginia and North Carolina, which makes our case federal because we crossed state lines. Uncle Sam *loves* the death penalty, and we can waive all our appeals."

Only briefly had Bert betrayed his tension, his fear for his ladylove. Now that he sensed a chance to help her—to improve her life, instead of making it worse—he seemed to be growing more relaxed as he talked.

Sheriff Fleury hated him for that. Mask on, mask off … truly, the mark of a sociopath. "Start talking," he ordered grimly.

"I can't remember everything," said Bert honestly. "Having a partner in crime is like being married, you know? You remember the very first time you made love, and a few memorable experiences after that, but you don't remember everything."

"Then tell us," said Bill, "about that first time."

"Death penalty!" said Bert firmly.

"You have my word," said the sheriff dangerously, "that I will do everything in my power to fry *both* your asses! It'd be my pleasure."

"Thank you. May I have a water, please?" asked Bert politely. "It sure is hot in here."

"Go get him a water, Rodriguez," ordered Sheriff Fleury curtly. "Just bring in the cooler, would you? We're gonna be here a while."

"What do you want to know first?" asked Bert, as Deputy Rodriguez left the room. "And thank you for the water."

"You're welcome," said Bob tersely. "Tell us how you met, which I believe was on a crime scene."

Bert bowed his head for a brief, silent moment, and held his breath. No one could have known that he was silently praying to the god that he'd abandoned, long, long ago. *Please don't let them ever catch her*, he begged internally. *But if they do, let my story be enough to kill us both. Throw me into the darkest pit in Hell if you must, but spare her.*

"So how did you meet?" prodded Bob. "Can we talk about that?"

"Oh, sure," said Bert, letting his breath out. "It was a cooler summer, not nearly as hot as this one. And it was late, maybe around three in the morning…"

***

Bert stepped on the gas pedal, rolling down the country road as he sang happily along to "Friends in Low Places." He'd always loved that song, with its theme of finding happiness after surviving a painful situation. It never failed to cheer him up, reminding him that the world was, indeed, a very happy place most of the time.

The flashy pickup truck bounced and careened along, steered as much by the cracks and potholes as by its driver. Watsonville was coming up soon, but it was just a little mud-puddle of a town. He'd pass through it soon enough and be on his merry way, disappearing into the swamps that he loved so.

"Friends in Low Places" segued into "The Devil Went Down to Georgia" as Bert reached the outskirts of Watsonville. He was careful to take a side road through town. Although he and his buddies had often joked that Watsonville always "died" at nine o'clock, a few stores along the main thoroughfare might be open all night. Bert couldn't say for sure, though. He never went to Watsonville at night, not even to the bars. He much preferred to drink out in the wild, out in his own vast stomping ground.

He turned a dark corner …

And then the truck sputtered to a stop.

"Dang it!" moaned Bert, eyeing the gas gauge as he climbed out. "*Really?*"

He walked around to the front of the truck, surveying the mangled grill. The front end and hood were completely covered in blood, making the headlights rather dim. He hadn't noticed the headlights before, probably because he knew these roads so well that he could have driven them even in the dark.

As Bert stood scratching his head, wondering what to do, he heard a noise behind him. He turned, wondering what could be stirring at this hour.

There was a young woman standing there, just watching him.

Bert eyed her in wonder, taking in her pretty face and form in the feeble, red glow of the headlights. She was short, but decidedly curvy.

Her stylish auburn bob blew in the slight breeze, framing her heart-shaped face, her freckles, and attractive features. Her brown doe eyes reflected the light in a bewitching shade of rust, sparkling and soft.

She was dressed lightly, as befitted a North Carolina summer, in a short denim skirt. Her dark shirt was a "concert tee", with Megadeth's name and grinning skull logo printed on it. That was odd, thought Bert wordlessly. She looked so sweet, so pretty, certainly nothing like one of those raucous "metal chicks" he'd known in high school.

And she was holding a gas can.

"What's wrong with your truck?" asked the young woman, in a distinctly musical voice.

"Out of gas," said Bert. "What are *you* doing out here, miss?"

"Taking a walk," she said. "I meant, what's wrong with your grill?"

"Oh, that," said Bert. "Hit a deer."

"Was it wearing a plaid shirt?"

Bert turned, eyeing the tatters of a plaid shirt hanging from the mangled bumper.

"Sure was," he said brightly. "Damndest thing I ever saw."

"*That's* weird!" laughed the young woman. Her nose wrinkled prettily as she laughed, almost like a rabbit, causing her freckles to make a momentary shadow across the bridge of her nose.

He'd told an obvious lie, and the stranger clearly saw through it. That she was laughing about it—instead of panicking—warmed his heart in a way that he'd never before felt. Bert was about to offer the pretty stranger a walk home, when something stumbled screaming out of the nearby alley.

It took him a moment to make sense of what he was seeing. That "something" was a man...

And he was on fire.

The burning figure staggered around the street, looking like a cross between a zombie and an oversized tiki torch. Bert and his new friend glanced idly at him, and then turned their attention back towards one another.

"I'm Herbert," said Bert, ignoring the shrill screams of the burning man. "Herbert Ray, but my friends call me Bert. I'd be honored if *you* did, too."

The young woman blushed and set down her gas can. She looked bashfully away for a moment.

As she did, the burning man fell through the window of the antique store, shattering it. The dusty window displays went up like kindling, instantly setting the building ablaze.

"I'm Romary," she said, flirtatiously fluttering her eyelashes. "Romary Anne, but my friends call me Romy. I … I'd be honored if you did, too."

Bert took a step forward and gently took her slender hand.

"It's lovely to meet you, Romy," he said softly, relishing the feel of her quivering hand as he lifted it. He let the kiss linger for moment, tasting the sweat on her soft skin.

"*Such* pretty manners!" she giggled as he released her hand. "You charmer, you."

The burning man fell headlong into a pile of un-collected garbage bags, setting them alight in very short order. He thrashed around in the melting bags and blazing garbage, still screaming.

"I have a confession to make," said Romy, wrinkling her nose from the smell. "I don't have any gas left."

"Were you taking the can to get filled up? Is your car out of gas?"

"No," admitted Romy. "I kinda poured it all out."

Bert looked at the burning man, and then at the empty gas can, and then back at Romy. Dank, foul smoke began to overwhelm the street as the garbage pile, the hapless victim, and the antique store began burning even more brightly. The hardware store next door was starting to burn as well. Yet somehow, amidst all the chaos and horror, all Bert did was give his pretty acquaintance an amused smile.

"Would you like to get some ice cream?" asked Romy abruptly.

"At this time of night?"

"Trip's Truck Stop isn't far, and it's open all night." She was blushing again, as though she was surprised by her own temerity. "They have the *best* ice cream! If … if you're not busy, that is. I understand if you are."

Romy looked both hopeful and terrified at the same time. Bert looked at her a moment, wondering if he dared…

He did.

"There's nothing I'd rather do," said Bert sincerely, leaning forward and kissing Romy tenderly on her forehead, "than have ice cream with you."

Romy smiled from ear to ear, and her expression was so beautiful that it made Bert's heart ache. He had never met anyone so lovely in his entire life.

The burning man managed to extricate himself from the garbage, and promptly stumbled into a wooden, tar-covered telephone pole.

"What about your truck?" asked Romy, as the telephone pole lit up like a Roman candle.

"It's okay," replied Bert. "It's not mine anyway."

"What about your fingerprints?"

"Never had 'em taken."

"Me neither," said Romy, kicking over her gas can. "Shall we?"

Bert shivered as Romy wrapped her arm around his midsection and sidled close. On impulse, he stuck his hand in the back pocket of her jean skirt.

He gave her rear end a gentle squeeze as the two of them trekked companionably off through the smoke. And he thought to himself that life just didn't get any better than this.

## Chapter Two

"That 'burning man' had a name," said Bill, drily. "His name was Rufus Taylor. He started walking home from the local bar, and then he passed out in the alley. He thought all he had to worry about was a hangover. I'm pretty sure he didn't anticipate being set on fire."

"She does love her some fire, Romy," chuckled Bert. "It's kind of her thing."

"So we've heard," said Bob. "Now let's talk about *your* thing, shall we?"

"My thing?"

"You know exactly what he's talking about, you little *shit*!" snapped Sheriff Fleury, wiping the sweat from his brow. "Tell him about that friend of your little *girlfriend's* already!"

"Oh, they weren't friends," said Bert. "But of course I can tell you. We stayed at Romy's that night, since it was just outside of Watsonville. It was lovely walking her home, under the stars. It was even better waking up next to her. I've never felt so *alive*, you know? We felt that fate had brought us together, so we decided to spend the day celebrating…"

\*\*\*

Romy said something, but Bert couldn't make it out.

"WHAT?!" he shouted.

Romy reached over and turned the truck radio down. "Sorry," she said, as Megadeth slowly receded in volume. "I said, this truck rides really nice!"

"It sure does," said Bert, reaching down to tuck the mangled wires back into the ignition opening. "I wonder who it belongs to?"

"Let's find out," said Romy. "Here, hold this."

Bert reached for the offered half-gallon of Jim Beam and took a long tug as Romy rifled through the glove box.

"Here," she said. "It's registered to some guy named Buford Harrison."

"Oh, I went to high school with him. We called him Big Bubba. I'm surprised he has a truck like this. I always figured he'd end up in jail."

Romy took the bottle from Bert and helped herself to a deep draught. "Well, he doesn't own it anymore!" she said brightly, tossing the registration out of the open window. "Isn't it a *beautiful* day?" She licked her lips invitingly, playfully giving her new lover a sweet reminder of what she'd done with them the night before.

"It's the best day of my life," said Bert warmly, taking the bottle and having another gulp. "I think I just fell in love with you."

"You *think* you've fallen in love with me?!" said Romy with mock outrage, leaning over to give Bert a kiss on the cheek. "*I* don't think you 'think' anything, buster! And neither do I."

"You're right," said Bert, taking his eyes from the road to kiss her back. "I say we just call ourselves a done deal, you and I."

Romy squealed with laughter as Bert nearly swerved off the road. She took a slug of whiskey as he pulled a hasty course correction.

"I agree," she said, wiping her lips. "So what do you wanna do today?"

"What do *you* wanna do?"

"Let's find another one of those deer," giggled Romy. "You know, the kind in the plaid shirts."

"Perfect. I mean, it's not like we're keeping the truck, right?"

"Right!"

The new couple traveled happily along, occasionally passing the bottle back and forth. Even Megadeth's rambunctious, snarling music seemed oddly soothing as they weaved down the backwoods road.

"Hey, look!" said Romy excitedly, pointing. "*There's* our deer!"

Bert slowed the truck down, squinting. There was a woman in a red jogging suit running along the shoulder.

"I can't run over a woman!" protested Bert. "That just seems kinda… *wrong*, you know?"

Romy stuck her head out of the window, taking a longer look.

"That's not a woman. That's a barracuda in a woman *suit*!" she said sourly. "That's Tiffany Collins."

"Who's Tiffany Collins?"

"She used to slam my head in my locker door," said Romy darkly, as Bert slowed the truck even more. "And sometimes she'd pull my panties up to give me a wedgie. It got so bad by middle school that I stopped *wearing* panties most of the time."

"That's *awful*!" gasped Bert. "Here, let me help you with those bad memories. Put on your seat belt and hold onto the 'oh shit' bar, okay?"

Romy did as she was directed, after carefully setting the bottle on the floorboard between her calves. Bert waited until she was secured before he laid his foot into the gas pedal.

"*WHEEEEEE!!!*" howled Romy gleefully. "Now this is FUN!"

Tiffany turned to face the truck at the last possible second, her mouth open like a fish's and her blue eyes wide with horror...

*SPLAT!!!*

Romy held on as Bert slowly regained control of the vehicle. Coming to a stop, he put it into reverse and backed up.

"*Great* job, baby!" gushed Romy. "We didn't even spill our booze."

The truck came to a stop just in front of what was left of Tiffany Collins. Its occupants opened the door and climbed out, holding hands as they went to examine their handiwork.

"What a mess!" cooed Romy. "It's a good thing she was already wearing red."

"Yeah, no kiddin'," grinned Bert. "And look, we didn't even crack the radiator. I hate it when that happens."

Romy just smiled contentedly down at the scattered remains of her fallen tormentor.

"Wait!" said Bert. "Now we have to observe the Ritual."

"*What* ritual?"

Bert felt himself blushing. "It... it's one of those silly things that teenage boys come up with, but it turned into a superstition. Me and my best bud Eric came up with it. See, there's this ceremony you have to observe whenever you run someone over. If you don't, then the next time you drink you'll get sick. You know, because you didn't appease the great god Ralph. So if you fail to observe the ritual, you'll end up praying at his porcelain altar."

"Ew!" said Romy, making a face. "*I* don't wanna end up getting sick! I hate that!"

"I've never done this with another person before," gulped Bert. " 'Cept Eric, of course."

"Where's Eric now?"

"Serving life in prison."

"For what?"

"Running people over."

"Aw, that's *terrible*!" said Romy, taking Bert's hand. "Do you ever get to see him?"

"Every Saturday, at visiting time," said Bert, sighing. "You don't often find a friend like that. He told me to run before he was caught. He said they already had him, but there was no point in me getting busted."

"What a great guy," said Romy. "You'll have to take me to see him. So… how, exactly, does this ritual go?"

"You both point down at the mess, see," said Bert, pointing at the splatter that had once been Tiffany Collins, "and then you say this, in unison: *ooooooh… ahhhhh…* WOO-HOO!!!"

"That's it?" asked Romy. "That *is* silly! But I don't wanna get sick, so I'm in."

Taking a deep breath, she pointed down at the mangled jogger. "On three, okay?"

Bert nodded, feeling like he was going through a rite of passage. The Ritual was a very, very personal part of his past, but he knew that Romy would never truly become his soulmate until he shared it with her.

It was a nice feeling.

"One, two, three!"

"*Ooooooh…*"

"*Ahhh…*"

"*WOO-HOO!!!*"

## Chapter Three

"At least you knew *that* poor woman's name!" huffed Sheriff Fleury, as Deputy Rodriguez dug a bottle of water from the cooler. She returned to her post and took a long drink, still looking quite stoic.

"The truck was found two days later," said Bob, "completely torched. I'm going to go out on a limb and say that was Romary's doing?"

"Yeah," said Bert, yawning. "I always just dumped 'em in the swamp."

"And you admit to being Eric Walters' accomplice?"

"Oh, sure," he said, shrugging. "Anything to help my capital case!"

"Ask him about the killings at the Fincher farm!" interjected Sheriff Fleury. "We still need to piece that one together. The crime scene was a fuckin' *train* wreck!"

"Bert," said Bill calmly, "might you tell us about…"

"I heard him, Bill," interrupted Bert. "Romy called me one afternoon, while I was doing my shopping for the week…"

\*\*\*

Bert walked through the front door of the old farmhouse, looking guardedly about. It had taken him a few minutes to find the place from Romy's directions, so he hoped that nothing had happened to her in the meantime. He grew steadily more nervous as he walked inside.

He relaxed as he stepped out of the foyer and into the kitchen. Romy was sitting on the countertop, beaming at him. "Hey, baby!" she chirped.

There were two men duct-taped to chairs, one young and spindly, and the other old and prodigiously overweight. "How'd you tie 'em down?" asked Bert curiously.

"*This* dude was passed out drunk on the front lawn," said Romy, pointing to the younger man. "So I just dragged him inside."

She flexed her tiny biceps like a bodybuilder, causing both of them to laugh.

"The old man was already sitting in that chair," she continued. "He tried to get up, so I hit him over the head with the fireplace tongs before I taped him up. It's a good thing they had a whole case of duct tape in the garage. They *got* everything out there! Tools, camping stuff, fishing gear… you name it."

Bert pulled Romy from the countertop and spun her playfully around. She squealed with laughter, wrapping her legs around his waist as he covered her face with kisses.

"Nice work!" he said at last, setting her gently upon her feet. "I'm proud of you. What do we do with 'em?"

"I already thought of that," said Romy. "Here, look!"

The kitchen was open to the living room, and Romy walked over to the gun case. Its glass door was already broken, presumably by her.

She pulled out two shotguns. "I already loaded 'em," she said. "They're both semi-automatic, so they're pretty dummy proof. Do you know how to use one?"

"No," said Bert.

"How'd you grow up in North Carolina without learning to use a shotgun?"

"We were never allowed to have guns in the house, at least not after Dad shot Grandma."

"Was it an accident?"

"No."

"Oh," said Romy. "Is… is that why you didn't think it was right to hurt a woman?"

"What?! No!" laughed Bert. "Grandma was a nasty old cow. Nobody cared that Dad shot her. Except, you know, the sheriff. But yeah, Dad taught me that it's not nice to hurt a woman unless she's an awful person, like panty-yanking Tiffany, or my bitchy ol' grandmother."

"That's good. I'm glad you weren't sad when she died," said Romy. "Your grandmother, I mean. I'm pretty sure nobody gave two shits about Tiffany."

Bert nodded in agreement as his lover handed him a shotgun. "Here," she said, "I just turned the safety off for you. Now it's hot, so keep your finger off the trigger until you're ready to shoot."

Bert took the gun gingerly, pointing it toward the floor. "I'm not sure I like these things," he said uncertainly. "They're just so… *quick*, you know?"

"So's running someone over," said Romy brightly, sighting her gun. "But they don't have to be. Watch!"

*BLAM*!!!

Romy's shot hit the younger man square in the kneecap. He came to at that, screaming at the top of his lungs.

"Oh, quit whining!" ordered Romy sternly. "You still have one-and-a-half legs left, you big baby! Okay, *you* try it. Hit his other knee."

"PLEASE!!!" cried the old man, snapping out of his pseudo-catatonic state as he looked on in horror. "I'll give you anything, ANYTHING!!!"

Bert strode forward, and matter-of-factly smashed the old man in the forehead with the butt of his shotgun.

*BLAM*!!!

Romy screamed, ducking as the dusty, tacky chandelier overhead crashed to the floor. "I TOLD you that thing was hot!!!" she screeched.

"Sorry," murmured Bert sheepishly, lowering the weapon.

"I *might* forgive you," said Romy, "if you give me some extra special attention later."

"If I do, will you wear that cute black lacy—"

"NOT in front of Drunkie McGurk here!" interjected Romy. "That's *our* business! But yes, of course I will. I *love* the way you look at me when I get all sexy for you! So… shall we carry on?"

Bert sighted carefully, pointing the shotgun at the younger man's surviving kneecap. He was grateful that the old man was momentarily silent; he always hated it when people begged for their lives, and so did Romy. Life is short, and when it's over, that's it. Both he and she were offended that people would so often debase themselves seeking a mere few minutes more of panicking, wretched life.

*BLAM*!!!

Bert lowered the gun, aghast.

"Ooh," said Romy, biting her lip. "That … that wasn't his knee, Bert."

"*AAAAAAAUUUUGGHH*!!! *SHIT*!!! *AH CAIN'T FUCK NO MORE*!!!"

"Maybe we should give this guy a free pass," said Bert regretfully, raising his gun again.

"Yeah."

Bert sighted more carefully this time…

*BLAM*!!!

"Well," said Romy, waving away the acrid gun-smoke as she wiped the spattered blood from her pretty face, "at least you hit his *head* just fine. What should we do with Jabba the Hutt over there?"

"Let me see what I can find," said Bert, opening the silverware drawer. "Can you gag him for me, baby? He's gonna come to soon enough, and I can't take any more begging."

"Oh, sure."

Bert pulled forth a large butcher knife as Romy stuck a strip of duct tape over the old man's mouth. "How's this?" he asked.

"Now *that's* some pig-sticker!"

"Right?"

Bert walked over to his shaking victim and stabbed him in the belly. "*Mmph*!!! *Mmmm*!!!"

"Did you even hit anything?" frowned Romy. "He's not even bleeding, he's so big. Try his chest."

"Good call," said Bert, stabbing him again.

The two lovers stood for a moment, eyeing their victim.

"I'm not sure this is gonna work," said Bert dubiously, as the old man squirmed and jiggled. "There's just too… *much* of him, you know?"

"Maybe give him a scarlet necktie?" suggested Romy helpfully, running her finger across her throat.

"Oh, yeah."

Bert walked around the old man's chair for a moment, shaking his head.

"I can't tell if he even *has* a neck!" he said in exasperation, throwing down the knife. "Screw this. I'll be right back."

Romy waited patiently as Bert left and returned in a few minutes.

"*Now* we're talkin'!" he hooted, triumphantly raising a large chainsaw.

"What?! *No!*" protested Romy.

"Why not?"

"The exhaust burns my eyes, and they hurt for days! I hate that."

"I'm sorry, baby," said Bert contritely, lowering the chainsaw. "What do you suggest?"

Romy thought for a moment.

"I got it!" she said excitedly. "Pull the stove away from the wall for me, would you? I'll be right back."

Bert pulled the gas stove away from the wall, beginning to suspect that he already knew what Romy had in mind.

She returned a few minutes later, carrying a bucket of tools.

"Okay, here we go," she said, stopping for a moment to tie her bob into a bouncy ponytail. "This will just take a minute."

"What are you doing?" asked Bert curiously.

"This is the flex connector," said Romy, pointing to a metallic yellow line running to the stove. "I'm just gonna shut the main valve—here— and cut it."

She pulled a pair of tin snips from her bucket and cut through the line.

"Now, see this?" she asked, pointing to an aluminum device that reminded Bert of the Starship Enterprise. "That's the regulator. It throttles down the gas pressure, because the stove doesn't need all that much gas. So we'll just spin it off."

"How do you know all this?"

"My dad worked for the gas company. At least, he did before he…"

Romy's face fell for a moment.

"Before what?" asked Bert softly.

"I was ten. I was playing with matches…"

"I'm so sorry," said Bert, kneeling down and gently lifting her face by the chin. He gave her a long, reassuring kiss. "But *you're* still here, and I can't even begin to explain how absolutely crazy I am about you. I *can't* wait for tonight! I love it when you…"

"Not in front of Jabba, goofy!" laughed Romy, interrupting Bert by briefly crushing her pretty lips against his. "That's private! But thank you for making me feel better."

Bert flushed, elated by Romy's affection.

"So," she said, pulling a couple of wrenches from her bucket, "we'll just remove the regulator here. You wanna grab me that oil lantern from the mantle?"

"*MMMMPH!!! MMM!!!*" protested the old man, jiggling in his chair.

"Sure. Where do you want it?"

"Take it down to the end of that long hallway, off the living room. We want lots of gas to build up before the house catches fire."

"Won't that blow the building up?"

"*MMMMMMPH!!!*"

"Contrary to popular belief, a gas fire can't actually blow up a building. Most of these systems have less than two pounds of pressure, and there are backflow devices on the feeds. But it *can* burn a building down really, really fast. Okay, there goes the regulator. You wanna go light that lantern?"

"Got matches?" asked Bert.

"You kiddin'?" laughed Romy, fishing in the pocket of her shorts. "Here."

"Thanks."

"Grab some booze, too! There's a liquor cabinet in the living room."

"Got it!"

After he'd lit the lantern, Bert opened the liquor cabinet. "Check this out!" he said excitedly. "Johnny Walker *Blue* Label! Fancy, fancy, fancy … This stuff goes down like iced tea."

"Nice!" said Romy, still kneeling behind the stove. "Can you set some lawn chairs up? At the very edge of the yard, over by the trees. I'll be right out. I'll wait 'til you're gone before I open the valve."

"On it!" chirped Bert, heading for the door with his prize bottle of Scotch.

The old man fought mightily to free himself, but he ended up falling over sideways in his chair, making a loud crashing sound as he did. "*MMMPH*!!!" he shouted through the duct tape.

"See what you did, you big silly?" scolded Romy, rising a little. "I had you sitting all nice and comfortable. *Now* you can just stay like that, since you wanna be so cranky!"

Bert was opening up the folding lawn chairs as Romy came running out of the house, slamming the door behind her.

She threw herself backwards into her chair as Bert took a leisurely seat in his. He uncorked the bottle, and offered it to Romy.

"Not yet," she objected. "Kisses first!"

Bert bent over as Romy reached for him. He held his breath as she kissed him deeply, passionately, drinking in the manly scent of his sweat.

"Okay," she said at last, pulling away. "I'll take that drink now."

She took several deep gulps from the bottle. "Wow!!!" she said, wiping her pretty lips. "That is good! Here, have some."

*FOOMP*!!!

As the old farmhouse went up in flames, Romy sat bolt upright in her lawn chair. She stared at the burning building, her eager doe eyes eerily reflecting the raging fire.

She looked so beautiful, so… *alive.*

For her, thought Bert, he would be willing to set fire after fire. For her he would set the entire *world* ablaze, just to make her happy.

"I love you, Romy," whispered Bert.

Although she would have absolutely believed—and returned—his heartfelt words, he also knew that she'd not heard them…

There was no hearing *anything* over her epic blaze!

## Chapter Four

"Their names were Delbert Fincher and Delbert Fincher Junior," said Bill. "It was lucky that Martha Fincher was visiting her sister at the time."

"Oh, Romy wouldn't have hit the place if she'd been home," said Bert serenely. "Messing with an old lady just seems kind of… well, *mean.* Romy's not like that."

"NOT LIKE THAT?!" shouted Sheriff Fleury, red-faced, pounding his fist on the table. "We couldn't even put that fire *out*, you little shit!

Just had to shut off the gas and let it burn."

"Sheriff, please," said Bob, raising a hand. "When the state police tried pulling you over, Bert, they said they saw two people in the truck. When they finally caught up with you, you were alone. Would you like to tell us what happened?"

"When Eric took the fall for me," said Bert, leaning forward, "I promised him I'd pay it forward, and I did. I only fled long enough to get around a couple of bends, and then I let Romy out so she could hide in the woods. I love her, Bob. I'd do anything for her. If you didn't already have her nailed based on the evidence, I'd never have told you anything. As it is, it feels good to talk about the good times."

"GOOD TIMES?!" roared Sheriff Fleury, rising. He shoved Bill and Bob roughly aside, so he could lean over and look Bert in the eyes.

"Good times, you say?" he whispered dangerously. "Tell me, you little psycho... Tell me how you *do* it. Tell me how you sleep at night?"

"It's easy," said Bert. "You just lie down and close your eyes. Why?"

"Doesn't it bother you? Remembering what you did?"

"Should it?"

"*Why* do you do it?"

"Why do people do anything?" asked Bert reasonably. "Is there really any point to analyzing everything? Love is accepting a person's dark side as well as their good qualities. Then you realize that their dark side is *really* fun, and after that it all just kinda runs together."

Sheriff Fleury rose slowly, unable to break his gaze away from Bert's calm, placid eyes. Morality, he realized with horror, is utterly impotent in the face of raw apathy.

True monsters aren't vicious.

*True* monsters are footloose and carefree, and that's what makes them so very, very frightening. It's not that they're malignant...

They're just indifferent, and that's more terrifying than malice could ever be.

"I got *news* for you, asshole!" snarled Sheriff Fleury. "We lied about finger-printing your little girlfriend's home! Oh, Rodriguez here reported her, all right, for some weird goings-on. But when we showed up, her place was burned to the ground, and she'd disappeared. What do you think of tha—?"

*BLAM*!!!

Bert turned his head as his face was splattered with blood. Sheriff

Fleury remained standing for a moment, but only for a moment. It *is* rather difficult to keep one's feet without a head, after all. Slowly, his body fell to the floor.

Bill and Bob jumped up, reaching for their concealed sidearms. Deputy Rodriguez blasted Bob square in the middle of the chest, sending him flying across the room. He was dead before he hit the floor.

Bill managed to get his pistol out before the deputy shot him, but he had no opportunity to return fire. Rodriguez blasted him in the shoulder, sending him sprawling and his gun flying across the room.

She retrieved the pistol and tucked it into her belt. Pulling a set of keys from her pocket, she freed Bert's hands, and then knelt to unlock his leg shackles.

"Thank you," said Bert, rising. "Why... Why did you *do* that?"

Deputy Rodriguez laid her shotgun on the table and reached for her hair.

She pulled out the tight bun and shook out her jet-black bob. Then she took off her dark glasses...

"*Romy*," breathed Bert, meeting her affectionate gaze with relief.

"I've never dyed my hair before," said Romy. "Do you like it?"

"It suits you," smiled Bert, putting his arms around her and pulling her close. "How long did you have to sunbathe for?"

"Spray tan," grinned Romy. "I just hope it doesn't turn orange as it fades. Is this a good look for me?"

"Well, you *do* have a bubble butt," said Bert, kissing her on the forehead. "Kind of a 'Jennifer Lopez' caboose, you know?"

"*Jerk*!" murmured Romy, pressing her lips against her lover's.

Time itself came to a stop, and it seemed that the universe had suddenly come back into alignment. Sometimes two people are just meant for each other, and the world is out of balance whenever they're forced apart.

"Wait," said Bert, pulling away. "Where'd he go?"

"What?"

"Bill. Where'd he go? He's not here."

"Whoops," said Romy ruefully.

Bert ran to the door, looking outside. "I can see the blood trail," he said, squinting. "Must be Bob has the truck keys. Get them, would you?"

Romy fished in Bob's pants pocket and retrieved the truck keys. "Let's go!" she said, chasing Bert at a dead sprint towards the truck.

Thankfully the truck had running boards, because otherwise she would have had trouble climbing in. She could barely see over the steering wheel, and she had to move the seat forward, but she managed to reach the gas pedal.

"I could've driven, you know," said Bert.

"I *got* this!" said Romy stubbornly, throwing the truck into gear.

The truck careened down the gravel road, kicking up a cloud off chaff as it tore off in pursuit of the man who called himself Bill.

"I knew he wouldn't make it far," said Romy smugly. "Look!"

"He'll throw himself into the swamp before you get him," said Bert, nervously clutching the dash.

"He's probably in shock," said Romy. "Just following the road on instinct. Anyway, it's worth a try, and we can always shoot him later. Hold on!"

Romy floored the gas, surprised at how well the truck handled the rough terrain.

She'd been right about the shock. Bill seemed oblivious to the approaching truck.

*SPLAT*!!!

Both the driver and passenger-side airbags exploded in an instant, making it impossible for Romy to see. She just stomped the brake, hoping for the best.

The truck spun around several times, but thankfully it didn't roll over. It came to a stop facing the opposite direction from which they'd come.

As the airbags deflated, the lovers had trouble seeing through the windshield.

Bert reached soberly over and turned on the windshield wipers.

As the wiper fluid slowly washed the blood from the windshield, Romy and Bert surveyed their handiwork.

"The front end's toast," observed Bert. "We'll have to walk back and take the sheriff's truck. Good thing Bill didn't make it far."

Romy sat quietly for a moment.

"Do you wanna get a drink?" she asked abruptly.

"*Do* I? I've been in jail for weeks!"

"I thought so," said Romy, opening the truck door. "Well, I guess we'd better get to it, then. Don't wanna end up getting sick, you know?"

"What happened to Deputy Rodriguez?" asked Bert curiously, climbing out of the truck.

"Well, I couldn't very well steal her identity with her still alive, could I?" asked Romy, walking around the truck and taking Bert's hand. "Somebody would've noticed. Besides, I needed somewhere to stay after I burned down my own place."

"How'd you do her job?"

"It wasn't that hard," said Romy. "I just said 'yes, sir' whenever the sheriff told me to do something, and then I did it. Pretty mindless, honestly."

"You're *so* clever!"

"So … the Ritual, then?"

"Yeah," said Bert. "Exactly *how* are we gonna do the ritual? I don't even know where to point."

"Me neither," agreed Romy. "I mean, there's a lot of him on the road. But there's also a lot of him in the mud, and quite a bit dripping from the trees. There's a fair amount of him stuck in the grill, too."

"Well, let's just find the biggest pile, then."

The lovers looked around for a few minutes, and then agreed upon the best spot to perform the ritual.

But before they did, they held hands and looked into each other's eyes, just thinking, just enjoying the moment.

And in that moment, Bert suddenly discovered the answer to the erstwhile sheriff's question.

*Why do you do it?*

Because pushing other people out of this life bought him room to breathe, room to live. Space in which to enjoy this world, to enjoy *her*. It was a simple answer, but a profound one. He was surprised that he hadn't thought of it earlier.

"Bert?" whispered Romy.

"Yeah?"

"You… you'll have to drink alone. I'm pregnant."

Bert stood in stunned silence for a moment.

"Bert?" prodded Romy, looking insecure.

"That's *wonderful!*" gushed Bert. "You're gonna be the best mom ever!"

"Aw, really?"

"Yes!"

"I love you so much, Bert," said Romy, leaning up to kiss him. "Can I still do the Ritual if I'm not drinking?"

"Of course. And I love *you* even more."

"Okay, on three then. One, two, three!"

"*Ooooooh…*"

"*Ahhh…*"

"*WOO-HOO!!!*"

Bert took Romy's hand, and the two started the trek back to the abandoned post office.

"So where do we go?" he asked. "Now that we've avoided the death penalty?"

"Somewhere remote," said Romy. "Somewhere where hardly anyone lives, and the technology is fifty years behind the times. Somewhere where people mind their own business, because messing around with other people's business will get you shot."

The lovers paused, looking at each other for a moment…

Then the light bulb turned on.

"*West Virginia!*" they said, in perfect unison.

They laughed as they shared a quick kiss and began walking hand in hand towards the setting sun.

"Hey," said Romy abruptly. "Should we burn down the building, so we can hide any evidence that you were there? You know, buy us some time?"

"Baby, that building is made of cinderblock," objected Bert dubiously, "with a concrete floor. I'm not sure it'll burn."

"I'll go 'cowgirl' on you while we watch it burn," offered Romy, shaking her bust invitingly. "Right on the lawn. Whatcha think about *that?*"

Bert caught his breath, feeling a sudden tingle in his nether region. "Okay, you got me there," he conceded, "but are you sure it'll burn?"

"Oh, everything burns," said Romy sagely. "You just need a little patience."

The End

# The Substitute
## F. Burn

Monday morning staff briefing. I hated it. I groggily sipped my coffee, motivating myself for the long day ahead. It seemed no matter how strong it was, I just couldn't perk up. Why would anyone be happy about a two-day weekend that went by in a blur? I couldn't stand the fresh-faced newbies, eager and not jaded by the amount of admin that accompanied teaching. Since when did teaching become more about data and producing pointless documents? And meetings. How they loved to say something in the longest and most boring way they could. For fuck's sake, didn't they have lives outside of work? Evidently not.

"Morning, Tasha."

I snapped out of my bitter thoughts and turned toward my partner teacher. We had both been lumped in Year Six because apparently we were the best teachers for the job. I had requested Year Five for the last two years, but of course, senior management knew best. What I wanted didn't matter. It was all about what was best for the school. My well-being meant nothing.

"Morning, Mikey. How are we today?"

"Pretty damned good, after bumping into the sub this morning."

"Sub?"

"Oh my god, haven't you seen? Look across the room, but don't make it obvious."

I rolled my eyes. Everyone got excited when a male made an appearance. There was certainly too much estrogen in the place, but I humored him anyway and turned nonchalantly towards the left of the room.

My jaw dropped. He was exquisite. Tall, dark hair, chiseled features and broad shoulders. I drank him in from top to bottom, admiring his physique as he stood waiting for the meeting to start. He must have come in later, as most of us were seated somewhere in the badly designed, garish staffroom. He stood out like a model in a rubbish dump.

He slowly turned his head in my direction, and I quickly averted my eyes, wanting to appear cool and disinterested. From the corner of my eye, I could feel him looking at me. I feigned interest in the meeting that had just started.

'We'd like to welcome Seth to our school today. He'll be supporting in Year Six until the summer term,' the head teacher, Steven, announced.

I was taken aback, because Michael and I had been asking for teaching support to help plug the gaps in our class, and each time we had been given a convoluted story about budget cuts. Perhaps the poor results of the first assessment had been enough to convince them. And in typical senior management fashion, they hadn't discussed hiring a support teacher with us at all. However, this was certainly a pleasant surprise. The fact that he was hot as fuck was a bonus I hadn't even considered.

I zoned out for the rest of the meeting until Michael nudged me to return to our adjoining classes. I busied myself by preparing for the morning's maths activity but stopped when I saw Steven walking towards my class with Seth. I just stood and stared. All my ex-boyfriends were nothing compared to this magnificent specimen of a man. As if he could read my thoughts, he locked eyes with me. They sucked me in, and his gaze pierced through me.

There was something almost predatory in his stare, something feline. There was something different about him besides looks, but I couldn't quite put my finger on it. It was as if I could feel an electrical current thrumming in the air. I suddenly felt an overwhelming desire to get closer to him. I wanted to know more about this mysterious man.

Then he released me by breaking the gaze. It left me feeling dirty, like I needed a shower, but strangely it felt good. I desperately tried to tidy myself up as Steven entered with Seth.

Seth immediately held out his hand and said, "Natasha, I presume? A pleasure to meet you."

"The pleasure is all mine," I responded, more demurely than I had intended.

I didn't pull my hand away until Michael burst through the adjoining door and practically skipped toward us. He introduced himself with a giggle. Bloody hell, he was even worse than me, flirting shamelessly.

"I'm sure Natasha and Michael will make you feel welcome and fill you in on all the gory details."

"Oh, we certainly will," Michael replied a little too enthusiastically. My gosh, what must this man think of us!

Seth spent the morning just supporting in class. I'd give him his own groups of children to work with eventually, but I just wanted him to settle in and get used to things today. Plus I wanted to look at him. He flitted between both our classes with the grace and ease of a panther. I perked up each time he entered my room.

Thankfully, Michael was on duty in the playground for morning break, so that left me alone with Seth. As the children left the classroom in single file, I turned to find Seth standing right behind me. I jumped up, startled by the unexpected closeness. His pale grey eyes stared into mine and my heartbeat quickened. A member of staff had never had this kind of effect on me. I'd also never been particularly self-conscious about my looks, but he was standing so close that I was sure he could pick out every flaw on my face. I cleared my throat and took a step back.

"Would you like a drink? Coffee or tea?" I managed to ask.

"No, thanks. I don't drink tea or coffee. I prefer my drinks stronger," he hinted with a conspiratorial wink of his eye.

I chuckled and replied, "Is that so? Well, we normally go out for a drink on Fridays after school, so you're welcome to join us."

"That's very nice of you. I might just do that."

I decided to ignore my need for caffeine, just so I could savor the next fifteen minutes left of break alone with Mr Arden.

We sat at my computer desk, and I showed him the week's plans. He was lucky that I had actually completed the plans because I usually never had it done on time, but with a looming Ofsted inspection inching ever closer, senior management had been cracking down on planning in recent weeks. It was probably the reason why they had finally provided extra support, unless they really thought Michael and I were simply shit teachers.

When I laid the plans on the table, Seth brought his chair closer to mine, so close that our knees were almost touching. I couldn't help but run my eyes along his well-shaped muscular thighs. I could see the muscles tense as he shifted his long legs. He shrugged out of his blazer and leaned forward, looking at me expectantly. I almost forgot why we were sitting there, and it took me a moment to find my words. I was so distracted by the closeness of his body.

"Um… so, these are the plans. I guess we could start looking at maths. I must warn you, though, this class is really low in maths. You could either work with the middle group or the lower group. Sometimes the higher group need a challenge too. How do you feel about taking a group out tomorrow?"

"That sounds great. Whatever way you think I would be best utilized. I don't mind supporting in class either." I couldn't help but envision him naked when he said the word "utilized". There were many ways he would be best utilized.

Taking a deep breath, I tried to pretend my thoughts were purely professional. "Well, I'm sure you don't want to just sit around listening to me droning on. You probably have your own skills and plans to bring to the table."

"I don't have any problems listening to you drone on and on," he replied, almost flirtatiously. For a moment I wondered if he'd read my thoughts. A man as fine as him wouldn't be interested in a woman like me, would he? I urged myself to continue speaking.

"I think, for this week, we'll have you supporting in class, so you can get to know the children and get an idea of their strengths and areas for development. It's pretty self-evident, to be honest. You'll probably spot the lower achievers and end up gravitating toward them. Obviously, you will split your time between my class and Michael's class. I've got more children on the special needs register that aren't getting enough support, so you might be in my class more often. There might be some other interventions needed as well, like speech and language. You see, normally, we would have had a teaching assistant doing some of those interventions, but due to staff restructuring, they're covering classes rather than supporting. That's why I'm so grateful that you're here." I realized I was rambling on and needed to stop to breathe before I embarrassed myself even further.

He waited for a second, as if he expected me to say more. Then he replied, "Well, I'm glad to be here, Natasha. I want to help in any way that I can. Anything you need, please just tell me." A quiver went up my spine when he said my name. Why did everything he say sound sexual to me?

"Thank you, Seth. That means a lot. I think we'll get along really well." *I think we'll get along well?* Why did I say that?

"Oh, I hope so," he practically purred. For once, I was at a loss for words. He went silent for a moment, waiting. He wasn't afraid to make eye contact for longer than necessary, and it didn't seem to make him feel awkward as it would most people. I felt the heat rise to my face, and I was worried that he could see my embarrassment and that he would figure out that I found him extremely attractive.

When I said nothing, he smiled, and I automatically smiled back. I saw that he had unusually long canine teeth, which somehow made him look even sexier. His eyes appeared different, as if they reflected the light. I blinked, assuming it was a trick of light, and when I looked again, his eyes appeared as a pale shade of grey like before. I wasn't sure what had got into me – I'd seen attractive men before. Why was this one making me respond like this? The truth was that it had been a long time since a man had piqued my interest. After a few failed relationships and one marriage, I had pretty much given up on men.

However, all the late nights with Michael at the local pub were a blast. My parents had started to think he was my boyfriend because of the number of times I mentioned his name, until I'd told them that he was, in fact, attracted to men.

Just then, the bell went, signaling the end of break. I got up to help collect the children from the playground, when Seth stood up, put his hand gently on my shoulder and said, "No, it's okay. Don't worry, I'll get them. You focus on preparing for the lesson."

"Okay, thank you." The warmth of his hand lingered on my arm. I was enjoying the perks of having a support teacher. Not only that, he had a lovely manner about him. He had a sense of humor, yet he was very charming and polite. When I spoke, he looked me in the eyes, and he waited for me to finish without interrupting. He made me feel as if I was worth listening to. It was strange, considering that we'd just met that day. He also seemed experienced. I just hoped that he wasn't too good to be true.

As the class came back into the room, I saw that Michael and Seth were talking to each other and that Michael was giggling yet again. I felt a pang of jealousy because I didn't want to share Seth. As selfish as it sounded, I wanted to be the person that he bonded with most in the school. I didn't want him to make loads of friends who he'd like more than me. I didn't want him to join any of the cliques that had formed in the school. I wanted to be his confidant, his mentor, his friend, and maybe even more. Something dangerous was lingering in the air, and my adventurous side was responding. My inner voice seemed to say, *Life is short. Jump in with everything you've got. Don't hesitate.*

As the children settled in their seats, I told my mind to quieten down. I didn't have time for schoolgirl fantasies, which I should have outgrown by now.

My arm still tingled where he had touched it, and it lingered even after he'd gone to Michael's class. Part of me wanted him to support in class while I taught so that I could look at him throughout the day, but then the other part of me knew that I would not be able to focus on teaching children if he was constantly in the same room as me.

I hoped that we would spend lunchtime together too, but Seth said that he needed to go out for a walk and that he would be back soon. Whilst he was gone, Michael joined me for lunch, and instead of going into the staffroom like we normally did, we stayed in our classroom just so we could gossip about Seth.

"Tasha, this guy is hot. I couldn't stop looking at his tight arse. I'd do him any day. Do you think he's into guys or both?"

"Mikey, you are so –"

"Oh, come on, you can't say that you weren't looking. So, tell me, what do you think?"

"Okay, I think he's gorgeous. But don't they always say, 'Don't mix business with pleasure'?"

"Yeah, they also say, 'Don't shit where you work'. I couldn't give a toss. If I have a chance, I'm going for it."

Deciding to humor him a bit, I responded, "I reckon we wait till Friday when we go for a drink."

"Oh, I get it. He gets a little bit drunk and then we drill him for information. That sounds like a plan. Tasha, I'm so glad that we're on the same wavelength here."

"Well, I guess we need something to motivate us, don't we? We've had to deal with all this crap recently, and now we've got something that will actually make us want to come to work, so…" I joked.

"Just imagine, Tasha – us comparing notes on his penis size."

Chuckling, I said, "You make me laugh. You're such –"

"And I'm proud. Maybe you should have a little fun." I felt a little hurt that he was implying that I wasn't having any "fun", but who was I kidding? He was right.

"Yeah, maybe it is time for me to make a change. Maybe I should be a bit more free-spirited and take some risks."

On that last word, Seth entered the room and immediately we changed the subject. "So, about this afternoon," Michael said coolly.

"It's all in the plan. All in the plan."

Michael chuckled softly to himself, looked up and said, "Hey, Seth. Ready for the afternoon?"

After an interesting day at work, I got home feeling a little bit sexually frustrated. I was tempted to call Josh – an ex who would be well up for some no-strings-attached sex. I decided against it. I didn't want to be pathetic and desperate. And on second thought, I wasn't all that excited about him. I needed to be alone with my fantasies of Seth. My handy little friend would be busy tonight.

I looked in a mirror before going to bed. Light brown skin, long curly hair with natural, reddish highlights and amber eyes had always made me appear racially ambiguous. A DNA test had once revealed a very mixed background. Was I attractive enough to get someone like Seth?

I was pushing forty, but my body was a lot slimmer nowadays, and people said I looked young for my age. Now was the time to take advantage of that before I got too old to attract a younger man. I assumed he was in his thirties. The thought of getting closer to him and the thrill of taking a risk turned me on.

***

The next morning, I almost arrived late due to me taking ages picking out an outfit that enhanced my figure. Unfortunately, it was painfully obvious that I needed a shopping trip. Many of my clothes were two sizes too big and I hadn't yet replaced them since losing weight. I chose a simple long-sleeved, black dress which was well-fitted and emphasized my curves. Though, I probably wouldn't be able to eat anything at all throughout the day. A little over the top, but it was the only good thing I could find.

When I walked in, Seth had made himself comfortable in my chair. The classroom looked different, like it had been reorganized. He didn't even turn around when he said, "Good morning, Miss Chanté. What time do you call this?"

"Time to kick you off my chair," I joked, but I kind of meant it too. He laughed and turned with the smoothness of a snake uncoiling.

"Well, that was a cold greeting," he said, smiling.

Purposely ignoring his observation, I commented, "Mr Arden, you've made some changes."

"I have indeed. I hope you don't mind. I only wanted to help." I immediately softened at his words. The room did look better.

"For a minute there I thought you were trying to take my job."

"Sorry. Not the case. You're irreplaceable," he said, as I walked toward him. I stood there waiting for him to move but he didn't. Instead, he smirked. He was enjoying this. Wasn't he a bit too new to be so cocky? I leaned over, gently removed the mouse from his right hand and logged off the supply teacher account. Even though my backside was pretty much in his face, he didn't move. I turned to face him, planting myself between his legs, and only then did he roll the chair backward. He blatantly moved his eyes up and down my body from my hips to my face. The air crackled with static energy. He laughed in disbelief, and his eyes dilated more than I thought humanly possible. He reminded me of a cat eyeing its prey. He was the first to break eye contact, though.

"I need to get to the bathroom," he said very quickly, just before he disappeared out of the door.

Did I just imagine all of that? He sounded nervous. I had a knack for scaring men away with my direct manner. Perhaps I'd gone a bit too far this time. Maybe it had been flirting only and I had complicated things. I looked down at my outfit, feeling stupid. I'd never paraded myself like a piece of meat in a buffet before, and I certainly didn't want him to think less of me. He was to be based in Michael's class this morning, so I would see him later.

I didn't get a chance to speak to him until lunchtime.

"Hey, Seth, is everything okay?" I said, as he put his jacket on. I assumed he would be going out for lunch.

"Yes, everything's fine, Natasha."

"Going out for lunch?" I probed.

"Yes. Actually, would you like to come along?" he asked almost hesitantly.

Even though I had photocopying to do, I replied, "Why not?"

I guessed that everything was fine between us after all, or he wouldn't have asked me to come out.

We walked to a local park and talked about various things. I found out that he had tried a number of jobs in the past and had recently become a teacher, which meant that he wasn't experienced. I found that surprising, as he'd always given me the impression that he was experienced. He just seemed knowledgeable, like he'd been teaching for years.

He played the piano, loved classic horror literature, as did I, and kept a journal. I told him about my poetry and my ambitions to publish them, and my first novel. He asked to read my writing, which had always been too dark for the average, normal person. Never had a man ever asked to read any of it. So far, this man was too good to be true.

The first week went by very quickly, and to my delight, Seth agreed to join Michael and me for a few drinks on Friday. Neither of us wanted to share Seth with any other member of staff, so we went to a different pub further down the road. One might say it was an *irregular* haunt. Throughout the evening, Michael was all over him, but Seth didn't seem uncomfortable in any way. He certainly was confident with his masculinity, or rather just tolerated it in an attempt to be polite. When Michael went to the bathroom, Seth noticed that I had a tattoo, as my sleeve had ridden up and part of the ornate rose peeked through. He boldly pulled my sleeve up to look at it.

"It's beautiful. Can I touch it?" I nodded, feeling overwhelmed by his touch. He ran his fingers over it and up to my wrist, where his fingers seemed to linger over my vein which seemed to pulsate and become a deeper blue under his touch. He licked his lips and ran his tongue over his teeth as if he was hungry. It seemed a bit strange, but it was very provocative and quite arousing knowing that I was giving him just a minuscule amount of pleasure. We had him until the SATs tests in May, so who knew what the future would hold. I couldn't wait to find out.

We had such a great time that we stayed until closing. We put Michael in a taxi, and Seth offered to escort me home. It was a short walk away and he gave me his elbow, as a gentleman would, and let me lead the way.

"Well, this is my stop," I announced as we approached my door. I gathered my courage and asked, "Would you like to come in for a drink?" He raised his eyebrows in amusement, surprised at my forwardness.

"I don't think you're quite ready for that, Miss Chanté," he purred mischievously. He leaned forward, moved my hair aside and kissed me lightly on the cheek. What a tease, I thought to myself as he walked away, leaving me hanging. Well, that was the last invitation I'd extend, I thought, irritated. However, deep down I knew it wasn't over yet.

I wasn't at all surprised when I saw Seth sitting at my computer on Monday yet again. Bloody hell, he was enjoying this game wasn't he?

Well, I wasn't going to rise to it this time.

"Morning," I said brusquely.

"Oh, good morning, Miss Chanté. I trust you had a pleasant weekend?"

"Yep, not bad." He frowned.

"Is everything alright?"

"Yeah." He wasn't the only one who could play games.

Of course, I couldn't keep up the charade, and eventually the flirting started up again. I would often catch him observing me, and he would see me admiring him. Every Friday we would go out, get drunk, and he'd walk me home, always ending with a kiss on the cheek. I never asked him to come inside again. If he was interested, then he could make a move. It was down to him.

***

Seth had been supporting target groups of children for writing, maths and reading, and had already produced good results. The children loved him, especially when he offered to run a football club. He now taught physical education regularly and wanted to teach music next term.

After dismissing the children, I showed him the music room, so he could see what a meager supply of instruments we had. When he saw the piano, he started tinkling with it, but then he made himself comfortable, stretched his fingers and started to play. What followed was a hauntingly beautiful melody. I stood frozen on the spot, the sting of tears threatening to spill. It spoke to me in a way nothing else ever had. I immediately wanted to get my poetry book and write something as dark and haunting. I had no clue how long I stood there.

"Natasha? Are you okay?" he asked, concerned at the sight of my expression.

"Sorry… it's just… that was lovely. It was very moving," I sputtered, feeling silly. I must be premenstrual or something, I thought.

"Really? Don't think I've ever had a reaction like that to any of my pieces." He got up and walked towards me, looking over me to see if I was alright.

"You composed that?" I asked, sniffling slightly.

"Well… yes," he said as he smoothed his hair back in a nervous gesture – something I wasn't used to seeing. "It was about a very sad time in my life." He paused as if deciding whether or not to continue. "When my wife died," he added, his head bowed.

"You were married?" I asked, surprised.

He nodded. "It seems like a long time ago now."

"You must have loved her very much," I said solemnly.

"I did." The mood became somber, both of us deep in thought. I wasn't quite ready to speak of my past tragedies.

After a while, I broke the silence. "Would you mind sending me your songs?"

A gentle smile brightened his dark expression. "Of course, but only when you bring in your poetry – like you promised."

The next day, I brought my wad of paper to school, and he took it home that evening, promising he would read my poems. I felt nervous about letting him read some of my innermost and darkest thoughts, but he'd shared his song with me, and that had been a privilege.

Later that night, I was woken by a text from Seth. We'd exchanged numbers originally for work purposes only, but over time we had texted each other on a social basis – never this late, though. I blinked my eyes a few times to unblur my vision. He wanted to tell me that he'd read my poetry and he especially liked a particular poem that didn't have a title. He sent a photo of it, so I knew which one he was referring to.

By a strange twist of fate, he had chosen my favorite one, which was of the most sentimental value. In the next text, he asked if he could have a copy of them, and I hastily agreed. Then he sent me recordings of his songs, and I closed my eyes as I listened to the evocative melodies. They lulled me to sleep.

As the evenings and weekends of constant texting passed, I started to feel that we could be something more than just a passing fling. I still didn't want to invite him over, and he offered me no invitation to his. I sensed a note of hesitation on his part. Why was such a great guy still single and nervous to get close? Surely he'd had many women throwing themselves at him; any woman at work would give it up to him. All he had to do was turn up – no wooing necessary.

Michael eyed us suspiciously when Seth greeted me affectionately, like an old friend who he had not seen in years. Admittedly, we hadn't talked as much as we used to, and although we still hung out on Fridays, we were not as close. There were no more conspiratorial references to plans of seduction. Nothing had actually happened with Seth, I thought to myself frustratingly. And I didn't want to lose Michael as a friend. He'd definitely made life more bearable during his time here. He had looked upon me like a mentor – whether or not that was a positive experience, I didn't know. I wasn't always the best of influences when it came to following school policies. He'd helped me too. He had helped loosen me up a great deal, and if it weren't for him, I may not have had the confidence to even consider a guy like Seth. And for that I owed him a great debt. I had been more of a loner before he'd come along.

As time progressed, I could sense that something was different between Seth and me. I could feel it in the air around us. Our feelings, which remained unsaid for now, grew like a virus. Although we still joked around and flirted a lot, we still felt inhibited somehow. I was ready to take things to the next level, but I felt as if he wasn't. Maybe the memory of the woman who he had once loved so dearly had caused a mental block. He'd said that it had been such a long time ago, but it couldn't have been that long. How old could he possibly be? Or perhaps I just didn't live up to her memory.

It wasn't until one Friday that things progressed. Michael had claimed tiredness and gave the pub a miss. I suspected that he could sense the tension in the air between Seth and me. I tried to convince him to stay, feeling bad about pushing him away, especially after we had decided to pursue Seth at all costs. In hindsight, it had been a silly conversation. Now that I knew Seth, I couldn't just objectify him. There was a lot more to him than looks.

Rather than sit opposite me, Seth chose to sit right beside me in the booth seat – closer than I would have expected him to, considering we were still friends. Throughout the evening, he inched closer and closer, even putting his arm around me. I was surrounded by his scent and the warmth of his body, and my body started to respond to his. Our legs were practically rubbing against each other. After a while, he turned to face me and moved aside strands of loose hair about my jaw. He then leaned in closer, to place a soft kiss on my lips. I was too stunned at first, and all the initial bravado I had displayed with Michael disappeared. My body betrayed me, becoming flushed and heated until I could feel my cool exterior start to slip.

Soon, my tongue joined his caressing tongue. I was becoming really aroused. I wanted him here and now. I didn't care that people could see me.

He then did something unexpected. He started to trail kisses along the right side of my jaw, which was closest to him. They continued down my neck, where he paused and inhaled deeply. I hoped I smelt fresh, because a long day at school didn't produce the best of aromas. He hovered there, and I could feel his warm breath against my skin. I waited with anticipation, wondering what he was going to do next.

Just when I thought we had publicly displayed quite enough, he licked my neck, as if he was savoring the flavor. We had to take this elsewhere, I thought. When I turned to tell him, his eyes were silvery, and his teeth were sharp. I reared back in fear. Realization dawned on him, and he closed his eyes and placed a hand over his mouth, mumbling something about feeling sick and needing to go. He quickly grabbed his jacket and fled.

I was left sitting there totally baffled, because one minute we were kissing passionately with promises of more to come later on that night, and the next minute his face had taken on a feral appearance, and he disappeared. I was a little shaken by what I saw, but I couldn't trust my judgment in this state. I was confused. Perhaps I'd had too much to drink. It was time for me to go home.

Once home and in bed, I lay there reliving what had happened, or rather, what hadn't happened. The truth was that I really liked him, and despite my initial fear over his alarming appearance, I didn't know if I was quite ready to give up on him. He intrigued me in a way that no other man had. He certainly hadn't harmed me in any way. I decided to text him just to say that I hoped that he was okay, though, I sensed it was something more than feeling ill that made him flee so suddenly.

In the early hours of the morning, I was disturbed, not by a sound or a physical touch, but by a sensation that I could only describe as intuition. There was a presence in the room. I slowly opened my eyes, only to be confronted by a looming shadow above me. Too paralyzed to scream, I froze. The entity sped away through my door at a speed that wasn't humanly possible. I immediately turned my lamp on.

I knew it probably wasn't the wisest decision, but I decided to inspect each of the rooms in my small flat. It didn't take a genius to work out that I was alone. The strangest thing was the smell that hung in the air. I could have sworn that was the cologne that Seth wore. I had smelt it last night at the pub. Strangely, I felt no fear. Surely, alarm bells should have been ringing, but instead, there was only curiosity.

\*\*\*

The next morning, I was woken by the doorbell. To my surprise, no one stood on the doorstep, but a fresh coffee and a bag of doughnuts did, accompanied by a note that said, "Sorry". I assumed that this was from Seth to apologize for his hasty departure at the pub last night. I greedily consumed the offering, wondering what my next move should be. Approach with caution, I decided.

I texted him just to say thank you and acted as if I suspected nothing. I needed to lure him out and get him to confess. Confess what, I did not know. So, I took a bold step: I invited him over for drinks. I could almost feel him ruminate over the decision as the hours passed by. To my delight, not only did he accept, he also offered to bring sushi. Food was always a bonus.

I gave the place a tidy up, had a bath and picked out one of the new dresses I had purchased. As the sky darkened, I set the mood. A candlelit, intimate setting was hopefully what I had created.

When the bell sounded, I quickly immersed myself in a single puff of perfume and reapplied my strawberry-scented, tinted lip-gloss. I decided on no shoes, only sheer stockings with suspenders underneath my low-cut, blood-colored dress. My painted nails and toenails added an additional splash of red.

The sight of Seth took my breath away; he was ravishing, in a black suit and a burgundy color shirt. In his hands was a bouquet of red roses. His cheeks were flushed pink, probably from the cold weather. It was February, after all. Curiously, when he took my hand to kiss it, his hand was warm. Perhaps the flush in his cheeks was because he was embarrassed. I needed to make him comfortable.

"Hello, Natasha."

"Good, evening, Mr. Arden." My greeting teased a little smile from him, relaxing him slightly.

I set up the sushi on the coffee table, and he poured us glasses of wine. We settled on the sofa, and I purposely sat further away than I usually would. He took his blazer off and laid it on the armchair to his right.

"You look beautiful, Natasha," he said, as he took in my appearance. "Red becomes you."

"Thank you. Well, you look great in anything you wear." He looked down at himself, as if unsure of whether that was true. That brief moment of self-doubt was actually quite adorable on him, and I almost laughed at how endearing it was. I stopped myself, as my tendency to make fun of men had been my downfall in the past. It was banter to me but it was not always received well.

He'd picked an interesting array of dishes, and being adventurous when it came to food, I was happy to sample each one. I made no secret of the fact that I was enjoying the food immensely, and he made no secret of the fact that he was enjoying watching me eat.

"Oh, how rude of me. Please eat some before I demolish it all," I offered through a mouthful of food.

"No, thanks. I'm still feeling a little fragile after last night," he responded with a pat of his stomach.

"Not too ill to drink wine, though?" I teased before I had a chance to stop myself.

Luckily, he didn't take offense and instead played along. "I'll never be too ill for that. It has many healing properties, I'll have you know, Miss Chanté."

I giggled and shoved another roll into my mouth. I'd been drinking too fast, and it was having an effect on me. Oh well, to hell with caution, I thought to myself. Carpe diem!

My well-conceived, or should I say *ill-conceived*, plan went out of the window. I blatantly moved closer to him and ended up putting my foot on his leg. He couldn't take his eyes off it.

"What lovely feet you have," he said as he held it. He proceeded to massage it, and when he was finished, I cheekily gave him my other foot, and he massaged that one. He didn't stop there. His hand running softly up my calf almost undid me. I stretched out on the sofa so he could take in all of me and continue running his hand up my leg. It was an open invitation, and he knew it. As his fingers reached my inner thigh, where the suspender held the stocking, he leaned forward until he was above me, moved my hair aside and kissed me. It was a sensuously slow kiss which deepened with every stroke of his tongue. His hand skimmed over my hip and waist and settled on my breast. He expertly swirled his thumb around my nipple, and I felt wetness gathering in my famished interior. I was in heaven and hell at the same time. The sensations were more than enjoyable, yet the build-up was torture. I wanted instant satisfaction.

I reached down to touch myself. To my disappointment, he moved my hand away.

"No, we need to stop."

Those were the last words I expected to hear.

He sat back up abruptly. I straightened myself up, the arousal I felt fading away and being replaced with anger and confusion. What the hell? What a fucking tease. I felt humiliated. I had let my guard down, only to be let down again.

"What the fuck, Seth. That is not cool."

"I know. I'm sorry, I've got to go."

"No fucking way. Tell me what the fuck is going on. I'm not playing games here." When he still didn't turn to face me, I shouted, "At least fucking look at me!"

He stiffened but still did not turn. He reached for his blazer. I immediately got up, planted myself in front of him, grabbed his face, and made him look at me. I gasped. "Oh my god… your face… your eyes…"

"Don't look at me!" he cried, covering his face with his hands.

My anger dissipated as quickly as it had appeared. "So I didn't imagine it all," I murmured to myself rather than to him. After a moment, a strange sense of calm took over and I knew I had to ask, "What are you?"

I pried his jacket from his hand and rubbed his arm. His gaze was firmly pointed down. "Stay away from me. I might hurt you," he warned.

"No, you won't, Seth. Tell me. I want to understand."

He let me lead him to the sofa. This time, when he met my gaze, his features had returned to normal.

"Here," I coaxed, as I handed him his glass of wine. He sat staring at his glass, so I went first. "So, your eyes reflect light, your pupils dilate more than normal, your canines extend…" Still no response. "That was you in my bedroom last night, wasn't it?" He nodded. "And you're super fast. Are you some kind of mutation or government experiment?"

A loud noise erupted suddenly, and I realized it was the sound of his laughter. I let him laugh it out at my expense. When the laughter died down, he responded. "No, far from it. I'm just a plain old vampire."

"Vampire?" I whispered incredulously. How was that even possible? But why would he lie? The evidence was almost plain to see. *Almost.* "Okay. Prove it."

"Would you like me to demonstrate on you?" he said sarcastically.

"Will it hurt?"

His eyes widened. That was the last thing he expected to hear. It pleased me that I could have that kind of effect on him.

"No. It can be quite pleasant actually." He moved closer as if he was about to do so but stopped. "Are you sure?" he asked softly.

I nodded and waited, preparing myself to feel a bite. He didn't move a muscle, so I looked up at his face. Shaking his head, he blurted, "No, I can't."

That answer wasn't good enough for me. I reached for my shoes by the front door and grabbed my coat. "Right. Let's do this."

His jaw dropped, stunned by my brashness. "Let me get this straight, Natasha – you want to watch me hunt?"

"Well, how the hell are you going to prove it if you won't drink from me?"

"Alright. You win. I may regret this for eternity but here goes…" Grabbing his jacket again, he waited quietly while I opened the door.

As I locked up, he put his jacket back on and took a deep breath, as if he was motivating himself to do this. Performance anxiety perhaps, I thought, amused. I took his hand and said, "Lead the way. Show me your world."

"I've never done this before," he muttered, almost defensive of his hesitant behavior.

"Never done what?" I asked, needing clarification.

"Hunted with a human watching."

"What about the people you drink from? Don't they watch you?"

"No, they don't normally see me coming," he drawled, with a slight hint of pride.

We walked the dark streets of London, actively looking for alleyways and unsuspecting victims. I must admit that the anticipation was kind of exciting. What that said about me and my depraved sense of fun was another matter. I was really going to get to know a part of Seth that no one knew about or find out whether he was delusional or not.

Eventually, we spotted a well-dressed man urinating in an alleyway with almost no lighting. I let go of Seth's hand, and he pretended to undo his fly, as if he was going to urinate too. However, as the man zipped up, Seth moved so fast that I didn't see him until he was standing right behind the man. He opened his mouth wide and plunged his teeth in. I moved closer to get a better look. The man seemed to enter what looked like a swoon, and a tranquil expression relaxed the tension around his jaw, which slackened. I moved closer. Seth drank deeply for a few minutes, and then he carefully let the man go. He fell into an unconscious heap. At least he wasn't really harmed, I thought. Seth threw his head back, enjoying the rush of blood running through his system. Then he looked at me, unflinchingly, daring me to see him. His thin irises blazed with a silver light, like mother of pearl, and his fangs were coated with blood.

It was sexy as fuck.

I pulled his face towards me and kissed him, blood and all. It didn't take him long to respond, and soon the blood mingled with our tongues. He pressed the length of his body against me, until I backed up against the brick wall. Whilst he fondled my hardened nipples, I felt his erection grow as it pressed against my navel. I became slick with arousal.

"I can smell you," he said through his protruding fangs, as he placed his hand under my dress.

I unzipped his trousers, slid my hand under his boxers, and grabbed his engorged shaft. He bucked his hips and I parted my legs, giving each other better access. I felt his fingers part my lips and slide inside me. They moved in and out, making me grab him harder. Then his fingers were slowly encircling my clit and I took a sharp intake of breath. I moved my hand up and down his hard length, rotating my wrist, creating more friction. I felt his sharp teeth graze my earlobes and his hot, panting breath against my neck.

With each stroke of his fingers, my heart rate skyrocketed. His body tensed and he sped up his movements dramatically. I clung to his neck as we climaxed together. I rode the wave of ecstasy until my breathing slowed down. When I looked up at him, he was watching me, his face almost back to normal now. He kissed me passionately before untangling himself from my grip.

"I never thought in a million years…" he trailed off. Taking my hand, he led me away and headed in the direction of my flat. There was a sense of reverence in the air, like we'd made a life-changing discovery. This experience certainly would change my life. There had always been something missing, and now I truly felt alive.

Looking at his side profile, I admired his perfectly smooth skin, his angular cheekbones and his dark hair, which was almost blue-black in the darkness. "How do you have such a beautiful, olive complexion if you're dead?" I asked.

He smiled and responded, "Not dead. Undead. Only my human body is dead, but the vampire is very much alive."

"And now so am I, thanks to you, Seth." I slipped my arm through the crook of his elbow and laid my head against his shoulder. Something about it felt so right, especially when he lifted his arm and put it around me in a kind of half embrace.

***

This time, Monday morning felt very different. Rather than greet each other in the usual fashion, I was greeted by a sultry gaze. I guessed somebody must have missed me. I popped into Michael's class to say good morning and to say we missed him on Friday. Seeing that we hadn't forgotten about him, he promised we'd all go out for a drink at the end of the week.

The morning was busy, as we were reassuring parents about booster classes and upcoming tests. Thank fuck Seth and Michael were there to assist, otherwise I would have ended up telling them to get lost. My enthusiasm and patience had decreased over the years. Teaching was a dying profession run by bureaucratic leaders. They didn't care about the children. It was all about test results. I'd always promised myself that I would leave the profession, yet here I was, after nearly twenty years.

When the kids went out to play, I stood in the large storage cupboard near my computer desk, trying to look for a science activity for the Evolution and Inheritance unit coming up. I had stupidly said I would plan it, so that Michael could plan next week's history lesson.

I felt him before I saw him. Seth was standing behind me. "That's twice you've sensed my presence now," he observed. When I turned, he looked me up and down, appreciating my body. "You do look a bit witchy – maybe that's why I'm under your spell." He closed the cupboard door behind us.

"Seth, the class will be back soon."

"Not for at least fifteen minutes," he whispered, eyes shining slightly. He undid my zip, pulled my trousers and knickers down, threw them to the side and hoisted me on top of a filing cabinet. I gasped, taken aback by his forceful approach, but I craved his touch. The cold metal made me break out in goosebumps, making me shift, and it wobbled precariously under my weight. Even that couldn't stop my excitement building. After he loosened his tie, he pushed my legs apart, and began to kiss my inner thighs. My breath quickened in response. He pulled me forward a bit, so that his nose nuzzled my clit. I felt his hot tongue enter me.

"You taste delicious," he moaned, sending vibrations over my clit. Licking from my opening to my sweet spot, he proceeded to flick, nibble and suck. I held his head and grabbed his hair. I let out a cry, hoping no one had heard. The speed increased until I was bursting with pleasure.

I didn't have time to turn into jelly, so I hastily located my clothing on the floor and we exchanged a quick kiss. Luckily, I was back in class just before the kids returned. Seth coolly slunk away to take a target group from Michael's class. Feeling flushed, I downed some cold water and started maths. I would have to plan science another time.

Despite wanton looks from Seth, the next few days were uneventful due to impending deadlines. We had some planning time on Thursday, so all three of us headed to the meeting room where the staff computers were. Michael had a meeting with his mentor during our planning session, so off he went.

Seth and I continued tapping away at our computers, but the tension was too much for me. I stood up quickly, before I changed my mind, and commanded, "Stand up." He obeyed. He didn't object when I pulled him in for a kiss either. "My turn," I murmured softly in his ear, before giving his lobe a gentle nip.

I unbuckled his belt and unzipped his trousers. My simple action elicited quite the response from Seth. A bulge formed in his pants. I pulled them down, and this time I knelt before him as he made himself comfortable in the chair. His thighs spread open awaiting me, and for the first time, I truly had the chance to admire the view. His smooth head glistened, and the veins throbbed.

He gripped the armrests of his chair as he enjoyed the sensation of my tongue running along the ridges. I took most of him in my mouth and sucked softly at first, then harder. I was met with quiet groans of approval. Feeling his hand gripping my hair only fuelled my efforts. I held the bottom of his shaft, giving it a little squeeze while sucking. It had been a long time since I'd given a man oral, and giving him pleasure like this was quite empowering. His breathing became more labored, and he gripped the armrests harder as he reached the pinnacle of pleasure. He was putty in my hands.

When it was over, he laughed for no apparent reason, but I knew why. We both felt alive, enjoying the simple pleasures in life, not bound by laws. It was exciting, and I was the happiest I'd been for a long time, but something niggled in the back of my mind.

Michael returned to the planning room none the wiser.

"So, what have you been up to while I was away?" he asked jokingly.

"Why, awaiting your return of course," I bantered back.

"Tell him the truth, Natasha. Tell him about the wild orgy." We all laughed, but Seth snuck a sneaky smile at me, and the look in his eyes promised more to come.

***

As the weeks went by, there were more brief, risqué encounters, as well as the usual flirting. Although I'd hinted at wanting more, he'd turned down my invitations to hang out at mine. It seemed as if he was deliberately avoiding going all the way with me but couldn't quite stay away from me. I wondered where I stood with Seth. What were we? Were we colleagues who merely had kinky urges, fuelled by the risk factor? As fun as it was, I wanted something more. I was too old for a quick fling and didn't just want to be somebody's plaything if that was all I'd ever be. What was the point in even telling me that he was a vampire? Why share something so personal? I wanted companionship as well as physical closeness, but I had so many questions. Could or would a vampire have a real relationship with a human? How long did vampires actually live? Could a human and a vampire really make it work, given the age difference? Could we be something more than what we currently were?

At our usual haunt, Seth, Michael and I shared a drink and a few shots. I found myself not being able to follow the conversation. Recently, I had been overly consumed by our antics and my wandering thoughts. Even my work had suffered. I'd had to make the excuse that I was unwell or tired. The confusion overwhelmed me, now that his hand was resting on my thigh under the table. We needed to talk.

"Guys, I'm feeling shattered. Gonna go home now, but you stay and be merry."

Seth immediately stood up, a look of concern etched on his face.

"I'll walk you," he announced. Michael looked between us, obviously disappointed.

"No, you stay with Mikey. I can make my own way home." He stood there unsure of what to do, so Michael came to give me a parting hug, which broke the awkwardness of the moment. "See you on Monday."

Reluctantly, Seth sat back down when Michael did. It would have been rude if he'd left because of me, and he knew it. It seemed that he was so afraid of people knowing about us – whatever we were. Well, no more. I needed to regain control of my life. I didn't like the direction it was headed in.

***

The phone blared in my ear, making me jump up. Wow, that's what you call a wake-up call. It was Seth.

Instead of my usual greeting, I said, "Bit late to be calling isn't it?"

He remained quiet, surprised by my tone.

"But it's Friday," he tried to tease, but it didn't have the desired effect.

"What of it?" I snapped impatiently.

"I'm outside, would you let me in?" Oh, so now he wanted to communicate with me.

"What for?" I responded, trying to remain tough. But who was I kidding – the thought of being alone with him was extremely appealing. Also, maybe now he would listen.

"Natasha, please." He sounded distressed. Mr. Arden sounded nervous. Did I make him feel like that? I'd made a vampire feel unsure of himself? I couldn't help but feel slightly proud of myself, because now he knew how I'd been feeling.

I opened the door, stepping aside to let him in, and we both stood in the darkened hallway waiting.

"Is everything alright?" he asked cautiously.

In a slightly softer tone, I answered, "Yes, I'm okay."

"It's just that you left suddenly and we normally…"

"I know, Seth. I just needed to think about us." His eyes dropped in a gesture of guilt. He knew that he'd been avoiding getting any closer, but just then I understood.

He was afraid.

"I thought we were having fun," he postured a little too casually. He wasn't fooling me.

"We were but the truth is I want more. I really like you. If we're gonna do this, I want all of you. I don't just want a bit here and there. Don't be afraid, I won't hurt you."

What I said may have seemed strange, because how could I possibly hurt him? I was just a human, but he knew what I meant. He opened his mouth as if he was about to deny being scared but closed it again.

"You're right, Natasha. I am afraid. I don't want to lose you, but I'm not good for you…"

His admission resonated deep inside me. He was worried about my future. We both knew there was only one way for us to truly be together. I didn't have the strength to face that now. I took him into my arms and kissed him, while he pulled me close. Sometimes, when words fail, actions speak louder than words. I felt something deeper in the urgency of his kisses. I felt love. I was ready for whatever he wanted to do to me.

My heart thumped as he grabbed me by the buttocks and caressed my curves, almost too roughly. His strength far exceeded mine. I was totally at his mercy, but I didn't care.

"Take me, Seth," I whispered breathily. He looked into my eyes, which burned dangerously with desire. I shivered with a mixture of fear and anticipation.

I watched his every move, transfixed by his fingers undoing each button on his shirt, revealing more of his toned, broad chest. Practically drooling, I was totally helpless to resist. He proceeded to remove all his clothing. I didn't make a move. I wanted to see what he would do to me. He slid my nightie up, tantalizingly slow, and I raised my arms to assist. As he eyed my naked body, his eyes transformed before me into something inhuman and it set my fire alight.

He was going to feast on my flesh.

"I don't know if I can control myself," he uttered in a guttural tone.

"Then don't," I exhaled.

He fondled one breast while taking the other into his mouth, his fangs nipping at them slightly. Lifting me up like I weighed nothing more than a feather, he carried me to the bed. Whilst I lay there at his mercy, his tongue trailed up my thigh over my pelvic bone and to my belly button. I spread my legs, inviting him to give me a taste.

He feasted on me like it gave him nourishment until I was close to climaxing. I reached down, trying to locate his erection, but he pulled my hand away and held both of them above my head. He nuzzled my neck, and I turned my head, giving him access to my carotid artery. He sighed as he rubbed his cheek against mine, and instead of drinking, he nipped me playfully. I felt his kisses raining down on me like snowflakes. He licked my lips before my mouth was overcome with hot, sweet kisses. His swollen member nudged my opening, which was dripping wet after being teased mercilessly by his exploring tongue.

"Do it now," I pleaded. "I can't take anymore." I gripped his body, trying to hold him closer, encouraging him to drink. Fangs immediately pierced my neck. Despite the initial sting, it was a pleasurable sensation, and it only heightened my arousal. After only taking a little, he suddenly withdrew his sharp teeth. Before I could protest, he placed a well-timed kiss to quieten me.

Feeling the length of him fill my eager opening was pure bliss. The relief it offered me was so long overdue. I bucked my hips, wanting him to go deeper and harder. He slid almost all the way out and plunged back in deeply, again and again. It felt so right, like we were meant to fit together. The taste of my own metallic-tasting blood mingled with my saliva as he kissed me and thrust into me simultaneously.

"You feel so good," he gasped into my hair.

Untangling my legs from around him, I pushed him back slightly, indicating that I wanted to change position. I wanted to see him beneath me in all his glory. I pushed him onto his back roughly and he welcomed my ferociousness. I watched his face intently as I eased onto him. I cried out at how deep he was. I bounced up and pushed down over and over again until his head hit me in just the right spot.

I lowered my head, overcome by something primal. I wanted to taste what he tasted, and I didn't think my own blood quite cut it, so I bit down on his neck as hard as I could. I wanted to taste his blood. He snarled and inhaled through clenched teeth. Mistaking the action for pain, I reared back, but he pulled me down, wanting more. I bit down again until a little blood trickled out. As I swallowed, my body seemed to tingle, and a surge of power flowed through my veins like a powerful current. His thumb massaged my clit, whilst he thrust upwards until we found the perfect rhythm. Our cries filled the air. We gripped each other's hands, fingers entwined, as we tensed up and exploded with an indescribable rush. Bombarded with wave after wave of euphoria, the pleasure was too much. I collapsed in a heap on top of him, and he embraced me, holding me close to his chest. I listened to his heart beating powerfully as I lay there, energy spent.

As my eyelids became heavy, I turned the lamp off, plunging the room into darkness. The sounds of our breathing filled the room as we became one with the shadows.

\*\*\*

Over the next few months, we prepared for SATs exams. Whenever Seth and I got a moment, we couldn't help but steal a kiss or sometimes something more. We almost got caught a few times, and I'm fairly sure Michael did catch us at one point, but he tactfully turned and walked away. He never asked questions, but I think he knew we were seeing each other.

In the evenings, I often had to work and was too exhausted to see Seth. He required a lot of energy. But every weekend I was his for the taking. Every Monday was a countdown to a weekend of intense lovemaking. Seth restricted the amount of blood we took from one another when he noticed my senses becoming sharper. I enjoyed my extra keen senses immensely, totally getting rid of my glasses at one point.

Ultimately, Seth's stay at our school was coming to an end, as senior management had decided there would be no use in keeping him on any further. In their eyes, he had served his purpose now that tests were nearly over.

It was the weekend preceding his last week at work. We held each other after another bout of passionate lovemaking. I sighed longingly. "How long can we carry on like this, Seth?"

"As long as we have to," he said with a hint of melancholy.

That was an answer I just couldn't accept. "No," I stated firmly.

"No? Are you saying you want to leave me?" He sat up abruptly, pulling me up with him. I looked into his eyes, willing him to understand.

"Of course not, my love. What I'm getting at is…" I took a breath, trying to get out the words I needed to say.

"Tell me, Natasha – what is it?"

"I love you. I'll never love anyone like this. I want to be with you forever." He closed his eyes like it hurt to hear my fateful words, placing a hand on his heart like it physically hurt.

"I love you too," he declared fervently.

I squeezed his hand, and a hot tear trickled down my face. I was incredibly moved by his admission and my realization of my feelings. His eyes glistened as he reached out to wipe the tear from my face.

I decided that the right time was now, so after taking another deep breath, I simply stated, "I want you to change me."

He pulled back, horrified by my words.

"You don't know what you're asking."

"Yes, I do. I've been thinking about it a lot."

"But, you could have a family and grow old with a human man."

"You can't tell me you love me and then say that." He shook his head resignedly. "You don't understand, Seth. I already had a child, and she died. I can't go through that pain again," I said, fighting tears. It was a wound that I didn't want to reopen.

He pulled me into his arms and said, "Oh, I'm so sorry. I had no idea.

I've always sensed sadness in you, and I thought something was missing in your life that I couldn't give you."

"But there is something missing, Seth. I did have a child and a husband. I tried that life. I don't want that life again." Taking a moment to calm myself, I tried to find my inner strength. "What I want to say is I want a new life. I want to be reborn. I want to hunt. I want to feel the wind in my hair and the grass beneath my feet. I want to be free."

"But are you sure? We don't age like humans. We can't settle anywhere for long or we'll arouse suspicion. You'll have to cut all ties."

"I can do that; let's do it on Friday after the tests are done. The sooner the better. I'm done with all of this."

\*\*\*

Sitting in Seth's living room, I was nervous. I'd handed in my notice at work, to everyone's shock and horror. There were tears from the students, and senior management were panic-stricken about losing their Year Six lead. Michael was beside himself, and I must admit that it almost undid me.

I fed everyone stories full of lies, including my family, who thought I was just having some kind of midlife crisis. We'd never been particularly close, so that one was easier than expected. They had always been disappointed in me for not following the path they had chosen, and I believe that they even blamed me for my marriage breakup, after our child had died from sudden infant death syndrome. I didn't want bitterness in my heart, so I wished them well.

I'd put all of my stuff into storage and ended my tenancy agreement for the flat. Seth packed up everything we would need to stay at a cottage he'd rented in the Lake District. He thought a quiet and peaceful area would give us more privacy and space to hunt.

"Are you ready to go? It's not too late to change your mind, you know."

"Let's do this," I affirmed, standing tall.

The moon's luminescence bathed the landscape with an uncanny light, but it wasn't cold on this summer's night. It seemed a fitting background for tonight's task. Doors locked and candles lit, Seth set up the room to make the change as comfortable as he could. After I'd had a soothing bath, he lay naked on the bed waiting for me to join him. I dropped my towel and settled in beside him in the little nest of cushions he had created for us.

We made love for one last time as human and vampire. It was different this time – no frenzied lust, only gentle and loving. The love we had for one another was plain to see, and I knew he was the right one for me. He placed a soft kiss on my lips, then on my neck. His fangs entered my skin and the blood flowed freely. Seth drank and drank until I swayed, weakened by the blood loss.

My vision darkened when his bleeding wrist hovered in front of my face. "Drink, my love," he coached. The thick liquid flowed so quickly that I had to take long deep gulps to keep up. It tasted like red grapes, only not as sweet, and thicker, rich with other flavors. The different notes danced on my tongue, and when it entered my bloodstream it tingled at first, giving me a rather pleasant feeling. Soon the tingling gave way to a dull burning sensation which increased by the second.

I was on fire.

"It hurts!" I cried, clenching my fists, wildly grabbing at the cushions and sheets.

Restraining me in a solid embrace, Seth whispered, "It's only the venom. It will pass. Trust me." He rocked me back and forth. My vision darkened further, and I heard a faint humming – it was a familiar tune that I once heard being played on a piano. That faded too. The darkness closed in, and everything went black.

***

I heard crickets chirping. I smelled damp grass. I felt silk beneath my touch.

My eyes flew open. It was light, but it wasn't daytime. The waxing crescent moon hung in the inky, night sky like a scythe.

Someone was asleep in the chair beside the bed. A man. No, not a man. A vampire. Seth. I opened my mouth to speak, but it was so dry and parched that I could only croak. I tried again.

"Seth?" I rasped. He looked around the room in a panic and stood up as soon as he saw me.

"Natasha? Thank goodness you're okay."

I must have been out for quite a while, judging from his anxiety. "Yes."

Relief washed over his face.

"How do you feel?"

I held my cramping stomach. "Hungry."

Seth held out his hand and I held it, immediately comforted by his touch. He helped me up, and I stumbled, but his reassuring hands steadied me. I took a few more steps, and my balance quickly improved. The cobwebs cleared in my mind, and there was a newfound spring in my step. I pushed the patio doors open.

Hand in hand, we walked out into the night. We merged with the shadows. I could smell prey in the air, and I ran so fast that I was flying. I felt the wind in my hair, the grass beneath my feet and the humidity on my skin. I wasn't confined by the laws of human nature.

I was free.

## The End

# Stille Nacht
## Deborah Kelsey

### Part I

"Shall we toast once more, Major?" Faber raised his glass. "To Christmas?"

Strasser quickly raised his glass. "To Christmas." As he drank, he found he couldn't take his eyes off the gentle movement of Faber's throat as he swallowed his own champagne. He had dreamed for ages of an evening just like this, of time spent alone with Faber in the Standartenführer's sumptuous Parisian townhouse. He had been in love with Faber since he'd first been assigned to his command, and now, at long last, they were spending an evening alone together

Hermann, Faber's long-time driver and manservant, came in with coffee and cake and began to clear the dishes from their Christmas Eve feast.

"You may leave once you've finished the washing up," Faber told him. "Frohe Weihnachten."

"Danke, Standartenführer. Frohe Weihnachten."

Faber sliced a piece of the cake, a fine Buche de Noel, and handed it to Strasser on one of the delicate porcelain plates that came with the townhouse, once owned by a prominent family of Jews.

"This cake is quite good," he told Strasser. "Hermann found it in a little pastry shop near the Bois. I'm afraid I have quite a weakness for good pastry," he added, "which is why I must constantly exercise to keep myself trim." He lightly patted his flat stomach.

Dieter gazed at that graceful hand. He found it hard to believe that Faber had any weaknesses at all. Though taller than Faber, Dieter always felt as though he were looking up at him, rather than the other way around. Faber was, after all, the notorious Jew Killer, the single greatest investigator in the Reich's armed forces.

"You're awfully quiet tonight, Major. Have you somehow abandoned your highly skilled powers of speech?"

"Not as skilled as yours, Standartenführer."

Faber grinned at that. They could hear cheerful laughter in the street below. "It's getting late," Faber said as he glanced out the window toward the passing voices. "About time for Saint Nicholas—or Père Noël—to put in an appearance, don't you think? Will he bring the Krampus with him?"

Dieter laughed. "Not likely, sir. The French have no dark undercurrent in their yuletide celebrations."

"That's why they've lost to us twice in the last fifty years," said Faber. "They're simply unprepared for terror. Whereas we thrive upon it." Both men chuckled at that.

"I was terrified of the Krampus as a boy," Dieter suddenly said. "So terrified that I would run and hide under my bed or in my closet, missing the December fifth celebrations entirely."

Faber poured himself some coffee and took a sip. "And what terrified you so? Afraid to look in the face of the devil? He's nothing more than a wicked hobgoblin, you know."

"Not to me," Dieter replied. "I always felt—I knew he would hurt me."

"So, a little pain, a few scratches here and there, a bump on the head—what terror is there in that? These are nothing more than the common slings and arrows of boyhood."

"No," Dieter went on. "It was that I knew he would hurt me. He wouldn't hurt the other boys, but he would hurt me. I knew I would be his victim."

"Come now, Dieter. You can't say that the Krampus was only after you. How solipsistic can one boy be?"

"It wasn't like that," Dieter snapped.

"Calm down, my boy. You're upsetting yourself."

"One did hurt me. My cousin—"

He stopped and was silent.

"Your cousin?"

"My father and my cousin—my cousin Dieter, the one with whom I shared my name—used to dress up on Christmas Eve. Father would play Saint Nicholas and Cousin Dieter, well, he was the Krampus.

"From the time I was four years old he would chase me all around the house, inside and outside, into the old, abandoned barn we had on our property. I was ten or twelve when he finally caught me. You'd think I'd be harder to catch as I got older, but in fact, I was easier to catch.

"I wanted to be caught," Dieter continued. "And I wanted Cousin Dieter to catch me. I wanted him to be the one to catch me because I wanted him to touch me. I wanted him to touch me the way I'd seen boys touch each other in the changing houses at beaches and lakes like Wannsee.

"But it wasn't the rapture I thought it would be. It hurt. It hurt terribly, and I was humiliated. I was never able to feel the same about Cousin Dieter after that—and I've had to share his name all my life.

"I closed myself off after that. I was numb. I couldn't feel. I was like that for years. Then, when I was fourteen, I was alone in my dormitory at school. I had to stay back from our field hike because I'd been sick with a cold.

"I was all alone in my dormitory—in my bed, when I—thought of it again. And this time it excited me, remembering it—and afterwards, I wanted to die. I wanted to hurt myself—and I did.

"And somehow, hurting myself freed me from it. I no longer felt I was to blame for what had happened. And a part of me that had died when it happened also came to life again. The shock of the pain brought it back."

"What was that part of you?"

"The part of me that…"

Dieter's voice trailed off. He had said far more than he had expected. The drinks before dinner, the wine with it, had loosened his tongue significantly more than he wanted.

They were silent for quite a while after that. It had grown still and quiet in the streets, now empty. People were home with their families, basking in the hushed tranquility of Christmas Eve, that calm and spiritual prelude that always precedes the festivities of Christmas Day. Even in wartime, it was there as it always had been when Dieter and Hans were boys.

Finally, Faber spoke. "We are the sum of all our desires—and all our fears," he told Dieter. "And what they say about us is usually quite revealing.

"It may surprise you to know this, Major, but I am quite a student of the Jew, Freud. Shocked? You shouldn't be. To capture my prey, I very often have to open its mind and peer deep within to find its secrets and desires. And when I find these, I find its weaknesses. And no one knew better than Freud how much can be found when one unlocks another person's psyche.

"You see, Major, Freud had a theory, that one's sexuality begins taking shape from birth, when the infant first responds to the touch of its mother. As a child grows up, it finds itself responding to all manner of stimuli—at home, at school, and at church. A simple bath becomes a delicious self-caress of the body with a slick bar of soap. The strong legs of a fellow schoolmate as he climbs a ladder to reach for a book sends shivers down one's spine. And in church—you are Catholic, are you not, Major?"

By now Dieter's heart was pounding, and all he could do was nod in reply.

Faber smiled. "I thought so. Well, then you are as familiar as I with that image of the nearly naked Christ, slender and pale as porcelain, delicate arms outstretched, graceful feet stacked neatly for the penetration of the nail, clearly suffering—and yet in radiant ecstasy."

Faber leaned forward in his chair then, his razor-sharp eyes fixed on Dieter in an appraising gaze so clear and so frank it unnerved the major.

"I have my own Freudian theory," he continued, "about Catholic boys, as you and I once were. There are, you see, three ways for a young boy to respond to that image of suffering on the cross. The one that is most talked about is of course the one that finds both humility and inspiration in the profound divinity symbolized by that act of supreme self-sacrifice.

"But then there are the two others, the ones never spoken of, both a combination of exhilaration and desire. There is the one that wishes he had inflicted the wounds on that deceptively soft-looking white skin, that he had tortured that gaunt body, that he had been the source of such exquisite suffering.

"That boy, of course, is me."

Faber paused for a moment to let those words sink in. His usually hazel eyes were now a blazing and brilliant emerald green, and Dieter, transfixed, thought that he had never seen more beautiful eyes, a more beautiful face, a more beautiful man. He swallowed and caught Faber's glimpse at the clear bob of his Adam's apple.

"Then there is the other," Faber continued. "The one who wishes it was he upon that cross, he whose flesh is peppered with wounds and punctures, he who has suffered the thrilling agony of unspeakable torture and humiliation, he who glories in such complete and utter submission."

Again Faber paused, giving the meaning of his next words even greater weight.

"And that boy, my dear Dieter, is you."

Dieter's breath caught in his throat. A hot flush suffused his body. He felt the sharp stab of desire in his belly, and he was suddenly, achingly erect.

The weight of silence filled the room, broken only by the steady ticking of the grandfather clock in the hallway. The air seemed thick and heavy.

The clock sounded, then began to chime. Dieter turned toward those chimes, counting each one. Four… six… eight… twelve. Midnight. It was Christmas Day. He turned back to Faber and was met with a gaze of fiercely bold determination—and raw, naked desire.

"You will stand up now, Dieter," Faber said quietly, "and remove your uniform."

Without hesitation, Dieter, who now believed he had never loved anyone more than the man before him, rose to his feet and began to undo the belt around his tunic.

## Part II

### Hide 'n' Seek

Without uttering a word, Dieter slowly removed his uniform, taking the time to neatly drape his shirt and tunic over the dining room chair, and carefully fold his trousers and place them on the chair's seat. Faber smiled at every meticulous little move.

When he was clad only in his underclothes, Dieter stood up straight in front of Faber and tried to meet his fiery gaze. He felt flushed and hot, and he was acutely aware of the growing damp spot on the front of his undershorts. He ached to touch himself, to smooth that silken fluid around the exposed head and the sheath that clung so much more snugly to him now. But he was also anxious to see how the man he loved would react to him.

Faber gazed at him with a mysterious, dark smile, cocked an eyebrow when he spotted the front of his shorts. "What an excitable creature you are," he said, openly admiring the swelling in those undershorts, which clung tightly to two taut, smooth white thighs. "The undershirt, now. Please." He shifted in his chair to accommodate his own arousal as Dieter unbuttoned and then pulled off his undershirt, exposing a pale, white chest with no more than a few sprinkles of hair around the nipples, something Faber considered a special treat in a man. He had always enjoyed licking those little hairs, and tugging at them with his teeth.

"Now that I find myself confronted with an embarrassment of riches, I'm almost at a loss regarding what to do next," he told Dieter with a chuckle. "Pull down those undershorts for a taste of that sweetness? I imagine you taste very good indeed, Sturmbannführer. You certainly have an intoxicating scent." With that Faber closed his eyes and inhaled deeply, as though he were savoring that scent.

Dieter began to shiver almost uncontrollably, although not from the cold—Faber kept his townhouse unusually warm—but because each and every word Faber uttered was like a caress, and he felt himself grow even harder.

"How lovely it would be to step over there and touch that smooth, pale skin of yours, Dieter," Faber went on, his voice huskier. "As pale as porcelain, soft as a woman, yet firm like a man… oh, to bite those tender nipples, to kiss that beautiful, slender throat. To slide my hands beneath that soft cotton and grasp that firm behind. Just talking about it makes me very hard indeed, and—unless my eyes deceive me, and I don't believe they do—my words seem to have the very same effect on you."

Dieter blushed and lowered his head. He had never been more embarrassed and aroused in his life, and yet there was something wonderful in such humiliation. He had never felt happier, nor more in love.

"Look at me, my boy," Faber said firmly. "Do not look away."

Dieter raised his head, and struggled to meet head-on that clear, sharp gaze.

Faber stood up, walked over to Dieter, and with one graceful hand reached out to stroke that pale chest, dragging his fingers down to one brown nipple, pinching it lightly, then twisting it roughly. Dieter winced in pain but the bulge in his shorts lurched upward.

"Ah, you like that," Faber exclaimed. He pinched the nipple harder, saw the tears well up in Dieter's large blue eyes. "A little twinge here"—Dieter moaned softly—"a sharp twist there." Dieter gasped. "It's not difficult to make you sing, is it? Like a little bird…"

"Oh, what to do, what to do," Faber suddenly groaned. "I have fucked many women and many men, but you are easily one of the most beautiful creatures I have ever seen. Still, I mustn't be greedy, mustn't rush into things…"

Faber snapped his fingers. "I have it," he said cheerfully. "Let's play a little game, shall we? A game of hide 'n' go seek. You shall hide, and I, the hunter, shall seek. Yes. That's exactly what we'll do."

Dieter stared at Faber, completely dumbfounded. He was expecting to be seduced, and now Faber wanted to play a game?

"Why are you looking at me that way, my boy? Do you begrudge me a little fun? You were expecting me to simply bend you over, pull down those shorts and take you without putting any thought into it?"

"No, Standartenführer, of course not, but…"

"I would think by now you should know to always expect the unexpected from me. I'm going to cover my eyes now and begin my countdown. You be a good little bird and fly away."

Faber turned his head toward the wall and began to count. Still dumbfounded, Dieter didn't move.

"Fifty-nine, fifty-eight, fifty-seven…" Faber stopped. The townhouse was suddenly engulfed in silence, broken only by the distant ticking of the grandfather clock. Without turning around, Faber spoke very quietly, very clearly and very firmly.

"Go hide, Dieter. *Now.*"

The promise of a threat was unmistakable in that voice, and Dieter backed out of the room, then turned and ran, his heart thudding in his chest.

This game was not unfamiliar to Dieter, and as he flew from room to room, looking for a suitable place to hide, he had the odd sensation that something very primal was being enacted; some deeply buried feeling was being uprooted, if not torn from him. And then of course, he understood. He was running from the Krampus again, as he had for so many years as a child—and that this had been Faber's intention all along. The thought filled him with exhilaration as he bounded up the staircase to the second floor of the townhouse.

"Thirty-six, thirty-five, thirty-four…" Faber's voice drifted upstairs, ticking off the numbers like a metronome, and Dieter was suddenly acutely aware of the fact that behind one of the doors at the top of the stairwell lurked Faber's bedroom. But which one? He decided he would try all of them until he found it. After all, where else could he hide if he wanted the rest of the night to follow what he thought should be its natural progression?

He found it behind the third door. It was large and sumptuous and very tidy, dominated by an enormous bed that was neatly and properly made. Faber's comb and brush were on the dressing table, and within that brush Dieter spied a single, silky strand of dark blonde hair. He wanted to touch that hair, but turned away to look elsewhere in the room.

He opened a drawer in the bedside table and found a book. Curious, he took a look. Freud's *Das ich und das Es.** Obviously a lucky find in a French used bookstore, since there were no more copies in the original German anywhere in the Reich. That it was, of course, a forbidden book, only gave Faber greater allure in Dieter's eyes.

Faber's voice drifted upstairs again. He was nearing the end of his countdown. There was no more time to think about where to hide. Dieter spotted Faber's wardrobe, went over to it and climbed in, closing the door behind him.

He found himself surrounded by Faber's uniforms, which dominated the narrow wardrobe. To one side hung an emerald-green smoking jacket and a few pairs of civilian slacks, most likely worn only at home. Faber never appeared out of uniform outside of that townhouse.

The uniforms themselves were immaculate, and all bore Faber's distinct scent, a mixture of pipe tobacco, fresh soap and the special imported ink he used to write all his reports. Faber never wore cologne, the way Dieter often did; he considered it merely "perfume for men," and he didn't like much perfume on his women, either. Faber's olfactory glands were acutely sensitive and easily bothered by artificial scents.

Now it was Dieter who inhaled deeply, breathing in Faber's special scent. In front of him hung one of Faber's daily uniforms. Dieter wrapped his arms around that uniform, embraced it as though he could conjure up Faber's body within it and embrace the man himself, whom he loved so deeply. He rubbed his lips and nose against the rough cloth and breathed deeply, lost in the pleasure of it. Soon, very soon—he would be in Faber's arms—

"I have a feeling, my dear boy, that you are not downstairs at all," Faber's voice boomed. "No, indeed you are not."

There was something different in Faber's voice. The mirth that had been there at the beginning of the game was now gone, and the menace had returned. Dieter shivered as he heard Faber's slow footfall start up the stairs.

"That was quite a little tale you told me tonight," Faber said. "Poor, innocent little Dieter, who wanted only love from his cousin and suffered such violation instead. Such a sad little story—but that's exactly what it is, isn't it? A story."

Dieter froze. A chill ran up his spine.

"Made up with the intent to arouse my sympathies as well as my love, no doubt. But you should know by now that you can never fool me, Dieter. I will always find you out."

Dieter's mind was racing. He knew. Somehow, Faber knew. He had been a fool to think that he could have deceived Faber. A stupid, stupid fool.

"And such a pathetic attempt. I expected more from you, much more."

Dieter backed up against the rear of the wardrobe. He had heard that tone in Faber's voice before, and what usually followed was far from pretty.

"You have a story, Dieter my boy, but that isn't it."

Dieter was terrified now, more terrified than he had ever been in his life.

"No, your story is much more shameful, is it not?" Faber had reached the top of the stairs.

"Now where would I hide," he mused, "if I wanted to be easily caught? Really, Dieter, this is so beneath you."

The bedroom door opened.

"Tsk, tsk, tsk. So ridiculously easy. And what was the purpose of this little tale of yours, my boy? What on earth were you hoping to accomplish by acting out your idea of a confession to Father Faber?

"The truth is that your adored Cousin Dieter rejected you, didn't he? He refused the pathetic offering of a scrawny, pallid little boy. And from that moment on, he treated you with all the contempt you deserved."

Faber stood right in front of the wardrobe. Inside, the sweat began to run down Dieter's brow.

"And that experience shaped your entire future, didn't it? Molded you into the bully you are now, a bully identical to all those who tormented you throughout your youth.

"What is that American saying? If you can't beat them, you must join them? You certainly did very well in that regard didn't you? Even down to that ridiculous pomade in your hair."

Faber swung open the wardrobe doors, reached into the back, pulled out Dieter and flung him to the floor. He knelt over him and, with one hand, grasped him by the throat and began to squeeze.

"We are both hunters, you and I," Faber told him, as Dieter struggled in his grasp. "The difference between us is that I don't feel the need to bully or torture my prey. I get exactly what I want without resorting to violence—either physically or verbally."

The tears began to spill then, and Faber snorted in disgust. "I'm rather appalled that I want you at all," he told the quivering figure, "but I do." He ran his free hand down Dieter's bare chest and onto the white undershorts, squeezing the undiminished bulge there.

"Yes," Faber went on, his voice thick. "I want you very much indeed, Dieter. And I will have you. But not necessarily in the way you'd like me to."

The tears were running faster now, and Dieter's shoulders began to heave with barely suppressed sobs. In one swift move, Faber flung him over onto his stomach and knelt over him, covering him with his body. He undulated his hips gently, rubbing his arousal against those cotton-clad buttocks, and slowly ran his hands up that trembling torso.

"Such soft, soft skin," he breathed into Dieter's ear before sinking his teeth into the tender lobe. Dieter flinched.

Faber sat up. "This isn't much fun for me, I'm afraid," he said. "I expected you to struggle a bit more, not just lie there like a rag doll. What's the fun in that?" He leaned over Dieter once more, who shivered when he felt Faber's hot breath in his ear again. "Fight back, my boy," he whispered, and bit his ear again.

Dieter bucked back then, pushing Faber off him. The two men tumbled on the floor together, clawing, scratching, and pulling at each other. Dieter tore at Faber's uniform, struggled to pull off the tunic and reveal the man within. Faber fought back by sinking his teeth into every bare patch of Dieter's flesh that came in contact with his mouth, eliciting a sharp cry with each bite.

Faber somehow managed to shed his tunic, and Dieter gazed hungrily at the lean torso outlined in his undershirt and the golden hair on his arms. He wanted to bite those arms, to fill his mouth with that golden hair, and he was straining towards one arm to do so when Faber grabbed him and held him with that same arm securely around his throat. Dieter struggled to break free, clutching at that beautiful arm, straining to bite down into that warm flesh.

Faber brought his mouth back down to Dieter's ear, tracing it with his tongue. "That's better," he breathed. "How much more beautiful you are when you struggle. Now I am like Jacob, wrestling with the angel—'I shall not let thee go unless thou bless me'—"

He brought his other arm around Dieter's waist and pulled him closer, almost into an embrace. The words that followed were like a purr, and they set Dieter on fire.

"My beautiful angel. I cannot wait to be inside you, to feel you tight around me. To feel those long pale legs wrapped around my waist…"

Dieter moaned—a long, low moan so filled with primal need that it made Faber shudder and growl in return. Then something seemed to take over in Faber, some raw, feral power, and he flung the trembling creature from him onto his back. Faber stood up then and stepped over Dieter, one uniformed and boot-clad leg on either side of that pale, thin body.

Faber smiled sweetly down at Dieter as he began to undo his trousers.

"Rise up my boy," he said, as he freed himself, revealing a darkly sheathed shaft that rose and thickened further, one glistening drop on the pink tip that peeked from within.

Like a baby bird, Dieter rose up, mouth opened wide.

\* *The Ego and the Id*

## Part III

### Little Bird

Dieter rose, mouth open and hungry with both love and lust. With one hand Faber reached out and placed his index finger on that slender chin, his thumb on that red upper lip, and pressed the younger man's mouth closed.

"What a hungry little bird you are," he told Dieter, his thumb slowly and sensuously caressing those unusually red lips. "And such a beautiful mouth." He brought the moisture-slick head of his cock to that mouth, and began lightly painting it, leaving sweet, wet trails along those pretty lips.

Dieter's breath quickened, and his lips parted slightly. When Faber drew away from him he followed, leaning forward, his tongue sneaking out, ready to gather the silken, glistening fluid that now coated the tip, poised to sweep up every last drop. But Faber pulled away.

"Ah, ah, ah," he chastised the now trembling younger man. "My little bird is indeed hungry, I know, but I need time to enjoy the sight of you on your knees before me, those lovely red lips quivering, that sweet, pink tongue poised and ready. What a beautiful sight to behold, and look at what it does to me to do just that. I'm starting to drip, my boy."

Dieter's breathing grew more labored, emerging now in short, sharp and shuddering gasps. He looked up at Faber, blue eyes now blazing with an almost feral need, a sight that made Faber himself shudder in an equally powerful answer.

"Oh, my hungry, beautiful little bird," Faber breathed, his voice thick, his own breath just as labored. He uttered one more word, just one, but that one word was enough to light a fire deep within Dieter.

"Open," Faber said, his voice soft yet full of lust.

Dieter's lips parted, the lower one trembling. Faber stepped forward slightly and poised over that open mouth. He brought his hand slowly up his stiff shaft, squeezing out two fine, syrupy drops—Dieter's tongue darted out and caught them both.

"That's my boy," whispered Faber, as he continued to slowly stroke himself squeezing out a few more drops, all quickly captured by Dieter's nimble tongue.

That tongue had not even touched him yet, but Faber knew he was dangerously close to completion. He paused for a moment, closed his eyes, and gently squeezed that pressure point which would stave off the urgency, holding the hunger at bay while allowing him to remain fully aroused.

"Now," Faber said, holding himself ready. Dieter leaned forward, mouth open wide once more, barely stifling a trembling moan as Faber's thick shaft slid slowly, surely down his throat, leaving a fine coat of moisture on its way.

It was so wonderfully, so wickedly pleasurable that Faber let loose with a rich, throaty groan, his hips pitching forward slightly until he was fully encased in that slender throat. Dieter began to swallow, and the motion rippled along Faber's aching shaft. The older man was trembling all over now, and he watched closely while Dieter slowly drew back until just the head remained inside that lovely mouth.

"What a pretty sight," Faber breathed, one hand coming down to stroke Dieter's cheek, the other laying claim to a fistful of his hair. "My beautiful little bird feasting on me." He gripped Dieter's hair tightly, began to gently thrust between those sweet, red lips. The hand that had almost tenderly caressed Dieter's cheek snaked around to the back of his neck and roughly pulled him in closer as his thrusts grew harder and deeper.

He could lose himself in every sensation, Dieter thought. His mind was in a daze, yet every one of his senses was acutely attuned to that very moment, the taste and smell of Faber, the thick slide of his flesh between Dieter's eager lips, the almost honey-like flavor of the steady stream of fluid that oozed out and coated Dieter's hungry tongue.

Faber's breathing was now heavy and ragged, and every so often he let loose with a softly ecstatic moan of pleasure. Both his hands now gripped Dieter's hair as his thrusts increased in speed and depth. His whole body now trembled with the sheer, unbridled pleasure of every motion of his hips.

Suddenly Faber stopped, abruptly pulled out of Dieter's mouth, and with two fingers, once again pinched the tender head of his cock. He closed his eyes, and a mighty shudder ran through him, but he did not come.

"That," he told Dieter with a broad grin, "was what the Americans would refer to as a 'close call'."

He closed his eyes and shuddered once more. "A *very* close call," he breathed. He opened his eyes and reached out to once again brush his thumb against Dieter's tender, moist lips.

"As delightful as it would be to come deep in that lovely, slender throat"—he stopped abruptly, took a deep breath—"and as you can see, the thought excites me beyond words—I want to savor every moment. This is, after all, my Christmas gift. The greatest gift I have ever received—and shall ever receive." The smile he gave Dieter at that moment was warm, almost tender.

Then Faber suddenly whirled around, filled with renewed energy, and fell back into an easy chair in one corner of the room, legs outspread, trousers still undone, cock still erect, another broad grin spread across his face. He gazed at Dieter for a moment, watched his prize rise to his feet.

Dieter stood up, gazed evenly at Faber, saw the raw lust grow in his eyes, watched the man's grin grow slack with desire. It was moments like these when Dieter felt immensely powerful, when he knew he could control another man more completely and utterly than he ever could with violence or threats, and that incredible realization always left him slightly dizzy, almost drunk. It was tremendous, almost overwhelming to feel such power, and Dieter trembled with the pleasure of it.

Eyes locked, for a moment the two men simply gazed at each other, drinking each other in with their eyes, absorbing the sight and smell and sounds of each other. The air was thick with the mixed scent of male arousal and sweat, the sound of heavy intakes of breath, and the distant but ever-constant ticking of the grandfather clock.

The clock chimed. It was now two in the morning on Christmas day.

As they stared at each other, unable to pull their eyes away, the shared hunger of the two men—and, yes, love—grew stronger, shone brightly in their eyes. Dieter slipped a hand into his briefs, grasped himself, tugging gently. Faber did the same, taking hold of his cock and stroking it, slowly drawing his foreskin back and forth over the ruddy head.

"Come here, my boy," he told Dieter, the words a command, the voice husky and rich with passion. "My pet, my treasure, my love…"

Dieter slowly walked over, hand still tugging at himself. He stood between Faber's open legs, his knees nearly brushing the older man's arousal. Faber closed his eyes, inhaling deeply the younger man's musky scent. When he opened them once more it was to at last to pull down Dieter's by now by very damp briefs, and to bat the boy's hand away from himself.

Faber grasped Dieter's hips and pulled him closer until the young man's erection bobbed within inches of his mouth. Without warning, his tongue darted out and swept across the slick head, gathering the moisture there.

Again, Faber's intake of breath was heavy and sharp. Suddenly he leaned forward and engulfed that tender head. Dieter gasped with pleasure at the sudden invasion. Faber moved forward, took the boy deep into his throat and held him there, just for a moment, before drawing back slowly, letting Dieter's cock pull from his lips with an audible pop. Then he took the head in his mouth once more and sucked on it, filling his tongue with the sweet fluid that oozed from it. He drew on it for a while, eyes closed, drinking as though from a well, absorbing as much of the young man's arousal as he could, all the while squeezing and caressing those firm, white buttocks.

He grasped Dieter's slim hips more tightly, began to draw him in and out of his mouth, fucking the boy with his face, losing himself in the scent and taste of him, drunk with pleasure and power and passion, until he pulled back once more, let Dieter's cock fall from between his lips and watched it bob damply in the warm air of the bedroom as he struggled to hold back, his breath ragged and rough. Finally, he looked up at Dieter and smiled.

"Is that not the most amazing of all sexual acts?" he asked him. "To have a man's cock in your mouth. It is at once the most powerful and the most submissive act in human existence. There is no other experience that is anything quite like it, and I could no more forsake it than I could forsake the intimate taste of a woman, not only because I enjoy them both so much but also because I hunger for them both.

"But right now…" Faber's voice trailed off as he drew his hands slowly up Dieter's waist, "…at this very moment…there is nothing I hunger for more than you."

He leaned forward, kissed Dieter's belly, lightly sucked at his navel, then nibbled his way up that pale, white chest, pausing occasionally to lap up the light pools of sweat that had gathered along a fold of skin here and there. If he hadn't been so hungry for all this beauty for so long he would have licked and kissed every inch of him. But there was always time for that later, after he had satisfied his lust and left his seed deep inside the boy, marking him forever with his presence. The thought of doing so was so powerfully arousing that Faber began to nip and bite as well as to kiss the soft, warm skin beneath his lips.

Dieter trembled and moaned at Faber's every touch. He was aching now, aching to be held close and kissed on the mouth by this man who so masterfully manipulated the very darkest of his desires. He had never wanted to be loved and taken by a man as much as he wanted to be loved and taken—no, not just taken but ravished, devoured—by this elegant, sensual and brilliant Standartenführer.

Faber licked all around Dieter's nipples, soaking the tiny hairs there, pulling them into his mouth, tugging at them with his sharp, white teeth, all the while avoiding the two small nipples, which now stood proudly erect. Suddenly Faber sank his teeth into first one taut brown nipple, then the other. Dieter cried out, grabbed Faber's hair and pulled his face closer—

Faber drew back sharply, eyes dark yet fiery, and shot Dieter a look so contemptuous and cruel that the younger man shuddered in fear.

"Never pull at me like that," he told him fiercely. "Never. Don't *ever* try to bend me to your will."

"Bitte," Dieter begged, falling to his knees. "Bitte…"

"I know what you want," Faber said, his voice icy. "I've always known what you wanted, from the moment I first caught you staring at me when you rather stupidly thought I was completely unaware of those longing looks of yours."

"Bitte." Dieter was sobbing now, and the tears ran down his cheeks again. Faber drew back and scornfully surveyed the trembling, naked creature that slumped before him.

"Somehow that part of you that disgusts me also excites me," Faber told the shivering heap. He grabbed Dieter by the hair and pulled him back to his feet, ignoring the younger man's wince of pain, until the two were face to face, their mouths within inches of each other.

Faber's breath was even more labored now, and Dieter could feel the solid bulk of his erection pressing against him.

Suddenly Faber pulled him into a fierce embrace.

"I do the taking, my boy," he growled thickly, just before pulling Dieter into their first kiss, one so hungry and so violent and so passionate that it nearly overpowered them both…

## Part IV

### Brute, Brute Heart

That violent kiss took Dieter by complete surprise, but he fell headlong right into it, and Faber followed him. For a moment the two were lost in passion. Then Faber's lips and tongue took control, moving firmly but sensuously over Dieter's mouth. When he felt Faber's arms wrap around his waist, drawing him closer, Dieter slid his hands up Faber's back to clutch at his shoulders.

Faber's lips caressed Dieter's, his tongue darting out occasionally to tease lightly at that tender mouth before plunging deep inside. Their groins were pressed close together now, and Dieter moved his hips slowly, deliberately, rubbing his arousal against Faber's.

Faber gasped into Dieter's mouth, pushed him roughly up against the wall of his bedroom, his kiss hungrier and more insistent than before. He reached up and took hold of Dieter's face, pulled away from the kiss to gaze into those clear blue eyes. There was lust in that gaze, but something else as well, something Dieter hadn't expected: tenderness.

"I could eat you up," Faber breathed, "you delicious, delicious, glorious creature."

He kissed Dieter again, this time lightly, first on the lips, then on the cheeks, then nibbled along his jaw line. Dieter's eyes closed, his head fell back against the wall, and he moaned at the gentle yet firm press of those lips against his skin.

Gott, the boy was so responsive, melting at his touch—it excited Faber beyond belief. He couldn't remember ever having been so feverishly aroused. He dragged his lips all over Dieter's beautiful face, then down to his soft, tender throat. He ran his hands all over his pale, firm body. The boy was thin, but clearly not as fragile as he looked; his skin was as soft as velvet, and the sweet yet tangy taste of his sweat utterly delectable.

A tiny pool of sweat had gathered in the hollow at the base of Dieter's neck. Faber dipped his tongue into that warm pool, lapped it up eagerly. He began to nip and bite at that soft skin and found that the groans and gasps he elicited from Dieter only fed his hunger further, made it more urgent. He mimicked Dieter's movements, pressing his groin back against the boy's. They were both leaking a steady stream now, and Faber brushed one hand over and around both cockheads, coating them with their mixed fluids, then grasping both cocks and stroking them together with a steady, sensuous rhythm.

Dieter let out a quivering moan so needy that Faber couldn't help but answer with a rich moan of his own. He grabbed the younger man by the hair and pulled him into another eager kiss, his tongue thrusting as deep as it could go.

Without breaking that kiss, Faber pulled Dieter away from the wall, dragged him over to the bed and pushed him down on it. He stepped back to remove his boots, undershirt, trousers and underwear. Dieter's breath caught in his throat when he saw Faber naked at last. The older man's body was compact and masculine in its maturity, slender yet strong and very, very beautiful. He looked like a small but sturdy angel, and Dieter felt as though he had now become Jacob, ready to wrestle Faber wholeheartedly.

Faber's nipples were small, brown, erect, surrounded by a soft dusting of dark hair covering his pecs. His very hard cock rose proudly from a nest of soft, brown curls, the foreskin drawn back just below the head, which glistened with moisture. Dieter's breath had now lapsed into a series of irregular pants, and he reached out to Faber, his eyes an entreaty.

"You're so hungry." Faber's voice was seductive. "So desperately hungry and in love with me, aren't you?"

"Ja…bitte…"

"Ah, I do like it when you beg." Faber reached down, took hold of his own cock and stroked it slowly, suggestively. Dieter was mesmerized by the sight, and his breath grew even more labored.

"I love you… and I need you to touch me," Dieter breathed.

The boy's aching desire was so clear, so raw, that it thrilled Faber to the very core of his being. He climbed onto the bed and over Dieter, leaned down to give him a deep kiss. His cock slid more urgently against the boy's cock as he caressed every part of his body, unable to resist that silky, smooth skin.

He broke away to kiss the side of Dieter's face, then traced his tender earlobe with his tongue.

"Do you want to feel my love inside you?" he whispered, his breath hot against Dieter's ear.

"Ja, bitte, bitte, bitte," Dieter moaned, both hands groping at Faber's body, luxuriating in the feel of Faber's warm, damp skin against his own.

"Oh, you want it badly, don't you? I can feel how much you want it," Faber breathed. He reached into the drawer of the bedside table, shuffled around in it, pulled out a tube of lubricant. He sat up then, snapped open the cap and began coating two fingers. Dieter spread his legs in anticipation, brought his knees up, and heard Faber's quick intake of breath at the sight.

"You're so desperate for it," Faber said. He squeezed out a small glob of lubricant onto his fingertips, lifted Dieter's left leg over his shoulder, spreading him open. Dieter lifted his right leg over Faber's other shoulder, opening himself fully to him, his breathing now rapid and harsh.

Faber exclaimed softly at the sight, brought his fingers up, worked that blob against the boy's entrance and just inside, gently spreading the lubricant. Dieter moaned and pushed back against those fingers, tried to capture more of them.

"Stop right there," Faber said sharply, his voice cold and dispassionate. Dieter gazed up at him fearfully; Faber's face was cold and stern.

Then Faber leaned forward slightly. "What's the rush? Love must take its time," he said, as he slowly slid his fingers inside, a wicked grin spreading across his face. Dieter gasped, let out a low groan, and lifted his hips to pull those fingers in deeper. Faber slowly stroked his fingers in and out, twisted them, scissored them, then slid a third finger inside, eliciting another sharp gasp from the boy, who bucked up his hips to take them deeper.

"Mein Gott," Dieter begged, "please…"

Faber leaned over, bending the boy's legs back towards the bed, ran his tongue along Dieter's jaw and dragged it up to tickle the sensitive spot just below his ear. Dieter shivered with pleasure. Faber brushed his lips against his ear, sank his teeth into the tender lobe once more.

"I need to be inside you," he whispered hotly.

Faber slowly withdrew his fingers, and the dull ache that remained instilled a craving in Dieter so intense it was almost unbearable, and his head began to roll.

"Bitte," he cried out, "bitte, bitte, bitte, bitte—"

Dieter's voice caught in his throat as he felt Faber's cock slide deep inside him, and he let out a long, ragged groan.

Faber let out a deep moan when he was all the way in. He leaned his forehead against Dieter's, biting back his need. "I have thought about this… wanted it… for weeks," he breathed. "And now—it feels—"

"It feels good," Dieter cried, "so good—"

Faber interrupted him with a passionate kiss. "My beautiful boy," he whispered. And then he began to move, sliding the full length of his cock in and out, savoring each long, slow thrust.

"I want your legs around me," he breathed. "I want to feel you wrapped around me while I make love to you…"

Dieter brought his legs down, wrapped them around Faber's waist, then slid his hands up to grasp his shoulders, bracing himself.

"Ja," Faber moaned. "It's good…" his own breath was becoming more labored now. Dieter began to move in tandem with him, his heels pressing him in even deeper, his hips rising to meet each thrust.

"Oh, you love to be made love to, don't you," Faber said, his voice thick with passion as his thrusts increased in speed.

"Gott, Ja," Dieter cried out, "Ja! Faster, bitte, harder…"

Suddenly Faber pulled out completely. Dieter's legs fell from his hips as he watched him move back and away from him. Dieter looked up at him in a fog of confusion and lust.

"You weren't expecting that, were you, my boy? Have you forgotten what I told you earlier?"

Dieter couldn't muster up the wherewithal to answer, but continued to gaze up at Faber, puzzled. Faber returned that gaze with a chilling smile.

"I told you I would have you—but not necessarily in the way you wanted me."

Faber grabbed Dieter's hips and roughly flipped him over onto his belly, then pulled him up to his knees. He slapped the boy's pale, white buttocks, then parted them tenderly. He was sorely tempted to lick and probe that sweet, pink rosebud, but he knew all he'd get was a mouthful of lubricant for his efforts. Oh, well. Next time he would take as long as he liked to taste that part of his new lover.

Still, it was terribly tempting, and Faber couldn't restrain himself. He leaned forward and planted a firm kiss on that pretty hole, swiped his tongue quickly against it before drawing back.

Dieter shuddered and let out a groan so loud Faber was sure it must have echoed throughout the townhouse. Gott, if the boy reacted that way to a single kiss there, how would he react when Faber thoroughly explored him with his tongue? He shivered at the thought of what he had to look forward to, but quickly regained his composure.

"Quiet," he ordered, rising up and landing a sharp slap against Dieter's right buttock. He admired the reddened spot for a minute, then brought both hands up and began gently caressing those firm, young buttocks. Dieter moaned with pleasure.

"This is, without question, one of the most beautiful asses I have ever fucked," Faber said, his voice raw and husky. He bent down to plant several tender, almost reverent kisses all over it. Dieter writhed at the soft brush of Faber's mouth against this rarely kissed part of himself. Each whisper of those lips felt feather-soft against his skin, and he trembled violently. If only these kisses could go on forever; it was so rare for a man to genuinely worship his behind. An older boy had first done it to him when he was only eleven, and ever since, Dieter had craved it more than anything else. He closed his eyes and sighed in ecstasy.

Faber opened his mouth and let his tongue dance soft circles around that slender yet taut rear. He had never tasted sweeter skin and could easily have devoted a good hour to this exquisite endeavor. But he had something else in mind, something quite different. He leaned to the right to plant a kiss in the hollow of Dieter's buttock, and at the same time reached under the bed.

When Faber's lips were suddenly removed, Dieter shivered, aching for their return.

He heard the snap before he felt it, and then the sting came, sharp and acute. It came again, and again and again on both buttocks, and Dieter jerked at the painful shock of each strike. He turned to look over his shoulder—Faber was whipping him with a very thin cane, more like a switch, really, and the sensation of pain so soon after pleasure inflamed him. The impact of each strike slowly increased in speed and intensity, and Dieter couldn't help himself. A quavering, passionate moan emerged from his lips. He was close, so close. He was going to come…

Faber must have sensed it, because his hand was suddenly on Dieter's cock, pinching the head, preventing him from attaining the release he so desperately needed. Dieter's eyes stung with tears of frustration. Faber leaned over his back, and he felt the man's hot breath in his ear once more.

"I'll decide when you come, my boy," he hissed, and Dieter trembled at his words. Faber's hard cock was sliding along the crack of his ass, and he pushed up against it.

"Oh, did you want me inside you again?" Faber asked, his voice teasing.

"Ja…bitte…" Dieter was breathless now. Faber brought the head of his cock to the boy's entrance and rubbed it slowly around the hole, occasionally stopping to tease him with a light press against it. He repeated the motion again, and again and again until the tears of frustration finally began to spill from Dieter's eyes.

"*Bitte!*" Dieter shouted, anguished and desperate. "*Bitte, bitte, bitte—*"

And then the head of Faber's cock pressed into him and held still. Dieter tried to move his hips back to capture more of it, but Faber drew back every time he attempted it.

"*Please, no more,*" Dieter cried. "*Please, please, please make love to me, please—*"

He was cut off by a thrust so savage it nearly knocked him forward into the headboard. Faber grabbed his hips and held them fast in a bruising grip, shoving rapidly in and out, and Dieter grunted with each deep thrust.

"Fuck me," Dieter groaned. "Fuck me, fuck me, fuck me…"

He braced himself against the headboard, clinging to it as he violently slammed his hips back to meet each hard thrust. His prostate was being rubbed raw, and he was desperately clutching the headboard to keep himself from crashing into it. He couldn't let go to stroke himself and relieve the burning pressure. But he felt it rapidly build inside him, expanding and flowing throughout his body, until he was suddenly hit by a bolt of pleasure so powerful he couldn't contain it. A harsh shout erupted from his lips when he came, his untouched cock jerking as it spewed forth.

Faber leaned back over Dieter, wrapped one arm around his belly while bracing himself against the mattress as he drove into him relentlessly. He made one final violent thrust, sunk his teeth into the boy's shoulder and let out a long, loud groan. Dieter felt each powerful throb of Faber's cock as his hot semen spilled into him.

Dieter collapsed on the bed, and Faber collapsed on top of him, both men panting heavily. Faber rolled off Dieter and flopped onto his back, closing his eyes. Both men lay silent for a few moments, awash in the heady scent of semen and sweat.

In the distance, Dieter heard the grandfather clock chime once more. It was four o'clock. He thought back to those chimes at midnight when all of this had first begun—it seemed as though days had passed. He knew that he and Faber had taken a step forward together. He didn't know what that step was yet, and he was both frightened and exhilarated by it. But he knew there was no turning back. The relationship between the two had been changed irrevocably on this Christmas day.

Faber opened his eyes, turned to look at Dieter, and smiled. It was a smile of triumph and satisfaction, and somehow it brought a sense of relief to Dieter. He smiled back.

"Frohe Weihnachten, Standartenführer," he said.

"Frohe Weihnachten, Sturmbannführer."

Faber reached out and gathered Dieter against him. Dieter settled into his arms, rested his head against Faber's shoulder. They lay quietly together for a few minutes, basking in the tranquility of their shared afterglow. Although he had no idea what was to come, Dieter felt at peace. He had wanted this for so long. It had finally happened, and it had been everything he had hoped for and more.

Faber grasped Dieter's chin and drew him into a tender kiss. When he pulled back he smiled the same familiar, sly grin Dieter had witnessed in a wide range of situations, from the interrogation of a resistance fighter to the first assessing sip of a restaurant's finest wine.

"And so it begins, my boy," Faber said. "You'll soon learn that I am a man of many unusual needs. What you experienced today was only the very tip of a quite large, jagged iceberg."

Dieter shivered at his words.

"The question," Faber continued, "is will you be up to the task? Can you fulfill my love?"

Dieter didn't respond. He had learnt a great deal about Faber this odd Christmas Day, and he knew no response was needed. After all, neither of them could possibly know the answer at this point.

Only time would tell, Dieter thought. Only time. All he knew was that he loved this man profoundly, deeply, and he couldn't wait to see what happened next.

The End

# Electrifying
## Gibby Campbell

Alex was exhausted. It had been a busy week in the hospital, and she had stitched up one gunshot wound after another. The gangs of Rochester were at war again. By Saturday night, she had worked well over one hundred hours in the emergency department. Another trauma surgeon was coming in to relieve her at midnight. Alex was looking forward to going home and getting some sleep.

At 11:15pm, Joel Goldberg came in by ambulance. He was not their typical patient. Joel was a wealthy chairman who sat on the hospital board. He was also seventy-two and a lifetime smoker. He presented with shortness of breath, and Alex quickly diagnosed a ruptured bleb. She put a chest tube in and moved on to the next patient.

When she came back to check on him, she discovered the man was unconscious and hypotensive. A FAST check of the abdomen showed it was full of blood, and she realized she had accidentally punctured his liver. Joel was whisked away for surgery and spent four weeks in the hospital. By the end of his stay, a lawsuit had been filed.

This was the first one filed against Alex where she was truly at fault. Normally the hospital overlooked such matters, particularly when the doctor in question was so talented. But Joel sat on their board, so they had no choice but to fire her. She went home that night in shock.

Things got worse when she arrived at her apartment. Alex was a Domme, and she had a live-in male sub, Jeremy, who had been with her for over two years. That night she found him in bed with another woman. It was not just any woman, either, but a real Barbie-type who looked to be all of twenty years old.

Jeremy jumped out of bed and tried to look contrite. He even knelt down and bowed his head, but Alex didn't have the energy to punish him. Instead, she pointed to the door and said, "Get out."

Once they were gone, she methodically packed his things and left them on the stair landing. Only then did she allow herself to sink down on the bedroom floor and hold her head between her hands.

Where in the hell had it all gone so wrong?

\*\*\*

It took a month to wrap up loose ends, pack her stuff, and move to Boulder. That's where she grew up, and it felt like the safest option. Alex made the drive in her pick-up truck, with her beloved thoroughbred horse, Scott, in the trailer behind. She had arranged for Scott to be boarded at a local ranch. It had the best reviews, and she would settle for nothing less than the best for her baby.

She pulled into the JH Mountaintop Ranch two days later. It was bigger than she expected. There was a line of heated barns along one side, and a sprawling two-story house on the other.

Alex parked the truck and got out. In the distance she could see a purple mountaintop with the sun just beginning to set behind the peak. She had forgotten how pretty this part of the country was, and she breathed in the country air with a smile.

As she unloaded Scott from the trailer, she heard a deep voice call out from the house. "We're closed."

Alec turned and saw a tall, good-looking man walking toward her. His stride was forceful, and he had an angry expression on his face. God, how she loved a man who thought he was powerful. She ignored him and led Scott around in a circle to stretch the horse's legs.

The man finally stood next to her. "Didn't you hear me? We're closed."

Only then did Alex turn and look up at him. He was a good five inches taller than she was and had a muscular build. His tanned complexion spoke of hours working outdoors. His hair was brown and wavy under a cowboy hat, and his green eyes were sparking in anger. She placed him at about forty-five years old.

She thrust her hand out. "Alex Jones. I arranged to board my horse here."

He stared at her hand for a beat before shaking it. "You're Alex? I was expecting a man."

She nodded. "Yep, I get that a lot. It's short for Alexandra."

He barely moved his head in acknowledgment. "Josh Hanson. I own the ranch. You were supposed to be here two hours ago."

"I know. I got caught in rush hour. I'm here now, though."

He grunted and turned to look at her horse. "Let's see what you got." He peered at Scott and ran his hand down the horse's neck and shoulders. "He's a beauty, and he looks to be in fine shape."

"He used to be a racehorse," she proudly responded.

"I can see that. He's rather feisty, isn't he?" Then he turned and looked at her. "Quite a handful for a little gal like yourself."

Alex didn't bat an eye. "He is a handful, and most can't ride him. That's why I want to remind you that no one is to ride him here but me. Is that understood?"

Josh grunted. "A horse like this needs exercise, Ms. Jones."

"I'm well aware, Mr. Hanson."

He peered down at her. "And what is it you do for a living?"

"I'm an ER surgeon." She saw his eyebrows rise up in surprise.

"Sounds like a busy job," he murmured.

"It is."

He sighed. "I have excellent and experienced staff. If you prefer, I could even ride him. I've been on the rodeo circuit, so this here thoroughbred is nothing I haven't seen before."

"Nonetheless, I don't want anyone riding him but me, and that includes you, Mr. Hanson. Is that clear?"

"Crystal clear." He had an amused expression on his face.

Alex wanted to grab his balls and drop him to his knees. Instead, she said, "Why don't you show me where he'll be staying."

An hour later, they were done. Alex kissed Scott on the nose and gave Josh the briefest of nods before heading to her car. She adjusted the rearview mirror as she pulled out of the ranch. She could see the stud cowboy walking back toward his house. His head was held high, and he walked with an arrogance she found amusing. What she wouldn't give to take him down a few notches. But Alex didn't have time for a sub now. Instead, she needed to concentrate on getting her career back on track.

***

It wouldn't be easy. Alex had landed a job at a level 2 trauma hospital in town, and it was quite a step down from what she was used to. She now spent her nights evaluating abdominal pain and suturing minor cuts. On the rarest of occasions she got to do a surgery, but even those were of the simple gall bladder or appendix variety.

This was not where she wanted her life to be. Alex was an optimist, though, and she knew she would eventually move on to a better hospital. Until then she would hang in there and try to combat the boredom as best she could.

The staff in the emergency department helped. They were a lively bunch who worked the night shift, and they kept Alex in stitches with their antics. One nurse in particular, Janet, had become an unexpected friend.

Janet was a down-to-earth woman who never got upset. Her quiet and soothing nature worked well with the patients, and they all thought she was an angel. Behind closed doors, though, there was another side to the nurse the patients didn't see. She had a wicked sense of humor and often played pranks on the staff. She also gave everyone she encountered a nickname.

Once, Alex had to step in when a lab tech learned Janet was calling him "trauma trooper." He took exception to this, even though the moniker fit. The man showed up to work in combat boots and camouflage every single night. What the heck did he expect? Alex was able to calm him down before taking Janet aside. She made it look like she was going to scold the nurse, but instead she whispered, "We need to give him a better nickname than that."

"Like what?"

"I was thinking pencil dick," came the serious reply.

Both women immediately burst out laughing, and just like that they became friends. It had been a long time since Alex had a female friend, and she was enjoying the camaraderie. She was also settling down into her new life in Colorado, and the months passed quickly.

***

One particularly boring night at work, Janet popped her head in the break room. She had an excited expression on her face.

"Heh, doc. We've got a live one out here."

Alex sighed. Usually, that meant a mental health case. She closed the book she was reading and stood up, mentally bracing herself for the encounter to come.

Janet continued, "He's really unstable but walked in on his own. I have no idea how. He looks to be in a lot of pain. The best part is, he is one fine specimen of manhood."

"Which room is he in?"

"The Randy Rancher is in room four."

Alex chuckled as she headed down the hall. She stepped into examining room four and immediately went to the sink to wash her hands. Then she turned and looked at the man in the bed. Josh Hanson looked back at her.

His breathing was ragged, and there was a blue tinge around his lips. Someone had slipped a nasal cannula into his nose, but the oxygen wasn't helping. The man was clearly struggling, and he clutched his right side in pain.

"Mr. Hanson, you don't look so good. What happened?"

Josh stared at her in surprise and managed to gasp, "I thought you were a surgeon?"

"I am, but I work in the emergency department," she explained. "Now tell me what happened."

"Fell. From a horse," he gasped. She noticed he wasn't looking her in the eyes.

"Did you fall on your right side?"

"Yes."

She eyed his vitals on the monitor and saw his blood pressure was low. She turned to Janet and ordered a chest image. Then she reached down and pulled Josh's hands away from his body. "I need to see what we're dealing with," she said before gently feeling around the area. He gasped in pain.

"Right," she murmured. Then she looked at him. "I'm fairly sure you broke at least one rib, and you may have punctured a lung. We're going to take you down and do some imaging to be certain. Is anything else hurting? Your arm or leg?"

He shook his head. "No. Just the chest hurts. Is the lung thing serious?"

"It can be."

Just then a staff member came to take him down to imaging. As he rolled past, Alex called out, "Mr. Hanson. You weren't by chance riding my horse when you fell, were you?"

He looked up at her, and the guilt on his face was obvious. "You hadn't been out in a while, and he was getting skittish. I thought I could handle him. I'm pretty tough, Ms. Jones. I just didn't think it would be an issue."

Alex glared at him.

Ten minutes later, and Josh was wheeled back to the emergency department. Imaging had confirmed two broken ribs and a punctured lung. He had a hemothorax and would need a chest tube. Janet got everything ready and explained what they would be doing. Her soothing nature was putting Josh right at ease, but then Alex walked into the room.

The surgeon nodded at him before washing her hands, putting on gloves, and picking up a scalpel. "I usually use sedation, Mr. Hanson, but I need to get this tube in fast. You are very unstable, and it will take too long to sedate you." She cleaned the area as he looked on in panic. "The good news is you're tough. Wasn't that the word you used? I'm confident you can handle this." With that, she made a quick incision with the scalpel.

Josh gasped in pain, but Alex had already moved on to spreading his ribs and inserting the tube. His blood pressure immediately improved. Alex eyed the numbers on the monitor and looked down at her patient. "You did good, Mr. Hanson. I'll be back to check on you in a bit."

Once she left the room, Janet smiled down at the cowboy. "You're lucky she was on tonight. It would have been much worse with some of the other doctors." Then she left the room and went to hunt down Alex.

"Oh my god. What the hell was that about?" Janet whispered. "He was a bit sketchy, but you still had time to sedate him."

Alex gave a wicked smile. "I know. But I didn't want to, and I knew no medical board would question my actions. Tough guy, my ass."

"Wow. What did Randy Rancher ever do to you?"

"He rode my horse without my permission."

Janet nodded. She knew all about Scott and how much Alex loved that horse. "Is that all he did? Because if I didn't know any better, I would say the two of you had a thing going."

Alex shook her head. "Nah. Not that I wouldn't mind taking him for a ride, but he's really not my type."

"You have a type? Who needs a type with a body like that?"

Alex ignored her and headed into the next patient's room.

An hour later, she signed Josh's discharge papers. She wanted to admit him overnight for observation, but he flat out refused. After arguing about it for fifteen minutes, she finally agreed to give him an AMA (against medical advice) discharge. In return, he agreed to stay one more hour, and he also agreed to let her check in on him out at the ranch the next day.

Alex sighed as she watched him walk out of the emergency department. He held his head high and walked evenly, despite the pain she knew he was in. Maybe he was her type after all. The man had taken pain better than some of the most seasoned subs she knew. She idly wondered how he would take being bound and gagged, but then a gall bladder case came in, and her thoughts were interrupted.

\*\*\*

The next day Alex drove out to the ranch before her shift at the hospital started. It was after hours, so the place was quiet, but she still spotted Josh out by a barn. He was kneeling down mending fences. She shook her head in disbelief.

"When I sent you home and told you to take it easy, this is not what I meant."

Josh slowly stood and turned to look at her. "Yah. Well, tell that to the fences. They don't repair themselves, you know."

She pulled gloves out of a bag and started to put them on. "You don't have staff?"

He glared at her. "Some things I only trust myself to do."

"Like ride my horse?" she goaded.

"Yah. Well, I wanted to apologize for that. I should have listened to you. It won't happen again."

She nodded. "That's right. It won't. Now take off your shirt. I need to change the dressing and make sure everything is draining properly."

"That's okay, doc. I'm feeling just fine. I checked it earlier, and there's no issues." He started to walk toward the barn.

Alex followed him in, and the pungent smell of horses and manure hit her at the door. "I wasn't aware you were a doctor, Mr. Hanson. We had an agreement. Now take that shirt off, or I will take it off for you."

He arched one eyebrow. "Oh, is that right?" Then he turned and arrogantly walked away.

Alex watched his receding back in shock. She looked around and saw a lasso hanging on the wall. She grabbed it and chased after the retreating cowboy. Before he could react, she had the loop over his head and down around his shoulders. Then she hooked her right ankle around his legs, pulled on the lasso, and managed to bring him down on a bed of straw in the corner. His body made a solid thud when it hit, and she knew it had to hurt his ribs, but she didn't care. She was livid.

Alex quickly straddled him and squeezed his balls hard. "You need to obey," she barked. Then she unbuttoned his shirt and took in the bandage below. It was saturated with blood and fluid.

All Josh could do was stare up at her in shock and wonder. His ribs were throbbing, but he also felt oddly aroused. It didn't make sense, as she was being one hell of a bossy bitch, but he felt compelled to remain still. It was almost like he wanted to obey her, and that confused him even more.

Meanwhile, Alex had cut away the old bandage, cleaned the area, and placed a new bandage on the incision. When she was done, she helped him sit up and brushed a few bits of straw off his body. She could feel his heart pounding in his chest and saw the bemused expression on his face. She leaned in and gave him a chaste kiss on the forehead. It was something she would do with a sub during aftercare, and the thought startled her. Josh wasn't her sub, but she realized he would make a damn good one. She hurriedly stood up, reached down with both hands, and helped him to stand.

"I'll be back tomorrow to take the tube out," was all she said, and then she was gone.

Alex spent the rest of the night thinking over what had occurred. Josh was the epitome of a tough cowboy, and she knew he did rodeos, but part of her wondered if he might not have a submissive side as well. She had certainly seen glimpses of it, and for the first time in a long time, she felt interested in a man again.

***

The surgeon was true to her word and showed up the next night to take the tube out. Josh had worried about it all day long. He anticipated feeling some major pain, but it wasn't nearly as bad as he imagined. He was so grateful for this, and while she cleaned the area and put on a fresh bandage, he offered to pay her.

"I really appreciate you coming all the way out here, doc. How much do I owe you?"

She smiled. "You don't owe me anything."

"Sure I do. I would have needed to go to the hospital again if it weren't for you, and I really hate hospitals. Please. I'll feel better if I pay you."

She finished the wrap and leaned back. Then she looked up at him with a thoughtful expression on her face. "Well, I don't really need the money, but maybe there's another way you can pay me."

"Okay. Were you thinking of some free boarding time for Scott?"

She laughed. "Nope. I was thinking of something much more

intimate. Do you have a girlfriend, Josh?"

He frowned. "No. Most gals don't like my rodeo schedule. Too much time on the road."

"How about a booty call? Do you have someone you hook up with every now and then for a good romp?"

He shook his head in confusion. "No. Normally I just meet groupies at rodeos." Then he looked at her in surprise. "Are you asking to be my booty call?"

She laughed. "Actually, I'm asking you to be mine, but I'm not your typical roll in the hay. Remember when I lassoed you and cupped your manhood?"

He nodded.

"Well that's the kind of stuff I like to do. Much more than that, actually, and some of it can be scary. If you really want to thank me for treating your wound, then let's head into your house to discuss this in more detail. I would love to tie you up and take advantage of you, but only if you're willing. Not all guys can handle that. If this is too weird, then we can forget all about it, and you can give me a free week of boarding for Scott instead. It's your call."

Josh stood before her, and she could see him mulling things over. Then his face broke out into an uneasy grin. "I'm ashamed to admit that I'm intrigued by the idea. I guess it can't hurt to discuss it further." He took her hand, and they headed into his house.

They sat at the kitchen table. The house had an open floor plan, and Alex could see into the great room. What she saw was typical masculine décor including bold colors, comfy furniture, and paintings of horses on the walls. There was a stone fireplace in the corner with a few trophies on the mantle. She noted he was neat and tidy, and she could detect what smelled like stew simmering in a crock-pot on the counter.

"Can I get you a drink? I have a good selection of beer, or bourbon, if you prefer."

She could tell he was nervous. "I'll take some water. You should know, if we agree to do this, there will be no alcohol involved. It's too dangerous, and I prefer my subs sober and feeling everything I do to them."

He blinked as he handed her the water. "Sub?"

"Short for submissive. You know, one who obeys."

He pulled out a chair and straddled it. "I've never been one to meekly follow."

"You might be surprised to find you like it, Mr. Hanson. It can be very freeing to let go and let someone else take the lead. Kind of like a wild horse when you break it in." She took a sip of water. "Plus, it usually leads to some mind-blowing sex."

He took his hat off and placed it on the table. Then he ran his hand through his hair. "Well, that part certainly sounds appealing, but how would this all work?"

She smiled. "First and foremost we agree to keep things confidential. I have a reputation to uphold in the medical community, and I'm sure you don't want people knowing I'm tying you up like one of your steers."

He gulped. "So that's what you do? Tie me up?"

"Yep. And strike you with things. And play with your body. Basically, anything I want to do to you that's not off limits. You always have the option to tell me to stop if you can't take it, though. I can be pretty vicious when I want to be."

"That doesn't surprise me in the least," he replied drily.

"If your reaction in the emergency department is any indicator, you take pain quite well, Mr. Hanson. I would like to explore that side of you. But you're going to have to trust me, and we'll need some time for that trust to develop. The good news is, we have six weeks. It's going to take your ribs that long to heal."

"Are you saying I have to wait six weeks to get laid? I'm a fast healer, doc, I think we can bump it up a bit."

"Somebody is horny," she teased. "Don't worry. If you're a good boy, I will reward you at the end of those six weeks, and it will be well worth the wait."

He grinned at her. "I'm holding you to that. Okay, then. I'm in."

"Just like that? You don't want to think about it some more?"

"What's to think about? I like taking risks. Plus, I'm very attracted to you."

Alex peered into his eyes and got a bit lost in there. He seemed genuine enough. She proceeded to explain everything she wanted, and an hour later she drove off. They had hammered out all the details, and she had even given him a few tasks to get him comfortable with the submissive role. It had gone better than she expected. She knew he might balk at any moment, but she could see a hint of arousal in his eyes and also some curiosity. Only time would tell.

***

Five weeks later, and the ribs were finally healed. Alex had put Josh through some gentle training in the interim. He was a fast learner and had done better than she could have hoped. Each time he completed a task to her satisfaction, she rewarded him. Sometimes that was in the form of praise or a gift, but sometimes it was more sexual in nature. With the latter, she would take his cock in her hand or mouth and work it up until he was just about to orgasm. Then she would remove the stimulation and walk away. The poor man was left in a perpetual state of blue-ball agony, and he often complained.

Alex smiled as she thought about this on the drive over to the ranch. Tonight she planned to finally give him a release. He had earned it, and she couldn't wait to see his reaction.

"Babe." He had opened the door before she had a chance to ring the bell and smiled down at her.

She grinned back at him. "How's my good boy? I've been thinking about you all day, and thinking about what I might like to do to you tonight." She could see his pupils constrict. He had obviously been thinking about it as well. She knew if she reached down below his waist, she would be able to feel his hard-on through his jeans. It sent a thrill up and down her spine.

"I need you to strip down, darling, and then get into position on the kitchen table."

They had discussed her plans on their previous date, and Josh knew exactly what to do. He eagerly shucked his jeans and almost fell over as one foot got caught in the leg of his boxer shorts. Once he was free of clothing, he strutted to the kitchen and bent over so he was hugging the table. In this way his ass was proudly on display.

Alex reached down and eased the belt from his discarded pair of jeans. It made a swishing sound as she pulled it out of the belt loops. She walked over and gently caressed his ass cheeks with her right hand before dipping her fingers down into his crack. Her index finger teased his puckered opening, and she felt him stiffen.

"Relax, baby. I'm just having a little fun. Now be a good boy and spread your legs. Then put your hands behind your back."

As he did so, she used his belt to tie his hands together tightly at the wrists. Once he was secure, Alex pulled a wire brush from her purse. She proceeded to rub the bristles up and down his back and watched with satisfaction as the skin rippled with goose bumps. She did the same with his arms, neck, and the back of his legs before concentrating on the flesh of his bottom. Gradually, she started pressing harder, and now there were red streaks where the bristles had been.

Josh was still and quiet during all of this, but he let out an occasional groan of approval, which Alex found amusing. She gave no warning when she switched from massaging his flesh with the bristles to striking him with the wooden side instead. His muscles tensed as he sucked in some air, but then she watched him slowly relax and breathe in and out. They had been practicing this, and she was proud to see how well he was doing.

After the brush spanking, Alex moved on to a riding crop. She purposefully used one of Josh's from the barn, and she put it out in front of him so he could see it. His only response was, "Babe." She could hear the admiration in his voice, and also the arousal, and that made her smile even more.

Alex moved back behind and slowly began to strike his ass cheeks with the crop. "Try exhaling each time I hit you," she suggested. The strikes were soft at first, but slowly she began bringing the crop down more forcefully. She was also striking other areas of his body, and she felt the hum of power course through her arms as she worked him over. Occasionally she stopped to check in on Josh, but he was enjoying the session as much as she was, and he begged her to continue.

Alex could have gone on all night, but she knew Josh was too new to the scene, so she finally brought it to an end. He had done so well, and it was time to reward him with an orgasm. It didn't take long. She sensed when he was getting close and increased the speed and pressure of her hand. She could hear the guttural sounds he was making as he came, and she squeezed the last drops of semen out of his balls before finally releasing his manhood. Then she untied him and led him over to the couch. He collapsed with a grunt, and she sat on his lap and cradled him with her arms.

It took a few minutes, but then he began to stir. "Now it's your turn, babe," he said, as he reached for the drawstring on her scrubs.

She pushed his hand away. "Not tonight, my sweet sub. You have to earn that honor, and we're not there yet."

He whimpered like a child, and she kissed his pouty face. "Now then, how are you feeling? Do you need to discuss anything?"

He grinned at her. "Fuck, no. I think that was the best orgasm of my life."

She laughed. "You haven't seen anything yet. This is just the beginning of where I can take you, if you let me."

Josh leaned his head back and closed his eyes. "Oh, I'm fairly sure I'll let you do whatever you want to me. I'm a goner." He wasn't looking at her, but she could hear the emotion in his voice.

She was feeling it as well. Their relationship was more than just a Domme and sub hook-up, but Alex had been burned before, and she didn't trust her feelings now. She knew they were getting closer, but she wasn't ready to discuss it yet. Instead she pushed the hair off his forehead and gave him a chaste kiss. "Good boy," was all she said.

***

After that, their relationship fell into an easy rhythm. In public she allowed Josh to act like the protective, stud cowboy the world expected. But in private, he was to obey and submit. When he didn't, she quickly punished him. Once he really ticked her off at a rodeo event. She made him ride a carousel on the fairgrounds in front of all his friends. It was the first public punishment she had ever given him, and she worried it would end the relationship right then and there.

It didn't. Josh had a furious expression on his face, but he straddled the pink pony she picked out for him and rode it for all it was worth. As his buddies hooted and howled, Josh kept his eyes fixed on Alex. That's when she knew he was in it for the long haul. The realization scared her, but it also tugged at her heart.

They had only been dating three months, but she decided to take things further and suggested breath play on their next date. She explained what it was and then looked over at him. He had a stunned expression on his face.

Alex bit her lip. "I know what you're thinking. This is really hard-core shit. I've always wanted to try it, but I never had a deep enough connection with anyone to feel safe doing it."

Josh shook his head. "Wasn't this just all over the news with that baseball player? Why would anyone want to do this?"

She grinned. "You've heard of men hanging themselves for a good orgasm, right? This is the same principle. Only in this case, you would have a surgeon squeezing your carotids who knows what the heck she is doing, so there is less danger. It would still be a frightening experience for you, though." Then she laughed, "Well, until the end. Then it would be one incredibly euphoric feeling."

Josh chuckled. "Kind of like every time I hop on an eight-hundred-pound bull, strap my hand in, and take it for a ride? Yah. That's scary too, until the end, when I beat my record and claim another trophy."

She nodded. "In this case, your orgasm would be your trophy."

Josh pushed his hat up further on his head. "Okay. I can see it from my viewpoint. But why do you want to do it?"

That one made her uncomfortable. Alex knew if this scene was going to work, or their relationship for that matter, then she had to be brutally honest with him. "There's something inside of me that likes playing God, I guess. When I'm operating on someone, and I know I hold their life in my hands, it's such an awe-inspiring and humble moment. It gives me this wonderful feeling inside. Breath work would give me the same feeling… I don't know… one of power… one of control." She looked down at her hands self-consciously and then back at him. "I guess that makes me a bit crazy, huh?"

He shook his head. "I don't know. I worry more about what this says about me, not you. I mean, I'm basically putting my life in your hands."

She shrugged. "So we're both fucked up."

"Yep. I guess there's a pot for every lid, eh, doc?" he laughed.

They did the scene the following weekend. They talked it through in meticulous detail, came up with hand signals Josh could use to back out, and made sure Alex could see his eyes the entire time. Afterward, she cuddled with him on the couch and spoke softly as he came down from his high.

"That was incredible," he whispered.

"I know."

He looked into her eyes. "How about for you? Was it incredible for you? I mean, you still haven't had an orgasm with me."

She smiled. "I told you. That is a major reward for you, and we're just not there yet. But, yah. I got that feeling all right."

They smiled at each other, and Alex could feel their connection growing stronger. She found herself telling him all about Jeremy and then the lawsuit back in New York.

Josh was back to being protective. "If I ever see that loser, I'll deck him for you, that's for sure. But the lawsuit. It's not worth dwelling on, babe. You're human and make mistakes like everyone else. Seems to me it was a blessing in disguise. You're not nearly as stressed out here in Colorado, I'm thinking, and it brought the two of us together. Let it go."

Alex marveled at the wisdom of his words. In that moment, she felt herself letting go of the anger and embarrassment of the lawsuit. It was another step forward in her life and in their relationship.

***

Six months later, and the two had done just about everything Alex could dream of from a kink perspective. It was so liberating acting out all her fantasies, and she realized Josh truly was the lid to fit her pot. There was one more thing she wanted to try, though, and that was electrical play. This tapped into the darkest side of her psyche, and she was afraid to even go there, but she knew she had to. She brought it up over dinner that night.

When she was done talking, Josh started laughing. "Truth be told, I've always wondered what the steer feels when I use a cattle prod."

Alex rolled her eyes. With her man, everything could be linked back to the rodeo. "Well, I'm not going to use an actual cattle prod on you. That wouldn't be safe. But I would use something similar and specifically made for humans. The shock will whip through your body like a freight train, and you won't be able to resist it at all. That's actually what I like about electrical play. I will have utter and complete control over your body, and the sensation you will feel will be very uncomfortable."

"Damn, babe. Sadistic, much?"

She looked worried. "The DSM no longer considers that a disorder, but I do wonder if there's something wrong with me."

She was staring off into space with an almost childlike vulnerability in her eyes, and not for the first time Josh realized he was truly the one with power in their relationship. He put his big hand over hers and offered some reassurance. "I will always tell you if I don't want to do something you ask. You can trust me to be honest." Then to lighten the mood he added, "Like ass stuff. I keep telling you, there ain't no way in hell you're ever sticking anything up my ass."

And just like that, Alex was in control again. "Oh, we'll see about that, little boy. We'll see."

Josh just chuckled and rolled his eyes.

She added, "But seriously. Before I try shock on you, we'll need to make sure your health is up for it. When was the last time you had a physical? I need to get your heart checked, and it won't hurt to run all the usual blood tests on your cholesterol and such, just to be safe."

He sighed. "Why do I think you thought up this new round of kinky just to force me to see a doctor?"

She shrugged. "Like you had a choice. If I want you to get a physical, and I do, then you'll get a physical. You're not exactly a spring chicken. I know you hate medical stuff, but you should be checked out once a year. It can be with me or with your own doctor."

His eyes softened. "It's nice having someone who cares." Then he mischievously added, "And it's adorable you think I actually have a doctor."

She was appalled. "Joshua Hanson, what am I going to do with you?"

"Well, I'm hoping something naughty that involves me blowing a huge wad at the end, but we've already established that's up to you and not me."

She laughed. "Oh, my dear boy. You have so much to learn." She crooked her finger and led him back to the bedroom.

***

They attempted electric stimulation a week later. Alex started with a TENS unit and attached the pads to his inner thighs. She turned the unit on to a low voltage at first and asked Josh what he thought.

"This actually feels pretty good. It doesn't hurt at all."

She nodded. "I'm not surprised. People actually use these things on sore muscles as a form of massage. You should try it after a rodeo." She continued to place the pads on different parts of his body, but was careful to avoid the carotids, heart, and eye area. Once she was satisfied he could handle the sensation, she pulled out her newly purchased wand. It came with excellent ratings and a voltage that would be safe but still allow her to take control of his body.

Alex set the wand down and pulled out her stethoscope. She listened to his heart and carotids while he watched in amusement. She noticed the look.

"You should be grateful I'm a doctor," she said. "It comes in handy when you're in the scene."

"The scene?"

She put the stethoscope down and fiddled with the probe. "That's what they call all the kinky stuff we like to get into."

He raised one eyebrow. " 'They' being all the pervs out there? Can't argue with that, as you are one kinky chick."

"Says the man about to get his body jolted by some serious electrical juice."

His pupils constricted, always a sure sign he was turned on, but Alex needed to try the wand on herself first. She pressed the button and placed the wand on her inner thigh. It made a loud cracking sound and emitted a spark. She knew this was coming, but Josh didn't, and he immediately jumped up and grabbed her arms.

"Are you okay? That thing is defective. It could have killed you."

She reassured him. "It's supposed to do that. It's all part of the sensation. And I needed to test it on me first before I tried it on you. I am nothing if not cautious."

Now he was angry. "I don't like that. I'm the one to take the pain, not you." He was in protective mode, which Alex loved, but not when they were in a scene.

She stepped back and gave him a stern look. "Who's in charge here?"

"Well… you are," he stammered, "But—"

"But nothing. Get back on that bed and don't you dare move again."

He hesitated for a second but then gave her a slow smile. "Yes, Ma'am." He lay down on the bed and waited. He felt Alex sidle up on the bed on top of him. She rubbed her hands all over his body and started massaging his muscles. The massage slowly went deeper and seemed to go on forever. It felt great, and his entire body was warm and relaxed. When she moved off his body and the bed, he suddenly felt cold.

The first jolt hit him on his thigh and made the loud cracking sound with the visual spark. Even though he knew what to expect, the sound still startled him. The sensation was sharp but manageable, and he gave his Domme a cocky grin.

"Oh, baby," was all she said as she shook her head. Her face had a determined expression he had grown to love and fear, and then she brought the wand down on his body again. This voltage was stronger, and it zipped through his body like a thunderbolt. As hard as he tried to resist, there was no way to avoid the sting of the wand. With a crop or belt he could tense his muscles in anticipation, but the wand left him completely helpless and vulnerable.

Alex only zapped him a few times. Then she straddled his semi-hard erection and sunk down on it so he was deep inside of her. It took him a moment to realize what had happened. He opened his eyes and gave her a startled and lustful look. She had never allowed him to bang her before.

"Ma'am, may I?" he managed to croak.

"You may," she smiled sweetly at him.

That's all Josh needed. He sat up and fucked her like he was pounding his seed into mother earth itself. They were both making animalistic sounds, and Alex was meeting him on each thrust and squeezing his ass cheeks and hips as if to pull him in deeper. It was an intense and mind-blowing moment. Josh held on with every ounce of restraint he had until he finally heard his Domme howling out an orgasm. Then he let go and ejaculated so hard he swore his balls would explode. They finished and clung to each other in a mass of sticky and sweaty limbs as they waited for their heart rates to slow down again.

It took Alex a while to regain her composure. Then she started on aftercare, although truth be told, she needed it almost as much as he did.

"How are you feeling?" she asked.

He gave her a lopsided grin. "That was electrifying, babe. Get it?"

She laughed and snuggled against his chest. "Ha, ha. But seriously, was it okay? I didn't push you too far, did I?"

He wrapped his arms around her body and sighed contentedly. "Nah. It was an intense sensation and hurt like hell, but it wasn't terrible. Mostly I liked finally being allowed to fuck you. I'd been waiting for that moment for what seemed like forever."

She propped herself up on one elbow and kissed his forehead. "Well, you earned it. You gave yourself over to me completely, and I couldn't have been prouder. Thank you."

He nodded. "Right back at you, babe. This is more than just crazy sex, isn't it?"

She lay down by his side and stared up at the ceiling. "Yah," she sighed. "I have never felt this way for another man before. Truth be told, it scares me a bit."

"Me too. But I also like it."

"Me too," she whispered. Then to lighten the mood she added, "But seriously, can I shock you again? I really liked it."

His chest rumbled with the laughter. "Of course you did. But yah, you could do it again. The shock kind of reminds me of our relationship."

She frowned. "How so?"

Now it was his turn to prop himself on one elbow. He tried to find the words. "I don't know. You're not a typical woman. You're exciting. You take me on these intense rides, and it's even better than how I feel riding a bull. You're like a bolt of electricity to my system. You make me feel alive."

"Hopefully not in a bad way."

"Nah, babe. You're the real deal. I love you." He looked her right in the eyes when he said it.

She smiled and returned the gaze. "I love you too, Josh."

And just like that, they were in a long-term relationship. Sure, it might be unconventional to the rest of the world, but it worked for the two of them. Alex provided Josh with the excitement and risk-taking lifestyle he craved. She in turn found a level of stability and control in her life she had never experienced before. The two together were truly electrifying and lit up each other's lives.

The End

# Beginning Forever
# Virginia Wallace

## Prologue

I jumped at the sound of a loud bang, nearly cutting myself as I did.

Setting the knife down on the kitchen countertop, I wiped off my hands. No, I realized, my home wasn't being invaded…

It was just the doggy door.

I knelt down on the kitchen floor as a small wolf cub frolicked towards me. He was white, and slightly fluffy, with that roly-poly look that all small canines have. I'd never quite figured out why humans had such a fascination with puppies… and then this little guy came into my life. Then I understood.

"*Hey*, Charlie!" I said gaily, ruffling the fur on his head. "Whatcha got there?"

Charlie sat on his haunches, proudly showing me his prize: a dead field mouse. He wagged his tail furiously as he pushed his snout toward me, holding the bloodied rodent by its tail.

"For me?" I said. "You caught that all by yourself, didn't you? What a good *boy* you are!"

Charlie relinquished the mouse as I took it. I'm not over-fond of mice, but then, I don't particularly dislike them, either. Besides, his feelings would be hurt if I didn't accept his gift. He was only four years old, after all, and quite pleased with his handiwork.

At least *this* mouse was pleasantly plump, having gorged itself upon the fall abundance. I swallowed it down and scratched Charlie behind the ears.

"Thank you!" I cooed. "Now, no more snacks before dinner, okay? Mommy will call you when it's ready."

Charlie sniffed the air and barked in eager anticipation. I hadn't cooked the chicken on the counter, and I didn't intend to. But its scent, I knew, was as strong to Charlie as if it'd been deep-fried.

"Soon, honey!" I smiled, rising. "Now go play outside, but don't go too far. I'll whistle for you when dinner's ready."

Charlie took off across the open kitchen and living room, his claws clacking on the laminate floor as he lunged toward the doggy door. He crashed through it and took off across the front yard.

I reached for the sliced chicken breasts, getting ready to spice them and mix them with some vegetables.

And then I paused.

I walked across the kitchen and opened the glass door that opened onto the screened-in porch.

I stepped outside and looked through the screen, breathing in the twin scents of blossom and decay, death and life. The waters of North Carolina's Back Bay spread out before me, lapping gently at the rock barrier near the kitchen wall.

This rustic house had once been a hunting lodge, owned by a conglomerate of wealthy sportsmen. Surrounded on three sides by water, it was nestled deep in the swamps. Here, Charlie had room to run and play, space in which to figure himself out. This verdant heaven was nothing like our old home in urban Virginia Beach, and I treasured the sense of peace that it provided.

Normally, waterfront property costs a small fortune, but when this place went up for sale it went cheap. The hundred-acre lot upon which the old lodge sat was condemned as "wetland," and thus couldn't be developed. The lodge itself was grandfathered in as an existing structure. It was too far from the seven cities of Hampton Roads to make for an easy commute, and it was almost impossible to get a cell phone or wireless internet signal. Thus, the old lodge held value only for fishermen, hunters…

… and werewolves.

My name is Jillian. And things weren't always like this.

*I* wasn't always like this…

## Chapter One

### August, 1975

I set down my mug of beer, wiping the foam from my lips.

I'd been here all evening and was probably on my twelfth beer, just out of boredom. But my kind—the Deista'ari—are made of sterner stuff than men. I didn't even have a buzz.

I was just drinking because I *really* like beer, and upstate New York has some of the best brews in the world. It always did. Trust me, I'd know; I was born around the dawn of the twentieth century.

The joint was a restaurant called Wally's, in one of the old buildings in downtown Plattsburgh, New York. I'd been there for two weeks and found myself eating there nearly every night. The food was basic, homespun really, but tasty enough in its own way. Plus the old décor was pleasant and the staff were quite friendly.

It was busy that night, and the half-drunk patrons—college students, mostly—were talking loudly and stumbling about. Those that were under the legal drinking age had X's drawn in black marker on their hands, alerting the waiters not to serve them. Most of the marked patrons looked pretty glum about their situation and watched the stumbling drunks with obvious envy.

"Would you like another beer, Miss Jillian?" piped up a young voice.

"Hello, Dave!" I said warmly, ruffling his curly black hair. "What are you doing here so late?"

"It's not a school night," said Dave, giving me a wink with his large, dark eyes. "And Uncle Wally says we're busy."

"You sure are," I said, looking around. "I'd love another beer, if you wouldn't mind. Thank you."

"Everybody else is pretty drunk by the time they've had that many beers," observed Dave. "Especially the girls. But you're not. You *do* smell like a keg, though."

I laughed at that. "Maybe I'm just tougher than the other girls," I said. "Now run along before you miss an order, kiddo."

"Yes, ma'am," replied David politely.

He took off at that. I don't remember what the law was, back then, about having children serving beer late at night. But it *was* the seventies, you know?

America was a freer place back then.

The north wall of the restaurant was mirrored, creating the illusion that Wally's was bigger than it actually was. I eyed my reflection, occasionally interrupted as it was by the images of tottering patrons.

I'm fairly petite. And I suppose that most men would say I'm pretty. Actually, they have, although some didn't live very long after professing their infatuation. I'm blonde-haired and blue-eyed, and at a glance—at least in the mid-seventies—I could pass for eighteen. Which is why little Dave 'carded' me the first few times I came in to eat.

So why was I there? What was I doing at Wally's that night? I guess I should start at the beginning…

I'm from Virginia Beach, Virginia. That region is the world's second largest natural sea-harbor, and a massive hub of commerce.

And let's face it. Where there's commerce, there's crime.

My people—the Deista'ari, the hidden nation of werewolves—have had their thumbs on the pulse of the world's underbelly for millennia. It's only natural, I suppose. Our species is used to hiding in the shadows, preserving our bloodline by keeping our true nature concealed. So of course our world began to merge with that of human outlaws. Or at least, that was true for many of our families. Others still lived in the wild, preferring their more tribal customs.

Maybe those tribal customs are healthier, and better for our society. I wouldn't know. I was born of the "werewolf mafia."

I was in Plattsburgh, New York, because a gang lord named Lionel "Pimp Daddy" Owens had approached my family with an offer. My father, Fyodor Gwinblaidd, was always a powerful player on the maritime smuggling scene. He was known to his contemporaries as Theodore Gibson, and he was *not* someone who tolerated failure… or meddling.

Pimp Daddy's offer was simple: he would run my father's massive profits through a string of phony businesses that he funded with prostitution and drugs, thus sanitizing the income so the Internal Revenue Service wouldn't notice it. For his help, of course, he would take a cut.

Now, my father made deals like that all the time. Such arrangements were business as usual. But there was just one small problem: Pimp Daddy wasn't supposed to know about my father's operation, and that made his very existence a security risk.

When the Deista'ari decide that someone is a threat, we have a simple method of eliminating said threat: we deploy a Bloody Fang—an assassin.

*I* was such an assassin.

Pimp Daddy's people tipped him off that there was a price on his head, so I lost him in Norfolk, the city adjacent to Virginia Beach. I knew he'd fled, but I didn't know where.

A little research revealed to me that he was a native of Plattsburgh and had begun his criminal career there by running a string of underground strip clubs, all of which he'd started up with drug money.

So there I was, just waiting. I'm the patient sort. My kind doesn't reckon time the same way that humans do.

But on that night, my patience paid off.

I couldn't believe it when Pimp Daddy just walked in like he owned the place. How *stupid* can a man be?! He was dressed to the nines, in flashy colors and way too much jewelry. All he was missing to suit the stereotype was a gold cane. Pimp Daddy was a scrawny red-head, almost laughable in appearance. He only commanded respect because he truly was a criminal mastermind.

Until, of course, he pissed off my father.

I started to rise, thinking that Pimp Daddy was going to take a table. But he didn't; he walked toward the kitchen instead.

I cocked my head, listening. Pimp Daddy had also run extortion rackets when he was in Plattsburgh. Was he up to his old tricks already? Didn't he have enough sense to lay low, as he was being hunted by the most powerful cartel on the planet?

Apparently not.

I could hear shouting in the kitchen. The shouting was clearly coming from Pimp Daddy and old Wally—young Dave's granduncle.

I rose, heading for the kitchen…

And then a gunshot rang out.

I barely held my feet as the patrons scattered in terror. As the place emptied out, the kitchen door flew open.

Wally stumbled out, clutching his chest. He stared at me with bulging eyes, gasping. I could smell his blood in the air, hot, dank, and reeking of fading life.

Then he fell onto his face.

I heard the back door being thrown open, so I bolted through the front door. I ran down the sidewalk and ducked into the alley into which the kitchen door opened.

You can't outrun a Deista'ari. It's simply not possible. If we come after you, say your fucking prayers and hope you don't bleed out before you get your last rites.

I slammed Pimp Daddy against the wall, snarling.

"WHY?!" I demanded.

I was tempted to shift into my most terrifying form: the half-wolf.

Humanoid in body, but furred, and wolven in the head. That shape is strong, powerful, even more so than the full-wolf form that my kind can also take.

But the half-wolf is a bit noticeable in public, so I settled for a partial shift. I allowed my teeth to elongate and my claws to emerge from my slender fingertips. My eyes were glowing yellow, I knew; I could feel them burning.

"WHY?!" I repeated. My voice sounded bestial, raspy. I couldn't help it.

"Why *what*, bitch?" whimpered Pimp Daddy. "What the fuck do you *want*?!"

That was a bad choice of words on Pimp Daddy's part. I *hate* being called a bitch! The elders among my species often call their women that, and the word always made me cringe. It seemed so demeaning, so dismissive.

I roared as I slashed Pimp Daddy's throat, spraying his blood all over the alley. I could smell it clearly; it was hot and sweet, and beautifully flavored with adrenalin.

I slammed Pimp Daddy down on the asphalt and raised my hand.

I wanted his *heart*!

The human heart has always been my favorite thing to eat. It's toothsome and savory. I always looked forward to that first bite, when the nerves are still making the tissue quiver, and the blood is still hot.

I'd been hunting this clown for weeks. I'd *earned* this!

Pimp Daddy spat a mouthful of blood as I plunged my hand into his chest, breaking his ribs like toothpicks. I wrapped my hand around his still-beating heart, relishing the feel of it pulsing against my palm.

Flexing my shoulder, I ripped it from his chest.

The aorta sprays blood for about six feet whenever it's violently severed or torn. I howled as Pimp Daddy's blood splattered all over the alley yet again, overwhelming my senses with its deliriously delicious smell.

I held the quivering heart to my face, taking a deep whiff. Oh, this was going to be *wonderful*!

I opened my mouth, preparing to sink my fangs into that delicacy of delicacies…

"Miss *Jillian*?!"

I paused and looked toward the kitchen door.

Young Dave was staring at me, his dark eyes wide with terror.

I stood up and dropped the heart.

I was appalled, aghast. The dark doings of adults should be *reserved* for adults. There are some things that children simply should not see!

Confused and ashamed, I fled the alley.

## Chapter Two

### March, 1999

"Let's run through this one more time," I said sternly, resting my hand on my holstered sidearm. "Without the theatrics, shall we?"

"Dammit, I *told* you already!" moaned our witness. "I saw a wolf chase that guy down and tear him to shreds. I was just taking a walk in the *park*, for God's sake!"

"The evidence says otherwise," I said coolly, nodding to my partner. "Show him, Chuck."

Chuck was an older man, and somewhat portly. People often mistook him and me for father and daughter when we went out. Either that, or some creepy guy with a late-life crisis and his gold-digging girlfriend.

Chuck opened a file and threw a picture down on the table.

"The man you said was torn apart by a wolf," he said flatly, "was found shot in the back. His wallet was missing, as was his watch. Does this body *look* mangled to you? Do you know what the consequences are for making a false statement to an officer?"

"I… I know what I saw," quavered the witness. "Please, you have to believe me!"

"I think we can write this off as a delusion born of stress," I said, tapping on the mirrored glass window. "But if you speak of this to anyone—and I *do* mean anyone—expect to face charges for impeding a police investigation. Am I understood?"

"So I can go, then?"

"Yes," I replied. "On the condition of silence. Start blabbing this story around, and the Virginia Beach Police Department will come knocking on your door. Now get the hell out of here."

Our witness lunged up as the officer outside unlocked the door to the interrogation room and took off like a shot.

"Hopefully that's the end of that," sighed Chuck, running a hand through his thinning hair as we left the room. "Who actually offed that guy, anyway?"

"My cousin Eddie," I moaned. "He's a right bastard sometimes. I had to hunt for half the night before I found someone who resembled his victim. Then I had to drug the coroner—again—so I could switch the bodies. Then there was swapping out the reports, the fingerprint files…"

"That coroner's going to end up completely addled from all the drugs. It's a good thing your dad pays you," said Chuck, holding open the door to our shared office for me. "I'll be damned if *I'd* do all that shit on a detective's salary."

"He pays *you*, too," I said with a wink, pulling out the chair at my desk.

"Don't sit down just yet, Jillie," said Chuck, unlocking the top drawer to the filing cabinet. "You have another assignment. It's not from the captain; this one's off the books."

"*Again?*" I moaned. "Good grief, which dumb pup did what *this* time?!"

Chuck opened the folder and dropped a picture on my desk.

"Well," I said, picking it up. "*He's* a handsome one!"

"He won't be for long," said Chuck grimly. "He's a crane operator, down at the docks in Portsmouth."

"Does Mr. Crane Operator have a name?"

"No, at least not yet," said Chuck. "He often unloads ships with government ties—weapons, mostly. Since he does, he has a high security clearance and his records are pretty hush-hush."

"Oh, c'mon!" I said. "We can get his records. We always do."

"We will," said Chuck firmly. "But it'll take some doing. That picture was enhanced from ATM footage near the docks. We hacked the camera, but we haven't gotten his banking information yet. We also got a picture of his car leaving work last night."

"Why the hell am I hunting this guy, again?"

Chuck just lowered his glasses and gave me a look.

"Right," I sighed. "He unloaded one of our ships, didn't he? We're worried he got a look at the…"

"Cargo manifest, yes," finished Chuck.

"So did we get his license plate?" I asked.

"We will. But this photo was taken last night and he's not back to work yet. Must have the day off."

Chuck handed me another photo, the grainy image of a white car pulling out of a parking lot.

"Nice ride," I said. "Camaro Berlinetta. Looks to be around an '82. This guy's got taste."

"Fat lot of good it will do him."

"So… do you want me to hunt him down, while you clean up the mess? Or do *you* wanna kill him, and leave me with handling the details? Who's doing what here, Chuck?"

"You covered up Eddie's little fiasco, Jillie. I figured I'd let you handle the hunt this time. I'm getting too old to chase people down."

"Well," I smiled, giving my partner a wink. "I suppose if *I'd* fought in the War of 1812, I'd be a little tired too."

"Don't remind me," groaned Chuck, pulling a pack of cigarettes from his desk. "I don't remember which was worse, the redcoats or those damn French pirates. They both gave me a headache!"

"Go have a smoke, old man," I said, taking another look at the ATM mug shot. "I got this one covered."

"Of course you do," said Chuck. "You always *do*, Jillie-Jill."

## Chapter Three

I waited outside the gate of the Portsmouth docks, listening to the car radio.

It wouldn't have been that difficult to finagle my way inside, if I'd wanted to. But I had to play it safe; the U.S. Federal Government had a strong presence here, and besides I was out of my jurisdiction. This wasn't Virginia Beach.

As I sat waiting, I wondered idly why southeastern Virginia had so many cities jammed tightly together. The cities of Norfolk, Portsmouth, Chesapeake, Virginia Beach, Hampton, Suffolk, and Newport News comprised the sprawling metropolis known as Hampton Roads, and their borders were all pretty squirrelly. When I'd first started with the police department, I accidentally pulled someone over without realizing that I wasn't in my own city. I was only outside its borders by a few blocks, mind you, but the mistake earned me a reprimand anyway.

I sat up in my seat as a car approached the guard shack…

*There* it was!

The gate lifted, letting a white Camaro through. I started my car and pulled out of the parking lot. It was broad daylight, for which I was grateful. It's actually harder to tail someone at night, because your headlights are always the giveaway.

It was past rush hour, so there wasn't much traffic. I followed the car onto the main drag, heading toward the interstate.

It was hot, so I turned the air conditioning up. The car headed out of Portsmouth in fairly short order. No surprise there. Anyone with half a brain heads out of Portsmouth in short order; it's the Chicago of the south.

I followed the Camaro through Norfolk, until it took the off-ramp onto Little Creek Road. My prey was heading for the oceanfront. He would soon be within the borders of Virginia Beach, if he didn't stop first. I could throw my portable police light onto the dash and pull the car over, of course, but I felt like I owed it to Chuck not to make too much of a mess. It'd be better if I caught this guy somewhere private.

Soon we were heading down Shore Drive. Maybe this fellow had a beachfront condo, or perhaps he was going to The Jewish Mother for drinks after work…

Maybe he had a beachfront condo, or maybe he didn't. But he wasn't heading for The Jewish Mother, either.

I grinned as the Camaro turned down a side road.

Seashore State Park.

This clown was heading into a park. Suddenly, my job just got *way* easier! I turned off the main drag, and followed him in.

Seashore State Park is an expansive chunk of wilderness, smack in the middle of an asphalt jungle. It's part woods, part cypress swamps, and part of it borders on the Atlantic Ocean. It's interspersed here and there with trails, and my kind are quite fond of the place. I often went deer hunting in Seashore State Park.

The Camaro pulled up to the gate and parked in the small parking lot.

I watched as a tall man exited the vehicle. He locked the door, and started walking down the trail, past the visitor's center.

Only when he was out of sight did I pull up beside his car.

I simply waited. I wanted my quarry to be as far into the park as he was willing to go, before I took off after him. Werewolves and serial killers have one thing in common: seclusion is ever their ally.

After a while, the sun began to set. Soon, the park would close. Any cars left inside after that would be imprisoned behind a locked iron gate until the next morning.

It was time.

I climbed out of my car and took off my belt, along with my badge and my gun; those I tucked under the front seat. Then I locked the car and walked into the woods.

I took off my shoes, and then my top and jeans.

I smiled, suddenly feeling more feral as I unhooked my bra and slipped out of my panties. *In wildness is the preservation of the world,* Henry David Thoreau had once written.

Yes. Yes, it is.

After hiding my clothes underneath a bush, I took a moment to appreciate the feeling of freedom. I smiled at the rising moon, opening my mouth to set free my fangs.

I dropped onto my hands and knees, feeling a delicious sense of relief as my bones shifted. I could feel the fur sprouting from my body and my tail growing and elongating. The dank, sour smell of nearby swamp-water grew more pungent as my snout elongated, and the clacking of cicadas became a deafening cacophony as my ears lengthened.

Only when the Change was complete did I take off into the woods. Simply walking by the Camaro had already given me the scent I needed for the hunt.

I was tempted to howl at the waning sun out of sheer exuberance, but I knew better. This park *was* inside a major city, after all.

My prey had taken the trail, and so did I. But I took care to run alongside it, staying under cover. I could smell my kin all around me; Seashore State Park was our sanctuary. My quarry would be safe here, though, at least from the others. The Deista'ari were always forbidden to kill humans within these borders, lest we draw undue attention to our refuge. There was only one exception to the 'no killing' rule…

It didn't apply to Bloody Fangs hunting a sanctioned target.

I charged alongside the trail at a dead run, glorying in my un-leashed canine form. My prey's scent became increasingly easier to follow, as he shed drops of sweat onto the dirt path. After ten miles or so, his scent was so strong that I could almost taste him.

I veered off the path, slowing my pace as I slipped into the brush. The sun was setting now, and the moon was rising. The air smelled of salt and brine; the ocean was near. I could hear seawater lapping gently against a sandy shore.

I crouched low as I approached the beach, keeping to the brush as

I looked about for my soon-to-be victim. I wanted to see *him* before he saw *me*…

And there he was.

I raised my ears, listening. I could tell by his breathing that my intended victim was asleep.

I crept softly across the sand, silently, stealthily, until I was standing next to him.

He was lying on his back, using his now-discarded shirt as a pillow. His scent was nearly over-powering now, musky, masculine, and…

Well, somewhat arousing.

I padded softly around his slumbering form, admiring him against my will. He was in perfect shape, and obviously worked out often. I crept a bit closer, eyeing the face that I'd only seen in an ATM photo.

He was almost Italian in appearance, with a slight olive complexion. His long, black, sweaty curls were a mess, and I thought in amusement that he'd have trouble washing the sand out of his hair later.

And he was handsome…

Very, *very* handsome.

I sat on my haunches, just watching him sleep. I could kill him anytime I wished, I told myself. There was no hurry.

Something about the man was strangely familiar. Had I known a relative of his, perhaps? Or did he just remind me of someone else?

I must have gotten lost in my thoughts for a few minutes…

Because when I looked down at the man's face again, he was looking back at me.

"Hello, you," he whispered, his dark eyes reflecting the silver moon. "Are you lost?"

I was insulted, but I knew that I shouldn't have been. I'm smaller than most of my kin. And I'm white, not gray, so I'm easy to mistake for a husky, or a German shepherd hybrid.

"What are you doing out here?" The man reached for my snout, slowly, careful not to make any sudden moves.

*Kill him*, I told myself.

"It's okay," cooed the man, moving his hand ever closer to my snout. "Don't be afraid."

*KILL him*!

I looked into his eyes, hoping to see some trace of fear, something that would summon a sense of contempt in my heart. Something that would make me feel… *justified.*

I saw nothing of the sort. I saw only kindness and concern.

Confused, I bolted.

I ran back to the parking lot, as fast as my legs could carry me. I charged recklessly down the middle of the trail, making no attempt whatsoever at stealth. I dressed hastily and headed for my car.

The gate was locked. I snapped the chain impatiently, pulling it apart like a rubber band, and threw the gate open.

I roared off down Shore Drive…

But not before noting the license plate number of the Camaro.

\*\*\*

I shut the office door behind me, grateful that Chuck wasn't in. I'd come straight here from the park, still panting from exertion.

I turned on my computer and accessed the Division of Motor Vehicles database.

I froze when I ran the Camaro's plate number.

*No*, I thought. *This can't be!*

My fingers trembled as I typed in a request for the driver's license number of its owner…

I jumped up, kicking my chair as I stared at the image before me. There it was, the image of the man I'd been hunting, the man who'd nearly touched me.

*Now* I knew why he looked so familiar. I whispered his name aloud, feeling my heart pounding in my ribs: *David Wollstonecroft.*

David Wollstonecroft…

His family, once upon a time, owned a restaurant called Wally's. David, once upon a time, called me Miss Jillian.

To me, he had simply been Dave.

And I realized suddenly that I could never kill him.


## Chapter Four

"What's gotten into you, Jillie?" asked Chuck softly. "This isn't like you at all."

"There's no point in killing him," I said, knowing that I was lying to my dearest friend. "He doesn't know anything. Given his security clearances, his job, why put ourselves on the radar over him?"

"How do you *know* he doesn't know anything?"

"I've been researching him." Which was true. I had, but not for the reasons that Chuck would have expected. "He doesn't have any shady connections, especially not to us. He even messes up his paperwork half the time, because he hates filling it out. And we think he's a threat because he may have glanced at a manifest? All he wants to do is run his crane."

Chuck gave me a long, hard look.

"I'll have a chat with your father," he said at last. "Old Fyodor won't like your position, but he'll listen to me. Have you and he talked lately?"

"No." My father was a hard man, and we'd never been close.

"Well, I'll handle this. I'll call you and let you know how it goes, okay?"

"You can get him out of this?" I pleaded.

"I can get him out of this," assured Chuck. "But remember, this kind of behavior is only ever forgiven *once*, understand?"

"I've been a loyal Fang for most of my life, Chuck. I would think this shouldn't be too hard."

Chuck rose and took his hat from the stand next to the door. "It shouldn't be, but it will. But don't worry, I'll come through. See you later, Jillie-Jill."

I leaned back in my chair, sighing with relief.

***

I left shortly after Chuck and took off for home.

Somehow, it didn't occur to me that Shore Drive was out of my way. Maybe I was just bored. Maybe I was just reliving a recent memory.

Maybe I was *looking* for something.

Or maybe I wasn't… but either way, I found it.

The white Camaro pulled out in front of me as I waited at a traffic light, turning down Shore Drive ahead of me. I don't know what I was thinking, but for some reason I threw my portable police light onto the dashboard and flipped it on.

The Camaro turned into a parking lot, and I pulled up behind it, aghast.

What the fuck was I *doing*?!

My legs were actually shaking as I stepped out of my car and walked toward the Camaro.

The window was already rolled down, and there he sat: David Wollstonecroft.

"Hello, Officer," he said pleasantly. "May I see your identification, please?"

That was supposed to be *my* question, but I knew what he meant. I was in plain clothes and driving an unmarked vehicle. My service weapon was concealed in my waistband, underneath my blouse. David had every right to request identification.

I pulled out my badge and police ID and held them out for his inspection.

"Jillian Gibson, Detective," read David, still smiling as he kept his hands on the steering wheel. "What can I do for you, Detective Gibson?"

Dammit, *now* what?!

I'd spent a lifetime lying my way out of tough situations. Why was I suddenly so nervous? I stood there for a moment, looking like a fool, right out in the open under the shining southern sun.

"Miss?"

"You… Your car matches the description of a vehicle used in a robbery," I said. "It was stolen in North Carolina. Is this car registered to you, Mr. Wollstonecroft?"

"How'd you know my name was Wollstonecroft, Detective?"

*DAMMIT!*

"I called in your plate," I lied, knowing that I was blushing. "If your identification matches your plate, and your plate matches your vehicle's VIN number, you'll be free to go."

"Of course," said David. "Just a second."

I watched as he reached for his wallet, and then pulled his registration out of the glove compartment.

*Dear god*, I thought with a feeling akin to terror, *he really is handsome.*

"Here you go, Detective," said David, handing me everything.

"Thank you," I said. "Wait here, please."

"Well," said David, actually giving me a wink, "I can't go anywhere without my license, now can I?"

"Of course not," I said, barely managing a wan smile.

I threw myself into the front seat of my car, not even bothering to turn on my radio. I wasn't calling in his information; I was simply collecting my thoughts.

Why was I *doing* this? I was attracted to David, and I couldn't deny it. But why? Shouldn't I still have been thinking of him as a boy?

I knew better than that. I'd watched dozens grow from boys to men, and I'd learned to look at them differently as they aged. That's the curse of coming from such a long-lived race.

Was I just looking for a good time? Oh, I'd had a few lovers over the years. Nothing serious, much to my family's dismay. I was a Deista'ari "blue-blood" and meant to marry one of the same, but I never had. I eventually knocked off having occasional flings, because they just felt so... *empty*. Fun for only a little while, and then came the sense of cheapness and self-betrayal. That wasn't what I was looking for by stalking David.

No, *I* was just lonely.

And *he* was handsome, friendly, and kind...

Maybe I was hoping that he was lonely, too.

I walked back to David's car and handed him his effects. "Thank you, Mr. Wollstonecroft, for your cooperation," I said. "You're free to go."

"Thanks," said David, taking back his license and paperwork.

I stepped away as he put his car into gear, giving me one last, easy smile.

"Wait!" I said.

"Detective?" asked David, putting the gear shifter back into park.

"I... Well, there's been a rash of car thefts in this area," I said, reaching into my back pocket. "If you see anything suspicious, I'd be grateful if you called me."

David took my card and held it for a moment, looking deep into my eyes. Then he glanced down at the card.

"When I call the station," he asked, "should I request your personal extension?"

I flushed crimson and looked away.

"You can ask for my line," I said softly, quite against my will.

"Thank you," said David, putting the card in the center console. "I'll be sure and do that. You have a lovely day, Jillian."

As he drove away, I knew that I'd completely lost control of the situation. I felt as though David had stripped me naked with his eyes, but not in a creepy way. No, he'd just seen right through me. A part of me hoped that he already had a wife, or a girlfriend, so that I'd never have to feel that exposed again.

And another part of me hoped that he didn't.

## Chapter Five

"Dammit, Chuck, who *did* this?" I asked irritably, looking at a photo. "This couldn't have been done by a Fang. It's too sloppy."

"I know," agreed Chuck, sticking a cigarette in his mouth.

"Don't you light that thing in here!" I warned.

"I won't. The body was too mangled, and I couldn't find a close enough match to switch it out. So I called in a bomb threat to the crematorium, and while the building was evacuated I just stuffed the corpse into the nearest oven. I know, we prefer to close our cases. But this one's just gonna have to stay open as a missing-person case."

"Well, it's better than the know-nothing officers trying to find out who butchered a jogger in public," I sighed. "The less the Flock knows, the better."

"You hardly ever use that word," observed Chuck.

"I try to keep a less condescending view of humanity," I said. "But it's hard some days. I just wish…"

Then my phone rang.

"Are you gonna get that?"

I don't know why I was afraid…

"Jillie, you're phone's ringing."

I picked up the receiver, clearing my throat. "Detective Gibson."

"Hello, Detective!" chirped a masculine voice.

*Dear god*, I moaned inside. *It's him.*

"How may I help you?"

"This is David, David Wollstonecroft. You pulled me over the other day? Said I should call you if I saw anything suspicious?"

"Go on," I said tersely.

"Well, it's like this," said David. "I've noticed some sketchy fellows hanging out at the oceanfront, mostly in the parking lot of the Hilton. Do you know the place?"

"I do."

"Well, they seem to be keeping an eye on the valet parking. I think they're casing cars, you know? And sometimes I see them around back, talking to the kitchen staff while they're taking smoke breaks. It seems the kitchen guys work for Salacia, that restaurant inside that overlooks the ocean."

"Your surveillance is most impressive. Can you give me descriptions of these men?"

"I could, but don't you think we should check it out? We could take my car; it's a classic, so you could put a tracker in it. Then we'll go inside, see, and have dinner in Salacia. It'll give those guys plenty of time to notice my car. And then we might also see the kitchen staff pulling something."

I felt my apprehension melting away, and now I was sorely tempted to giggle. "So *that's* your plan? Tracker in the Camaro, dinner inside, and see if someone steals it?"

"Sure. Dinner's on me. You guys work hard, so I'm more than happy to support local law enforcement."

"If we're taking your car, would you be able to pick me up at the station?"

"Friday at six? Sorry, I'd make it sooner but there was a waiting list for reservations. I hope too many cars don't go missing in the meantime."

"We could do tomorrow, you know, and eat at the Wendy's down the street," I teased.

"No way!" laughed David. "Wendy's is where a guy takes *ugly* girls!"

I blushed from the facetious compliment. "Thank you for your assistance, David," I said primly. "Friday at six it is."

"Thanks. See you then!"

Chuck was staring at me, with his mouth wide open.

"What?" I asked innocently, hanging up the receiver.

"Did that guy just ask you out by proposing a mock stakeout?"

Damned werewolves and their hearing, he'd listened to both sides of the conversation. "Maybe," I replied. "Why?"

"Clever boy," smiled Chuck.

## Chapter Six

"Should I wear the blue dress or the green one?" I asked, holding up both.

"Damn, Jillie-Jill, you brought your whole *wardrobe* to work!" laughed Chuck.

I was standing in our office, clad only in my underwear. I'd pulled the blinds shut and locked the door, of course, but it didn't occur to me to bother being modest around Chuck. Undress—and even nudity—isn't the same thing among my kind as it is the humans. It just kind of goes with our species.

"The blue dress matches your eyes," said Chuck, "and the green one compliments your hair. So just *pick* one already!"

I chose the green cocktail dress, and slipped it over my head. I'd considered bringing pantyhose, but I didn't want to over-dress for my date. But then, I didn't want to *under*-dress, either. In that sense, Deista'ari girls and human ones aren't so different.

I spent nearly an hour fussing with my hair and makeup. It was funny, I hadn't really used makeup since before I made detective, when I was the best fake hooker in the VBPD. Honestly, it felt weird to be donning makeup without also putting a wire underneath my dress.

I jumped as the phone speaker buzzed to life.

"Detective Gibson, there's a man to see you at the front desk."

Chuck smiled as he leaned over the phone. "Tell him she'll be right out, Stiles."

I gave Chuck a helpless look as I picked up my clutch.

"Have at him, Jillie-Jill," smiled Chuck, rising and kissing my cheek. "You *got* this, kiddo!"

"I love you, Chuck," I said sincerely. "Thanks for being here for me."

"Always," smiled Chuck. "Now *go!*"

I walked to the front desk, feeling strange in my high heels.

And there he was…

David stood at the reception desk, clad in a tailored gray suit. His crimson necktie had a perfect knot in it and rested neatly against his off-white shirt. He'd pulled his hair back into a ponytail, and my keen senses could pick up the smell of his cologne even across the room.

"I'm sorry, Miss," he said, giving me a smile as I approached. "But I'm looking for a stuffy police officer. Have you seen her?"

I paused, stricken by the compliment…

And then he handed me the bouquet of flowers.

My heart melted as I took them. I come from a world of bloodshed, lust, and arranged marriages. A world in which savagery ever intermingles with duty and overwhelms the usual social niceties that humans so cherish.

I'd *never* been given flowers before…

I must have looked like a fool as I wiped away a tear.

"Shall we?" asked David, holding out his arm.

"I forgot to grab a tracking device," I said stupidly. It was the only thing I could think to say.

"Oh, well," smiled David. "They can *keep* the car, so long as we make it to dinner."

I was so overwhelmed that I spent the entire ride to Salacia staring down at the bouquet in my lap. David didn't try to force conversation from me, for which I was grateful.

He opened the door for me as we arrived at the hotel and gave his car keys to the valet. He walked me inside, and the hostess brought us to our table.

David pulled out my chair for me, and I took my seat. He sat down across from me, still smiling. We had a small, cozy little table next to the fireplace. The far side of the room was all glass, letting in merry shadows that danced prettily around the ornate dining room.

"Thank you," I said impulsively, "for this."

"Aren't you supposed to say that *after* a date?" asked David.

"But I feel so grateful *now*," I replied. "I'm glad you called me."

"So am I, Jillian."

That was the second time that he'd called me by name, and I blushed like a schoolgirl. There was something intimate about the way he said "Jillian." The fire was dancing in his dark brown eyes, giving him a slightly impish look.

"Would this be a good time," he said, "for us both to admit that we're full of baloney?"

"I suppose," I agreed. "I pulled you over because your crane company came up in an investigation, and I saw your picture. I… I thought you were attractive. Is that weird?"

A part of me was wondering exactly what the hell had happened to my inhibitions, and a part of me was grateful that something *had* happened to them.

"No, it's not weird. I called you because you pulled me over, and I thought you were beautiful."

I smiled and set my bouquet on the table. I'd carried the flowers inside because I didn't want them to wilt in the car; they'd suddenly become very precious to me.

"That's sweet of you. I appreciate…"

We were interrupted by the waitress, who took our drink orders.

And then my internal dam broke.

There was something about David that shattered my guard. I

told him about my childhood, about my terrible father and simpering, kowtowing mother. I told him about how I'd come to work at the police department, and how I'd made detective.

I left a lot out of my story, mind you. But what I *did* tell was truthful. I couldn't lie to this man, even if I did have to make omissions.

We'd ordered dessert before I finished talking. "Oh my god!" I said, appalled. "I've been yapping away all this time! Tell me about *you!*"

David reached across the table, and gently took my hand. "Listening is just that," he said gravely. "Listening, not simply waiting your turn to speak. My story probably isn't any shorter than yours, though. Maybe we'll have to take a walk along the beach after dinner, so I can share it with you."

I squeezed David's hand, watching the flames flicker in his eyes.

"I'd like that," I murmured.

## Chapter Seven

And that was that. I'd fallen hopelessly in love.

I'd never before felt what it was like to kiss a man out of honest affection, rather than selfish, temporary desire. I'd never known what it was like to be held, and to *want* to be held. David and I grew closer and closer over the next few months, enjoying afternoon dates and romantic evenings on the beach.

I couldn't bring myself to make love to him, though. I was terrified that if I did, I'd be hooked, forever ensnared by this beautiful man that I'd once meant to kill. I wanted him more than anything, mind you, but I also knew what it would mean for me. I'd become *alltudwyr*: outcast. My family would disavow me, and I would lose my inheritance. I'd be alone...

But I'd have David.

And even that small comfort brought a stab of fear. I'd outlive David, and that by a long shot. I'd watch him grow old, watch him die, and then resume my life as a widow. If we had children, they would become fatherless fairly young. The children of Deista'ari are always Deista'ari, even with a human parent; our blood runs strong.

David was gentle with me and accepted my awkward, contrived explanation as to why I was hesitant to be overly physical with him... and that just made me love him even more. He respected me. He loved me for *me* and asked for nothing that I wasn't ready to give him.

He had to know. About me. About my world, my people… and what a future with me would hold for him.

***

David pulled into the parking lot at Mount Trashmore and parked the car.

"You've been quiet," he said, looking over at me. "You okay?"

"I'm fine," I said, unbuckling my seatbelt. "It was just a long day, that's all. I need to relax."

David exited the Camaro and walked around to my side of the car. He opened the door for me, as he always did. Most would consider that a small gesture, but I always found it wonderfully sweet.

I smiled as David kissed my cheek and gave me an affectionate pat on my rear end. I'd changed into a sundress before David picked me up at the station, and it felt good to leave my badge and gun in my desk.

I took David's arm as we walked into the park. There was a slight breeze tonight, and the sun was already setting. Fall was coming, but it was still warm out. The breeze carried the scent of the people and dogs playing in the park, but I could tell that there were only a few of each.

Mount Trashmore had once been a landfill, hence the name. The park had a small pond near the parking lot, and its man-made hills were a popular spot for joggers and kite flyers. I knew where David was leading me, because we'd come here before.

One of the hills overlooked Interstate 264, and its far side was always dark at night. It was a peaceful spot upon which to sit, to reflect, and idly watch the cars passing on the interstate.

I climbed the hill with David, enjoying the companionable silence.

It would end soon, the silence…

Because *I* was going to break it. We'd come too far now for David not to know the truth about me, and I couldn't procrastinate any longer.

David stopped at our usual spot and waited for me to sit before he flopped down beside me. I smiled down at him for a moment as he lay on his back, looking at the night sky. Then I fell down beside him, laying my head on his chest as he put his arm around me.

"Whatcha thinking?" I asked.

"I miss the stars," said David.

"Well, *there* they are!" I said brightly. "I'm pretty sure they didn't go anywhere."

"I know," sighed David. "But the city lights make them so dim, and half of them disappear entirely. When I used to go camping with my dad, I'd just lie on my back and stare at them for hours."

"Do you miss New York? The Adirondack Mountains?"

"I do," said David. "More than anything. But the area has such a depressed economy. I'm better off here, where I don't have to struggle. I never stop missing the stars, though."

"Maybe you can take me there someday," I said.

"I'd like that," said David, kissing the top of my head. "I'll show you where I grew up, in Saranac, and where my family's restaurant used to be, in Plattsburgh. It's a bookstore now."

David had never mentioned his granduncle's murder to me. Did he even remember it? He obviously didn't remember *me*, but still…

It was time. I could feel it.

I pulled David's arm gently off me and rose to my feet. "David, I have to tell you something," I said firmly.

"What's that?" asked David lazily, crossing his arms behind his head. "You have a kid you were afraid to tell me about? You were married before?"

"No," I said. "Nothing like that. But I… I'm not what you think I am."

"What do you mean?" asked David, furrowing his brow.

"For starters," I said, "my name isn't Gibson. It's Gwinblaidd. And I'm not exactly what you'd call a normal woman."

"Jillian, just *what* are you trying to tell me here?!" demanded David.

"Perhaps," I said, as I peeled my panties from beneath my skirt, "it'd be better if I *showed* you."

"Please tell me you're not really a man," moaned David. "Dear god…"

"Nothing like that," I said reassuringly. "Would you close your eyes for a moment? I'll tell you when to look."

David obeyed, and I pulled my dress over my head. I wasn't wearing a bra, since my dress had a support top sewn in. I kicked off my sandals, and took the ponytail tie out of my hair.

"Okay, you can look," I said.

David opened his eyes, both of which promptly widened as he stared at my naked body.

"Okay," he said. "So you're gorgeous. I kinda already knew that. Jillian, we're in *public*!"

"There's no one around," I said, sniffing the air.

"Jillian, it's not like I mind seeing you like this, but what are you *doing?*"

"This…" I said.

David sat up as I dropped to my knees. I closed my eyes, unwilling to look at him. My kind were a myth to his, legends, story-book monsters…

How would he *react?!*

As my body shifted, I could smell the fear on him. Adrenalin was coursing through his blood, carried by veins and arteries just beneath the skin. As my ears lengthened, I could hear his frightened breathing, his raspy, shallow breaths.

When the Change was complete, I opened my eyes.

David was staring at me in shocked silence, with his mouth completely agape. He looked like a statue, so still was he.

I took a couple of steps toward him, wagging my tail invitingly. I couldn't talk, but I tried to convey friendliness in that endearing way that only a dog can.

David rose and took an unsteady step backward.

I lowered my ears, whimpering a little as I took another step forward.

David's arms were hanging limp at his side, and I licked his hand. I sat on my haunches, trying to look less threatening as I looked up at David, meeting his brown eyes with my feral yellow stare.

He looked down at me for a moment…

"*AAAAAAAUUUUUGGGGGHHHHH!!!*"

With that, he was off like a shot, tearing over the top of the hill and galloping down the other side as fast as he could run.

I followed him, careful not to overtake him but unwilling to let him go. Couldn't he see that I wasn't going to hurt him?

David passed a few people on his way to the parking lot, and they stared curiously at us as we passed. I skidded to a stop as David reached his car and fished his keys from his pocket in a blind panic. Throwing open the door, he started the Camaro and roared off, burning rubber in his haste to escape.

I sat down in the grass next to the asphalt, whining pitifully.

What had I *done?!*

## Chapter Eight

I sat in my living room, watching the sprinkling rain through the screen door.

I took a slug of whisky and set the bottle down on the coffee table. I'd have to chug the entire bottle at once just to feel anything at all, and I was tempted to do just that.

My house was on the outskirts of Virginia Beach, not too far from the semi-rural region of Pungo. I had neighbors, but my suburb wasn't as densely populated as the area in which I worked. It suited me.

I'd taken a leave of absence from the VBPD. Not because I'd lost David, although that broke my heart. No, I'd taken a leave of absence because *Chuck* died.

Even a werewolf can't live forever, and Chuck had been a heavy smoker for over two hundred years. It was ironic, I thought, that a Deista'ari could survive a bullet through the heart, but not a massive coronary episode.

Chuck's passing cemented my crushing sense of depression. He was my oldest friend, and the closest. He was the father-figure that I'd needed so badly as a girl, a good man in every way that my father was not.

Now he was gone, and so was David.

Watching the slow, light rain falling outside, I ran my hand distractedly through my hair for a moment…

Then I reached for the bottle.

The whisky burned my throat as I began chugging it. The powerful libation overwhelmed my senses, drowning out even the scent of the rain-sodden grass. After a few hard gulps, all I could smell was bourbon…

***

Today

I pulled Charlie close to me, lovingly running my hand through his disheveled shock of dark hair. How like his father he looked, at least in this form.

When he shifted, he definitely favored his mama.

Charlie was fast asleep, snuggled next to me on the couch. The gas fireplace was burning brightly, and its warm, comforting glow was the only light in our cedar-paneled living room. I pulled the blanket more tightly around Charlie and me, appreciating the moment.

Some days I wished that Chuck had lived to meet his namesake. I knew he'd be proud of me, of the life I was living…

Knowing he'd be proud was good enough.

I cocked my head, listening; I could hear a vehicle coming down the driveway. I gently lifted off my blanket and extricated myself from Charlie, laying him gently down on his side.

I walked to the front door, looking through its glass panels. The sensor on the porch light tripped as a station wagon pulled into the front yard. I smiled as the car came to a stop. It wasn't a Camaro, but then…

That's how things are when you have a family.

My favorite person in the world climbed out of the car and began walking toward the house.

Things weren't always this way…

*I* wasn't always this way.

I wasn't always "Mrs. Wollstonecroft."
***

October, 1999

I paused for breath about a third of the way through the bottle, and then prepared to toss it back once more.

But then something pierced the fog of reeking whisky, a tantalizing, familiar aroma…

*David.*

I dropped the bottle, noting dimly the sound of bourbon gurgling onto the carpet. I walked slowly toward the screen door.

There he was, leaning against a telephone pole. His long, dark curls stuck to his neck and shoulders, and his sodden shirt clung to his muscled torso. I would've thought that the sight of him was sexy, if only I wasn't so afraid.

I walked slowly toward him, crossing the yard and the sidewalk. The rain was warm and falling so gently that I hardly noticed it. My senses were already coming back, and I could smell the ozone heavy in the air.

"Hello, David," I whispered, standing before him.

"Hello, Miss Gwinblaidd," said David evenly.

"What are you doing here?" I asked. "You haven't picked up any of my calls."

"It was you, wasn't it?" asked David. "I don't know how, because you look too young… but *you* murdered Uncle Wally's killer, didn't you? I've never forgotten that night, although I never talk about it."

"Yes," I said, wiping my soggy bangs out of my eyes. "It was me. I'm sorry you had to see that."

"You've killed other people, too."

That wasn't a question. It was a statement of fact.

"Yes, many."

"Are you going to do it again? Kill someone, I mean."

"Probably." My answer was self-damning, but I couldn't lie.

David looked away, with a reflective expression on his face.

"Soldiers kill people all the time," he said. "We're told it's for freedom, for country… but most of the time our wars just turn out to be about resources, influence, or global power. Police kill people fairly often, too. It's supposed to be for public safety, but half the time the laws they're enforcing when they kill are pretty suspect. But we don't blackball police officers and soldiers from society, do we? I suppose that's maybe because there are far fewer moral absolutes than I used to believe."

"I wish I could tell you my killings were for a good reason," I said. "They were just… Well, it was *my* world versus *yours*, and my kind has always done what they had to do to stay hidden and get ahead. I'm sorry."

"Isn't that why *anyone* kills, at the end of the day?" asked David, shrugging. "Their own world versus another's?"

I was feeling a ray of hope. "David, can we… Can we start over? Now that you know the truth about me?"

"I'm not sure I could ever be with a Gwinblaidd, Jillian," said David flatly.

Tears poured down my face, and I felt suddenly crushed by a sense of overwhelming disappointment.

But I collected the pieces of my heart a moment later, as I stood looking at David.

He was still *there*…

I stepped forward and took David gently by the hands. He resisted a little as I pulled his arms around my waist, but to no avail. I'm stronger than any man, and now was his chance to learn that.

"So you can't be with a Gwinblaidd, huh?" I whispered, laying my head against David's chest.

"That's a lot to ask of any man, Jillian."

"Then maybe," I whispered, "I'd rather be a Wollstonecroft instead."

"That's a big 'maybe'," said David, holding me a little tighter.

"It's the only 'maybe' I want," I whispered. "Please don't leave me."

I never thought I'd say something like that. I never imagined myself being willing to bend my pride, my sense of dominance, in order to connect with someone on an emotional level. But I was broken. I'd been alone for too long, cut off from the types of relationships that make life worth living.

*Please don't leave me.*

I'd be throwing away everything I knew.

*Please don't leave me.*

My future would no longer be entirely my own to plan.

*Please don't leave me.*

I couldn't un-say those words, and I knew it.

David pulled me gently away from his chest and leaned down a little. I locked my lips with his, kissing him fiercely. I was both surrendering and seizing everything that I wanted. I had both won and lost; Defeat and Victory had become one and the same. The wolf may have allowed herself to become trapped, but the woman was set free.

Life, I realized, isn't about being happy "forever." Forever is too fickle, too fleeting, and too vulnerable to tumultuous change. Life is about learning to seize a single moment, a breath-taking moment frozen in time, and *keeping* that moment…

Forever.

## The End

# Ryker's Destiny
## Zia Westfield

### Chapter One

The massive beast loping toward him seemed more horse than dog. It stopped about six feet in front of Ryker and raised its head. Despite the darkness, Ryker easily saw the great shaggy head, the powerful muscles, and the black, appraising eyes. A rumble sounded from its chest.

His brother's weight sagged against him. "Think he'll eat us?" Cole chuckled weakly.

Ryker kept his eyes on the animal. "We'll know soon enough."

They needed a healer, and the best healer in these parts was the widow Ismene Dayann. Her name was whispered in a combination of respect and fear. Respect he understood, but fear raised questions.

Still, he didn't have a choice.

Cole's condition was deteriorating. He'd be dead before they rejoined their clan in northern Washington.

He waited for the healer to invite them in.

They didn't wait long for the cabin door to open. An elderly female voice said, "Bear, get back inside."

Ryker stiffened as the dog curled its lip and gave another growl before turning and running back to the cabin.

His brother's shoulders started shaking. "Did she just call that behemoth 'Bear'?"

"You can bring your friend in," the voice called, forestalling Ryker from having to answer.

His senses on high alert, he urged his brother towards the cabin. They climbed the two wooden steps to the front porch and crossed the threshold. Ryker felt a wrenching sensation as they moved indoors and realized the cabin was warded. Yet he hadn't noticed wards when he'd driven up the narrow drive.

The woman directed him. "In here. Lay him on that couch near the fireplace."

He entered a small, neat living area, immediately identifying the entrances and exits even as he noted homey touches around the room. It was a female room with comfortable wooden furniture, colorful throws, and flowers and herbs that covered every surface.

The elderly woman bustled towards them. She had tan skin, made leathery from years of being outdoors, and wrinkles that mapped a life lived to its fullest. Wispy white hair stuck out from a bun that she had haphazardly piled on her head. She paused about two feet in front of him and tilted her head back. "You're bigger than I expected. Let me see your hand."

Ryker's brows crashed downwards. "It's my brother who needs the help." He hadn't missed her remark about expecting him.

She held her hand out in demand. "If you want my help, your hand."

Ryker ground his teeth and held out his hand. She took it in both of hers. One finger traced over the lines in his palm. Her touch was soothing and something more.

He sensed her probing. Rather than repelling the intrusion, his beast responded like a cat being served cream. The woman murmured in a language he didn't recognize, though he'd swear his beast did. Ryker's wariness increased further.

The elderly woman gazed up at him with eyes that bored into his soul. "I'll have your name, please."

"Ryker Bernard. This is my brother, Cole." He glanced towards the couch where his brother lay pale and with sweat dotting his brow. "He got caught in a witch's trap and poisoned. We tried purging him, but the poison continues to spread." Ryker clenched his fists at his sides. "Can you save him?"

She cocked her head to the side. "I'll need to examine him first." She made a shooing motion. "You're big like Bear. Go find a place and sit down."

He ignored the reference to the dog, whom he assumed to be the alleged "Bear," and focused on what concerned him most.

"If you don't mind," he said, "I'll check that the cabin's secure." She nodded, but she had already shifted her attention to his brother, pulling down the skin under his eyes and feeling under his jaw. He watched to assure himself the healer knew what she was doing. Normally, he'd have stayed for protection and let one of his people inspect the premises. Only there was no one else. His people had orders to move northward. He and Cole would catch up. At least, that was the plan.

He opened a door to a room decorated with an iron bed, a homemade quilt, and a wooden dresser topped by an antique mirror. The healer's, he was certain. He opened another door and paused. The room had a double bed and a wooden rocker. Wildflowers sat in a vase on the dresser. Ryker inhaled, and a scent unlike any he'd ever smelled before penetrated to his core.

He shook his head to clear it and checked the rest of the tidy, compact dwelling. It was secure. He needed to check outside. The lack of wards when they drove up disturbed him. He'd check on Cole and then head outside.

In the living room, the healer was burning a mixture of herbs. She squeezed a wet cloth and bathed his brother's pale face. Unless the healer could work her magic, it might be just Ryker leaving this cabin—a possibility he refused to contemplate.

"Ryker Bernard," the healer said without turning around. "I'll make a deal with you."

Ryker tensed. What would the healer ask for? He'd do anything for his brother. "Name your price."

She paused, examining him, and then appeared to decide. "I'll save your brother. In exchange, you save my granddaughter."

Ryker absorbed the shock of the request. It was not what he'd expected.

"And if my brother dies?" he asked.

The woman stared at him, steady and determined. Only the flexing of her knuckles on the cloth she held betrayed her inner emotion.

"Then my granddaughter dies."

## Chapter Two

Lana switched on the high beams as the sky darkened along the mountain road. Tall fir and spruce trees towered over the lonely road.

She'd driven this stretch thousands of times, yet tonight her nerves jumped with each treacherous curve.

It was probably all the talk of an impending war between the clans. People were scared. As she'd delivered her grandmother's remedies to her clients, Lana had listened. Humans continued to encroach into the magical realm carved out by supernaturals after the Great Schism, which had occurred at the end of the Dark Ages. Some supernaturals had hidden amongst the humans, while most had chosen to live in their own magical world. Now, however, as their territory decreased, tensions were rising. Various powerful factions saw it as an opening to increase their domination over the supernatural communities.

Lana eased up on the pedal, aware that she was letting her emotions rule. In the rearview mirror, a set of twin lights appeared and disappeared in the distance. Unease slithered down her shoulder blades.

She should have left town before twilight descended, like she usually did. Instead, she'd let the rumors and speculation being bandied about distract her and she'd lost track of the time.

She cracked open the window and sent her senses outward, seeking an animal of the night. A northern spotted owl shrieked in a crescendo, and Lana felt the connection between her and the bird of prey take hold.

"Show me what you see," she said in a whisper.

While part of her mind stayed focused on driving, another part deciphered the images from the owl. It flew over treetops and captured the mountain road's twists and turns. The car behind her sped around one curve, confirming her fear that it was trying to catch up to her.

"Show me the driver." With her mind, she directed the owl to complete a sweeping pass over the vehicle.

It swooped low in front of the vehicle before pulling up by flapping its powerful wings. That moment was enough to see the features of the two men inside.

They were Fenton's men.

Her hands clenched the wheel as she digested that fact. The rogue pack alpha had picked Lana to be his mate and hadn't taken kindly to her rejection. It looked like he intended to force matters.

She wasn't far from the cabin she shared with Granny. Once she was on their property, the wards would protect her.

She bit down on her lip, aware of the truth she'd been avoiding. The wards were weakening, a sign that Granny's powers were diminishing.

The lights in the mirror grew, so she pressed down on the gas and clutched the steering wheel.

As the road curved, she eased up on the pedal, afraid of taking the turn too fast. Images from the owl flooded her mind. One image made her suck in a breath. It showed the road up ahead, where it straightened after coming out of the curve. Across the dark blacktop, a truck had pulled sideways, blocking travel from either direction.

Lana's stomach lurched.

She didn't want to confront Fenton or his men. As the curve ended, she jerked the steering wheel hard to the right. The jeep bounced onto an old logging trail. Given the rough terrain, she doubted anyone had driven this way in years. Scant light penetrated the dense foliage and overhanging limbs that scraped against the sides of the jeep.

Her connection with the owl remained, and she saw her pursuers had twigged onto her maneuver and were following.

The jeep's headlights illuminated a toppled tree that leaned against another tree trunk, barring the path forward.

Lana slammed on the brakes.

It was foolish to run. Fenton's pack could track her easily by scent.

But if she could reach the cabin's circle of protection, she'd be safe.

She ducked under the tree trunk, swatting away the branches that reached out for her, catching her hair and tugging. Although she wasn't without defenses, she'd prefer to make her escape than to go up against Fenton and his men.

A wolf howled, followed by another wolf's responding cry, and then another.

From the owl's images, she realized the men now ran in wolf form through the forest.

They'd be on her fast.

She burst into a clearing and turned. She would have to make her stand.

The wolves charged out of the forest, the alpha in the lead, with his two soldiers flanking him. Their teeth gleamed, and growls rumbled from each of them.

Lana raised her hands. Before she could utter a word or make any kind of movement, a loud roar sounded behind her. Something hurtled past her, moving straight for the wolves.

The creature stood, and Lana gasped. A bear, the biggest she had ever seen, stood on its hind legs, daring the wolves to attack.

Lana reached for the beast, a tentative probe, and then pulled back at the sparking sensation zinging between her and the bear. He had to be a shifter.

Who was he?

Two of the wolves came in low, lunging for the bear's midsection. The bear swatted one wolf away, a blow that sent the wolf sprawling to the edge of the tree line. The second wolf took advantage of the opening to clamp his jaw on the bear's hip. Fur flew and blood stained the dark bear pelt. The alpha growled and sat back on its haunches in preparation to launch itself at the bear for the kill.

Lana's fingers trembled and her heartbeat too fast. She took in a deep breath and centered herself.

Once more, raising her hands, she shut her eyes and reached for all the beings of the forest. Life pulsed in rhythm through the creatures and plants that inhabited the forest. She found the thread of life connecting them all and tapped into its energy. Energy crackled around her, and she felt it flow through her in waves.

Growls and roars brought her attention back to the fight in front of her.

The bear had raked its claws along the side of one wolf, but blood matted its hide.

They would fight to the death if she didn't stop them.

Sweat pooled between her breasts as she fought down her nerves. She'd never been this close to a shifter fight. Her presence was responsible for this attack, which meant she would stay and do what she could to end hostilities. Goddess willing.

She tapped into the energy and quickly shaped it into four balls that floated in the air. Pushing with her hand, she directed one ball and then another to each of the combatants, trapping them inside. Within seconds, they lost control of their beast and turned back into men.

Fenton and his two lieutenants shook their heads in confusion even as they placed their hands on their bleeding wounds.

"Go back home," Lana ordered. "Forget about what happened here." She sent a mental push to reinforce her command. Would it work?

The three men staggered to their feet and walked into the woods towards the road, the ball of energy surrounding them as they moved.

She shifted her attention to the last man, and she gasped. He stalked towards her with single-minded purpose and uncaring of his nudity.

He was magnificent.

He was also absolutely furious.

And he was nearly on top of her.

## Chapter Three

Ryker zeroed in on the woman like he would on prey. She didn't know it yet, but she was his.

His to protect.

He could have lost her before he'd even found her. Those three wolf bastards would have ripped her to shreds after they'd finished with her.

He stopped in front of her, ignoring the blood dripping down his thigh and the pain from where the wolf bastard had taken a piece out of him, and regarded the woman who held his destiny in her hands. About the height of his shoulder, she wore her thick, dark hair pulled back in a ponytail and sported the kinds of curves that a man could hold onto.

Odin's Knot, the mark carried by every member of his line, had awoken in response to this intriguing female.

"Bring it down," he said.

Big brown eyes widened, but she didn't step back in fear. Instead, her chin lifted and her shoulders stiffened.

"It's safer if I don't," she said.

"Safer for who?" Amusement coursed through him, replacing the pain gnawing at him.

"For me, of course." Her eyebrows drew together, and she studied his face. "Who are you?"

"The name's Ryker. Your grandmother is healing my brother." He waved in the cabin's direction. "We need to get back."

She hesitated, and he waited. Few people disobeyed one of his orders. This woman didn't know him yet. Didn't know that he would give his life for her. Already, he felt the pull as the binds inside him sought to complete the ties that rested within her.

Finally, she nodded, and the ball of energy around him winked out. "I'm Lana. You're right. We should get back. Granny will need my help." She turned away and began walking. "And please put some clothes on."

For her sake or for her grandmother's?

A zing of pain reminded him he needed to heal as well.

He rolled his shoulders to release the tension there and followed in her wake, planning as he went.

He'd promised Lana's grandmother to take her granddaughter north with him. How would either woman react when he changed the plan?

The woman wasn't what he had expected in a mate. But first impressions could be misleading.

What in the name of the gods had she done?

He knew shifters. Understood them. He was one, for Valhalla's sake.

He'd never run across man, woman or beast who could do what she'd done—manipulate energy and trap four shifters inside.

He had a lot to learn about his future mate and not much time.

War was brewing, and his people looked to him to lead. Lana was an unexpected complication he needed to solve before he brought her into their midst.

First, though, he had to dress.

## Chapter Four

Lana halted on the living room threshold. Thoughts of questioning Granny took a backseat to the unexpected scene. Lavender, ginger and other herbs and spices wafted towards her. Her grandmother murmured a healing spell and sketched rune patterns into the air.

On the couch lay a man, bare-chested, sweat glistening on his skin. His features were like the bear shifter's face, though younger.

A draft from the backdoor opening blew across her neck. Ryker.

She didn't have to look to know that he'd entered. She physically felt the difference in the air, which made little sense. Granny might explain it to her, but Lana wasn't sure she wanted to know. Sometimes ignorance was bliss.

The blasted man stood close behind her, his body heat seeping through her clothes and warming her down to her chilled toes. She could easily snuggle into that heat.

"How is he?" Ryker asked softly in her ear.

His breath caressed her cheek, and his outdoor, woodsy scent enveloped her. Her body melted.

Lana opened her mouth and shut it; the words strangled in her throat. She cleared her throat and ordered her traitorous body to behave. She didn't need this attraction. "I'm not sure."

Granny dropped her hands, the spell complete, and turned to face them. "Your brother will sleep now. I've slowed the poison, but it continues to spread." She shifted her gaze to Lana. "To remove the poison, I need the crooked thorn-stool."

"There's no other choice?" Even as she asked, she knew the answer.

Granny shook her head, wisps of white hair floating around her wizened face. "It's the only way to save him." She glanced back at the young man. "There isn't much time. You need to leave soon."

"What is crooked thorn-stool?" Ryker asked as he followed Lana to a closet.

She opened the door and reached inside for the backpack she kept supplied for occasions like this one. "It's a special mushroom that only grows in the cavern of the trolls." She pulled the backpack out.

"Let me take that," Ryker said, and he hefted it on his shoulder. "What else do you need?"

She tried not to look at him. It was as if every time he spoke or she glanced his way, tiny threads shot out from her to him, tying them together. She'd accuse her grandmother of magical meddling, but her grandmother's entire attention was on her patient. It was always that way when someone required her healing touch.

Lana bit back a sigh. "We'll need water and some food. We've got several hours of hiking ahead of us, depending on the condition of the trail and the weather."

In the kitchen, she filled two large, insulated canisters with cold, pure water from their well. "We have to reach the caverns before dawn."

Ryker took the two canisters from her. "Why?"

"Two reasons. The mushroom must be cut during the hours of darkness. The trolls who guard the cavern ensure it can't be accessed during daylight." She opened the refrigerator and eyed the contents. An apple, some carrots and a few of granny's cookies would do for her, but she'd bet the mountain standing next to her needed something more substantial. In the end, she made a few sandwiches and wrapped them in cloth before adding them to her pack.

"That's everything except for my bow and arrows," Lana said. Reluctantly, she lifted her gaze to meet his. Her cheeks flushed as she caught the desire lurking in those dark eyes. Once again, she felt tiny threads attaching the two of them together.

Maybe it was a dark spell. Then she mentally shook her head. Granny would know if the dark arts were being practiced.

"You must hurry." Granny thrust a jug into Ryker's hands. "It's elderberry mead. Give it to the trolls in exchange for cutting the crooked thorn-stool."

Ryker passed the jug to Lana. "Here. Pack this in or tie it to the outside of the pack. I'll be right back."

He strode to the front door and let himself out. By the time he returned, Lana had shifted some items around and secured the jug safely within the pack. He didn't have a backpack of his own, but she noted the wicked knife strapped to his thigh.

"Let's go," he said, and grabbed the pack.

"Wait," Granny said. She took a bottle and gave it to Ryker. "Drink this and it will heal your wounds."

She opened a drawer and removed two leather cords with a circular medallion hanging from each. "Wear these Troll Crosses around your necks. The trolls can be difficult. These will give you additional protection."

Lana slipped the cord over her head and then grabbed her bow and her quiver of arrows. Each flint tip was steeped in immobilizing magic. When her powers had been developing, she'd needed that extra edge. Now it was a comfort to carry the weight on her shoulders, and it provided camouflage. Granny had warned her against demonstrating her abilities with vague mutterings of danger and war.

She'd blown it with this stranger and Fenton and his men. She'd never used her abilities like she had tonight, and the strength of her powers alarmed her. She'd have to deal with the consequences. If she were lucky, her command to Fenton and his men would hold, and they'd forget about what had happened. Or their memories would be confused, making it difficult to know truth from lie. Either way, she and Granny would have to move. They were no longer safe here. They'd see Ryker and his brother on their way and then she'd persuade Granny to pack up and leave their home. It hurt to think about it, but she didn't see other options.

She blinked back the tears that threatened. Time to go.

She yanked open the door and let the night air flood in and calm her nerves. The smell of snow hung in the air. They'd have to hurry or risk not being able to cross the pass.

She looked back and frowned. Ryker was bent over and speaking quietly to Granny. It could've been about his brother, but she didn't think so.

The sudden flood of tears in her heart told her otherwise. What had Granny agreed to?

## Chapter Five

The first hour of their trek progressed in silence. Ryker let Lana set the pace while he brought up the rear. Fir trees towered over them on both sides of the trail, limbs dipping downward as if in preparation of the snow that would soon lay upon their branches. Clouds blocked the moonlight from penetrating the trees, but Ryker didn't need it. His night vision picked out obstacles with ease.

His brow lowered as he noted Lana's sure-footedness. It could be familiarity with the trail, since he didn't recognize the scent of a shifter on her. She was an enigma to him.

But he intended to learn every one of her secrets.

Ryker inhaled deeply, automatically sorting through the odors of the creatures inhabiting the mountainside a mile in any direction. A herd of elk foraged for food not far away, and in the distance a bobcat hunted. As far as human predators or shifters were concerned, Ryker detected none.

A lone owl hooted and flew overhead.

Lana halted and turned, her head cocked slightly upward. She'd bundled up in a navy wool knit scarf and hat that left little of her face visible, though what peeked out at him exuded a wholesomeness and an innocence at odds with his hard years of experience.

"A tree fell during the last storm," she said. "We can try to climb over it or go around it, but that will add time that I'm not sure we have."

Her melodic voice washed over him, and his beast lunged to the surface, causing Ryker to stagger at the unexpected action. Mastering his beast was for rookies, not for a clan leader of his caliber.

"Ryker," he heard her call out.

"Don't," he grit out. Coming closer could trigger another reaction.

As it was, he faced off with his beast, something he hadn't done in decades.

*Mine.* The forceful decree brooked no argument.

*Mine first.* Ryker asserted his dominance until his beast gave him a sign of acknowledgment. *We protect her together.*

Snow hit his face and then, as if Skadi, the winter goddess, had tipped over bucket after bucket of the white stuff, fat wet flakes poured down from the heavens. The thick white blanket obscured his view, but he didn't need it. The bonds forming between him and Lana ensured that he'd always be able to find her.

Did she understand what the bonds represented?

For him, it changed everything.

After delivering his people safely north, he'd planned to pass the mantle of leadership onto Cole. His younger brother had grown into a strong, respected warrior of the clan and would make a fine leader. Ryker would have disappeared into the mountains to live the life of a hermit until death claimed him.

The gods must have disapproved, because Lana's entrance showed that destiny had its own plans for him.

With unerring precision, he stomped after her, angry that his entire world had tilted on its axis and his plan for a future without responsibilities had slipped away. Ryker grimaced and swallowed his ire. He was a fool.

Every member of his family was born with Odin's Knot.

To find one's mate was a moment of celebration. It signaled a blessing from Odin himself and portended good fortune for the clan.

He flexed his fingers and then fisted them. Now wasn't the time to celebrate. Not when his brother could die if they didn't get the ingredient the healer needed to save him.

Through the cascading flakes, he spied Lana clambering over branches as she tried to get over the downed fir tree.

Movement above her caught his attention, and he froze.

Less than ten feet away crouched a bobcat.

"Don't move." Lana spoke firmly and with a distinct command. "I've got this."

The beast in him raised its head and roared in protest. Hackles lifted on Ryker's skin, and he struggled to prevent the change from taking over. The distance between himself and Lana was too far. The bobcat could rip her apart before he got to her.

The snowflakes falling around Lana turned yellow, followed by green, then blue and purple. A curious sense of peace stole over him, and even his beast sank back and watched. All about Lana, the snowflakes tumbled and spun like in a symphony of colors.

The bobcat padded its way down the trunk, its head lifted to the colorful snowflakes falling upon its face and body. Lana's melodic tones carried along with the wind. "We are only passing through your territory. It's important that we visit the trolls. I know you are hungry and wish to eat before the weather worsens. There's a herd of elk nearby. The eldest won't make it this winter."

The bobcat lowered its head and butted it towards Lana, who petted the creature as if it were a house cat. "Yes, I enjoy your company too, but if you don't go hunting now, you might miss a meal." She scratched the cat behind the ears and, with both hands, nudged it away. "Now, shoo."

The bobcat leaped from the branch and out of sight. Lana dusted her hands and, like that, the snowflakes returned to their normal shade of white.

A switch might have flipped. Ryker leaped across the distance and snatched Lana off the limb she'd been straddling in her quest to climb over the fallen tree.

She looked up at him in surprise. She should have looked at him in fear.

Except he didn't want her to fear him.

Ryker groaned. What in the name of the Valkyries was he going to do with this woman?

He did the only thing he could. The one thing he'd wanted to do since Odin's Knot had designated her his mate.

He kissed her.

## Chapter Six

Goodness. If Lana had needed a lesson in self-combustion, this was it. The snowflakes had to be melting on contact.

She'd been kissed before, but nothing like this.

Not this explosion of heat, this intense need or the bright flame of desire that had her in its grip.

She slid her arms up over his shoulder and hung on. A maelstrom of emotions skyrocketed like fireworks popping off in every direction. Sizzle. Pop.

His tongue stroked hers, and she was drowning in the sensations pouring into her. She could lose herself in this man. As it was, the ties binding them tightened, and more ties shot out to create new connections.

Where did she let off and he begin?

The sobering thought gave her the strength to wrench herself away.

She stood with her chest heaving and stared at the man who had lit her up like a Roman candle.

"What was that?"

He looked as shellshocked as she felt. He rubbed the back of his neck and lifted his face to the cold snow before dropping his chin. "That was Odin's Knot, and it's more potent than any mead created by man, woman or beast."

Before she could ask further questions, he grabbed her hand and tugged her back to the tree. He caught her by the waist and practically tossed her over it. She climbed down the other side after getting her footing.

Hands on her hips, she waited for him to join her. "Odin's Knot," she prompted when he reached her side.

Before he could answer, an owl screeched, the sharp rising sound interrupting her thoughts. Images came at her fast.

"We have to hurry," she said, gesturing further up the trail. "The mountain pass will be impassable in these conditions. We need to get to the cavern and back down before that happens."

She set a rapid pace, relying on her link to the owl to keep her informed of any obstacles ahead. Ryker stayed close behind her, his large presence a constant reminder of the explosive heat they had generated. Her palms sweated at the memory.

"You can talk to the animals." There was speculation in his voice, making it more of a question than a statement.

Lana hesitated. Usually, she would brush off such a suggestion, but she instinctively knew that the binds between them wouldn't allow her to lie.

"It's best to stick to the truth," Ryker said.

She whipped around to look at him, snow clinging to her face and his. "They're real, aren't they? These invisible bindings I feel. You feel them too, don't you?"

"I feel them. It's why I know there can only be truth between us." He stepped closer, close enough that the amber flakes in his dark eyes glinted. "Lies corrupt. Odin's Knot was bestowed upon one of my many great grandfathers and represents the purity of love that binds a fated pair for the rest of their lives."

She heard the truth in his words. No, that wasn't right. She felt the truth deep in her pores.

Except neither of them loved the other. How could they when they'd only just met? Spirals of panic coiled in her stomach at the sudden twist her life had taken.

"Can the binds be broken?" But she knew the answer. It was there buried in her soul, a seed that had been planted at birth and was now sprouting living threads that sought their other half.

Ryker was that other half.

But there was Granny to think of.

She held up her hand to forestall whatever he was about to say. "Never mind. Forget I asked." She offered a small smile. "You want to know if I can talk to the animals. It's actually more like establishing a link with them. I can't really explain it. It's an ability I've always had."

He took her hand in his and resumed their hike. "It's not the only talent you have."

His voice warmed her, filling in nooks and crannies inside her she hadn't realized were empty. It was all happening too fast.

"No, it's not the only talent I have," she whispered.

He squeezed her hand. "Since you're on this mission with me, why don't I tell you about your grandmother's patient, my brother Cole."

For the next hour, he regaled her with tales of his rascally brother, as he dubbed him. Affection permeated each of the stories, and Lana relaxed. Whatever fate had in store for her, at least Ryker appeared to be a decent man with a strong sense of loyalty and responsibility. Although the tales centered on his brother, Ryker's qualities shone through. He was also worried about his brother, an anxiety she sensed through the ties binding them.

And then they reached the mountain pass, dangerous to cross at the best of times, a death trap during a winter storm.

Lana stepped away from Ryker and drew an arrow from her quiver. She peered up at him, amused by his puzzled expression.

"Ryker, do you trust me?"

## Chapter Seven

Ryker's lips flattened as he grimly surveyed the tiny mountain strip, laughably called a pass. The stone bridge spanned a rocky gorge that was probably the repository of numerous bones from unlucky travelers who'd taken a header over the side—simple to do when there were no handrails and the width of the thing was barely three feet. A gust of wind would be enough to knock anyone off its perch.

Currently, the blasted bridge lay under a blanket of snow and ice. Unless one of Lana's talents included flying, traversing the pass would be a challenge both coming and going.

*Do you trust me?*

He faced Lana, who was making a notch in her arrow. Fate had chosen this woman for him. She was a woman of power, though the extent of her power remained a mystery to him, and she was capable of great compassion, as witnessed by her willingness to retrieve an ingredient in the wilds of the mountains that required a death-defying crossing over a tiny stone strip, all for a man she had glimpsed on her grandmother's sofa.

Sometimes a man had to take a leap of faith and trust in the gods.

"I trust you, Lana." He poured every ounce of conviction he could into that statement.

She shot him a smile, visible through the falling snow. "I'm going to shoot an arrow with a rope attached to the other side. It will serve as a guide as we cross. But I'll need you to help me aim. My vision is like any human at night. and if I try to use an animal to help, it might be more hindrance than assistance since their vision requires significant interpretation on my part."

Ryker lowered the pack. "I'll get out the rope."

He rooted around and found two coils of rope, which he pulled out, handing one to her.

"We'll tie the second rope around our waists," he said. "It'll give us additional security."

Not long after, she told him she was ready. Lana brought the bow up to her right shoulder and fit the arrow, which was now attached to a rope, to the bow's string. "I'm trying to hit an old spruce on the other side. With the snow and darkness, I'm relying on instinct more than anything else."

He got behind her and concentrated on the spot she indicated. He placed a hand on her left shoulder as an anchor and bent his knees to bring himself to her eye level. Snow swirled every which way, obscuring the target.

He made an instant decision. "Connect with me."

"What?" She whipped her head around to look at him.

"You heard me. Connect with me as you do with the animals. You can use my vision to lock on the target." It made sense. Yet, if he were being honest, he knew he'd never let another person do what he was offering Lana.

It was a matter of trust.

Her nose wrinkled in consideration, and he resisted the temptation to lean down and kiss the snow-tipped spot. After that explosive kiss they'd shared, touching Lana could easily turn into an obsession, and even the most innocent touch probably risked his control. For a man who prided himself on always being in control, this was unknown territory.

Finally, she nodded. "All right."

Ryker braced himself for an uncomfortable pinch, his imagination equating it to an injection, and discovered, when her soft entrance came so seamlessly that he never felt it, that he'd underestimated her ability. But there was no missing her spirit, the way it flowed through him, lighting the darkness within his soul and spreading a soothing balm of peace over the nicks and scars gained from years of fights and battles.

For a warrior, the feeling was addictive and dangerous.

He focused on the tree, and Lana took her shot. As soon as the arrow hit its target, Lana withdrew her connection.

Cold invaded him, and his beast growled in displeasure.

"I'm sorry," Lana said, concern coloring her voice. "I usually loosen the connection gradually, but I thought it better to get out fast."

She busied herself with tying off the end of the rope to a tree stump, although she threw several anxious glances his way.

He breathed in and centered himself. Their world was all about power: who possessed it, who wielded it, and who lost it. He'd seen her manipulate energy, reduce four shifters to human form, and communicate with animals.

Lana's power existed outside the boundaries of what he knew and understood.

Her grandmother's words took on new meaning. *Save my granddaughter.*

Once word got out about what Lana could do—and it would— supernaturals would want to steal her power, subvert it or kill her.

And he'd thought he could walk away from his responsibilities.

The universe had a warped sense of humor.

## Chapter Eight

With the mountain pass behind them, Lana led the way to the troll caverns. She'd accompanied Granny a few times, though usually not in the middle of a snowstorm. Granny liked to stop and examine plants along the way. Her healing skills were legendary.

But she was fading before Lana's eyes, age catching up to her.

A hand on her arm jerked her back to the present. Ryker pointed ahead on the trail. "Troll trap."

"Where?" she asked. Visibility had deteriorated, making it hard to see beyond a few feet in front of her.

"See those two overhanging branches? Follow the trunks down to the ground. There's a brown stain that no matter how much snow falls upon it, stays brown, like a large puddle."

Lana nodded. "I see it now. It's one of the troll's more basic traps. Crude, but effective. As soon as someone or something touches that puddle, the muck traps them. The trolls sense the disturbance and come out. Often as not, the poor creatures end up served for dinner."

"I don't plan for either of us to be on the menu," Ryker said. "Can you leap over it, or shall I carry you?"

She grinned at him. "I'm good, but why don't you jump first?"

She admired the smooth athleticism of his movements. She already knew he looked marvelous stripped, and her cheeks heated over the memory.

He beckoned for her to leap across the brown sludge, and she did it, landing in his arms, which she hadn't expected. He held her close, his face mere inches from hers. Dark eyes with amber flecks glittered with an emotion that caused her stomach to flutter, and that woodsy scent that she'd noticed belonged to him drifted her way and made her senses tingle. If he were a warlock, she'd swear he'd caught her in his spell.

Slowly, he released her. "We'd better go." Regret tinged his tone.

She hustled around him, certain that if he hadn't let her go when he had, she would have kissed him.

They trudged uphill through the snow, when a gravelly voice hollered out, "Who goes there?"

Ryker put a hand out, halting her. "We've come for the crooked thorn-stool."

"Don't know it. Go away." Annoyance mixed with the grumbled

response.

"Let me try," Lana said. "Birger, it's Lana Dayann, granddaughter to Ismene. I've brought something for you."

There was a shuffling sound, and a squat, round figure became silhouetted against a cave entrance, accompanied by a pungent odor. "What is it?"

Lana plugged her nose and breathed through her mouth. "Elderberry mead," she said. "But I'll only give it to you if you let us have some of the crooked thorn-stools."

"Three," he said hurriedly. "You can have three. Now, give me the mead." He looked back over his shoulder and then stepped out of the cave, reaching out with both hands. Tufts of wiry gray hair stood out from a balding scalp. Bushy eyebrows covered heavy-set eyes that were nearly hidden by a bulbous nose.

"We'll exchange at the same time," Ryker said, showing no signs that the smell bothered him. "You bring us the three crooked thorn-stools and we'll give you the mead."

After a short standoff and a lot of grumbling, Birger stomped back inside the cavern, and Lana waved her hand in front of her nose. "Birger and his wife, Ulfhild, are the caretakers who guard the passage to the caverns. They are not friendly, and they don't like visitors."

"Sounds like we have something in common," Ryker said. He lowered the pack and opened it to pull out the jug of elderberry mead.

Lana chuckled. "Maybe. But I don't think you eat your enemies."

Ryker didn't have time to respond, because Birger lumbered out of the cave holding a sack. "Here. Now, give me the mead."

"Show us the mushrooms," Ryker said as he stood up.

Birger loosened the string holding the sack closed and thrust his hand inside. When he brought his hand out, he held three crooked thorn-stools. "Bring me my mead."

"All right," Ryker said, "I'll take two steps and you take two steps until we meet, and then we'll exchange."

Lana pulled out an arrow and fit it to the string of her bow.

"Here now," Birger said, "no need for weapons."

"Insurance only," Lana assured him, certain Ulfhild was somewhere in the background, ready to protect her spouse. Between the Troll Crosses she and Ryker were wearing and the trolls' need for Granny's healing spells, Lana doubted the couple would pull a fast one. But it was always best to be cautious.

Birger snuffled his discontent, but he came two steps at a time until he and Ryker stood an arm's distance apart and made the exchange.

"Pleasure doing business with you," Ryker said, never taking his eyes off Birger, as he walked backwards with the sack in his hand.

Birger eagerly clasped the jug and pulled the cork free. He was raising it to his lips, when a loud holler shook the ground around them and a second troll stood in the entrance. "Bring that mead inside, Birger or—"

Whatever else Ulfhild uttered was lost in the wind, as Lana and Ryker rushed down the slope towards the pass. Ryker insisted they tie the ropes around their waist again before attempting to cross the stone bridge. Using the rope she'd shot with the arrow as their guide, they made their way slowly over the slippery surface.

By the time they reached the other side, Lana's neck and shoulder muscles were bunched up tight and she was gasping for breath. Twice she'd nearly lost her grip and once actually had slipped on an ice patch and dangled over the side until Ryker had pulled her up.

She was bending over to catch her breath as Ryker packed the rope away, when she heard familiar barking.

A dark shadow barreled toward them, the barking frantic.

"It's Bear." She stumbled forward through the snow. "Granny! She must be in trouble!"

## Chapter Nine

Ryker observed the mammoth black dog, its sides heaving. "Can you link to Bear to see what's wrong?"

Lana kneeled in the snow and wrapped an arm around his massive head. "I can't retrieve memories of the past, but I might get a sense of what brought him."

Energy surged in the air and the snowflakes danced in a rainbow of colors above Lana and Bear's head. Ryker wondered if he'd ever tire of seeing that incredible display. He shook his head and focused on the issue at hand. Bear wouldn't be here if there weren't trouble. The problem could be related to Lana's grandmother, or his brother might have taken a turn for the worse.

The colors faded, and Lana buried her head in the dog's neck before raising her head. "I sense men near the cabin and waves of hostility."

He helped her to her feet and brushed a loose strand of hair off her cheek, his heart no proof against the plea swimming in those brown eyes. "Sounds like your pals came back. We'd better go."

About a mile from the cabin, Ryker motioned for Lana to stop. "Stay here with Bear. I'm going to check things out." He didn't give her time to argue. He dropped a swift kiss on those tempting lips and shifted.

He trusted the ties binding the two of them to inform him if she was in danger. Meanwhile, Bear would protect her.

Ryker used his powerful forelegs to run through the forest, pausing at regular intervals to draw in the scents of the forest and process the information.

He recognized the scents of the three wolf bastards he'd tangled with earlier. Whatever Lana had done had worn off. They were back, and they'd brought reinforcements.

He returned to the spot where he'd left Lana to find her with her bow at the ready and an arrow pointed right at the center of his forehead.

She lowered her bow and watched him shift. He'd barely returned to human form when she threw herself at him.

"What did you learn?" She clutched at his arm.

"Woman, let me dress before I freeze my manly parts off." He winked while he considered his words. He wanted her far away from any battle that occurred, and she would fight him every step of the way until her grandmother was safe.

Once he'd dressed, he spoke. "That fellow chasing after you is back, and he's brought more men. They're watching the house. They may think you're inside, or they may be waiting for you to return. Hard to say."

Lana paced in front of him. "It doesn't matter. We have to get inside the cabin." She tilted her chin up at him at a stubborn angle. "Your brother needs the crooked thorn-stool if he's going to survive, and I am not leaving Granny to deal with Fenton and his goons." She picked up a stick and drew an X on the snow. "We're here, and this circle is the cabin. About half a mile between, there's an entrance leading to the root cellar and tunnels to the cabin. We can get in that way."

Ryker studied the crude map. She was right. They had to deliver the crooked thorn-stool. But he also couldn't leave her alone.

"We will go through the cellar," he said, deciding. "I take the lead and you do exactly what I tell you."

She kicked snow over her drawing. "Fine. Go in that direction," she said, pointing, "and when you see a tree split in half by lightning, head due north."

They made their way at a stealthy, rapid pace, Ryker alert to potential ambush, while relying on Bear's canine radar to give additional warning.

Thirty minutes later, they climbed out of a trapdoor and into the kitchen of the cabin. Lana rushed to her grandmother's side and put an arm around her.

"Are you okay, Granny? We've brought the crooked thorn-stool. We returned as quickly as possible. Bear met us on the way." Lana said anxiously.

"Give me that mushroom and don't dawdle." The healer concentrated on Cole. "We don't have a lot of time, so do as I say."

While the two women busied themselves, Ryker crossed over to his brother. Sweat trickled down Cole's forehead, and Ryker took the wet cloth lying nearby and bathed his brother's face. Cole's breathing appeared shallow and fast, and Ryker willed the two women to hurry and bring whatever foul-smelling concoction they were making and let it work its magic.

Cole's eyes opened, a feverish glow in them. "I know they're out there. One of them demanded the girl to come out. The healer told them to go away." He lifted a hand and caught at Ryker's sleeve. "Leave me. Take the women and go away. They don't want me. They'll leave me alone." His hand fell away and fell to his side.

Ryker glanced back and saw Lana's grandmother pouring dark liquid into an earthen mug. "Save your breath. If there's any leaving to do, we leave together."

The healer carried the steaming brew, and Ryker raised his brother and made sure that every drop disappeared.

"It takes time to work," the healer said. Then she chanted and sketched rune signs in the air that appeared in a smoky form and dissipated.

Glass suddenly spewed inward from the window by the front door and a rock sailed inside. Bear got to his feet and barked ferociously, intermixed with deep growls. Lana grabbed the dog about the neck to prevent him from stepping on the shards.

"Get out here, Lana." Fenton said, anger bursting with each word. "You've got five minutes. Next time, I'll be breaking more than glass."

Lana looked over at her grandmother and then at Ryker. "He's mean.

He'll do what he says if I don't go out there."

"I'm meaner," Ryker said, striding over to the trapdoor.

Lana tugged Bear with her as she followed him. "What are you going to do?"

Concern swam in those brown eyes—concern for him. He hooked an arm around her and reeled her to him. He kissed her rosy lips and felt how more and more ties continued to tighten between them. Heat curled in his stomach, and then detonated, fanning outward, until every cell in his body burned, and there was nothing more that he wanted than to strip them both and make love to her.

"I take care of my own," he said when he reluctantly released her, his voice rough with the passion he held inside. "And I gave my word."

With that, he dropped into the tunnel and took off running.

## Chapter Ten

The ticking of the clock pounded in Lana's ears. Two minutes to surrender to Fenton's deadline. Ryker was one man. While he was a powerful bear shifter, Fenton had his pack to back him up.

If Lana went outside to assist Ryker, it would mean leaving Granny alone in the cabin with a sick patient. She couldn't do it.

She had to trust in the bonds that tied them together to warn her if he needed her.

Trust.

It had been her and Granny for so long that it never occurred to her she might find a man she could trust.

*A man she could love.*

"Time's up!" Fenton yelled. "You should've listened when you had the chance!"

A roar bellowed so loud it shook the cabin's foundations. Snarls, growls, and yelps erupted in the front yard.

"Bear?" Ryker's brother called out weakly from the sofa.

Lana switched her attention from the fighting to Cole. His color was better, which told her that Granny's remedy was working.

"Bear's right here," Lana said, bringing the giant dog alongside.

Cole feebly chuckled. "Not that Bear. My brother, Bear."

"Ryker?" Lana checked his pupils for dilation. Maybe Cole had suffered a concussion.

"It's what we call him," Cole said. "He's leader of our clan and the biggest, strongest bear around." He paused and caught his breath. "I need to help him."

He struggled to sit up as Lana pushed him back down. "You need to lie down and rest. You'll only get in Ryker's way."

Cole shook his head. "There's too many of them. They'll wear him down, then go in for the kill."

Lana worried her lip and reached inside for her connection to Ryker. Would she be able to tell if he'd been captured or was injured?

The ties held strong. She went deeper still, examining each strand. Here and here she discovered a difference. Red tinged these strands.

Blood.

Ryker was hurt. How badly, she didn't know.

She had to go to him. It was crazy, and she didn't understand the connection they shared, but intuitively she knew that Ryker's death would leave a gaping hole in her soul she might never recover from.

She squeezed Cole's shoulder. "I won't let anything happen to him." She put on her jacket and grabbed her bow and arrows. Granny, will you be okay? I have to go outside."

Granny looked up from the pot she was stirring on the stove. "Be careful, child. Do what you have to; trust your instincts. Cole and I aren't going anywhere."

Lana kissed her cheek and ordered Bear to be on guard. Then she strode to the front door and let herself out onto the porch.

The gray streaks of dawn filtered through the clouds and snow. Five mangy wolves surrounded Ryker. One dived in low, aiming for his legs, while another attacked his back. Fenton stood in human form, arms crossed and a smirk on his face, as he ordered his soldiers to fight while he watched.

Lana pulled an arrow out and set it on the string. Picking out one wolf, she took aim and pulled the arrow and string back. About to release it, she was yanked up against a hard chest and her bow wrenched away from her grasp.

"Got her, Fenton!" a raspy voice said in her ear as he held a knife to her neck.

Lana froze. The stale odor of tobacco from her captor made her want to gag, but she forced her mind to stay focused.

Ryker fought brutally, his massive jaws clamping around a wolf's neck, and he tossed the animal against a tree where it landed with a thwack! Blood matted his fur on his right thigh and left shoulder.

The man holding Lana dragged her towards Fenton, the knife never leaving her throat.

"If she raises her hands, cut her, but don't kill her," Fenton said. "I've got plans for her."

She could imagine what those plans were, and she shuddered.

*Think! Think!*

She couldn't use her hands, but did she need them? She closed her eyes and blocked out everything. There wasn't room for anger or hate. No room for fear. She sent her mind out seeking and expanding, searching for the thread of life that ran through all creatures in the forest.

Energy flowed into her, lighting up her insides, energizing her, and empowering her.

"What the—" The knife disappeared from her neck.

"You fool!" Fenton shouted.

Part of her realized he'd pulled out a gun that he was aiming at her. A tremendous roar came from Ryker, and he threw off another attacker as he ran towards Fenton.

So much energy swirled around her, lifting her hair and lifting her body. It was more energy than she'd ever known existed. Her body hummed with it.

Fenton fired the gun. Ryker threw himself in front of her, taking the bullet in his chest and landing hard on the ground. Upon impact, he shifted and lay still.

"Ryker!" Lana screamed.

A few of the bonds connecting them snapped inside her. Horror crawled its way up her throat as Ryker's blood leaked his life away. He'd taken a bullet for her.

Lana let out an anguished cry and then sent a stream of energy to lasso Fenton, jerking him into the air like a puppet, and then flung him into the highest treetop.

Shouts and growls erupted. She whipped toward Fenton's men and sent a charged rope of energy around each one, causing them to collapse in place.

Lana dropped to her knees, tears streaming down her cheeks. "Stay with me," she murmured as she placed her hands on the wound. She wasn't a healer. She needed Granny to save him.

*You are capable.*

The female voice came out of nowhere. Lana looked up to see a shimmering figure in the early morning light.

*Trust in yourself.*

A man materialized beside her, his form hazy around the edges.

*You hold the power of our people. Use your talents wisely. Live for us.*

"Mother? Father?" She barely choked out the words. Her parents had been killed soon after she was born. She only had a single photo of them. "Help me." She looked down at Ryker. "Help me save him." But the forms were fading.

"We'll save him together," Granny said as she knelt down beside her.

"Granny?" Lana's voice quavered, her emotions raw.

"I'm here, child. Now, keep that pressure on." She took a worn leather pouch from a pocket in her vest and, taking a pinch of something out of it, sprinkled it over Ryker. "Cassia and Avery, I believe it's time for your daughter to step into her powers."

*It is time.* They spoke in one voice and melted away.

"I don't understand any of this," Lana said, energy still pinging inside her like shooting stars, while her world rocked off balance. "Who am I?"

## Chapter Eleven

A green meadow stretched before him, with a lone tree beckoning him in the distance. He walked and walked with no thought other than to reach the tree.

As he approached, two shadows detached themselves from the tree's shade and stepped into the sunlight.

*Diana. Odin.*

His brain supplied the knowledge, and he accepted it.

When he was close enough, he dropped to one knee and pledge his fealty to Odin, whose mark he carried.

"Ryker Bernard, you and your family have served me honorably," Odin's voice thundered. "The fates have chosen a fine mate for you. She is the only living descendant of the assassinated fae king and carries great power, with the potential to bring clans together. Will you offer her your protection?"

Ryker raised his gaze to his god's and placed his hand over his heart. "I will."

Odin nodded, his expression satisfied. "I grant you three favors. First, the ability to know truth from lie. Word will get out, and fae and shifters alike will wish to join your clan, but among the pure will be tricksters. Second, I increase your power and strength tenfold. Last, I will send you an advisor who will help you and your mate create a kingdom that will survive the coming war."

"My turn," Diana said. "On her mother's side, Lana descends from one of my beloved nymphs. Her daughter and every female descendant down the line has received special abilities from me."

"Lana communicates with the animals, and her grandmother is a great healer," Ryker said.

Diana nodded. "Yes. But Lana's father changed things. She carries a potent fae lineage. Besides Odin's favors, I decree you will have four boys and one girl. The boys will share in your power, wisdom and honor. Your daughter is mine to be blessed with whatever gift I choose."

Ryker bowed his head in acceptance. "As you both will it."

When Ryker raised his head again, the meadow was gone. He blinked several times, trying to put the scenery into focus.

He wriggled his toes and fingers, pleased to find himself alive. His head was muzzy, as if he'd awoken after a long sleep, and his chest felt sore.

Something warm snuggled against him. Make that someone. And lavender hung in the air.

Ryker lowered the heavy blanket covering him to see the top of a head with dark hair plastered against his side. At the cold air rushing over them, the woman burrowed closer.

*Lana.*

Memories came back, and he sifted through them quickly. Although he needed to check on Cole, most important to him was Lana, and she was where he needed her—right beside him.

She stirred and lifted her head, confusion clouding her eyes before they widened, and she tried to scramble away. He caught her and pulled her in tight.

"I had the night watch. How did I—? I should get Granny." The words spilled out and her cheeks pinkened. Once more, she attempted to edge away, but he wasn't having it.

"I feel fine. No need to bother your Granny." He recognized the tent they were in and, even without seeing outside, sensed it was the middle of the night.

"Cole?" he asked.

"He's fine. The remedy Granny brewed worked, and once he was on his feet, he took charge. He got us out of the cabin and on the road to meet up with your clan. He thinks we'll hook up in a couple of days." She sat up, shivering a little. "Let me check your wound. It was red and puffy yesterday. You ran a fever." She checked his forehead. "No fever." She undid his shirt and pulled away a bandage, catching some chest hair, which made him wince. "Sorry," she said and then sucked in a breath. "I don't understand. It's mostly healed, the puffiness and redness gone, just a small scar."

"Ah," said Ryker, thinking of the meadow. "It seems there was one more favor I was granted."

"What are you talking about?" Lana said, her nose wrinkling in confusion.

He drew her forward so that she tumbled upon his chest. "You're injured. I'll hurt you," she said.

"All better. Remember?" And then he kissed her, because the ache in his chest wouldn't close without the taste of her lips.

With or without the gods' blessing, this woman had become his everything.

***

Lana didn't think of resisting. It didn't matter that she'd known him for such a short time. In her heart, he was the man she'd waited for forever.

*And she'd almost lost him!*

So she kissed him back, putting the fear, the pain, the love into that meeting of lips, wanting him to understand that she accepted the bonds between them.

And there it was, a thousand lightning bugs taking wing, shining pinpoints of light in every part of her soul. She could almost feel herself flying with them, all from a kiss!

"Your wound," she said, pulling away reluctantly.

"It's a scratch," Ryker said as he kissed her nose and the corner of her mouth.

She framed his face with both hands. "You nearly died." Her voice caught, recalling that it had been touch and go at one point.

"Hey, I'm here and have no intention of going anywhere." He

hesitated before continuing. "My clan is a mixed group of survivors and misfits of other clans with nowhere to go. War is coming, and more people are looking for protection. It will get worse before it gets better." His tone was grim, and she glimpsed his beast peeking out, the warrior in him ready to battle.

She lay her head on his chest, taking comfort from the steady beat of his heart. "Granny told me that my father was the son of the fae king. I know little more than that. I could endanger your people.

"Never," he said, wrapping her in his embrace. "I'm fortunate to be gifted with such a powerful mate. And I will walk proudly at your side."

Lana raised herself so that she could look him squarely in the eye. "Bindings or no, I will always choose you, in this life or the next. You are my destiny, Ryker."

"You know, love," Ryker said with a grin, "we never stood a chance. So, what do you think about children? Five sounds like a good number."

"Five!" Lana nearly shrieked, shoving away from him. But he took her back in his arms, and because she couldn't resist and didn't want to, she gave herself up to the magic of Ryker.

The End

# The Wolf of Varg Island
## Estelle Pettersen

### Chapter One

Harper

Have you ever felt as if someone were watching you? All my life, I've felt it, but whenever I've turned around, I've caught only the glimpse of a faint shadow disappearing into the corner of a wall.

The shadow came and went in my dreams, always in the shape of a wolf. Maybe I imagined it, or perhaps I grew accustomed to the shadow. Either way, I was not afraid. Instead, I felt content, even protected.

I fell into a dark vortex of melancholy when it disappeared, and loneliness invaded my heart, burdening it with loss. I knew many people were afraid of shadows, but I ached for the wolf's shadow to return. Strange, huh?

\*\*\*

"Miss, wake up. We've arrived at Varg Island," the ferry captain said, tapping my arm. His name, Per Osling, was stitched in white, contrasting the darkness of his navy-blue jacket pocket.

Remnants of my dream disappeared as consciousness returned, bringing me back to reality. I stood up, grabbed my backpack and put it on. I freed the trapped strands of my untamed ebony hair from the strap and sighed. Gazing at the window, my eyes met a thickly forested island, lush with miles of green trees beyond the semi-circular bay.

The rain pelted from the heavens to the sea, creating a shimmery effect on the rocks by the jetty. I'd read on a few holiday websites that the island was an ideal place for anyone who wanted to escape from the world. They could leave their worries and troubles behind. Varg

Island had an abandoned schoolhouse, now a walk-in museum open to anyone, especially if visitors were willing to give a little spare cash, or a bit more, for its maintenance.

"I hope you like the rain," Per said. "But once it clears up, you'll enjoy the island."

"I look forward to seeing the sun," I admitted. It was a miserable northern European summer with weeks of rain, but I'd hoped for the best when I decided to rent a cabin on the island.

"What brings you here?" Per asked. "It can't be the weather."

"It's personal," I replied coldly, as I would rather not tell a stranger my life story. After teaching English as a second language to adult immigrants in the past year, I was finally on vacation.

Per squinted at me. "I hope you're not running away from anything."

"Why would you think that?" I demanded, offended at Per's critical interrogation.

Per stared at me. "Your face tells me the truth."

"The truth? What do you know about that?" I challenged, but the man ignored my question.

"A guy called Christopher Varg owns most of the island," Per said, changing the topic. "There are four cabins, and three are rented out, usually to tourists like yourself. Christopher lives in the fourth cabin. It's the white one near a yellow one. He's a carpenter, a jack-of-all-trades. If you ever need firewood to light up your fireplace, you can ask him."

I raised my eyebrows. "Firewood in the summer?"

The captain chuckled and rubbed his hands together. "It gets chilly at night. There's one more thing you need to know. If you put your trash outside after dark before taking it to the collective disposal in the morning, don't leave it on the ground."

"Why not? I always secure the bag." I tilted my head, confused by his instruction.

"Hang your bag up on the hook. Each cabin has hooks on the posts. There are wild animals that prowl at night, including a wolf," Per warned.

My amber-brown eyes widened. "A wolf? I thought they were mainland creatures."

Per scratched his bearded chin, then his thinning silver hair. "I might be wrong, but I believe someone brought a wolf to the island years ago."

"How odd." I tried to imagine a person having a wolf on their boat, perhaps wanting to make a pet out of it.

"There's one good thing about having a wolf on the island. These days there are fewer sheep, which caused problems back in the day. Tick infestation."

"Oh." I wrinkled my nose. I was about to bombard Per with more questions when he turned his back on me and started the engine to leave.

He waved as I hopped off the boat and onto the jetty. I waved back, remembering he'd given me his mobile number earlier. If I ever needed a boat trip to town, I could call him at least an hour beforehand.

I covered my mop of dark curls with the hood of my red jumper and hiked up a dirt path, which led to a yellow cabin beyond the trees. Rain still fell, not cats and dogs, but it was not a drizzle—the type of rain that would get my feet wet in the grass if I had not worn a good pair of shoes.

I felt exhilarated once I reached the hilltop. The timber cabin, freshly painted yellow with a rosebush near the porch, overlooked the vast Atlantic Ocean. I needed to remember where to find the front door key, having forgotten what Christopher wrote in his email.

*Think, Harper.* I lifted the doormat, taking a wild guess that the key would be under it. *Bingo!* I grabbed the brass key from the ground and unlocked the door. The sun would set in a few hours, so I was grateful to feel safe in a homely place.

***

Once inside, I dropped my backpack on the floor and inspected my vacation home. It was a quaint place, clean and tidy, with a hint of smoke that lingered in the fireplace. The bedroom was blessed with a magnificent window that revealed the island's coast and, further in the distance, a lighthouse surrounded by the ice-cold ocean. I wondered if sea monsters existed. If they did, they no doubt loved the ocean's darkness.

I returned to the living room and skimmed the pine bookshelf near the sofa. A velvet green album jutted out from one of the shelves, calling me to take it. I opened the album and studied old photographs of children from the Victorian era. Some of the little angels lay on their beds in their best garments, eyes closed in peaceful, eternal slumber. I'd heard stories that photos were taken of the dead, but had never seen an actual picture until now. I flipped through the pages and stopped at a photo taken years ago of a boy with startling gray eyes. His mouth was shut as he stood, staring at me.

Looking up, I noticed a photo on the wall of the same sullen boy.

He was next to his father, who held a rifle near a dead wolf spread on the ground. The boy's eyes were reddened, and his cheeks were stained with tears.

A sharp knock on the door caused me to jump and drop the album. Rushing to the door, I opened it, only to meet the same gray eyes. Except the boy was no longer a child.

"Harper Ross?" the man's deep voice growled.

"W–what do you want?" I whispered as his tall form overshadowed my body.

I gulped and stepped back, startled by his presence.

## Chapter Two

### Harper

"I'm Chris Varg," the man introduced himself, extending his hand. "I'm sorry, I didn't mean to startle you. I believe you got my email?"

"I'm Harper Ross, and yes, I received it. Thank you for sending me instructions on getting here via Per's boat. I appreciate it." I took the man's large hand and shook it, feeling its friendly warmth. Instinctively, I asked, "Would you like to come in for a bit?"

"Sure. I brought a welcome present for you," he answered, adjusting a bag on his right shoulder. His faded jeans and dark-blue T-shirt emphasized his lean frame.

"How did you know I was here?" I asked. I took off my jumper, feeling a droplet of sweat trickle down my neck. The fireplace was unlit, but the air was starting to heat up.

"I saw you arrive earlier," Chris said, staring at my thin blouse.

"You've got sharp eyes," I commented, then coughed. "I mean, to see me coming from the boat."

"Good sight is one of nature's blessings." Chris grinned and ran his fingers through his tousled, sandy blond hair, which highlighted his sharp cheekbones. His eyes played with mine as his lips continued to speak. "I'll leave your gift here. I thought you could use some wood for the fireplace. It gets chilly at night."

"Thank you," I mumbled, tucking away stray curls behind my ear. Chris released the bag from his shoulder and placed it next to the fireplace. He was gorgeous and virile, probably in his early thirties. I bet women flirted with him and kept his bed warm on chilly nights.

"You've got strong arms," I blurted.

He laughed softly and replied, "Years of hard work does that to a man. By the way, there's no need to lock the doors around here. It's a safe place."

"What about at night? I heard there's a wolf on the island."

"Wolves don't have hands. I doubt they can open doors with their paws or their jaws," Chris joked. "Anyway, the deck beyond the back door is a great place to sunbathe when the sun is out."

"I look forward to seeing some sun," I said, noticing the rain had stopped and the clouds were clearing.

Chris studied my fair complexion, a stark contrast to his tanned skin, and commented, "You may need sunscreen. The sun's strong here."

"I have sunscreen," I answered. Slightly embarrassed by his observation of my pale skin, I turned away.

"I switched on the hot water earlier so you can enjoy a warm shower tonight." His words put dirty thoughts in my mind. I pictured us showering together and blushed at the thought of Chris's hand lathering my breasts.

"You might want to keep your showers limited to ten or fifteen minutes," he continued, snapping me out of my erotic daydream.

"I guess the hot water runs out fast," I quipped. My nipples were hard pebbles pushing against my top's flimsy fabric. I wish I had worn a bra—I didn't think I needed one because I had a thick jumper to cover myself earlier today.

Chris's eyes widened as he stared at the peaks poking from under my blouse. "I'd better be leaving," he murmured huskily, then cleared his throat. "The sun's setting soon, but if you need anything—"

"Where can I find you?" I tried not to sound too desperate.

"I left my cellphone number in the email, but if you need me, I'm next door. You see the white cabin behind the apple tree?" Chris pointed at the kitchen window.

I nodded, catching a whiff of his manly scent. I became unusually light-headed, and wet excitement dampened my panties.

"I'll be at home, so just call or come over if you need me." Chris's gray eyes held onto me before he walked out the door.

\*\*\*

## Later that evening

"Shit!" I shouted, waking from a deep sleep. I'd dreamed of running in the woods, chasing a shadow that jumped from rock to rock, then from tree to tree, until it disappeared into a forest glade.

In the dream, I inhaled the fresh air—a mixture of the sea breeze and the dewy leaves. I moved toward the clearing, the earth soft beneath my bare feet. But there was another scent that lingered—a musky, animalistic one. Two wolves, one light gray and one with a dark-brown coat and narrower muzzle, slowly appeared from behind the leaves in the distance. They nuzzled each other with tender care. The larger wolf—with the lighter coat—rubbed its muzzle against the other wolf's hind leg affectionately, then positioned itself for copulation.

I hid behind a birch tree, rubbing my palm gently against the roughness of its bark. Closing my eyes, I silently prayed the predatory animals would not see me while mating. *Would they feel threatened because I'd invaded their territory? Would I be their next meal?*

A white mist surrounded the wolves, cloaking them completely. Now was my chance to run, and boy did I run. I felt the adrenaline rush through my body, my heart pounding and my arms and legs pumping with blood. My feet were soaked with dirt and moss when I reached the cabin. Opening the door, I clutched my chest and took heavy breaths as I heard howling coming from the forest in the distance.

I struggled to return to reality during the first few seconds after waking up. *Two wolves? Seriously, Harper! Get a grip.* I laughed, feeling silly for believing the dream was real.

An earthy scent lingered in the room. Was it in my hair, or perhaps it permeated into my skin? My eyes widened as soon as I glanced at my feet because my toes and soles were covered with soft, moist, dark dirt, dampened by the recent rain.

Had Varg Island bewitched me?

## Chapter Three

### Harper

### Three days later

I stared at the ocean.

Earlier this morning, its angry waves had lashed against the brown rocks, creating a frothy aftermath. The green trees shook with fear from the heavy wind, and the rain stamped the windows with countless droplets. A rebellious seagull dared to challenge the weather, flying in the sky during the turbulent weather.

Now, everything was still. The blue sky had replaced the angry clouds and highlighted the lone sun.

A howling wolf had woken me up and I could not get back to sleep. Alpha wolves howled to attract females and communicate their willingness to mate. But why did the female wolf—whether she was real or just a dream—remain silent?

I must be going crazy.

My sister rang me later in the day. I wouldn't have taken a call from anyone else, but she was my family, despite our differences. She was extroverted and carefree, while I was shy and reserved. We'd lost our biological parents when we were young, and she was all I had. Our parents' death had resulted from a hunting accident, the newspaper had reported. How I hated guns!

"Hey, Harp! Are you on vacay yet?" Romy had always called me *Harp* ever since we were kids. It was a pet name she had for me, though I didn't like it much.

"Yep, I'm on vacay, and please don't call me that. I'm not a child anymore. On another note, how are Princess and Charming? Are they house-trained yet?" The last time my sister visited me, she'd brought her dogs to my place, and they'd pooped on my favorite rug.

"My babies have always been house-trained. I think your scent throws them off," Romy joked. She was a vet who'd adopted two stray dogs she'd treated for fleas and ticks. The dogs were in good hands now.

"Haha, very funny. I don't smell that bad. At least I shower every day, unlike some people," I retorted.

"Have you gotten your vaccine yet?" Romy asked.

"You mean the Covid influenza vaccine?"

"No, dummy! Your rabies vaccine." Acerbic sarcasm dripped from Romy's voice.

"I've had my second vaccine dose, so I'm safe. How about you?"

"Do you have to ask? By the way, where on earth are you?"

"Varg Island."

"Oh." Romy remained silent for a while, then spoke again. "Be careful, Harp."

"My name's Harper, not Harp—you know that. And why would I need to be careful?"

"Harper, Harper. I believe the island is owned by crazy Bill Varg. You know, the guy who was on the news years ago."

"I don't know who you're talking about." My eyebrows furrowed. Romy remembered more of the past than I did, because she was a few years older than me.

"You know, the guy who murdered a wolf for supposedly killing his wife? She probably ran off with someone."

"I don't remember any of it. I met a guy named Chris Varg. He runs the show these days."

"That's his son. Apparently, the poor boy was traumatized by his mother's disappearing act and the dead wolf."

"Hmm, strange," I muttered under my breath. "I guess the island has some interesting secrets."

"Hey, I gotta go. Princess is begging me to feed her, and Charming is eating my favorite shoes."

"House-trained, huh?" I laughed at Romy's family life.

"Ciao!" Romy sang.

"Miao miao!" I teased before putting the phone back in my pocket.

Curious about wolves on the island, I plucked up the courage to pay a visit to my neighbor. Perhaps Chris could shed some light on the island's history.

After knocking on the door several times, I went to his garden, only to see him naked, fucking a beautiful brunette.

She lay on a sunbed, moaning and thrashing as he hovered over her. His ass cheeks moved in perfect rhythm while he grunted in unison with her moans. His lover's red lips formed a perfect O as she arched her back and yelled his name over and over again. He stiffened, growled, then cursed loudly, offloading his pleasure inside her.

Something primal inside me stirred at the sight of the couple. Perhaps I was in heat. Envy spread throughout my veins, and dark thoughts stirred my mind. I wanted to tie up the brunette with rope and make her watch me while I screwed her handsome boyfriend.

I'd hoped Chris was single, but such hopes were too good to be true. A guy like him always had a woman to keep him company. As for me,

I was a loner. A lone wolf who spent most of my adult life wondering why my relationships never lasted. I crept away from Chris's garden of delights and headed to the beach.

***

## Chris

"I'm spent," I said breathlessly, pulling my cock out of Roberta.

She removed the condom from me, got up from the sunbed, and joined me on the soft grass. We rested together, and her head nestled in the crook of my arm. I inhaled the coconut-scented oil that permeated her crown—it wasn't as dark as Harper's jet-black curls, but it was beautiful.

Yet Harper had got under my skin. I'd smelled her womanly scent earlier, and I wanted to taste her. I felt an instant arousal when she took off her red hoodie. Her dark nipples peeked through her semi-transparent blouse, a flimsy piece of clothing I could've torn with my teeth. I wanted to suck those nipples.

"Chris?" Roberta's green eyes looked at me quizzically.

"Hmm?" I molded her ample breasts with my hands. She usually loved it when I played with her body after sex.

"Can you please stop that?" She removed my hands and distanced her slim frame from mine.

"What's the matter?" I frowned. I tried stroking her hair, but she flicked my fingers away.

"I'm leaving Varg Island."

I sat up and cocked my head to one side. "Why?" I'd wondered why she hadn't answered my call last night. Or why she hadn't joined me for our usual nocturnal runs. The sex we'd just had was mechanical, a far cry from the usual passion we shared. "Roberta, baby—"

"Please, no more pet names."

"Why are you leaving?"

"You don't need me to be with you anymore because she's here now."

I frowned. "Who?"

"Her. That vacation tenant of yours. Hayley?"

"Harper."

"Exactly my point. You've marked her as yours." Roberta paused, then stared at me intensely. "You want Harper more than anyone you've ever cared about, except your mother, perhaps. The difference is your mother is dead, and this girl is alive. She's alone in the world."

I silently cursed Roberta's ability to read minds.

"Don't." She smiled bitterly. "I was born with it. I know your heart was never truly with me, but I couldn't stop my wishful thinking. We did have fun, though, didn't we?"

"Sorry. Roberta, please let me explain."

"What's there to explain? Your scent has changed ever since the girl arrived on the island. It was never me, was it, Chris?"

I said nothing. There was no point because my lover knew the truth. We never were serious. We'd seen other people from time to time over the years, and I'd felt something was missing in the relationship. However, I'd never fully admitted it until now.

"I tried, believe me, but I'm not in love with you," I confessed. I was angry at myself for trying to flog a dead dog to life. I believed I was cold-hearted, a result of losing my mother at a young age. *Roberta, you deserve better.*

"Don't blame yourself for it," she comforted me. "There's a pack on the mainland. Do you remember Tommy?"

"Yeah." I gulped, trying to hold back my guilt. *Men cry too when they farewell their lovers.*

"Tommy is sensitive to my needs," she said. "As you will be for Hayley's needs."

"It's Harper," I corrected.

Roberta giggled, then touched my arm. "I know. I was testing you. Promise me one thing?"

"It depends on the promise."

"Be patient with Harper, because she'll love you back one day."

"Love?" I scoffed. "What does love have to do with me?"

Roberta laughed. "You have no idea what's coming."

## Chapter Four

### Chris

It was two weeks since Roberta had left, but her sweet scent still lingered in the air. She'd left her soaked bra on one of the chairs in my three-bedroom cabin after we'd run in the rain together for one last time. "Keep it for old time's sake," she whispered, before kissing me goodbye.

"You deserve a good man like Tommy, who can love you the way I can't," I murmured after my lips parted from hers.

"I know. There's one thing I don't want you to forget, Chris. We were friends before we became lovers."

Roberta was right. She was not my soulmate, but we would continue our friendship.

Lost in thoughts, I didn't hear the soft knocks on my door until they grew louder. I cursed as I stood up from my comfortable lounge chair and slipped on an old, used shirt. *What now? Has a cabin tenant, maybe Liz, run out of hot water again?*

"Hey." Two bewitching amber eyes looked up at me as I opened the door.

*Damn, I could've put on a better shirt.* I folded my arms, hoping I didn't smell bad. "Is everything alright?"

"Umm, I need to leave the island."

I raised my eyebrows. "Oh?" *Don't go.*

"I need to go soon."

"You won't be getting your money back," I said sternly.

Harper waved her shaking hands in defense. "No, no! I didn't mean I wanted to leave for good."

"Then why do you want to leave?" I questioned, arms still folded.

"I need groceries and other stuff in town. I've run out of a few things."

*Is this small talk? Or does Harper need my help?* She and I were getting to know one another, engaging in plenty of small talk, talking about the weather whenever we passed each other. She invited me for coffee a few days ago, and she came over to try my home-brewed beer last night.

"I've got a few supplies if you need anything," I said, hoping we wouldn't have to go into town. I planned to show her the old schoolhouse today.

"There's something I need that you don't have," she replied.

"Try me," I teased, half-grinning.

"I ran out of contraceptive pills."

"Oh, shit. Well, I can't help you with that. But a drugstore can." We both laughed, and our eyes met again. I cleared my throat, then asked, "You got a boyfriend coming here?"

"As if. Nope, no boyfriend. I'm on the pill to keep my cycle regular," Harper admitted, then scratched behind her ear.

Neither of us spoke until I broke the ice. "So, you're an introvert, huh?" I chuckled, and she nodded, biting her lower lip.

"I'm a loner," she confessed.

"Ah, and you're also social. We talk a lot, you see. Ever since you got here, we've been yapping away like a pack of wolves. Don't you think?"

Harper smiled widely and answered, "You're easy to talk to, Chris."

"I suppose I am."

"I saw your girlfriend in town a few days ago. Sorry to pry, but she was with another man, and they seemed to be—"

"Roberta and I are just friends now. She's a good woman, and she deserves a man who can love her right."

"Oh." Harper blushed bright red, the color spreading from her cheeks to her bare neck. Right then, I wanted to kiss and suck that smooth neck. I detected a change in her scent and body warmth and knew she was in heat. Heck, I wanted to take her panties off and kiss her core until she would cry out my name. *Settle down, boy.*

"Why don't you call Per like you usually do to take you to town?" I asked, changing the subject.

Harper dug her hands into her skirt's pockets. "Per's off duty tonight, and I'm hoping to catch a ride with you if you're heading into town. I mean, it's Saturday and all. I thought—"

"Are you ready to go now?" I scratched my jaw, seeing the rain had cleared and the sun appeared from behind the clouds.

"Yeah, sure," Harper chirped, eyes all lit up like a kid about to eat cake.

"Alright, let's go," I instructed, grabbing the boat keys from the wall hook before shutting the door.

***

Paul's Hardware Supplies hummed with customers as I bought rope and weed killer while Harper shopped elsewhere. After returning to the island from our short town trip, I helped her step out from the boat to the jetty. Her skin felt smooth and supple, a combination of warmth and silk. It was a sunny afternoon, so she removed her red jumper and secured its arms around her waist.

I gazed at Harper's pretty face. "Have you seen the old schoolhouse yet?"

"Not yet, but it's on my list of things to do," she responded, leaning back against a large rock. "Chris, is it true that there's a wolf on Varg Island?"

"Hmm, yes, what about it?"

"I hear him howl at night sometimes. Do you know where he's from?"

"The wolf belongs to me," I replied. "I let the animals roam around this island because they're safe from hunters on the mainland."

"I love wolves. I dream of shadows of wolves, you know," Harper confessed. She sighed, basking in the sun's rays. My cock hardened as I watched her lift one leg to rotate her ankle, exposing her creamy thigh.

Not now, dude. Play your cards right, and she'll be begging for you later. I diverted my gaze to a rock. A boring, old rock.

"It's unusually hot today, isn't it?" Harper turned to me and smiled. Her eyes sparkled with a hint of mischief.

Needing her, I decided to take the risk of bringing her closer to me. Scratching my chin, I looked at the ocean and asked, "Harper, how open-minded are you?"

She slowly dropped her shapely leg and played with her skirt, raising it slightly. "I'd like to think I'm open-minded. Why?"

"Have you ever tried swimming naked in the sea?"

Harper shook her head. "It sounds like fun, with the right person. Is that something you and Roberta did?"

I nodded, then took Harper's hands. "If you're feeling warm and tense, we can cool down. The seawater might bite a little at first, but it's refreshing. What do you think?"

Harper's startled eyes blinked as she smoothed her skirt, pulling it down. "Skinny dipping? With you?" she squeaked.

I turned my head away, regretting I had ever asked. As sensual as she was, a girl as sweet as Harper would probably say no. Then, slowly, I felt her warm hand slip into mine. Harper's fingers weren't as firm as Roberta's, but her energy flowed smoothly into my skin.

"I want you to know one thing," Harper whispered into my ear. "I'm not a replacement for Roberta. Are we clear?"

"Yes, absolutely. Come," I coaxed, touching her smooth thigh. "I'll show you a nice, private place where we can swim."

Moments later, we stood on the large rocks, facing the calm sea. Apart from the waves washing up against the rocks, the only sounds were seagulls squawking near the abandoned lighthouse. Harper dipped her toe in the water, then turned to me. "Will anyone come here?" she asked.

"No. Nobody passes by this place anymore, especially after the new lighthouse was built," I explained, pointing at the landmark in the distance.

Harper pressed her lips together, then removed her skirt as I took off my shirt and cotton shorts. We already had our shoes off; her red sneakers were next to my gray ones. Our eyes met again, and she let out a little laugh as I threw a flirtatious grin.

"You go first," she encouraged, eyeing my boxer shorts with curiosity.

I stared at her. "What about your shirt and panties?"

Harper bit her lip. "I'm not wearing anything under my shirt."

"We're just going in for a dip. It's not a strip show." I smirked, remembering I hadn't been to a strip club for a while.

Harper toyed with her curly black hair, holding me captive with her dark eyes. "I want to feel safe with you."

"You are safe with me."

Harper slowly peeled off her shirt, showing off two perky breasts. They weren't big, but they were perfect. Her dark-brown nipples were erect, staring at me proudly. She was about to remove her panties but stopped.

"Keep going. I want to see all of you," I growled, moving closer to her. I breathed in her rose oil scent and kissed the nape of her neck.

She didn't resist, smiling a little instead. Her lips parted, inviting me to taste them. I brushed my mouth over hers and savored her sweet warmth. "Do you want this?" I whispered into her ear.

She nodded. Her eyes wide like saucers.

"Take this off," I touched the fabric of her panties.

"Actually, it's your turn," Harper murmured, pushing me back.

Feeling arousal stir in my body, I shucked my boxers and revealed my manhood.

"Oh!" Harper gasped as she watched my erection grow.

"You like this?" I massaged my cock. "It's been hungry for you since you first arrived."

"Are we… are we going to—?" Harper gulped.

"Let's go in the water first." I threw her a teasing smile, sensing her mixed feelings, then dove into the sea to cool down from the heat. I didn't want to pressure her into anything she was unsure of.

Her red lips pouted as I saw my rejection stab through her. She balled her fists into crimson rage and began to breathe rapidly.

Harper Ross was not ready for me.

Not yet.

## Chapter Five

### Harper

"Am I some kind of sick joke to you?" I shouted at Chris. "You did this to humiliate me!"

"It's not a joke, Harper. Come and join me," Chris yelled back, splashing the water as he swam.

I put my clothes and shoes back on and ran, speeding past the lighthouse and toward the cabin. I tried to hold back my tears, but they kept rolling down my face, staining it with sorrow. My ankles gave way to the crooked path, causing me to stumble. Reaching for the steadiness of the nearest birch tree, I leaned forward as my eyes caught sight of an old swing behind the forest leaves.

*Interesting.* I wondered how old the swing was. The ropes seemed sturdy and secure, despite being covered with moss, and the wooden plank seemed thick and sturdy. A gentle breeze shook the fragile leaves, and they parted, inviting me to try the swing.

I accepted the invitation, perched on the swing, and gripped the ropes. My feet pushed the ground and lifted off, launching me to my midair flight. Until I felt the plank's sturdiness sink into depression. I tried to get up, but it was too late. A violent gush of air whooshed out of my lungs as I fell hard on the ground. A shock wave traveled from my spine to my brain before pain bludgeoned its way throughout my buttocks and legs.

"Somebody, help me!" I shouted. Despair surrounded my soul like a blackened whirlwind, bringing me to a dark and haunted mental place.

I wept in agony, because my problems had caught up with me. I needed to unleash my pain. My anger. My despair. I howled, releasing the intensity of my anguish. Hell broke loose. Raw memories of my younger self took me back in time. I was the awkward, dark-haired dork next to my gorgeous blonde sister and our friends in high school and college. While they danced, laughed, and made out, I stood alone with the shadow. I always thought the shadow reminded me of a wolf. It kept me company.

Men called me names. Beanstalk. Ugly. Beak-nosed. Plain. "You're like a sister to me," the nice guys said. Always like a sister, but never a lover.

A low howl from the forest broke my lamentation, sending me back to the present day. My ears pricked as I got up from the ground and listened to more howls. Under normal circumstances, I would have panicked. Yet my animal instinct kicked in, and I felt calm—at peace.

A majestic animal, the king of the forest, padded slowly past the bushes and stopped at my feet. I gasped in awe of the gray wolf I'd dreamed about. He was magnificent—almost as big as a dire wolf—with thick, healthy fur and a powerfully built frame. He signaled a greeting with a fluid tail wag as he approached me.

"Aren't you the most beautiful animal on this island?" I kneeled and offered my hand, allowing the wolf to lick the salt from my skin. He stared at me with kind, gray eyes—the same shade as Chris's. There was a saying that animals looked like their owners, and I guessed it was true.

"You truly are Chris Varg's wolf, aren't you? You belong here," I said, stroking the animal's coat. He seemed to like the attention because he kept pawing and licking my hands and arms.

The wolf followed me to my cabin, keeping close to my legs. Moments later, after giving him a piece of salami, I sat on the bed and patted the space next to me. "Come here, boy. Rest up before you go out again. I've left the door open for you in case I fall asleep."

Understanding my invitation, he hopped on the bed, placed his paw on my arm, then tickled my neck with loving and affectionate licks. The tears emerged again as I continued stroking the wolf's fur. Except, these were tears of relief.

"Do you want to know the truth about me?" I asked Chris's wolf. "I got involved with the wrong guy. Jackson Smith. We worked at the same college, teaching adults. I thought he was kind and loving when we first started dating, but he humiliated me in the worst possible way."

The wolf turned his neck, and his eyes begged for me to tell him more about my heartache.

"Do you have a name?" I asked. The friendly predator placed his paw on my hand, then rested his head on the pillow.

"Jackson filmed us in bed without my knowledge. I was so stupid to trust him and believe he could love me. I mean, who could love Harper Ross, huh?"

The wolf's eyes lit up, full of surprise.

"Yep, my ex-boyfriend made a sex tape of me and published it online, calling it 'The Ugly Duckling.' Do you know, I had to resign from my teaching job after the film was distributed to some of the men in the faculty? And he kept his job! My 'vacation' is indefinite, at least until I find another job. That is how unfair the world is outside Varg Island."

Chris's wolf lifted its head and licked my fingers, giving them little nips.

"You and I are misunderstood animals. We're treated like outcasts," I lamented, caressing the wolf's muzzle.

"Now you know why I'm here. I don't want to go home, because I don't know where home is anymore." I rested my head on the pillow near the wolf's face.

*Chris, I need to talk to you. I'm ready for you now.* I regretted running away from him. He'd teased me, but he didn't mean to hurt me. Chris's teasing reminded me of my painful past, but I had to end the pity party. I needed to forgive myself and apologize to him.

He did nothing wrong.

Sleep began to possess my body, taking me to a world of dreams where I would howl together with the wolves. There was something therapeutic about it. It was as if I were giving the world back its problems and telling it to fuck off.

***

Slowly opening my eyes, I returned to reality from my peaceful nap and glanced out the window. Nightfall had hit the rocky shores, casting glorious darkness onto the ocean. I reached out to stroke the wolf's fur, only to feel a human arm. I tried to scream, but nothing came out. My heart pounded as I lay frozen, afraid to turn to my left to see who was there.

Shit, why did I leave the door open? Had the wolf abandoned me? Had my ex-boyfriend found his way to the island? He was a sadistic person, horrible enough to ruin people because it was fun for him. Who knew what he was capable of? Torture? Kidnap? Murder?

Slowly, ever so slowly, I turned my head and dared to look at the human by my side.

Oh. My. God.

"*Shit!*" I screamed as I sprung up from the bed. Shock gripped my shoulders, and my legs trembled, while my heart tried to lunge out of my body.

"What the heck?" I grabbed the pillow, preparing to attack.

Sure enough, there was a nude man in my bed—Chris Varg.

"Stop hitting me!" he barked, shielding my pillow slams with his elbow.

His deep voice triggered a calming effect, so I dropped the pillow. My shoulders started to relax, and my heartbeats slowed down. "Why the fuck are you naked in my bed? Did I invite you here? Don't you understand what consent means? Should I spell it out? C-O-N—"

"There was consent. You invited me here," Chris answered.

"You have some explaining to do. Where's your wolf?" I probed, placing my hands on my hips.

Neither of us spoke for a while as Chris stared at me with a half-grin. *Shit, that son of a—*

"That wolf you invited? You're looking at him."

"What do you mean? Stop playing with me, Chris!"

"I'm not playing with you, Harper. I am the wolf."

## Chapter Six

### Chris

"It doesn't make sense." Harper frowned as I handed her a cup of coffee. It took about fifteen minutes for her to calm down enough to have a conversation without shouting my name.

"Does anything make sense these days, Harper?" I answered her with a question. "I'm a descendent of the *kveldulf*, which means evening wolf. During the Viking ages, there lived a man named Úlfr Bjálfason, a shapeshifter who refused an allegiance with the king."

"Should I be scared of you?" she asked, then sipped her drink.

"I do bite." I grinned, running my tongue across my teeth salaciously.

"Stop that!" Harper huffed, and her body tensed.

"Stop what?"

"Stop teasing me when I don't know if you're going to make a meal out of me."

"I don't tease my food. I'm flirting with you because you're beautiful."

Harper touched my arm, sending a tingle to my heart. "You're the shadow," she murmured.

"The shadow?"

"The wolf's shadow that comes in my dreams. I've been chasing you for years. Except, I didn't think you were real until I came here."

"I'm flesh and blood. Here, touch me." My eyes begged hers as I placed her hand on my chest. Her fingers traced the contours of my muscles, feeling every scar, bruise, and scratch.

"You're handsome," she admitted, gazing at the towel wrapped loosely around my hips. It would take just one tug of the towel for my manhood to be exposed.

I pulled her into me, inhaling her rose scent. "I'm sorry for teasing you earlier today. I thought it was harmless flirting, but neither of us was ready. I got overly excited, as wolves sometimes do."

Harper pressed her head against my chest and whispered, "Our energies pulled us together too strongly. I reacted because of what happened to me in the past, and I was terrified of getting hurt again."

I frowned and tightened my lips. "I'm sorry for what happened to you. You didn't deserve any of it. I'll never hurt you, at least not intentionally. And if I ever hurt you, I'll be quick to apologize."

"I believe you and I trust you," she said.

"I might hurt your ex-boyfriend, Jackson. I can't promise what I'll do if I ever meet him. Heck, I might make a meal out of him!"

Harper giggled, then looked up at me. "Can you tell me your story?"

"I'll take you to the old schoolhouse," I answered, holding her hand. "I'll explain everything there, but first, I need to go home for some clothes."

"I prefer you without clothes," Harper admitted, blushing.

"I bet you do." I chuckled, adjusting the towel.

***

### Harper

"This place is amazing," I praised as we walked inside the old schoolhouse. The school was simple: it was one spacious room with empty desks and chairs facing a large oak bureau—the teacher's desk. Photos, drawings, and an outdated map decorated the timber walls, which emitted a crisp pine scent. Chris took my hand, guiding me to a wall photo of a small group of children.

"There you are." I pointed at a shy blond boy tucking in his chin and biting his lower lip. I recognized him immediately—he was the same boy in the picture in my cabin. It was hard not to miss the haunting stare in his gray eyes.

Chris's finger scratched my palm and his eyes creased from his weary smile. "There I am."

"You've got a haunted expression in the photo. It's as if you've seen a ghost. What happened?" I asked.

"I did see a ghost. I saw my mother's apparition floating in midair from time to time for forty days after she was murdered. She was like an angel surrounded by light. After that, she disappeared," he answered. "I also shifted for the first time, at the age of eight, right before her death. Don't you think it warrants prolonged shock?"

"You poor soul! Did anyone else know?"

"Come, look at this photo." Chris guided me to another framed photo on the wall. It was of Chris as a boy playing with a little dark-haired girl. She had a few freckles on her nose and green eyes like fresh forest leaves.

"Is that Roberta?"

Chris nodded.

"She knew all along?"

"Yes. She's a shifter, like me."

"Is she your soulmate?"

"No."

"I watched you make love to her before she left," I confessed.

"You did? Well, I hope you enjoyed the show," Chris scoffed, shaking his head.

"Why aren't you with her?"

"Roberta's been one of my closest friends since childhood, but I want you." Chris's gray eyes held me, captivating me with their mystery. He rubbed my shoulders, which shook from the cold gust of air blowing from the outside through the open doorway.

"You keep me warm from the cold," I murmured, inhaling his earthy scent. He smelled like the forest, hinting dark and sensual notes of cedarwood, bergamot, and sandalwood.

"I feel your moods and the energy around you. You are the only woman who affects me this way. We match, Harper."

"You sense me?" I stroked his strong arm.

"I do. I didn't mean to upset you yesterday, but I felt you weren't ready for me. That was why I jumped into the water."

Was I special to Chris? Where were we heading?

"You are special to me," he declared, pressing his lips against mine. *Could he read my mind?*

"I've been hunting for you all my life. And here you are," I said, breaking the kiss. Chris's shadow was always tied to me. "But tell me, were your parents also shifters?"

"My dad married a woman with Viking ancestry—my mother. When he took his new bride to the island, he didn't realize he brought a wolf. She kept her secret from him for years, fearful that he would no longer love or accept her as she was," Chris told me.

"That's so sad. Nobody should ever have to hide who they are to be loved," I remarked, shuddering at the thought of not being loved unconditionally.

"I shifted for the first time on my eighth birthday, so my mother and I spent a few days in the woods, camping out on the other side of the island. She taught me to hunt and survive in the wilderness," he continued.

"But what about your dad?"

"He went crazy during those few days. She left a note by the fireplace, but he never found it."

"Strange," I mused. "I wonder what happened with the note."

Chris shrugged his shoulders. "The locals said Dad went on a vengeance spree during those few days. He hunted and killed any animal that stood in his path—deer, a moose, and even a bear."

"Are there bears on the island?" I freaked out. "I can handle wolves, but I'm not so keen on bears!"

Chris chuckled. "Yeah, there's a family of brown bears, but they're harmless if they're left alone."

"So, your dad found you and your mom?"

"I'd transformed into my human form by the time he found us. I stood with a lone wolf next to my mother's torn clothes. Believing the wolf killed my mother, Dad shot her."

"Oh, my God!" I gasped, cupping my hands over my mouth.

"For years, I blamed myself for her death. I remained silent out of fear. Then Roberta helped me to see it was never my fault."

"She understood you and gave you comfort."

"She did. Come here, there's one last photo I want to show you." Chris led me to the teacher's desk. He opened the drawer and handed me a photo in a glass frame.

"Oh, she's beautiful," I exclaimed, staring at a pretty woman with gray eyes and flaxen-blonde hair. She stood in front of the schoolhouse and wore a mysterious smile. "Is this your mother?"

Chris nodded. "She was a teacher at the school. It shut down after her death, and many of the island's residents moved to the mainland. People feared Dad because he was impulsive, violent, and unpredictable."

"Did he ever hurt you, Chris?"

"He punched me in the gut during an argument when I was fifteen, so I called social services. They placed me with a foster family in town after that. People called my dad 'Crazy Bill,' you know." Chris sighed and wiped his brow. "He died of heart failure when I turned twenty, and I inherited everything he owned on this island."

Feeling a wave of emotions hit my heart, I caressed his arm. "Thank you for opening up to me."

"You're welcome," Chris answered with a half-smile. "How about you? Your parents? Do you see them much?"

"I visit them at Saint Mark's Cemetery in my hometown. They were walking in the woods when a bunch of gun-crazy idiots decided to shoot every animal they could find. Unfortunately, the animals they murdered were my parents. I was barely eight, too," I revealed.

*Enough of this melancholy.* "Let's talk about something else," I suggested. "There's too much darkness in the world."

"You want to know something kinda spooky?" Chris pulled me into him again.

"What could scare me?" I dared to ask. I glanced at the lone lamp on the school desk, which created an eerie glow surrounding Chris's form.

A flash of lightning struck the sky, followed by murderous thunder, causing me to jump and scream. Chris's grin was no longer sweet, but devilish and cunning.

"I'm starving, Harper. My appetite for you is insatiable."

## Chapter Seven

### Harper

I panicked, not knowing which option I should take. *Fight, flight, or stay?*

"Don't fight me," Chris whispered into my ear, holding my wrists tightly.

"I can't fight you. You're too strong," I answered. Wetness pooled between my legs as I imagined him dominating me, kissing my body, and giving me pleasure.

Rain besieged the schoolhouse, pelting hard on the ground and at the windows. "It looks like we're trapped here until the storm is over," I said, gazing out the dark window. I faced the handsome man in front of me, and desire permeated my body. I pictured Chris fucking me hard during the storm, and I wanted him to take me. I wanted to surrender myself to him.

"Your body is my sanctuary," he murmured, kissing my neck and shoulders. "Submit to me, Harper. Don't fight, because I crave you, and I know you want me too. Let go of all your insecurities and inhibitions."

I nodded, kissing Chris with hungry desire as he removed his clothes and mine, except my panties, which I clutched tightly. "I want to feel nothing between your skin and mine," he urged, rolling my nipples with his fingers and thumb.

"You're beautiful," I said, appreciating his broad chest, slim hips, and his thick, long cock, erect for me. His hand slipped beneath my panties, rubbing my mons first, then exploring the wetness at my entrance.

"Relax," he coaxed when my legs tried to snap shut.

"I haven't shaved or trimmed," I admitted sheepishly. Redness flushed my cheeks. Had I known that I would be having sex with a gorgeous hunk, I would have taken better care of my intimate grooming.

"I don't care. I want to see all of you," Chris growled. He pulled down my panties and threw them on the messy clothes pile on the floor. Instinctively, I tried to cover my pussy, but he removed my hands. He spread my arms like an eagle's wings as his eyes admired what he uncovered.

"Sit on the desk and lean back," he instructed, and I obeyed. "Now, spread your legs so I can see how sexy you are."

I moaned while Chris fingered my wet clit, slowly at first, then at rapid speed. He paused, sniffed my pubic curls, and kissed my mound before running his tongue along my clit, giving it hard licks and sucks.

"Not yet," he ordered when I cried his name, feeling the urge to come. He guided the bald tip of his penis toward my entrance and pushed.

"I want you to do it hard and fast," I pleaded as Chris continued thrusting in and out of me. I inhaled the scent of our sex, which heated the cold air and heightened my senses.

"Is that what you like, beauty? Hard and fast? I'll give it to you," he promised, speeding his lovemaking. I felt the light slapping of his balls on my anus while he grabbed my ankles, placing them on his shoulders so he could penetrate deeper.

The love we made together was intense, our bodies slamming into each other as the storm continued raging outside. One last, deep thrust from Chris undid me entirely as I cried out to the heavens, tears rolling down my cheeks.

"Oh, you're so fucking good, baby! That's it, that's my girl!" Chris exclaimed. He stiffened, then rammed into me, releasing his seed into my body. He shouted my name over again until his voice simmered into a low whisper. *Harper.*

Our bodies shuddered while our racing heartbeats regulated to a slower, steadier pace of exhaustion and bliss. The storm outside waned, now only light drops of rain kissing the blades of grass and tender leaves.

"You're special to me," Chris groaned into my neck before leaving my body.

*I'm falling in love with you,* I wanted to say, but it was too soon. Was it possible that loving someone could be so fast, intuitive, and natural?

***

One week later

It was time to leave Varg Island because my rental contract for the holiday cabin would soon end. Chris was away most of the week due to a work project in another town, and I didn't see him much. He gave me a gorgeous bouquet of red roses the day before he left, with a note:

*Harper, you once asked who could love you. Love yourself. I'll see you soon. Chris.*

Captain Per and his boat arrived early, as usual, to take me back to town. I glanced at the empty cabin and wondered if I would be back again. Would Chris still be here? I pictured him a few years later with a partner and family of small children. He would make a great dad and lover.

Once in town, I stopped at an Italian café for a bite to eat before catching the bus back to the city.

"Hi, can I sit here?" a woman's voice asked. "The rest of the café is full."

I glanced up and stared at Roberta. Dressed in tight jeans and a white tank top, she had a stunning figure. The brunette's cat-like green eyes contrasted with her hair, accentuating her high cheekbones and perky nose. I nodded at her request, moving my backpack to the floor to make room for her.

"I love your red dress. It's cute, and I'm sure Chris would adore it," she said, touching the fabric as she sat next to me. "I'm Roberta, by the way. We haven't formally met, but I'm Chris's friend, and I've heard quite a bit about you."

"Oh?" I raised an eyebrow. I wasn't sure which way the conversation was heading, so skepticism was my natural reaction.

"Don't worry, everything Chris has said about you is all good." Roberta laughed softly, patting my forearm.

We engaged in small talk until our drinks and meals arrived, then ate in silence.

"Mmm, now that was delicious!" Roberta exclaimed, finishing her pasta meal. "Not as delicious as a T-bone steak. Oh, have you tried Chris's T-bone steak? Now, that guy can cook."

I shook my head, feeling a little deflated. Roberta and Chris had a lifetime of friendship. He gave her a whole lot more love than I could imagine.

"Sure, we've been friends for a while, but don't you think he and I would still be together if we were in love?" Roberta asked as if she had delved into my thoughts.

"I, umm…"

"Sorry, honey. I didn't mean to read your mind."

"No, it's fine. Wait, can you really do that?"

"Mm-hmm." Roberta smiled serenely. "So, you're falling in love with Chris. What are you scared of?"

"I'm not scared!" I protested, tapping the table.

"You're in denial. Listen, you've got a good thing going on with him. Why are you leaving him? Besides, there are a few teaching jobs in the adult community college where I work. We always need teachers."

"I need to get back to the city to—"

"To what? To face your problems? You're not running away from them. You're leaving them behind because there's no point flogging a dead dog, right? I learned that expression from Chris." Roberta chuckled at the thought of her former lover.

"I lost my job, so I suppose I can start again here. My ex-boyfriend, Jackson—"

"Your ex-boyfriend is a sociopath, and your feelings about him were right. You should've listened to them when the red flags went up."

Roberta explored my mind just as I remembered Jackson kicking a stray dog that had got in his way during a stroll in the park together. The kick was light, but the intention was harmful. Why on earth had I been so weak and complacent? Or had I become like the many people around me who were numb or fearful of the violence surrounding them? Riots, robberies, people shouting at each other, physical abuse at pubs, clubs—the incessant violence.

"No more being complacent," I growled, curling my lip. "I'm done with being used by people who don't matter to me."

"Then do what you want. Fuck what your sister thinks," she said, reading my thoughts of Romy calling me to come home. I owed my sister nothing. In fact, she owed me a lot more. I remembered how she and her friends had laughed at me for being a loser in high school and college.

"Harper, you were *never* a loser." Roberta leaned closer to me and held my hand. "Romy had no depth to her soul. She's changing now, perhaps feeling guilty about the way she treated you. I gotta give her kudos for trying to make it up to you, but you don't owe her anything."

"You're right," I agreed. "I'm going back to Varg Island. About that teaching job. I think I'll apply for it."

Roberta laughed, then tucked a tendril of loose curls behind my ear. "I think you and I will be good friends. You can also tell Chris he owes me one."

I smirked, shook my head, then picked up my backpack. "See you around, Roberta."

I was no longer alone.

## Chapter Eight

### Harper

The clouds swirled like mist, low in the night air, as I stepped from the boat onto the jetty's wooden planks on Varg Island. Feeling the temperature drop, I put on my red hoodie and strode up the hill to Chris's cabin. His boat rested in its place, indicating that he'd returned from his out-of-town project.

"Chris," I called out, hoping to find him in his garden. There was no reply. I heard only the cry of seagulls near the lighthouse in the distance.

Noticing the front door was open, I walked inside the cabin and repeated Chris's name. The place was empty, so I made myself comfortable on the sofa and rested. Feeling the heaviness of sleep in my eyes and limbs, I drifted into a dream—but there was no shadow to chase anymore.

The sound of soft feet padding on the floorboard resurrected my body, stirring it to life. My tired eyes adjusted to the sight of a gorgeous gray wolf wagging his tail, his ears slightly off to the side.

"Hey there. How was your run?" I asked, stroking the creature's gorgeous fur coat. "Have you been hunting?"

The wolf howled, then licked my fingers, arm, and face.

"I'm not leaving you again," I promised, placing my arms around his sturdy neck.

The wolf suddenly barked, his eyes widening in alarm as a black shadow flew past him and hovered above me. He fled to the nearest corner, his hind legs crouching in fear. I gasped as an ominous mist seeped from the pores of my skin, enshrouding me.

"Chris?" My eyes blinked, swelling with tears from the suffocating smoke as my breathing quickened into short, shallow pants. My hands and feet twisted and shook while I drowned in the whirlpool of smoke.

"Chris, what's happening to m-me?" I rasped, losing control of my tongue. My incisors lengthened, cutting through bleeding gums. The hairs of my skin sprouted and thickened into a soft coat of ebony fur.

My mate stared at the animal emerging from me, while strong electrical currents pulsated down my spine, causing every muscle and nerve to ache. A howl lashed out from my lungs before darkness engulfed my body, only to heal my pain.

An enticing scent came from Chris's direction, and I immediately had an urge to sniff the supracaudal gland at the base of his tail.

Unleashing my inhibitions, I welcomed the dangerous thrill of transformation. It was time to embrace my true nature.

\*\*\*

## Chris

My eyes opened to the rising sun's blood-orange hues staining the morning sky with heat. After spending an incredible night with my amber-eyed mate, we now rested on the grass near the broken swing. Feeling a surge of pleasure from my groin, I glanced down at the creature taking pleasure in feeding on my cock. "Oh, fuck, Harper, that feels so good," I groaned.

"Mmm," the naked woman murmured, licking my shaft greedily. "You're my dessert."

Twigs and leaves were trapped in Harper's wild, black curls, which blew like crazy in the wind; she didn't give a damn about anything. The left corner of her mouth was covered with dried blood, a remnant of her first kill—a stag. Years of suppression could do that to a shifter, making her wild, hot, and hungry for venison or anything else that caught her attention.

I tried to move my feet apart, but my ankles were tied with some of the rope that once held the swing.

"Kinky," I remarked as Harper's sucks grew stronger, drugging me with pure seduction.

"I need you, Chris." Her cherry-red lips formed a sexy pout while her amber eyes glowed with passion.

"Don't stop," I begged, as her lips twisted into a sinful smile. The Lolita-like sweet girl who'd arrived on the island at the start of summer was gone. I now had a vixen in my hands… or on my dick.

"Do you want to play Red Riding Hood and the Wolf?" Harper teased me, throttling my shaft rapidly.

"Oh, God! Keep doing that!" I shouted, grabbing her hair roughly.

"That's it," she urged, licking her lips. "Be rough. I love it!"

I pulled her hair, feeling a surge of explosion as she fondled just the head—my most sensitive part—and released a flood of pleasure. She licked every drop of my cum, not missing in between her fingers.

"Oh, you are so yummy," she gushed, then left a trail of kisses on my stomach, chest, shoulders, and jawline.

"Don't stop there," I pleaded. "Kiss my mouth."

Harper bit her lower lip and shook her head. "Did you know I was a shifter all along?"

"Hmm, my senses kinda knew."

"What happened to me? Why did it only happen now?"

"I read about people transforming into *Canis lupus* when they're adults," I said, pulling Harper close to my chest. "You're a late bloomer."

"The shadow," she pondered. "I always thought it was you, but I was wrong. It was always me."

"Sometimes we need to tap into the shadows inside us, because they're telling us something," I explained. "Yours was telling you to let go of your insecurities and inhibitions. You needed to listen to your shadow to transform into the woman you are now."

"Chris Varg, how do you know so much about women?" Harper's eyebrows furrowed.

"I've been with a few." I grinned cheekily.

"Did you know I'd come back?" she asked.

"Hmm…" I pursed my lips, glanced at the trees, then back at Harper. "When you left the island, it felt like you ripped my heart to shreds. I was furious and disappointed, so I went for a run to release my anger."

"I'm so sorry," she whispered, stroking my naked skin. "I promise to talk to you first about how I feel, instead of running away."

"Or you can run with me instead." I grinned, kissing her forehead. "I'm excited you're back."

"I'm famished," Harper moaned as I nibbled on her ear.

"Again? But we just—"

"I'm falling in love with you, Chris."

I took her hand and kissed her palm. "I loved you from the moment you arrived, and I'm glad you've decided to stay."

"How could I not stay here? The magic and mystery of the island got to me," Harper confessed.

"Yeah, it really gets to you, doesn't it?" I smiled. "Now, would you mind untying my ankles?"

The End

# About the authors

### Alice Renaud

Alice lives in London, UK with her husband and son. By day she works full time as a compliance specialist for a pharmaceutical company. On Sundays she's a lay assistant in her local church. By night she writes fantasy and paranormal romance about shape-shifting mermen, lovelorn demons and thieving angels. A Merman's Choice is the first book in a trilogy inspired by the landscapes of Brittany (where she was raised) and Wales (her mother's homeland). She never completely grew up.

### Alan Souter

Alan is the author and co-author of more than 50 traditionally published U.S. histories, military histories, biographies, fine arts and auto racing titles. He graduated from the School of the Chicago Art Institute and the University of Chicago with a Bachelor Degree and graduate honors in photography. As a photojournalist, he has covered assignments in most of the world from the Arctic to sailing up the Nile and across the Egyptian Sahara on camelback, documented stories in the British Isles, South America, China, the Caribbean, and North America. His articles and columns have appeared in dozens of magazines and newspapers. Alan's background also includes the U.S. Merchant Marine, parachuting, and certified expert marksman. With his co-author wife, Janet, he founded the Avril 1 Group, Inc. in 1997 and has produced lectures on their books and adventures. They have three grown children in the arts and communications.

### Nancy Golinski

Nancy is married and lives on the outskirts of Amish country in the great state of Ohio. When she's not writing, you can usually find her hiking, crafting, traveling, or attending the theatre. She is also a part-time college professor and has written two nonfiction books on women's health.

## Dee S. Knight

A few years ago, Dee S. Knight began writing, making getting up in the morning fun. During the day, her characters killed people, fell in love, became drunk with power, or sober with responsibility. And they had sex, lots of sex. Writing was so much fun Dee decided to keep at it. That's how she spends her days. Her nights? Well, she's lucky that her dream man, childhood sweetheart, and long-time hubby are all the same guy, and nights are their secret. Dee loves writing erotic romance and sharing her stories with you. She hopes you enjoy!

## F.Burn

F. Burn was born and raised in Central London, which has been an inspiration for her stories. She writes fiction which explores the dark side of the human psyche.

F.Burn wrote songs and poetry before shifting to novelettes and novels. When she is not writing, she spends most of her time reading horror books, watching sci-fi movies, painting, going for long walks and cooking.

If you would like to know more about F.Burn and her blog, please visit her website at www.fburn2020.wixsite.com

## Virginia Wallace

Virginia Wallace is a native of the Chesapeake Bay region, on the Southeast coast of the United States. Nomadic by nature, Virginia has lived all over, from the mountains of New England to the rolling hills of the American Heartland.

She began her creative career during her late teens and early twenties, working as a freelance portrait and commercial artist. She slowly transitioned into writing, eventually self-publishing three novels for the indie book market.

As a writer, Virginia Wallace has always worked at meshing modern stories with a lush style reminiscent of 19th Century American and European literature.

## S.K. White

S.K. White is a lover of science fiction and enjoys inventing new worlds and situations for her characters to discover, grow, explore and fall in love in. She treasures writing in her journal and recording thoughts and ideas that flow from the experiences she sees and hears all around her. She uses many of those reflections to create the characters that appear in her novels, and in the poetry she writes. S. K. White resides in a small town in the west; she embraces glorious sunsets in the cool evening breeze, and savors the captivating western landscapes that surround her.

## Deborah Kelsey

Deborah spent the first 10 years of her life between California, Ceylon (now Sri Lanka) and India, with many trips throughout Asia and Europe. These experiences led to a strong interest in the Arts and in writing and storytelling in particular. A film major at university, she is the author of a critically acclaimed biography of film noir director, Robert Siodmak, under the name Deborah Lazaroff Alpi. Her first novel, *These Eyes So Green*, is also a Black Velvet Seductions publication. She lives in Southern California.

## Gibby Campbell

Gibby is no stranger to the perils of romance. Single until the age of 37, she dated many an interesting (dare we say crazy) guy until meeting the love of her life, Jim. The two are now married and live in the Cleveland, Ohio area. They are joined by their very spoiled dog, Scoob. Gibby believes there is no true norm when it comes to relationships, and they all take hard work and dedication. When she isn't writing, she can usually be found hiking in the park or attending the theatre. Check out her blog at www.gibbycampbell.com.

## Zia Westfield

Zia Westfield has a penchant for the quirky and the zany, qualities which often show up in her paranormal romantic suspense stories. Her contemporary romantic suspense tales follow a more traditional path, but there's always room for a dose of humor or a little snark. She makes her home in Tokyo with her husband and sons. She holds a full-time job, volunteers too much because she doesn't know how to say "no," and generally finds peace between the pages of a book or when she's writing out the stories in her head.

## Estelle Pettersen

Estelle Pettersen is an Australian author and former journalist whose romance stories explore empowerment, freedom, and finding one's strength. She has a Bachelor of Arts degree, majoring in Journalism and Psychology, from the University of Queensland, Australia. Her second degree is an MBA from Queensland University of Technology, Australia. She is a member of Romance Writers of Australia and is passionate about history, languages, cultures, traveling, food, and wine. She is happily married and living in Norway these days.

# More Black Velvet Seductions titles

Their Lady Gloriana by Starla Kaye
Cowboys in Charge by Starla Kaye
Her Cowboy's Way by Starla Kaye
Punished by Richard Savage, Nadia Nautalia & Starla Kaye
Accidental Affair by Leslie McKelvey
Right Place, Right Time by Leslie McKelvey
Her Sister's Keeper by Leslie McKelvey
Playing for Keeps by Glenda Horsfall
Playing By His Rules by Glenda Horsfall
The Stir of Echo by Susan Gabriel
Rally Fever by Crea Jones
Behind The Clouds by Jan Selbourne
Trusting Love Again by Starla Kaye
Runaway Heart by Leslie McKelvey
The Otherling by Heather M. Walker
First Submission - Anthology
These Eyes So Green by Deborah Kelsey
Dark Awakening by Karlene Cameron
The Reclaiming of Charlotte Moss by Heather M. Walker
Ryann's Revenge by Rai Karr & Breanna Hayse
The Postman's Daughter by Sally Anne Palmer
Final Kill by Leslie McKelvey
Killer Secrets by Zia Westfield
Crossover, Texas by Freia Hooper-Bradford
The Caretaker by Carol Schoenig
The King's Blade by L.J. Dare
Uniform Desire - Anthology
Safe by Keren Hughes
Finishing the Game by M.K. Smith
Out of the Shadows by Gabriella Hewitt
A Woman's Secret by C.L. Koch
Her Lover's Face by Patricia Elliott
Naval Maneuvers by Dee S. Knight

Perilous Love by Jan Selbourne
Patrick by Callie Carmen
The Brute and I by Suzanne Smith
Home by Keren Hughes
Only A Good Man Will Do by Dee S. Knight
Secret Santa by Keren Hughes
Killer Lies by Zia Westfield
A Merman's Choice by Alice Renaud
All She Ever Needed by Lora Logan
Nicolas by Callie Carmen
Paging Dr. Turov by Gibby Campbell
Out of the Ashes by Keren Hughes
A Thread of Sand by Alan Souter
Stolen Beauty by Piper St. James
Mystic Desire anthology
Killer Deceptions by Zia Westfield
Edgeplay by Annabel Allan
Music for a Merman by Alice Renaud
Joseph by Callie Carmen
Not You Again! by Patricia Elliott
The Unveiling of Amber by Viola Russell
Husband Material by Keren Hughes
Never Have I Ever by Julia McBryant
Hard Limits by Annabel Allan
Anthony by Callie Carmen
Paper Hearts by Keren Hughes
The King's Spy by L.J. Dare
More Than Words by Keren Hughes & Jodie Harrold
Lessons on Seduction by Estelle Pettersen
Rigged by Annabel Allan
Desire Me Again - Anthology
Mermaids Marry in Green by Alice Renaud
Holy Matchmaker by Nancy Golinski
Joshua by Callie Carmen
Whiskey Lullaby by Keren Hughes

Forgiveness by Starla Kaye
When the White Knight Falls by Virginia Wallace
Cowboy Desire - Anthology
The Bookshop by Simone Francis
Secret Love by F. Burn
Mischief and Secrets by Starla Kaye
Michael by Callie Carmen
Rainbow Desire – Anthology
All Gone by S.K. White
Fright Club by Stephanie Douglas
Creatures of the Night by Deborah Kelsey Lazaroff
The Sea of Love Box Set by Alice Renaud
The Legacy: Sins of the Fathers by Viola Russell
Tempting the Rockstar by Keren Hughes

Our back catalog is being released on Kindle Unlimited
You can find us on:
Twitter: BVSBooks
Facebook: Black Velvet Seductions
See our bookshelf on Amazon now! Search "BVS Black Velvet
Seductions Publishing Company"

Printed in Great Britain
by Amazon

85383975R00174